THEY WERE SEARCHING FOR A PLACE TO CALL HOME. . . .

BUTTERFLY

All she wanted was to be someone's little girl. . . .

CRYSTAL

All she wanted was a family to call her own. . . .

BROOKE

All she wanted was a mother's warm embrace. . . .

RAVEN

All she wanted was an end to broken promises. . . .

V.C. ANDREWS® ORPHANS

Collected in one riveting volume, here are four spellbinding novels from one of V. C. Andrews' most popular and beloved series.

BUTTERFLY

"I knew that someday I would have to break free, to be braver, speak louder, grow taller, but right now that seemed all too scary. The only way I knew how to keep the taunts and teasing of the other kids from bothering me was to stay in my own little cocoon—where it was warm and safe and no one could hurt me. But someday, someday I would soar. Like a beautiful butterfly, I would climb higher and higher, flying above them all. I'd show them. Someday. . . ."

CRYSTAL

"For someone my age, I know a lot about human psychology. I got interested in it after I read about my mother. Now I'm thinking I might be a doctor someday, and anyway, it's good to know as much as you can about psychology. It comes in handy, especially around orphanages. But it's not always an asset to be smarter than other people or more responsible. This is especially true for orphans. The more helpless you seem, the better your chances are for being adopted. . . ."

BROOKE

"When you're brought up in an institutional world, full of bureaucracy, you can't help but be very impressed by people who have the power to snap their fingers and get what they want. It's exciting. It's as if you're suddenly whisked away on a magic carpet and the world that you thought was reserved only for the lucky chosen few will now be yours, too. Who would blame me for rushing into their arms?"

RAVEN

"I looked beyond the street, out toward the mountains in the distance, and wondered what was beyond them. I dreamed of running off to find a place where the sun always shone, where houses were clean and smelled fresh, where parents laughed and loved their children, where there were fathers who cared and mothers who cared. *You might as well live in Disneyland,* a voice told me. *Stop dreaming. . . .*"

V.C. Andrews® Books

The Dollanganger Family Series:
Flowers in the Attic
Petals on the Wind
If There Be Thorns
Seeds of Yesterday
Garden of Shadows

The Casteel Family Series:
Heaven
Dark Angel
Fallen Hearts
Gates of Paradise
Web of Dreams

The Cutler Family Series:
Dawn
Secrets of the Morning
Twilight's Child
Midnight Whispers
Darkest Hour

The Landry Family Series:
Ruby
Pearl in the Mist
All That Glitters
Hidden Jewel
Tarnished Gold

The Logan Family Series
Melody
Heart Song
Unfinished Symphony
Music in the Night
Olivia

The Orphans Miniseries:
Butterfly
Crystal
Brooke
Raven
Runaways (full-length novel)

The Wildflowers Miniseries:
Misty
Star
Jade
Cat
Into the Garden (full-length novel)

The Hudson Family Series:
Rain
Lightning Strikes

My Sweet Audrina
(does not belong to a series)

Published by POCKET BOOKS

For orders other than by individual consumers, Pocket Books grants a discount on the purchase of **10 or more** copies of single titles for special markets or premium use. For further details, please write to the Vice President of Special Markets, Pocket Books, 1230 Avenue of the Americas, 9th Floor, New York, NY 10020-1586.

For information on how individual consumers can place orders, please write to Mail Order Department, Simon & Schuster Inc., 100 Front Street, Riverside, NJ 08075.

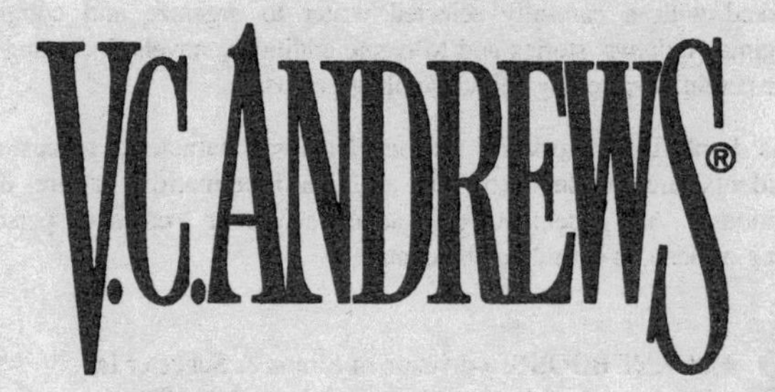

POCKET BOOKS
New York London Toronto Sydney Singapore

Following the death of Virginia Andrews, the Andrews family worked with a carefully selected writer to organize and complete Virginia Andrews' stories and to create additional novels, including the four herein, inspired by her storytelling genius.

POCKET BOOKS, a division of Simon & Schuster Inc.
1230 Avenue of the Americas, New York, NY 10020

ISBN: 0-7434-0361-4

First Pocket Books paperback printing August 2000

10 9 8 7 6 5 4 3 2 1

Cover design by Jim Lebbad
Front cover illustrations by Lisa Falkenstern

Printed in the U.S.A.

QB

Contents

Prologue

I was alone in Mrs. McGuire's office, waiting to meet the couple who had asked to see me. Sitting "properly" on the straight-back chair next to Mrs. McGuire's desk was making my back ache but I knew from past experience that I had better be on my best behavior. Mrs. McGuire was the chief administrator of our orphanage and pounced on us if we slouched or did anything else "improper" in front of visitors.

"Posture, posture," she would cry out when she passed us in the cafeteria, and we all would snap to attention. Those who didn't obey her had to walk around with a book on their heads for hours, and if the book fell off, they would have to do it over again the next day.

"You children are orphans," she lectured to us, "looking for some nice people to come snatch you up and make you members of their families. You must be better than other children, children with parents and homes. You must be healthier, smarter, more polite, and most certainly more respectful. In short," she said in a voice that often turned shrill during her endless speeches, "you must become desirable. Why," she asked, sweeping her eyes over each and every one of us critically, her thin lips pursed, "would anyone want you to be their daughter or son?"

She was right. Who would ever want me? I thought. I was born prematurely. Some of the boys and girls here said I was stunted. Just yesterday, Donald Lawson called me the Dwarf.

"Even when you're in high school, you'll wear little-girl clothes," he taunted.

He strutted away with his head high, and I could tell it made him feel better to make me feel bad. My tears were like trophies for him, and the sight of them didn't make him feel sorry. Instead, they encouraged him.

"Even your tears are tiny," he sang as he walked down the hall. "Maybe we should call you Tiny Tears instead of the Dwarf."

The kids at the orphanage weren't the only ones who thought there was something wrong with me, though. Margaret Lester, who was the tallest girl in the orphanage, fourteen with legs that seemed to reach up to her shoulders, overheard the last couple I'd met talking about me and couldn't wait to tell me all the horrible things they had to say.

"The man said he thought you were adorable, but

when they found out how old you were, they wondered why you were so small. She thought you might be sickly and then they decided to look at someone else," Margaret told me with a twisted smirk on her face.

No potential parents ever looked at her, so she was happy when one of us was rejected.

"I'm not sickly," I whispered in my own defense. "I haven't even had a cold all year."

I always spoke in a soft, low voice and then, when I was made to repeat something, I struggled to make my voice louder. Mrs. McGuire said I had to appear more self-assured.

"It's fine to be a little shy, Janet," she told me. "Goodness knows, most children today are too loud and obnoxious, but if you're too modest, people will pass you over. They'll think you're withdrawn, like a turtle more comfortable in his shell. You don't want that, do you?"

I shook my head but she continued her lecture.

"Then stand straight when you speak to people and look at them and not at the floor. And don't twist your fingers around each other like that. Get your shoulders back. You need all the height you can achieve."

When I had come to her office today, she had me sit in this chair and then paced in front of me, her high heels clicking like little hammers on the tile floor as she advised and directed me on how to behave once the Delorices arrived. That was their names, Sanford and Celine Delorice. Of course, I hadn't set eyes on them before. Mrs. McGuire told me, however, that they had seen me a number of times. That came as a surprise. A number of times? I wondered when, and if that was true, why had I never seen them?

"They know a great deal about you, Janet, and still they are interested. This is your best opportunity yet. Do you understand?" she asked, pausing to look at me. "Straighten up," she snapped.

I did so quickly.

"Yes, Mrs. McGuire," I said.

"What?" She put her hand behind her ear and leaned toward me. "Did you say something, Janet?"

"Yes, Mrs. McGuire."

"Yes what?" she demanded, standing back, her hands on her hips.

"Yes, I understand this is my best opportunity, Mrs. McGuire."

"Good, good. Keep your voice strong and clear. Speak only when you're spoken to, and smile as much as you can. Don't spread your legs too far apart. That's it. Let me see your hands," she demanded, reaching out to seize them in her own long, bony fingers.

She turned my hands over so roughly my wrists stung.

"Good," she said. "You do take good care of yourself, Janet. I think that's a big plus for you. Some of our children, as you know, think they are allergic to bathing."

She glanced at the clock.

"They should be arriving soon. I'm going out front to greet them. Wait here and when we come through the door, stand up to greet us. Do you understand?"

"Yes, Mrs. McGuire." Her hand went behind her ear again. I cleared my throat and tried again. "Yes, Mrs. McGuire."

She shook her head and looked very sad, her eyes full of doubt.

"This is your big chance, your best chance, Janet. Maybe, your last chance," she muttered and left the office.

Now I sat gazing at the bookcase, the pictures on her desk, the letters in frames congratulating her on her performance as an administrator in our upstate New York child welfare agency. Bored with the things decorating Mrs. McGuire's office, I turned around in my chair to stare out the windows. It was a sunny spring day. I sighed as I looked out at the trees, their shiny green leaves and budding blossoms calling to me. Everything was growing like weeds because of the heavy spring rain, and I could tell Philip, the groundskeeper, wasn't very happy to be mowing the endless lawns so early in the season. His face was screwed up in a scowl and I could just imagine him grumbling about the grass coming up so fast this year, you could watch it grow. For a moment I drifted away in the monotonous sound of Philip's lawn-mower and the dazzling sunlight streaming in through the windows. I forgot I was in Mrs. McGuire's office, forgot I was slouching with my eyes closed.

I tried to remember my real mother, but my earliest memories are of being in an orphanage. I was in one other besides this one, then I got transferred here when I was nearly seven. I'm almost thirteen now, but even I would admit that I look no more than nine, maybe ten. Because I couldn't remember my real mother, Tommy Turner said I was probably one of those babies that doctors make in a laboratory.

"I bet you were born in a test tube and that's why you're so small. Something went wrong with the experiment," he'd said as we left the dining hall last night. The other kids all thought he was very clever and laughed at his joke. Laughed at me.

"Janet's mother and father were test tubes," they taunted.

"No," Tommy said. "Her father was a syringe and her mother was a test tube."

"Who named her Janet then?" Margaret asked doubtfully.

Tommy had to think.

"That was the name of her lab technician, Janet Taylor, so they gave her that name," he answered, and from the look on their faces, I could tell the other kids believed him.

Last night, like every night, I had wished with all my heart that I knew something about my past, some fact, a name, anything that I could say to Tommy and the others to prove that once upon a time I did have a real Mommy and Daddy. I wasn't a dwarf or a test tube baby, I was . . . well, I was like a butterfly—destined to be beautiful and soar high above the earth, high above troubles and doubts, high above nasty little kids who made fun of other people just because they were smaller and weaker.

It's just that I hadn't burst from my cocoon yet. I was still a shy little girl, curled up in my quiet, cozy world. I knew that someday I would have to break free, to be braver, speak louder, grow taller, but right now that seemed all too scary. The only way I knew how to keep the taunts and teasing of the other kids from bothering me was to stay in my own little cocoon—where it was warm and safe and no one could hurt me. But someday, someday I would soar. Like a beautiful butterfly, I would climb higher and higher, flying high above them all. I'd show them.

Someday.

One

"Janet!" I heard Mrs. McGuire hiss, and my eyes snapped open. Her face was filled with fury, her mouth twisted, her gray eyes wide and lit up like firecrackers. "Sit up," she whispered through her clenched teeth, and then she forced a smile and turned to the couple standing behind her. "Right this way, Mr. and Mrs. Delorice," she said in a much nicer tone of voice.

I took a deep breath and held it, my fluttering heart suddenly sounding like a kettle drum in my chest. Mrs. McGuire stepped behind me so that the Delorices could get a good look at me. Mr. Delorice was tall and thin with dark hair and sleepy eyes. Mrs. Delorice sat in a wheelchair and was pretty, with hair the color of a red sunset. She had diminutive facial features like my own, but even more perfectly proportioned. Her hair floated around her shoulders in soft undulating waves. There was nothing sickly or frail looking about her, despite her wheelchair. Her complexion was rich like peaches and cream, her lips the shade of fresh strawberries.

She wore a bright yellow dress, my favorite color, and a string of tiny pearls around her neck. She looked like every other potential mommy I had seen except for the wheelchair and the tiny little shoes she wore. Although I'd never seen ballet shoes before, I thought that was what they were. If she was in a wheelchair, why was she wearing ballet shoes? I wondered.

Mr. Delorice pushed her right up to me. I was too fascinated to move, much less speak. Why would a woman in a wheelchair want to adopt a child my age?

"Mr. and Mrs. Delorice, this is Janet Taylor. Janet, Mr. and Mrs. Delorice."

"Hello," I said, obviously not loud enough to please Mrs. McGuire. She gestured for me to stand and I scrambled out of the chair.

"Please, dear, call us Sanford and Celine," the pretty woman said. She held out her hand and I took it gingerly, surprised at how firmly she held her fingers around mine. For a moment we only looked at each other. Then I glanced up at Sanford Delorice.

He was looking down at me, his eyes opening a bit wider to reveal their mixture of brown and green. He had his hair cut very short, which made his skinny face look even longer and narrower. He was wearing a dark gray sports jacket with no tie and a pair of dark blue slacks. The upper two buttons on his white shirt were open. I thought it was to give his very prominent Adam's apple breathing space.

"She's perfect, Sanford, just perfect, isn't she?" Celine said, gazing at me.

"Yes, she is, dear," Sanford replied. He had his long fingers still wrapped tightly around the handles of the wheelchair as if he was attached or afraid to let go.

"Did she ever have any training in the arts?" Celine asked Mrs. McGuire. She didn't look at Mrs. McGuire when she asked. She didn't look away from me. Her eyes were fixed on my face, and although her staring was beginning to make me feel creepy, I was unable to look away.

"The arts?"

"Singing, dancing . . . ballet, perhaps?" she asked.

"Oh no, Mrs. Delorice. The children here are not that fortunate," Mrs. McGuire replied.

Celine turned back to me. Her eyes grew smaller, even more intensely fixed on me.

"Well, Janet will be. She'll be that fortunate," she predicted with certainty. She smiled softly. "How would you like to come live with Sanford and myself, Janet? You'll have your own room, and a very large and comfortable one, too. You'll attend a private school. We'll buy you an entirely new wardrobe, including new shoes. You'll have a separate area in your room for your schoolwork and you'll have your own bathroom. I'm sure you'll like our house. We live just outside of Albany with a yard as large, if not larger than you have here."

"That sounds wonderful," Mrs. McGuire said as if she were the one being offered the new home, but Mrs. Delorice didn't seem at all interested in what she said. Instead she stared at me and waited for my response.

"Janet?" Mrs. McGuire questioned when a long moment of silence had passed.

How could I ever refuse this, and yet when I looked up at Sanford and back at Celine, I couldn't help feeling little footsteps of trepidation tiptoeing across my heart. I pushed the shadowy faces out of my mind, glanced at Mrs. McGuire, and then nodded.

"I'd like that," I said, wishing I was as good as Mrs. McGuire at faking a smile.

"Good," Celine declared. She spun her chair around to face Mrs. McGuire. "How soon can she leave?"

"Well, we have some paperwork to do. However, knowing all that we already know about you and your husband, your impressive references, the social worker's report, et cetera, I suppose . . ."

"Can we take her with us today?" Celine demanded impatiently.

My heart skipped a beat. Today? That fast?

For once Mrs. McGuire was at a loss for words.

"I imagine that could be done," she finally replied.

"Good," she said. "Sanford, why don't you stay with Mrs. McGuire and fill out whatever paperwork has to be filled out. Janet and I can go outside and get more acquainted in the meantime," she said. It was supposed to be a suggestion, I guess, but it sounded like an order to me. I looked at Mr. Delorice and could see the muscles in his jaw were clenched, along with his fingers on the wheelchair handles.

"But there are documents that require both signatures," Mrs. McGuire insisted.

"Sanford has power of attorney when it comes to my signature," Celine countered. "Janet, can you push my chair? I don't weigh all that much," she added, smiling.

I looked at Mrs. McGuire. She nodded and Sanford stepped back so that I could take hold of the handles.

"Where shall we go, Janet?" she asked me.

"I guess we can go out to the garden," I said uncertainly. Mrs. McGuire nodded again.

"That sounds wonderful. Don't be any longer than you have to, Sanford," she called back as I started to push her to the door. I went ahead and opened it and then I pushed her through.

I started down the hallway, overwhelmed and amazed with myself and what was happening. Not only was I going to have parents, but I had found a mother who wanted me to take care of her, almost as much as I wanted her to take care of me. What a strange and wonderful new beginning, I thought as I wheeled my new mother toward the sunny day that awaited us.

"Has it been difficult for you living here, Janet?" Celine asked after I had wheeled her outside. We followed the path to the garden.

"No, ma'am," I said, trying not to be distracted by the kids who were looking our way.

"Oh, don't call me ma'am, Janet. Please," she said, turning to place her hand over mine. It felt so warm. "Why don't you call me Mother. Let's not wait to get to know each other. Just do that immediately," she pleaded.

"Okay," I said. I could tell already that Mrs. Delorice didn't like to be argued with.

"You speak so softly, darling. I suppose you've felt so insignificant, but you won't feel that way anymore. You're going to be famous, Janet. You're going to be spectacular," she declared with such passion in her voice it made the breath catch in my throat.

"Me?"

"Yes, you, Janet. Come around and sit on this bench," she said when we had reached the first one along the pathway. She folded her hands in her lap and waited until I sat. Then she smiled. "You float, Janet. Do you realize that? You glide almost as if you're walking on a cloud of air. That's instinctive. Grace is something you're either born with or not, Janet. You can't learn it. No one can teach that to you.

"Once," she said as her green eyes darkened, "I had grace. I glided, too. But," she said quickly changing her expression and tone back to a happier, lighter one, "let's talk about you first. I've been watching you."

"When?" I said, recalling what Mrs. McGuire had told me.

"Oh, on and off for a little more than two weeks. Sanford and I came here at different times of the day. Usually we sat in our car and watched you and your unfortunate brothers and sisters at play. I even saw you at your school," she admitted.

My mouth widened with surprise. They had followed me to school? She laughed.

"When I first set eyes on you, I knew I had to have you. I knew you were the one, Janet. You remind me so much of myself when I was your age."

"I do?"

"Yes, and when Sanford and I went home, I would think about you and dream about you, and actually see you gliding down our staircase and through our home. I could even hear the music," she said, with a faraway look in her eyes.

"What music?" I asked, starting to think that Mrs. Delorice might be a little more than just bossy.

"Music you'll dance to, Janet. Oh," she said, leaning forward to reach for my hand, "there is so much to tell you and so much to do. I can't wait to start. That's why I wanted Sanford to cut right through all that silly bureaucratic paperwork and take us both home. Home," she repeated, her smile softening even more. "I suppose that's a foreign word to you, isn't it? You've never had a home. I know all about you," she added.

"What do you know?" I asked. Maybe she knew something about my real mommy and daddy.

"I know you were an orphan shortly after your birth and ever since. I know some very stupid people came to find children to adopt and passed you by. That's their loss and my gain," she followed with a thin, high-pitched laugh.

"What did you mean when you said music I would dance to?" I asked.

She released my hand and sat back. For a moment I didn't think she was going to answer. She stared off toward the woods. A sparrow landed near us and studied us with curiosity.

"After I picked you out, I observed you, auditioning you in my own mind," she explained. "I studied your walk, your gestures, and your posture to see if you were capable of being trained to become the dancer I was to be, the dancer I can no longer even dream to be. Beyond a doubt I am convinced you can. Would you like that? Would you like to be a famous dancer, Janet?"

"A famous dancer? I've never thought about it," I said honestly. "I do like to dance. I like music too," I added.

"Of course you do," she responded. "Someone with your natural grace and rhythm has to love music, and you'll love to dance, too. You'll love the power. You'll feel . . ." She closed her eyes and took a deep breath. When she opened her eyes I saw that they were filled with an eerie light. "You'll feel you can soar like a bird. When you're good, and you will be good, you will lose yourself in the music, Janet. It will carry you off, just as it did for me so many, many times before I became crippled."

"What happened to you?" I dared to ask. It was obvious that talking about dancing made her emotional, but the eerie look in her eyes made me nervous and I wanted her to do something besides stare at me so intently.

Mrs. Delorice lost her soft, dreamy smile and gazed back at the building before turning to me and replying.

"I was in a very bad car accident. Sanford lost control of our vehicle one night when we were returning from a party. He had a little too much to drink, although he'll never ever admit to that. He claimed he was blinded by the lights of a tractor-trailer truck. We went off the road and hit a tree. He was wearing his seat belt but I had forgotten to put mine on. The door opened and I was thrown from the car. My spine was very badly damaged. I almost died."

"I'm sorry," I said quickly.

Her face hardened, the lines deepening as shadows darkened her complexion.

"I'm past being sorry. I was sorry for years, but being sorry for yourself doesn't help one bit, Janet. Never indulge in self-pity. You become incapable of helping yourself. Oh," she said excited again, the light in her eyes returning, "I have so much to tell you, to teach you. It's going to be wonderful for both of us. Are you excited, too?"

"Yes," I said. I was, but everything was moving so fast and I couldn't help feeling nervous and a little bit scared.

She turned toward the building.

"Where is he? I never saw a man waste so much time. Oh, but you'll get to admire him for his compassion and sensitivity," she said. "There isn't anything he wouldn't do for me now, and now," she said with a wider smile, "there isn't anything he won't do for you.

"Think of it, Janet, think of it," she urged, "for the first time in your life, you will have two loving people who will care more about you than they will for themselves. Oh yes, it's true, dear, precious Janet. Look at me. Why should I worry about myself anymore? I'm a prisoner in this damaged body forever, and Sanford, Sanford lives to make me happy. So you see," she said with that tiny, thin laugh again, "if my happiness depends on your happiness, Sanford will cherish you as much as I will.

"You will be happy, Janet," she said with such firmness it frightened me. It was almost as if she was commanding me to be happy. "That," she said, "I promise you."

Sanford stepped out of the building.

"It's about time," she muttered. "Come, Janet, dear. Let us begin your new life. Let's think of this as your true birth. Okay? We'll even use this day as your birthday from now on. Why not? Yes? I like that idea. Don't you?" she declared with another thin laugh. "Today is your birthday!"

"Sanford," she called before I could reply. Actually, I didn't know what to say. My birthday had never been very special to me. He started toward us. "This day is more extraordinary than we imagined. It's Janet's birthday."

"It is?" he asked, looking confused. "But, I thought . . ."

"It is." She stamped her words in the air between them and he nodded.

She reached her hand out to me.

"Come along now," she said. "We're going home to celebrate."

When I saw the grim look on Sanford's face and remembered the crazy light that had come into Mrs. Delorice's eyes, I wondered just what I had gotten myself into.

Two

Despite the years I had lived at the orphanage, there wasn't anyone I was sorry to leave behind. My good-byes were quick. Those who had made fun of me for so long just stared with envy. No one had much to say. Only Margaret came up to me as I was getting my things together and whispered, "What kind of a mother is a mother in a wheelchair?"

"One who wants to love me," I replied and left her gnawing on the inside of her cheek.

Celine was already in the car, waiting. Sanford helped me with my things and then opened the car door for me as if he were my chauffeur. They had a very expensive-looking black car with leather seats that felt as soft as marshmallows. I thought the car was as big as a limousine. It had the scent of fresh roses.

"Look at her, Sanford," Celine said. "She's not the least bit sorry to be leaving that place. Are you, dear?"

"No . . ." The following word seemed hard to form, so alien. My tongue tripped over itself. "Mother."

"Did you hear her, Sanford? Did you hear what she called me?"

"I did, honey." He looked back at me and smiled for the first time since I'd met him. "Welcome to our family, Janet."

"Thank you," I said, but I knew I had spoken too softly for either of them to hear.

"We had a nice conversation in the garden while you were crossing T's and dotting I's, Sanford."

"Oh?"

"Janet told me she loves to dance," Celine said.

"Really?" Sanford sounded surprised.

I had said I liked dancing, but I hadn't done enough dancing to say I loved it, especially the sort of dancing she meant. She turned to face me.

"I was younger than you when I started training, Janet. My mother was very supportive, maybe because her mother, my grandmother Annie, was a prima ballerina. It broke my mother's heart almost as much as it did mine when I had to stop." She had turned to look at me and I could see the strange light had returned to her eyes.

She took a deep breath before continuing.

"Both my parents are still alive. They live in Westchester in the same house where my brother Daniel and I were raised," she explained.

My heart began to pound again. It was one thing to dream of having a mommy and daddy, but another to think up an entire family with grandparents and uncles and aunts. Maybe there was a cousin, too, a girl about my age with whom I could become best friends.

"Unfortunately, both of Sanford's parents are gone," she continued. She gazed at him again. "His sister Marlene lives in Denver but we don't see her very much. She doesn't approve of me."

"Celine, please," he said weakly.

"Yes, Sanford's right. No unpleasantness, never again. You don't need to know any of the unpleasantness I've had to bear. You've known enough during your poor little life," she said. "You don't have to worry about money, either. We're rich."

"You shouldn't say things like that, Celine," Sanford gently chastised. I could tell immediately that he was sorry he'd spoken.

"Why not? Why shouldn't I be proud? Sanford owns and operates a glass factory. We're not as big as Corning, but we're competition for them, aren't we, Sanford?" she bragged.

"Yes, dear." He looked back at me. "Once you've settled in, I'll show you the plant."

"You can show her, but she's not going to spend a great deal of time down there, Sanford. She'll be too busy with her schooling and her dancing," Celine assured him.

A cold drop of ice trickled along my spine.

"What if I can't be a dancer?" I asked. Would they send me back?

"Can't be? Don't be silly, Janet. I told you, you

have grace. You already dance. You dance when you walk, the way you hold yourself, the way you look at people, the way you sit. Having been gifted with this myself, I know how to recognize it in someone else. You won't fail," she said confidently. "I won't let you fail. I'll be your cushion, your parachute. You won't suffer the sort of disappointments I suffered," she pledged.

Even more anxious, I squeezed my arms around myself. When I was younger, I would pretend my arms were my mother's arms, holding me. I would close my eyes and imagine the scent of her hair, the softness of her face, the warmth of her lips on my forehead. Would Celine ever hold me like that? Or would her being in a wheelchair make that too difficult to do?

I gazed out the window at the scenery that flowed by. It was as if the whole world had become liquid and ran past us in a stream of trees, houses, fields, and even people. Few took any special notice of us even though I felt so special. They should all be cheering as we go by. I'm not an orphan anymore.

"Looks like some rain ahead," Sanford predicted and nodded at a ridge of dark clouds creeping toward us from the horizon.

"Oh phooey," Celine declared. "I want the sun to shine all day today."

Sanford smiled and I could feel the tension ease out of him.

"I'll see what I can do," he said. The way he looked at her, doted on her, I had no doubt that if he could, he would shape the weather and the world to please her. There was love here, I thought, some sort of love. I only hoped it was the right sort.

When I finally set my eyes on their house, I thought I had fallen into a storybook. No one really lived in such a house, I thought, even as we went up the long circular driveway with perfectly trimmed hedges on both sides. Evenly spaced apart were charcoal gray lampposts, the bulbs encased in shiny brass fixtures. Celine hadn't been exaggerating. They did have more lawn than the orphanage. There were large sprawling red maple trees with leaves that looked like dark rubies, and a pair of enormous weeping willow trees, the tips of the branches touching the ground to form a cave of shadows. I could just make out the shape of two benches and a small fountain surrounded by the darkness. Squirrels scurried around the fountain and over the benches, up trees and through the grass with a nervous, happy energy. I saw a rabbit pop out from behind the trees, look our way, and then hop toward the taller grass.

I turned to look at the house, a tall two-story with a porch that wrapped all the way around. Two robins paraded over the four wooden front steps. Alongside them was a ramp for Celine's wheelchair and a sparrow stood so still on it, he looked stuffed.

It all seemed so magical, touched by a fairy's wand and brought to life.

"Home sweet home," Celine declared. "We did a lot to modernize it after we bought it. It's Victorian," she explained. I didn't know what that meant, but from the way she said it, I understood it was impressive.

The house looked like it had been recently painted, a bright, crisp white. The paired entry doors had mirrored glass in the top halves of each and all the windows on the first and second floors had filmy white curtains in them. Only the attic windows were dark, with what looked like dark gray drapes pulled closed.

"Your room faces the east so you will have bright morning sunshine to wake you every day," Celine explained.

To the right and just behind the house was the garage, but Sanford stopped the car in front and got out quickly. He opened the trunk, took out Celine's wheelchair, and moved to open her door.

"Get her things," Celine commanded as soon as she was in her chair.

"Don't you want me to get you into the house first?"

"No. I asked you to get her things," she repeated firmly. "Where is that Mildred?" she muttered under her breath.

I stepped out and stared up at the house, my new home. Celine had gotten a little of her wish. The clouds had parted briefly and rays of light made the windows glitter as we stood there, but before we went up to the front doors, the clouds shifted and deepened the shadows again. Celine shuddered and tightened the shawl Sanford had placed around her shoulders.

"How do you like it?" she asked me expectantly.

"It's beautiful," I said.

However, most of my life homes with families in them looked beautiful to me, even if they were half the size and cost of this one. Behind closed doors and on the other side of curtains, families sat having dinner or watching television together. Brothers and sisters teased each other, but told each other secret things and held each other's dreams in strict confidence. There were shoulders to lean on, lips that would kiss away tears, voices that would warm cold and frightened little hearts. There were daddies who had strong arms to hold you, daddies who smelled of the outdoors and aftershave, daddies with love in their smiles; and mommies who were beautiful and soft, who were scented with flowery aromas, perfumes that filled your nostrils and stirred your imagination and filled your head with dreams of becoming as lovely and as pretty.

Yes, it was a beautiful house. They were all beautiful houses.

"Hurry along, please, Sanford," Celine said, wheeling herself to the base of the ramp.

He struggled with two suitcases and one of the smaller bags. I started toward her chair, but she turned in anticipation. It was as if she had eyes behind her head.

"No, Janet. I don't want you doing anything this strenuous. You can't afford to pull a tendon."

I stopped, confused. Pull a tendon? I had no idea what she meant.

"It's all right," Sanford told me and somehow

managed to take hold of the chair as he kept the suitcases under his arm. He pushed her up the ramp and I followed. When we reached the porch, he put down the suitcases and hurried around to unlock the door.

"Where is that fool?" she asked him sharply. I had no idea who she was talking about. Did someone else live in their beautiful house?

"It's all right," he said inserting his door key.

Celine turned and smiled at me.

"Now you can push me, sweetheart," she said, and I moved quickly to the back of the chair.

Sanford opened the door and we entered the house. The entryway was wide with mirrors on both sides. On the right was a coatrack and a small table on which were some sort of pamphlets. When I looked closer, I saw they were programs for a dance recital. On the front of one was Celine's picture. Above it in big red letters were the words *Sleeping Beauty.*

"I want you to see the studio first," she said when she saw what had captured my attention. "Sanford, bring her things upstairs to her room and see if you can find Mildred. We'll be along in a few minutes."

I saw there was a special elevator chair that ran up the side of the stairway. At the top was another wheelchair. Celine wheeled herself deeper into the house and I followed slowly, drinking everything in: the beautiful paintings on the walls, all of dancers, one who looked very much like Celine.

"This is our living room," she said, nodding at a room on the left.

I could only glance at it because she moved quickly down the hall. I saw the fancy pink and white sofa with frills along the base, a red cushioned chair, the fieldstone fireplace and mantel, above which was a grand painting of Celine in a ballet costume.

"Here," she declared, pausing at another doorway.

I stepped up beside her and looked into the room. It was large and empty, with a shiny wooden floor. All around the room were full-length mirrors and on one side was a long wooden bar.

"This is my studio and now it is yours," she declared. "I had a wall knocked out and two rooms connected. You can spare no expense when it comes to your art."

"Mine?" I asked.

"Of course, Janet. I will get you the best instructor, Madame Malisorf, who has trained some very famous Russian ballet dancers and once was an accomplished ballerina herself. She was my teacher and mentor." And again that faraway, eerie look came over her.

"I really don't know anything about ballet," I said, my voice trembling. I was afraid she would want to return me to the orphanage immediately when she learned how clumsy I was.

"That's all right. That's good. I'd rather you didn't know anything," she replied, taking my hand.

"You would?"

"Yes. This way you're pure, an innocent, an untouched dancer, not contaminated by any mediocre teacher. Madame Malisorf will be pleased," she assured me. "She loves working with pure talent."

"But I don't have any talent," I said.

"Of course you do."

"I don't think I've even seen a ballet on television," I confessed.

She laughed and I was glad to see her normal face returning.

"No, I don't imagine you did, living in those places with children who have had no opportunities. You mustn't be so afraid," she said softly, squeezing my hand. "Ballet is not as difficult as you might imagine and it's not some strange form of dance reserved only for the very rich. It's just another way of telling a story, a beautiful way, through dance. Ballet is the foundation of all Western theatrical dance. People who want to be modern dancers or dancers in show business are always advised to start with ballet."

"Really?"

"Of course." She smiled. "So you see, you will be doing something that will help you in so many ways. You'll have wonderful posture, more grace, rhythm, and beauty. You will be my prima ballerina, Janet."

She stared at me with her eyes so full of hope and love I could only smile back. Suddenly we heard a door slam and someone hurrying down the stairs. She turned her chair and I looked back to see a tall young blond girl come down the hallway. She was dressed in a maid's uniform. She had large brown eyes with a nose a little too long and a mouth a little too wide with a weak, bony chin.

"I'm sorry, Mrs. Delorice. I didn't hear you drive up."

"Probably because you had those stupid earphones in your ears again, listening to that ugly rock music," Celine quipped.

The maid cringed and began to shake her head vigorously.

"Stop sniveling, Mildred, and meet our daughter, Janet," Celine said sharply and then her voice softened. "And Janet, this is our maid, Mildred Stemple."

"How do you do," Mildred said with a small dip. When she smiled, her features shifted and she actually looked pretty. "Call me Milly."

"She will not," Celine corrected quickly. "Her name is Mildred," she told me firmly.

Mildred's smile wilted.

"Hello . . . Mildred," I said, not wanting to make waves.

"I was making sure her room was clean and ready, Mrs. Delorice," Mildred said, continuing her explanation for not coming to the front door.

"You're always leaving things for the last minute, Mildred. I don't know why I keep you. We'll have an early dinner tonight. You have the turkey roasting, I assume?"

"Oh yes, Mrs. Delorice."

"Well, see to getting the rest ready," Celine ordered.

Mildred glanced at me, smiled quickly, and left.

"That," Celine said, raising her eyes to the ceiling,

"is my act of charity. Anyway, back to what I was saying. Madame Malisorf will be here the day after tomorrow to meet you."

"The day after tomorrow?"

"We don't want to waste time, dear. In dance, especially ballet, training is so important. I wish I had found you when you were years younger. It would have been easier, but don't fret about it. You're at a perfect age. You'll begin with a sequence of exercises to build up your precious little muscles. There is always a great deal of stretching and warming up to prevent injury. You'll learn how to use the barre."

"Barre?"

"The bar there is known as a *barre,*" she said and spelled it out. "All the terms in ballet are French. Ballet began in France. You use the barre to steady yourself during the first part of ballet class. It provides resistance when you press down on it and helps to lengthen the spine." She laughed. "Think of it as your first partner. I used to give my barre a name. I called it Pierre," she said with a perfect French pronunciation. "I'm sure you'll find a suitable name for your first partner, too."

I gazed through the doorway at the barre, wondering how I could ever think of it as a person.

"Come along, dear. We have so much to do. I need to have you fitted for pointe shoes and buy you leotards first thing in the morning."

"What about school?" I asked. She kept wheeling and then paused at the foot of the stairway.

"Don't worry. I'm enrolling you in a private

school. We can do that later. First things first," she said. She started to move into the chairlift.

First things first? But wouldn't my schooling be the first thing?

"Let me help you, darling," Sanford called as he came down the stairs.

"I'm fine," she said slipping into the lift chair. She pressed a button and it began to move up the railing. I watched her for a moment. She looked radiant and excited as she rose above us.

"How wonderful," Sanford declared at my side. "Just your coming here has already filled her with new strength. We're blessed to have you, my dear."

I gazed up at him and wondered what I had done to bring such happiness to two people who only hours ago had been complete strangers. I couldn't help being afraid that they had mistaken me for someone else.

Three

When I stood in the doorway of the room that was to be my very own, I felt my mouth fall open. Never in any of my most wonderful fantasies could I have imagined a room as beautiful as this, or as big as this, or as warm and cozy. And this was the first time in my life that a room was all mine, too!

"How do you like it?" Celine asked excitedly.

For a moment I couldn't speak. Like it? *Like* is too weak a word, I thought. I was to sleep here? To live and do my schoolwork here?

"It's so big," I began. I was afraid to step inside, afraid that if I did, it would all pop and disappear like a nice dream. Celine wheeled herself forward and Sanford stood behind me with his hands on my shoulders while she inspected the room to be sure Mildred had done a good job.

"Good. At least your things have been put away,"

she said. "We're going shopping first thing in the morning to get you some decent clothes," she added.

"I'd like to check on the factory first, dear. I'll come right back and . . ." Sanford began meekly.

"You can stay away from your precious factory one more day, Sanford. Your manager is quite competent. Anyway," she said, gazing at me, "what's more important?" She looked at him pointedly. He said nothing.

Anxious to avoid their heated words and glances, I entered my room. The curtains were flamingo pink as were the canopy, pillows, and comforter on the four-pillar bed. There was an eggshell white desk with a lamp that had a base shaped like a duck. On the walls were paintings of ballet dancers.

"Those are scenes from famous ballets, Janet," Celine explained. "That's *Swan Lake,* and that's *Le Jeune Homme et la Mort.* That one is *Romeo and Juliet,*" she said, nodding at the one over the bed. "I want you to be surrounded in dance—sleep, eat, and drink it just the way I did. In time it's all you'll care about," she said, and again I felt it was an order.

She wheeled herself to a cabinet next to the closet and opened it.

"Here you'll find tapes and CDs of music I want you to listen to and get to know so well you can hum entire productions. The music must become a part of you. You'll surely do as I did, hear the music, even while you're away from the studio, and you'll find yourself wanting to pirouette or perform a *changement de pieds.*"

"What's that?"

She looked at Sanford and smiled.

"Frequently you need to change the position of your feet, from right foot in front to left foot in front or vice versa. That's a jump in which you land with the other foot in front. So, changement de pieds, change of the feet. Don't worry. It will be easier than you think, especially for you," she said.

I looked at Sanford to see if he had as much confidence in me. His eyes were filled with smiles.

"Let her look around at her new room, Celine."

"Of course," she said, backing away. "Your bathroom is through that door."

I peered in at the round bathtub and stall shower. All of the fixtures were shiny brass, and then I saw the towels on the racks. There was something written on them. I drew closer to read.

"My name is on the towel!" I exclaimed.

Sanford laughed.

"And on the glass and the little soap dish," he added.

Amazed, I took it all in.

"But how did you do all this so fast?"

"Remember, I have a factory, and connections," he said, clearly amused at my question.

"But how did you know I would come here to live?" I pursued.

He gazed at Celine, who had wheeled up to the bathroom door.

"I told you, dear, from the moment I set eyes on you, I knew you were the one. The only one. We were destined to be a family."

I thought I would simply explode from the way happiness filled my heart. A beautiful bed, furniture, personalized bathroom items, new clothes, everything I could ever want. It was Christmas in springtime.

"Are you happy?" Sanford asked.

"Oh yes." I practically shouted the words and thought, finally, I'm speaking loudly enough to please even Mrs. McGuire.

"Good. Change into something casual and I'll show you our grounds," Sanford told me. "There's a lake out back, and in the summer we get geese."

"I'm going to call Madame Malisorf," Celine said, "and confirm your first lesson for the day after tomorrow. I'm so excited—I wonder if we should change it to first thing tomorrow? No, tomorrow we'll have to get your pointe shoes and leotards. We mustn't get ahead of ourselves."

"Shouldn't you wait before buying her the pointe shoes, dear?" Sanford asked softly.

"Absolutely not." She turned to me. "She's going to be Madame Malisorf's best student. Since me, of course. What a wonderful day!" She reached for me and then for Sanford. "We're finally a family," she said, looking at us with that faraway gaze.

I thought the tears that were burning under my eyelids would go streaming down my cheeks, but they remained where they were to wait for another time.

After I changed into a pair of old jeans and put on a blouse and sneakers, I wandered along the upstairs hallway. There was another bedroom with the door shut tight and then Sanford and Celine's room. Celine was inside, resting in bed and speaking to Sanford. I didn't want to seem like I was spying on them, so I turned to go downstairs and wait, when I heard Celine mention my name.

"Janet will blossom like a flower in our soil, won't she, Sanford?"

"Yes, dear," he said. "Please. Just rest a bit now. It's been a very long and emotional day for all of us."

"And when she does," Celine continued, ignoring him, "she will dazzle audiences the way I was meant to dazzle them."

Dazzle audiences? I thought. Me? The one the other children called Miss Fraidy Cat for as long as I could remember? The one who couldn't speak loud enough for someone right beside me to hear properly? Perform before audiences and dazzle them? How could I? As soon as Celine and Sanford realized I couldn't, they would send me back. I was so sure of it, my heart shriveled into a tight little knot. The beautiful room, this home, the promise of a family, all of it really was just a dream. I bowed my head and slowly descended the stairs.

I wandered into the living room and gazed up at the painting of Celine that hung above the mantel. The artist had captured her in the middle of a leap, maybe that changement de pieds she had described. Her legs, the ones that were hidden under a blanket, lifeless and limp now, looked shapely and muscular in the painting. She resembled a bird, soaring, just as she had described how I would feel someday. How graceful and beautiful she looked against the dark background. The painting was so lifelike, I half expected her to land before me.

"So here you are." I turned to see Sanford in the doorway. "Celine's taking a little rest. Come on. I'll show you our grounds. We'll walk down to the lake," he added and I noticed that he spoke in an entirely different voice when Celine wasn't around.

When we got outside I saw that the sky had cleared as Celine had said it would. I was beginning to wonder if everyone and everything did as Celine asked.

"This way," Sanford said, turning right at the bottom of the steps. He walked with his hands behind his back, his tall, lean body leaning forward. He took long, lanky strides, one for every two of mine. "This house was a find. It was in very good shape for its age, but we made a number of changes and improvements," he said. "I'm sure you will be as happy here as we have been, Janet." He smiled at me and nodded at the descending hillside before us. "Just over the crest is our lake. I have a rowboat, but we haven't used it for some time. Can you swim?"

"No sir," I said softly, afraid to add another "can't" to my name. Can't dance. Can't swim. Can't stay.

"Oh, well, that will have to be remedied before summer, and please, don't call me sir. If you can't call me Dad yet, just call me Sanford, okay?" His eyes twinkled and I relaxed and smiled back at him. Somehow I'd already gotten the impression that Sanford was going to be a lot easier to please than Celine.

We walked on.

"I have a service that comes twice a week to care for the grounds," he said. He waved his long arm toward the east. "We own all this property and then some. I've left woods intact so we have the privacy and the feeling we're out in nature. We're really not that far from the city. The private school you'll attend is only fifteen miles away, actually. Celine has already made all the arrangements. I just have to bring you there to enroll you."

"She has?" It made me feel strange to think that Celine had been planning a life for me, for us, before I'd even met her. What if I had said no to going home with them? But then, I was an orphan, and orphans never say no.

Sanford laughed at the perplexed look on my face.

"Oh yes. Celine has been preparing for your arrival literally from the first moment she set eyes on you, Janet. I'll never forget that day. She was so excited, she couldn't sleep and she wouldn't stop talking about you. She talked late into the night and when I woke up the next morning, your name was the first word on her lips."

Rather than fill me with joy, these words sent tiny electric shocks of fear along my spine. What did Celine see in me that I couldn't see in myself, that no one had ever seen before? What if it was all untrue?

"How come you don't have any children of your own?" I asked.

For a few minutes he walked along silently, and I thought perhaps he hadn't heard me, but then he paused, looked back at the house, and sighed. The grim expression that I had seen earlier was quickly returning to his face.

"I wanted to have children. From the first day we were married, I planned on having a family, but Celine was too devoted to her career, and she believed giving birth would take away from her power as a dancer.

"Anyway," he said, continuing to walk toward the hill, "she would be the first to admit she didn't have the temperament for children in those days." He shook his head. "You would have had to look far and wide to find someone as moody. I felt like an inept weatherman, unable to predict the days of sunshine or the days of gloom. One moment she was laughing, light, and happy, and the next, because of some dissatisfaction with her rehearsal, she would become dark and sad, wilting like a flower without water. Nothing I did could cheer her. But," he said, smiling at me again, "now that you're here, that's all going to change. There'll be no more dark days."

How could I make Celine so happy that she'd forget about her legs? Would watching me dance really make her feel any better about never being able to dance herself? How was I to be responsible for Celine's happiness? I was too small and too shy. I'd never be able to do it.

"I used to feel like I was walking barefoot on shattered glass when I returned home from business every day," Sanford continued and his voice interrupted my worrying. It was nice listening to him, to hear him open his heart to me as if I was already part of his family or had been a part of it for years. I just wish the thoughts and desires he confided in me were pleasant ones, but the more Sanford spoke the more I realized how sad and bitter he was. "Celine's moods were totally unpredictable, and after the accident they got worse. Now, that's all going to be different," he emphasized cheerily. I could tell he was trying not to say anything else gloomy.

We stopped at the top of the hill and looked out at the lake. It shimmered in the sunlight, the water looking smooth as ice. There was a dock just below us with the rowboat he had described.

"The lake's not that big, only about a half a mile or so, but it's nice to have water on your property. And the geese who visit every year are quite a sight toward the end of the summer. You'll see," he said. I was happy to hear him plan on my being here for a long time.

"It's pretty," I said. I was thankful he'd changed the subject.

"Yes, it is." He thought a moment and then looked at me. "Well, I've been talking about us so much, I haven't given you a chance to talk about yourself. What are the things you like to do? Did you ever ice-skate or roller-skate?" he asked.

I shook my head.

"I'm sure you haven't ever gone skiing. Do you play any sports?"

"I only play sports in school. I usually don't play at the orphanage."

"What about books? Do you like to read?"

"Yes."

"Good. We have a very good library. I like to read. I suppose you like television."

I nodded.

"And movies?"

"I haven't gone many times," I said. Actually, I could count the times on my fingers.

"Your life is going to change so much, Janet. I'm almost more excited for you than I am for us. Come along," he added after a moment. "I'll show you the wild berry bushes."

I hurried to keep up with him. Berry bushes, a lake with a rowboat, beautiful flowers and personal gardeners, a private school, and new clothes. I was beginning to believe I really was Cinderella! I just hoped that I could hold off the stroke of midnight for as long as possible.

That night I had my first dinner in my new home. Celine wore a candy apple red knit dress with gold teardrop earrings and a necklace that had a cameo in a gold frame. She looked beautiful. Sanford wore a suit and tie. I had only the worn-out light blue dress I had worn at the orphanage for our first meeting.

The dining room was lit by a large chandelier over the table. All of the dishes, the napkins, candles, and silverware looked so expensive I was afraid to touch a thing. Sanford sat at one end of the long table and Celine at the other with me on the side. Mildred began to serve the food just moments after we sat down. Nothing felt as strange as having a servant. From the day we were able to do for ourselves at the orphanage, we took care of our own needs.

I watched how Celine ate, pecking at her food like a small bird. Meanwhile Sanford explained to me which piece of silverware to use and dining etiquette. Everything was so delicious and I was very hungry, but Celine didn't allow me to eat as much as I would have liked.

"Don't offer her seconds on the potatoes," she commanded when Sanford reached for the bowl. "From this day forward, she has to watch her diet. Dancers," she explained, turning to me, "have to maintain their figures. Excess fat just won't do. It will slow you down and make you clumsy. Even though I don't dance anymore, I still watch my figure. Habits become part of who you are, define your personality. Remember that, Janet. I'm passing all my wisdom on to you, the wisdom that was passed on to me by very famous and successful people."

I left the table that night still feeling a little hungry, something I never did at the orphanage. How strange it was to look at all those delicious things and have to keep from tasting them. I glanced at Celine every time Sanford passed something along, and if she frowned or looked displeased, I didn't take any of it. Passing on the delicious-looking chocolate cake with creamy white frosting made my stomach grumble loudest.

"You'll notice," Celine said, wheeling beside me as we went to the living room, "that you don't have a television set in your room. I know teenagers are fond of that, but between your schoolwork and your dancing, you won't have time for much else, especially frivolous things. I never did."

"I didn't watch a lot of television at the orphanage," I replied. "There was only the one set in the recreational room and the older boys always decided what we would all see. I'd rather read."

"Good. I have a book on ballet that I want you to start tonight," she told me and wheeled past me into the living room. I followed and watched her pluck a book from the shelves. She held it out for me and I hurried to take it.

"It's full of basic information," she said, "so you won't look stupid when you meet Madame Malisorf the day after tomorrow."

"Oh, she's far too excited to read and retain all that, Celine," Sanford said quietly. I couldn't help but think that if he just spoke more strongly, Celine might just listen to him.

"Nonsense. I'm sure she's tired, too, and she'll want to go up to her room, get into her bed, and read." She turned to me, obviously looking for my agreement.

I looked at Sanford, at the book, and then at Celine.

"Yes," I said. "I am tired."

"Of course. It's not every day that you get to start your life over again," Celine said. She reached up for my hand and held it. "We're so alike, you and I, it's as if you really were my daughter."

I saw tears in her eyes. They put tears into mine. My heart thumped with the promise of finding real love, real joy.

"Get a good night's rest," she said. "Welcome to your new home."

She pulled me down to her and kissed me on the cheek. It was the first time in my life someone who wanted to be my mother had kissed me. I swallowed back my tears of happiness and headed out the door. Sanford stopped me and kissed me on the cheek, too.

"Good night, Janet. Just call me if you need anything," he said.

I thanked him and hurried up the stairway with the ballet book in my hands.

Then I went into my room and just stood there gazing around in wonderment.

I had a home.

I was someone's child.

Finally.

Four

Celine was so excited about getting me ready for my ballet lessons the next day that she was up and at my door before I had opened my eyes. When I had finally laid my head on the fluffy pillow last night, I had turned and gazed at myself in the wall mirror. The bed was so large, I looked even smaller than I was. It made me laugh. But it was so comfortable, the most comfortable bed I had ever slept in, and all the linen smelled fresh and brand-new. The next thing I knew, it was morning.

"Rise and shine, rise and shine," Celine sang as she wheeled herself into my room. "We have a great deal to do today, Janet."

I rubbed the sleep out of my eyes and sat up.

"Oh, you slept in your underwear!" she cried. "Don't you have a nightie?"

"No," I said.

"How do they send you out into the world without a nightie? Up, up, up. Get washed and dressed and come down to breakfast in fifteen minutes. We're off to the shops," she said with a sweep of her hand. Then she turned and wheeled out of my room.

I hurried to do what she asked, and in ten minutes, I was on my way down the stairs. Sanford was already dressed in his jacket and tie and sitting at the breakfast table reading the newspaper.

"Mildred," Celine called as soon as I set foot in the dining room.

Mildred came from the kitchen carrying a tray with orange juice, buttered toast, and a poached egg. I had never had a poached egg before. I stared at it all when it was set before me.

"You start your diet today," Celine explained when she saw my curious expression.

"Diet?" I had never been accused of being overweight. Everyone always thought I was underdeveloped. "But I don't weigh a lot," I said.

Celine laughed.

"Diet isn't something you watch just to lose weight. Diet in this case means eating properly. A dancer is an athlete and has to eat and live like one, Janet," Celine explained. "Go on, eat," she ordered.

Sanford lowered his paper and gave me a sympathetic smile as I drank my juice.

"Did you sleep well?" he asked.

"Yes," I said.

Celine leaned toward me to whisper, "Daddy."

"Yes, Daddy," I corrected.

"Good," Sanford said. "Good." He returned to his paper while Celine went on about our schedule.

"I have appointments arranged at the shoe store for your pointe shoes, and then we'll go to the shop where I will get you your dancing outfits. After that we'll go to the department store and get you some more clothes, regular shoes, undergarments, and a nice jacket for you to wear," she cataloged. "Oh, and a nightie."

"What about school?" I asked between bites. I couldn't help thinking about what it was going to be like to have new teachers and meet new children my age.

"School can wait another day," she declared. "I'm sure you're a very good student and it won't take you very long to catch up."

I was a good student, but I was still surprised at how confident she was about my abilities. Sanford folded his paper, sipped his coffee, and nodded.

"After that, we'll swing by the factory," he added.

"If we have time," Celine corrected.

I had barely swallowed my last bite of breakfast when she pushed away from the table and declared I should go brush my teeth and "Do your bathroom business." We were to meet at the front door in ten minutes.

Everything was ten minutes, five minutes. For a woman in a wheelchair, she had an unbelievable amount of energy. Rushing up the stairs, I thought I had been woken to participate in some sort of marathon, but I was afraid to utter a single syllable of complaint. Sanford seemed very happy about Celine's excitement and energy and they wanted to do so much for me.

By the time I returned, Celine was already in the car waiting. Sanford was just putting her wheelchair in the trunk.

"Hurry," she called. "I want to get everything done in one day."

I ran to the car and got in. Moments later, we were off.

"Getting the proper pointe shoes is paramount to success as a dancer," Celine lectured as we drove along. "In ballet, maybe more than in anything, initial preparations are very, very important. Your shoes should fit like a second skin. There is no room for growth. When you put them on before practice, don't tie the drawstring too tight. You can damage your Achilles tendon. Let me see your feet," she suddenly ordered.

"My feet?"

"Yes, yes, your feet. I need to check something. I should have done it before," she muttered.

I took off my sneakers and peeled off my socks. She reached back between the seats and pulled my feet toward her and inspected my toes.

"Oh," she cried, "these toenails are too long. Didn't they teach you anything at that orphanage? You must keep your toenails short. Cut them every morning, every morning, do you hear?"

"Yes," I said, nodding.

She reached into her purse and found a nail clipper. She handed it to me and watched as I trimmed my toenails. My hands shook and I thought I might cut myself, but Celine was starting to sound angry and I wanted to please her.

"Are you sure the store will be open this early, Celine?" Sanford asked as we approached the business district.

"Of course I'm sure. I made a specific appointment. They know how important this is to me," she added, and her voice was finally calming.

I put on my socks and sneakers quickly and gazed out the window as we slowed down and stopped before the specialty shop. Sanford hurried around to get Celine's wheelchair out of the trunk.

"It's such an inconvenience having to wait for that damn thing, and Sanford moves slower than a turtle," she muttered. She was so anxious to get into the store and have me fitted with pointe shoes. I wished I could be as excited about it as she was, but I felt as if I had been caught up in a whirlwind and barely had a chance to breathe. As soon as she was in her chair, she called to me. "Come on, Janet. We're late."

When we entered the store, the salesman, a short, chubby bald man with thin wire bifocals planted on his thick nose, came waddling from the rear to greet us.

"Mrs. Delorice," he said. "Good morning. It's so nice to see—"

"Here she is," Celine interrupted. "Janet, sit and take off your sneakers and socks."

The salesman nodded at Sanford.

"Mr. Delorice."

"Good morning, Charles. How have you been?" Sanford asked.

"Oh, fine, just fine."

"Please, let's concentrate," Celine demanded.

Charles frowned and squatted to study my feet. He held them in his hands as if they were jewels, gently turning them from side to side. He felt around under my toes and pressed on my heels.

"Exquisite," he said.

"She may look small to you, but she is not fragile," Celine assured him.

"Oh, I can see the potential, Mrs. Delorice, yes. Let me get her fitted." He looked genuinely pleased.

He rose and headed back to the rear of the store.

"All pointe shoes are handmade," Celine explained. "There is no right or left to them, so don't be confused."

"They must cost a lot," I said. I hoped her money wouldn't be wasted.

"Of course they do if they're good ones, and you must have the best. Our equipment, our dress, all of our preparations are very important for us, Janet," she said. It was the first time she had included herself and it sounded funny. It was as if she would rise out of the wheelchair and do one of her pirouettes in the shoe store.

Charles brought three pairs and tried each on my feet. Celine tested them as much as he did. She had me stand and then walk across the store.

"Very graceful young lady," Charles commented. I was beginning to wonder if Celine was right. Maybe I could be a dancer.

"Yes, she is," Celine said, her eyes shining with excitement. "How do those feel, Janet? Remember, I want you to think of them as a second skin."

"Good, I guess," I said. I really wasn't sure. I had never worn this kind of shoe before, and I didn't know how they should feel.

"Those have Toe-Flo," Charles remarked, "the best stuff ever invented for padding."

"I don't want her to become too dependent on that. I want her feet to toughen quickly." Celine's eyes darkened.

"Oh, they will," he promised.

"We'll see. We'll take them," she concluded.

"Very good choice, Mrs. Delorice," Charles said and I could almost see the dollar signs floating through his mind.

I sat and began to take the shoes off.

"We have to have the best so we can develop quickly," Celine said. She smiled at me and stroked my hair. "We're going to become prima ballerinas."

I looked at Sanford, who stood near the doorway. Again, I caught him wearing an expression of very deep concern, his eyes dark and concentrated on Celine. Then he saw me gazing at him and he smiled quickly.

After the shoes were purchased, we went to a store that sold the dancing costumes, called tutus, and leotards. Celine bought me a half dozen outfits, and this was only the beginning of what soon became a shopping frenzy. We went to the department store and flew through the lingerie department, shoe department, and then the clothing department. The registers clicked and dinged, printing out reels of receipts. It was as if all the clothing I should have had since birth was being bought now. In one day I was catching up with children who hadn't been orphans. I barely had time to take a breath before I was being herded into another section of the store, measured, fitted, and dressed to model whatever Celine thought might look nice. Price tags didn't seem to matter. She never looked at a single one, nor did she blink an eye when the totals were rung up. All she did was hold her hand out to Sanford, who produced his credit card.

Just a day before, I had thought of myself as an object of charity, cast off, living as a child of the state, without parents, without family, without anyone really caring if I looked nice or felt comfortable in my clothing and shoes. Suddenly, I was a little princess. Who could blame me for being afraid that I would blink and be back at the orphanage, waking from a dream?

Almost as if it pained her, Celine reluctantly agreed to stop for lunch. Sanford took us to a nice restaurant and told me I could order whatever I wanted from the menu, but Celine intercepted immediately and forbade me from ordering a big juicy hamburger.

"Choose a salad," she said. "You have to watch your fat content now."

"She's growing," Sanford said softly. "She'll burn off any calories, Celine."

"It's not what she'll burn off that's important. It's

development of good habits, Sanford. Please. I know what I'm doing. I was the one who trained, not you. And I don't want to hear about you spoiling her when I'm not with you, Sanford," she said, warning him with her eyes wide.

He looked at me and laughed, but it was a weak laugh, a laugh of embarrassment.

"I like salads," I said to stop any more arguments.

"There, you see. She has a natural proclivity to do the right thing. It's in her nature. She's instinctive, just as I was, Sanford. She's me. She understands," she said, smiling at me. As much as it made me uncomfortable, I knew I could easily please her. I just had to agree to go along with anything she said. I think I was beginning to understand why Sanford looked so grim all the time.

Sanford wanted us to share dessert, but Celine refused.

"She can have something after dinner tonight," she compromised and we were off again, this time to buy toiletries Celine decided I would need.

"I want you to take special care of your hair, Janet. Your complexion, your looks are very important. You're a performer, an artist, a living, natural work of art yourself. That's how I was taught to think and believe and that's how I want you to think," she declared.

When we were in that section of the store, she pulled me aside so Sanford wasn't able to hear us.

"Have you had your period yet?" she asked.

"No," I answered softly. It embarrassed me to admit it because all the girls I knew who were my age and even some a year younger had already had their first period.

Celine looked intently at me a moment. Then she nodded.

"Nevertheless, we'll be prepared for it," she said, and bought what I would need.

By the time we left the business district and headed for Sanford's glass factory, I was getting tired. Celine, however, continued to look energized. She talked and talked about my ballet lessons, preparing me for my first session with Madame Malisorf.

"A ballet class is a carefully graded sequence of exercises lasting at least an hour and a half, Janet. You'll begin with stretching and warming-up exercises using the barre. Madame Malisorf likes to spend nearly an hour doing that. Next, you'll move to the center of the studio to work without support. This second part of the class we call *adage.* It consists of slow work emphasizing sustaining positions and balance. The third part of the class is called *allegro,* and that consists of fast work, combinations, sequences of steps with the big jumps and turns that make ballet impressive. Can you remember all that, Janet? Madame Malisorf will be happy if you do." It was clear from her tone of voice that I should memorize what she'd said.

I told her I had read some of it in the book she had given me and that I would be sure to mention it to Madame Malisorf.

"Good. You'll pick it up faster than anyone expects. I just know you will," she said.

"We're here," Sanford announced proudly. It

seemed that aside from pleasing Celine, the factory was the most important thing in Sanford's life. Maybe soon I would be added to the list.

The factory looked much bigger than I had expected and there were dozens and dozens of cars parked in the lot. Sanford owned all this? No wonder money didn't seem to matter, I thought.

"I'm really very tired, Sanford," Celine suddenly said. "I should take a rest."

"But . . . well, can't I show Janet the plant and check on some matters?" The smile and proud glow were gone from his face.

"Take me home first," she commanded tersely. "Besides, Janet's seen the factory. Why does she have to go in and be exposed to all that dust?"

"Dust? It's not dusty inside, Celine. You know how proud I am of our industrial environment." He was starting to whine.

"Please," she groaned. "Between you and Daddy, I hear more than enough about business. My parents own a printing plant," she explained. "Please, drive on, Sanford."

I could see his jaw tightening as he looked at her and then he gazed at his factory and shrugged.

"I just thought since we were already here . . ." He had already given up. He sounded like one of us orphans when we'd been passed up by yet another set of potential parents.

"She's not just visiting us, Sanford. She's come to live with us. There will be other times," Celine reminded him.

"Of course. You're right, dear. Home it is," he said and started off with a sigh.

But what about my school? I couldn't help but wonder. Shouldn't we go there now?

Celine seemed to read my thoughts.

"In the morning Sanford will take you to the private school and have you enrolled," she said. "And when you come home, Madame Malisorf will be there, waiting for you.

"Then," she added, her face filled with that eerie light and excitement from before, "we'll begin again."

Five

Later that evening when Celine began to question me about what I had read in the book on ballet, I felt as if I had already enrolled in a new school. She was like a teacher, correcting, explaining, and assigning me more reading. She wanted to be sure I knew the names of all the famous ballets.

"I haven't told Madame Malisorf anything about your background, Janet. She doesn't have to know you've lived all your life in an orphanage," she said. "You could be a distant relative whom I've adopted."

It was the first time she had said anything that made me feel ashamed of where I'd come from. I remembered the first time I heard someone refer to me as an orphan. It happened on the playground at school. I was in the fourth grade and we were outside at recess. There was a small sidewalk the girls used for hopscotch and we often partnered up. When one of the girls, Blair Cummings, was left with me, she complained.

"I don't want to be with her. She's too small, and besides, she's an orphan," she remarked, and the others looked at me as if I had a wart on my nose. I remember my face became hot and tears felt like boiling drops under my eyelids. I turned and ran away. Later, when our teacher, Miss Walker, found me sitting alone in a corner of the playground, she asked if I was sick.

"Yes," I said. It was a convenient way to escape any more ridicule. "I have a stomachache."

She sent me to the nurse's office and I was told to lie quietly after the nurse had taken my temperature even though she found that I didn't have a fever. I suppose that was why people thought of me as sickly. Whenever I felt singled out, I would often get these "stomachaches" and be thankful for the excuse to disappear. Being an orphan made me want to be invisible.

"Most of Madame Malisorf's pupils," Celine continued, "come from the finest families, people of culture who have raised their children in a world of music and art and dance. They have a head start, but don't you worry, dear," she added, reaching out to touch my cheek. "You have me and that, that is a much better head start than any of the more fortunate ones have had."

After dinner I sat with her and Sanford and listened to Celine's descriptions of some of the dances in which she had performed.

"Madame Malisorf compared me to Anna Pavlova. Have you ever heard of her?" Celine asked. I hadn't of course. She shook her head and sighed. "It's a crime, a crime that someone like you, someone who is a diamond in the rough, has been denied so much, denied the opportunity. Thank Heaven I saw you that day," she declared.

No one had ever even suggested I had any sort of talent, much less thought of me as a diamond in the rough. When I left Celine that night and went to my room, I stood in front of my full-length mirror in my new pointe shoes and my leotards and studied my tiny body, hoping to see something that would convince me I was special. All I saw was an underdeveloped little girl with big, frightened eyes.

I crawled into bed that night terrified over what was to come.

The next morning after breakfast, Sanford took me to the Peabody School, a private school. The principal was a woman named Mrs. Williams. She was tall but not too thin, with light brown hair neatly styled. I thought she had a very warm, friendly smile, and was nothing like the principal in my former school, Mr. Saks, who seemed always to be grouchy and unhappy, and who was always anxious to punish students for violating one rule or another. Often he perched in the corridors like a hawk watching and waiting. He was always charging in and out of the bathrooms, hoping to catch someone smoking.

Peabody was a much smaller school, and also much cleaner and newer. I was surprised when I was brought to a classroom where there were only eight other students, three boys and five girls. For my grade there was one teacher, Miss London, who taught English and history, and another teacher, Mr. Wiles, who taught math and science. Our physical education teacher, Mrs. Grant, also taught health education. I discovered there were only 257 students in the whole school.

"The classes are so small you know you're going to get special attention here," Sanford told me. He was right. All of my teachers were very nice and took the time to explain what I had to do in order to catch up with my classmates.

What I liked most of all was that I was enrolled and introduced to the other students as Janet Delorice, and no one was told that I had been adopted and had been an orphan before this. Everyone simply assumed I was transferring from another private school, and I did nothing to cause them to think otherwise.

I thought most of the girls were snobby as well as most of the boys, but one boy, Josh Brown, who wasn't all that much taller or bigger than me, gave me the warmest smile and greeting when I sat next to him in my first class. Afterward, he walked with me and told me about the school and the teachers. The color of his hair was so similar to mine, we could have been brother and sister. He didn't look like me, however. He had dark brown eyes and a round face with firmer lips and a nose that tipped up at the end. When he smiled, I thought he was cute, although I didn't dare say so.

"Did your parents just move here?" he asked me between classes.

"No. My father owns a glass factory," I told him as I thought of ways to avoid telling him I had come from an orphanage.

He thought a moment and nodded.

"Yeah, I know where it is." He seemed satisfied with my answer and I was happy to let the conversation drop.

Later in the day, the girls asked more questions, and I could see that one girl, Jackie Clark, was suspicious.

"You didn't attend a private school before, did you?" she pursued.

"No," I admitted hesitantly. I was really going to have to get better at creating a story for myself.

"Were you a problem child?" Betty Lowe asked quickly.

"No," I said.

"You didn't get into big trouble?" Jackie followed.

I shook my head.

"How are your grades, pretty bad?" Betty asked with a nod and a smile as if she hoped they were.

"No. I have good grades," I told her.

They looked at each other, confused and skeptical.

"Why weren't you in a private school before, then?" Jackie demanded.

I shrugged.

"My parents just decided," I said vaguely.

"I'd rather be in a public school," Betty admitted.

"Not me," Jackie responded, and they got into their own argument and forgot about me for the moment. That was when Josh offered to show me around some more and we left the others. I enjoyed my first day at my new school so much, maybe because of Josh, that I nearly forgot Madame Malisorf would be waiting for me when I got home.

At the end of the school day Sanford was waiting in front of the school to bring me home.

"There may be times when I'll have to have one of my employees pick you up, Janet. Whoever it is will be very nice," he assured me. "Oh, and you don't have to tell Celine, she never understands why sometimes work needs to come first. I enjoy taking a break to come get you, but I just won't be able to do it every day. Don't worry, Celine won't find out, it'll be our little secret."

I tried not to worry about there being yet another secret between us, another secret kept from Celine, and concentrated on the drive. There was some roadwork being done between our home and the school, and we got stuck in a traffic jam about a mile from the school. I didn't think it was so terrible, but Sanford was getting very nervous. He kept muttering, "Damn, damn," under his breath, and chastising himself for not taking a detour. Finally, we were sailing along again. He drove a lot faster and I couldn't help thinking about the terrible car accident he and Celine had been in. The wheels squealed as we turned up the drive and came to an abrupt stop in front of the house.

I carried my new books in my arms and hurried to the front door with him. Celine was waiting in the entryway, sitting in her wheelchair and scowling at us as if she had been waiting at the door for hours.

"Why are you so late?" she demanded as soon as we entered the house.

"Roadwork," Sanford began to explain. "It—"

"I don't have time for your excuses, Sanford. Just go on back to your precious factory." She spat the words through clenched teeth and then turned her angry face to me. "Janet, Madame Malisorf is waiting in the studio. Put your books down—come along."

I placed my books on the entryway table, gazed at Sanford with wide, frightened eyes, and then started after Celine. My heart was pounding as I entered the studio. The first thing that astounded me was how small Madame Malisorf was. From the way Celine had described her, I pictured a towering figure at least as impressive as Mrs. McGuire. Madame Malisorf looked to be no more than five feet tall. Her hair was all gray and her face was full of wrinkles, but she had such a trim, athletic body, she looked like a young person who had prematurely aged. Her eyes washed over me as I followed Celine across the floor.

Madame Malisorf wore her hair pinned up in a huge twist. She wore black leotards and pointe shoes like the ones Celine had bought for me. Her lips were scarlet and her eyes were charcoal smudges in her pale, pale face.

"Janet, this is Madame Malisorf," Celine said, and I was amazed to hear that she no longer sounded angry. It was as if crossing the threshold of the studio transformed her.

"Hello," I said and smiled weakly.

She simply stared at me and then turned to Celine.

"You know I don't like to put girls onto full pointe until they are thirteen, Celine, no matter how long they've studied."

"She'll be thirteen very shortly, Madame," Celine said.

Madame Malisorf smirked with skepticism.

"She looks no more than nine or ten."

"I know. She's small but she's precious and very talented," Celine said.

"We'll see. I want you to walk to the far wall and back," Madame Malisorf commanded.

I gazed at Celine, who smiled and nodded encouragement. Then I walked to the wall, turned, and walked back.

"Well, Madame?" Celine asked quickly. It was obvious she expected Madame Malisorf to agree with her assessment of me.

"She does have good posture and balance. The neck looks a bit weak, but that will be rectified quickly. Stand on your toes," she ordered, and I did. When I started to lower myself, she barked, "No, stay there until I tell you otherwise."

I did what she asked and waited. My calves began to shake and to ache, but I held myself up. I could feel my face turning red.

"Hold your arms straight out," she ordered.

I did that, too.

"Keep your head high, your eyes straight ahead."

It felt like some sort of torture, but because Celine was watching me with that smile on her face, I forced myself to endure. My whole body began to shake. I hoped it would be easier in pointe shoes.

"Relax," Madame Malisorf said. "Good strength, good balance for someone without any training. You might be right, Celine," she said, "but it will take a grand effort. As far as pointe work, we'll see how long it will take to get her ready." She turned back to me. "Change into your exercise outfit and be back in ten minutes," she ordered.

There was that ten minutes again. Celine nodded at me and I hurried out and up the stairs to my room to get into my leotards. Celine was right about how Madame Malisorf conducted her class. She demonstrated and then put me into one exercise after another at the barre. Repetition was the magic word. She barked her orders and expected me to obey instantly. If I paused to catch my breath, she sighed deeply and said, "Well?" And Celine would give a little cough from the doorway where she was sitting. She hadn't told me she was going to watch my lessons and was making me even more nervous. I performed each move so many times, I thought I would do each of the exercises in my sleep. Finally, Madame Malisorf had me move away from the barre and work on standing with my feet turned out.

"For various reasons having to do with the structure of the hip joint," she explained, "a dancer can obtain the greatest extension if the leg is rotated outward, away from its usual position. This rotation will enable you to move to the side as readily as to the front or back. This position is known as—"

"Turnout," I said quickly. I wanted to impress her with my knowledge.

"Yes," she said, but she didn't seem surprised or even very pleased. Instead, she looked annoyed that I had finished her sentence. From her reflection in the mirror I could see Celine's eyes fill with warning and I moved quickly into the position as it had been described in the book.

"No, no," Madame Malisorf cried. "You don't begin from the ankles. You do not force your feet into that position and let everything from there on up follow. Turnout begins at the hip joint."

She seized me at the waist and had me do it repeatedly until I satisfied her. It was too soon in my training to go on to jumps so we returned to the barre for more exercise.

"I will get you strong enough so you can attempt the moves I will teach you," she said confidently.

When we finished for the day, I was aching all over, especially in my hips and legs. The pain was so deep in places, it made my eyes tear, but I dared not utter a syllable of complaint. All the while as I worked with Madame Malisorf, Celine watched from her wheelchair, nodding and smiling after everything Madame Malisorf said.

"She'll be wonderful, absolutely wonderful, won't she, Madame Malisorf?" Celine asked at the end of the session.

"We shall see," Madame Malisorf replied, her eyes cold and critical.

"I have already fitted her for pointe shoes."

"We can't rush her along, Celine," Madame Malisorf snapped. "You, of all people, should know that."

"We won't, but she'll progress rapidly," Celine said undaunted. "I'll see to it. She'll practice and practice, Madame."

"I should hope so," she said directly to me. "You can't expect to become a dancer with only our sessions." She thought a moment and added, "Next time, I think I'll bring another pupil along." She turned to Celine. "It's good to have someone else work alongside her."

"Yes, yes, fine," Celine said. "Thank you. Tomorrow then?"

"Tomorrow," Madame Malisorf replied, and began to gather her things.

Tomorrow? Will I have lessons every day? I wondered. When will my poor little body have a chance to recuperate?

As soon as Madame Malisorf left, Celine wheeled over to me, her eyes blazing with excitement.

"She likes you. I know she does. I've known her a long time. If she didn't think you had potential, she would simply refuse to be your dance instructor. She doesn't waste her time on mediocre students, and for her to volunteer to bring along another one of her special students . . . well, you just don't understand what that means, Janet. That must be why you're not as excited as you should be. You have to be excited, Janet. Don't you see? Madame agrees with me. You're going to be a prima ballerina. This is wonderful, wonderful," she said, clapping her hands.

I tried to smile through my aches and pains. It made her laugh.

"Don't worry about your pains, Janet. Go soak in a hot tub before dinner. After a few more sessions, you won't be so sore. You'll see. Oh, I can't wait to tell Sanford about the lesson. I was right. I knew it. I was right," she said, spinning around in her chair and wheeling toward the doorway.

What had I done to make her so confident, I wondered, besides parading across the studio, rising up on my toes, balancing myself, and then performing some vigorous exercises that left me feeling like I'd been hit by a truck?

I followed her out and walked up the stairway to my room much slower than I had the day before. It wasn't until I was in my room and the door was closed that I permitted myself my first groan. Then I ran water for a bath and soaked my sore muscles. Later, at dinner, my work in the studio with Madame Malisorf was all Celine would discuss. Sanford tried to ask me questions about my first day at school, but Celine continually interrupted with advice about this and that work at the barre.

"I wish you could have been there to see her, Sanford. At times I felt like I was looking at myself in the mirror when my mother used to come around to watch me, too," she added.

I wondered when I was to meet my new grandparents, but there was no mention of their visit or our visiting them.

Celine wanted me to remain with her after dinner

and talk about dance some more, but Sanford reminded her that I had to catch up on a great deal of schoolwork.

"Schoolwork," she said disdainfully. "Someday and someday soon, she'll have a tutor, just as I had."

"You mean you stopped going to school?" I asked.

"Of course. Dance was everything to me, and it will be to you, Janet. You'll see," she predicted.

Just dance and have a tutor all the time, I wondered, but what about friends and parties and most of all, boyfriends? I didn't look very enthusiastic about it, I guess. Her mouth turned down in a frown.

"What's wrong?" she asked quickly.

"She's very tired, Celine," Sanford answered for me. "This has been a big day, one of the biggest in her life, I imagine."

Celine studied me a moment and then smiled.

"Yes, yes, I'm sure that's it. Go do your schoolwork, dear, and then get some beauty sleep."

I was excused and returned to my room. For a moment I just sat at my desk and gazed at the small mountain of reading I had to do. Getting a new home and a new family wasn't as easy as I'd always dreamed it would be.

When I stretched against the back of my chair, my lower back and the backs of my legs screamed out in pain. I looked at myself in the mirror and groaned. I had some news for my tired little body.

"There'll be much more pain to come."

Six

Madame Malisorf kept her promise. The next day when Sanford brought me home from school, there was an older boy waiting in the studio with her. I don't know why, but I expected the student she was bringing along for my lessons to be another girl. The sight of a boy in his tights took me by such surprise, I simply stood there gaping stupidly at him. He had to be at least fifteen or sixteen, and was at least six inches taller than me with raven black hair and eyes that glittered like black onyx. He had a dark complexion, but his mouth was so red, it looked like he was wearing lipstick. It didn't look like there was an ounce of fat on his body.

He had muscular shoulders and very muscular legs. His tights fit him like a second skin, so that there wasn't much left to my imagination. Sex talk was often the topic of conversation for the older girls at the orphanage, and I couldn't help but want to listen in on their experiences. Through what they'd told me and what I overheard, I thought I knew everything I was supposed to know at my age, despite not having an older sister or mother to take me aside to discuss the birds and the bees. However, I had never been in the same room with an older boy who looked so . . . so naked. I couldn't help blushing. I saw immediately that my embarrassment annoyed him, so I shifted my eyes away.

"This is Dimitri Rocmalowitz," Madame Malisorf said. "He is one of my best students and often instructs new students on the basics. Of course, he has a way to go, but he is a very talented and precise dancer. When he tells you to do something, you should treat him with the same respect and regard you would treat me. Do you understand, Janet?"

"Yes, Madame," I replied skeptically. Dimitri looked too young to be such an amazing dancer. It would be strange taking direction from him.

"Watching someone who has mastered as much as Dimitri has will help you understand what is expected of you," she continued. "Today and from now on, I want you to begin our sessions wearing these leg warmers," she added as she handed me a bright purple pair of heavy wool leg warmers.

After I put them on we proceeded immediately to the barre and I noticed that Celine had wheeled herself into the corner of the room, where she sat with her hands folded on her lap and watched.

Dimitri went right into a warmup drill and for a

moment all I could do was watch. He didn't seem shy or nervous to be dancing in front of us. It was as if he was in his own world. His legs moved with such grace and speed while he held his body in a perfectly vertical line.

"Begin," Madame Malisorf said, and I approached the barre, standing just a few feet from Dimitri. "No, don't hold the barre that tightly," she said. "See how Dimitri uses it only for balance."

I tried to relax and we began a series of exercises that included the *pliés,* the *tendus,* and the *glissés,* all that she had shown me the day before. From there we moved to the *fondus* and then the *ronds de jambe à terre.* First, Madame Malisorf would describe what she wanted. Then Dimitri would demonstrate, always with a proud look on his face as if he was dancing for an audience of thousands, and then I would begin, usually followed by Madame Malisorf's quick, "No, no, no. Dimitri, again. Watch him, Janet. Study the way he is holding his back and his neck."

Sometimes it took me so long to satisfy her, I was practically in tears before she let me go on to something else, always with the conditional statement, "We'll work on that." There wasn't anything I wouldn't be working on, seemingly forever and ever, I thought.

When we got to the turnout again, the pain of rotating my hips nearly made me cry out in pain. I was sure my face revealed all my new aches. Madame Malisorf seemed merciless, however. Just when I thought there would be a short break so I could catch my breath, she was on to something new with Dimitri demonstrating and then me trying to mimic his moves.

The session lasted longer than the one we had the day before. I was sweating so much, I felt the dampness in my leotards, which were now glued to my skin. Finally, Madame Malisorf did give us a short break and I collapsed to the floor. Madame Malisorf went to talk to Celine and Dimitri finally looked at me for the first time since we'd been in the room.

"Why do you want to be a ballet dancer?" he asked immediately and with a sharpness in his tone that made me feel guilty.

"My mother thinks I should be," I said defensively.

"That's your reason?" he asked with a smirk. He wiped his face with his towel and then threw the soggy towel at me. "You're dripping," he said gruffly.

I found a dry spot on the towel and wiped my face and the back of my neck.

"I think I'll like it," I said cautiously. Again, he smirked.

"Ballet requires complete and utter devotion, a total commitment of mind, body, and soul. It becomes your religion. An instructor like Madame Malisorf is your high priestess, your god, her words gospel. You have to think and walk like a dancer, eat and breathe it. There is nothing else that is half as important. Then, and maybe then, you have a chance to become a real dancer."

"I don't expect to become a famous dancer," I said and wondered why this boy made me feel like I had to defend myself . . . especially when I wasn't so sure that I even wanted to be a dancer.

He looked quickly toward Madame Malisorf and Celine and then back at me.

"Don't ever let Madame Malisorf hear you say such a weak, self-defeating thing. She'll turn and walk out of the room forever," he warned.

My heart, which was pounding madly from our exercises anyway, stopped and then pounded even harder. Celine would be devastated. She would hate me, I thought.

"Madame Malisorf will tell you what you will and will not be," he continued and then he shook his head. "Another spoiled rich child whose parents think she's someone special," he commented disdainfully.

"I am not," I said, nearly in tears.

"No? How many kids your age have a studio like this in their homes and a teacher who costs thousands of dollars a week?"

"Thousands?" I gulped.

"Of course, you little idiot. Don't you know who she is?" He groaned. "This isn't going to last long. I can just feel it," he said with a knowing shake of his head.

"Yes, it will. I'll do what I have to do and I'll do it well," I fired back at him.

I didn't want to tell him that I thought my life depended on it; that the woman who wanted to love me as a mother had her heart set on my success as a dancer and that I would devote all my strength and energy toward making her happy.

"My mother was going to be a famous dancer until she was in a terrible car accident. That's why we have this studio. It's not here just for me."

He smirked.

"You shouldn't look down on someone who is just starting out simply because you're a good ballet student," I added.

He finally smiled.

"How could I do anything but look down at you? What are you, four feet eight?"

This time tears escaped the corners of my eyes. I turned my back on him and wiped them away quickly.

"Are you really nearly thirteen?" he continued. His voice had softened and I wondered if he was sorry he'd hurt my feelings.

I began to answer him when Madame Malisorf returned and told me to take off the leg warmers. It was time to move away from the barre to repeat everything we had done, but this time without the aid of the barre. I couldn't help being tired and making mistakes. I knew I was looking very clumsy and awkward. Every time Madame Malisorf corrected me, Dimitri shook his head and smirked. Then, as if to drive home his disdain, he would do what she asked so perfectly, showing off, his spinning turns so fast he became a blur. Occasionally he would break out of the spin and do a leap that seemed to defy gravity and land without a sound. Whenever he demonstrated something for me, Madame Malisorf would cry, "That's it! That's what I want. Study him. Watch him. Someday you must be as good as he is."

His face filled with arrogant pride as he puffed out his chest toward me.

I wanted to say I'd rather watch a dead fish floating on the top of our lake, but held my breath and my words and tried again. Finally, mercifully, it seemed, the session ended. Celine clapped and wheeled herself to the center of the studio.

"Bravo, bravo. What a beautiful beginning. Thank you, Madame Malisorf. Thank you. And Dimitri, you make me want to get up out of this chair, forget my crippled legs, and dance in your arms."

He bowed.

"Madame Malisorf has told me how wonderfully you danced and what a tragedy it was for ballet when you were injured, Mrs. Delorice."

"Yes," Celine said softly, her eyes taking on that faraway, distant look. Then she smiled toward me. "But my daughter will do what I can't do anymore. Don't you agree?"

He looked at me.

"Perhaps," he said with that crooked smile on his lips. "If she learns to be dedicated, devoted, and obedient."

"She will," Celine promised and I wondered if just her command would turn me into a ballerina as easily as it had turned a cloudy, gloomy day bright and beautiful.

I tried not to look as tired and as sore as I was, but Dimitri saw through my mask and smiled cruelly at me. When I entered my room, I threw myself on my bed and let my tears burst forth freely.

I'll never be the dancer Celine dreams I'll become, I thought. I may never be the daughter she wants, but I'd rather die trying than disappoint her.

Once again at dinner all our conversation centered around the dance class and my progress. Celine talked so much she barely ate or took breaths between sentences. Sanford tried to talk about other things, but she refused to change the subject. He smiled at her and at me, his face filled with amusement. Afterward, he pulled me aside to tell me that it had been some time since Celine was as animated and cheerful.

"Thank you for making Celine so happy, Janet. You're a wonderful addition to our family. Thank you for just being who you are," he said. He smiled a genuine smile and I couldn't help but think that this smile looked so much better than the tight, grim one he usually wore around Celine.

Celine caught up to us in the hallway and noticed Sanford's beaming smile. "Why are you grinning like an idiot, Sanford? What are you two discussing?" Suddenly her eyes narrowed and turned dark and cold. "Janet, go to your room. You need your rest. You're obviously going to need all the help you can get to keep up with Dimitri."

I couldn't help but feel that Celine had scolded me and I moped up to my room to collapse.

The first two weeks of my new life flew by so quickly, they felt like hours. I was sure it was because each and every moment of my day was full of things to do. Unlike in the orphanage, there weren't long hours of emptiness to fill with distractions and daydreams. Here I was working on my school assignments, taking dance lessons, recuperating from them, and starting over again. I went to sleep early and ate from the strict dancer's diet Celine had designed. Although I thought it was too early to see any real changes, I believed my legs were stronger, my small muscles tighter. I even thought I was doing what Dimitri claimed I would have to do: walk and move like a dancer, even when I wasn't in the studio.

Because my after-school time was dedicated to dance lessons, it was hard to make new friends and Celine wouldn't permit me to join any teams or clubs.

"All we need is for you to sustain some sort of injury now," she said. She even tried to get me out of gym class, but the school wouldn't permit it and Sanford argued that it wouldn't interfere with my dancing lessons.

"Of course it will," Celine snapped. "I don't want her wasting her physical energies on nonsense."

"It isn't nonsense, darling," he tried to explain, but Celine would have none of it. She hadn't gotten her way and she didn't like it one bit.

"Don't do any more than you have to," she advised me, "and do what I used to do whenever you can: claim you have cramps from your period."

"But I haven't gotten my period yet," I reminded her.

"So what? Who's going to know? Lying," she said when she saw the expression on my face, "is all right if it's for the right cause. I'll never punish you for doing something to protect your dancing, Janet, never, no matter what," she said, her eyes so bright and big, they scared me. I wondered where she went when that look came over her.

Like most of the girls and boys my age at the orphanage, I used to fantasize about the people who would become my parents. I filled my head with dreams of fun things like picnics and trips to the park, and I saw myself holding my father's hand as we walked through the gates of Disneyland. I imagined big, beautiful birthday parties, and I even dreamed of having little brothers and sisters.

How empty and different the big house I now lived in seemed when I compared it to the house in my dreams. Yes, I had expensive things and a room bigger than I'd ever seen, and there was a lake and beautiful grounds, but none of the family closeness or trips or fun and games that I'd imagined. Sanford wanted to spend time with me, to show off his factory, but Celine just seemed to come up with one reason after another why I couldn't go. Finally, she realized how silly her arguments sounded and relented. I went to work with Sanford on a Saturday and saw the machines and the products. I met some of his workers and his executives. I was amazed at how pleasant and eager he was to show me things and how sad I was when our time alone ended. I think Sanford felt the same way—on the ride home neither of us spoke and for the first time that day the mood between us was gloomy.

When we returned home and I started to tell Celine about our day, she grimaced as if in pain.

"We need the factory so that we can afford the luxuries in life," she said. "What we *don't* need is to acknowledge its existence. And we certainly don't allow it to take up one iota of our time or thought."

"But some of the things that are made in the factory are beautiful, aren't they?" I asked.

"I suppose, in a pedestrian sort of way," she admitted, although I didn't understand exactly what she meant, and I saw it displeased Sanford. She didn't become animated and happy again until Sanford told her he had gotten us tickets to the Metropolitan Ballet's performance of *The Four Temperaments.*

"Now," she cried, "now you will see your first real ballet and understand what it is I want you to do and become."

Celine had Sanford take us to buy me a formal dress. I chose a long royal blue taffeta and Celine even had Sanford buy me some jewelry—a set of sapphire earrings and a matching teardrop-shaped necklace.

"Going to the ballet is a very special thing," she explained. "Everyone wears their very best clothes. You'll see."

She brought me to a salon where they styled my hair in a French twist and showed me how to apply makeup properly. When I gazed at myself in the mirror, I was amazed at how grown-up I looked.

"I want you to make a statement, to be noticed, to be someone everyone will look at and think, 'There's an up-and-coming star, a little princess.' "

I had to admit I was finally swept away in Celine's world. I permitted myself to dream the same dreams, to think of myself as a celebrity, my name up in lights, and when I saw the theater and all those rich and elegant-looking people in the audience, I was filled with excitement, too. By the time the curtain lifted, my heart was pounding. The ballet began. I gazed at my new mother beside me in her wheelchair, saw the happiness and radiance in her eyes, and felt as if I was leaping and soaring alongside her. During the first act, she reached through the darkness until she found my hand.

When I turned to her she whispered, "Someday, Janet, Sanford and I will be coming here to see you.

"Someday," she whispered, lost in her dream.

And I dared to believe it could come true.

Seven

Although I didn't hear them referred to very much, I couldn't help wondering when I would meet my grandparents, Celine's mother and father. I never heard or saw her talking to them on the phone and neither she nor Sanford mentioned speaking to them recently or on any regular basis. During the week, Sanford and I usually ate breakfast without Celine since it took her much longer to rise and dress. I knew Sanford would tell me about my new grandparents if I asked him, but I was having trouble getting up the nerve. Finally I decided I would settle into my routine and wait for Celine to bring up the subject of her parents again—then I would ask to meet them.

As the days wore on, my dance lessons seemed to be going better, and although I couldn't imagine myself ever liking Dimitri, I couldn't help being flattered when he complimented me on my technique.

Madame Malisorf didn't go so far as to say I was a special student, but she did offer that I was better than average, which was enough to make Celine happy and even more confident.

"I think," Celine said one night at dinner, "that it's time for my mother to see Janet. Janet's made significant progress. I'll have mother stop by during one of her dance lessons."

Sanford nodded without speaking, but I saw something strange in his eyes, a look of concern that I hadn't seen often before. Of course, I couldn't help wondering why I hadn't met Celine's parents before now. I knew they didn't live very far away. Why didn't we ever visit? I kicked myself for not having the courage to ask Sanford earlier since it was obvious from the look on his face that he had strong opinions about them.

"Isn't your brother returning from his holiday tomorrow?" Sanford asked her. His face didn't relax at all, and I wondered what it was about Celine's family that upset him.

"I don't recall. And what do you mean, return from his holiday? When isn't Daniel on holiday?" she asked and laughed a high, thin laugh.

Nothing else was said about Celine's family, but two days afterward, right in the middle of our dinner, the doorbell sounded and Mildred hurried out of the kitchen to see who it was. Minutes later, I heard a loud laugh.

"Mildred, you're still here! Wonderful!" A loud voice boomed from the entryway.

"Daniel," Celine moaned, shaking her head.

Moments later, Celine's younger brother burst into the dining room. His light brown hair was long and tossed about his head and face as if he had been running his fingers through it for hours. Not quite six feet tall with an athletic build, Daniel had hazel eyes set in a face much more chiseled than Celine's. I saw resemblances in their noses and mouths, but there was a sly smile on his lips that I would discover to be a habitual characteristic. He wore a black leather jacket, faded blue jeans, and black boots, as well as black leather gloves.

"Celine, Sanford," he cried. "How are you?" He started to take off his gloves. "I'm in time for dinner. What luck. I'm starving."

He slid into the chair across from me and reached for some bread before anyone could respond.

"Hello, Daniel," Celine said dryly. "Please meet Janet."

He winked at me.

"I heard you guys were finally parents. Mother gave me an earful." He studied me. "How are they treating you? Has Sanford negotiated your allowance yet? Better let me represent you. Ah, a veal roast," he said, stabbing a piece of meat. "Mildred's quite a good cook." He shoved the meat into his mouth and chewed.

It was as if a strong, wild wind had blown into the house. Sanford was so obviously stunned by Daniel's appearance that he sat with his hand frozen in the air, his fork full of peas.

"Hello, Daniel," Sanford said, his eyes softening. "I see you finally got that motorcycle you've been threatening to buy."

"You bet I did," Daniel said. "I seem to remember you used to throw around the idea of getting one of your own."

"I was never really serious," he said, glancing at Celine.

"How about you?" Daniel asked me. "You want to go for a ride after dinner?"

"Of course she doesn't," Celine said quickly. "Do you think I would place her in such danger?"

Daniel laughed and continued to eat. I was still too surprised and overwhelmed to speak. He winked at me again.

"I bet you'd like a ride," he said, and he stared at me so intently it seemed like he could see into my soul. I wondered if my soul wore biker leather!

"Stop it, Daniel," Celine ordered. He laughed again and shook his head in defeat.

"Where were you this time?" Sanford asked. Although he meant it to sound critical, I saw a look of envy in his eyes as he waited for Daniel to tell about his adventures.

"The Cape. You would have loved it, Sanford. We took the sea route through Connecticut and rode along the ocean. I swear, with the wind blowing through our hair and the smell of the fresh salt air, I felt like we could drive forever. Never come back."

"And yet here you are. I dare not ask who the *we* was," Celine said as she wrinkled up her nose.

"You dare not? Funny, Mother dared not either."

"I'll bet," Sanford said with a small smile.

"Actually, Sanford, she was a very pretty young damsel in distress when I found her, clothed and fed her, and bought her a motorcycle," Daniel told him between bites.

"You bought a strange woman a motorcycle?" Celine asked with a grimace.

"Actually, she wasn't so strange after a few days," Daniel said and winked at me again. "So, tell me all about yourself, Janet. How old are you?"

"I'll be thirteen in a few weeks," I said hesitantly. Daniel seemed larger than life and having him concentrate his questions on me was making me nervous.

"That old? You'll need to negotiate a retirement package as well then," he joked. "Seriously, are they treating you well here? Because if they're not, I have friends in high places and I can have things going your way in no time. They have to obey the rules of the Geneva Convention when it comes to prisoners."

"But . . . but I'm not a prisoner," I said quickly, looking from Sanford to Celine for help.

"Will you stop it. You'll frighten her with your behavior," Celine said. She paused and then asked, "How are Mother and Father?"

"Proper well," he said. He turned to me. "Our parents are slowly becoming statues. They sit still as granite and breathe only filtered air."

"Daniel!" Celine chastised.

"They're fine, they're fine. Of course, I saw them

only for a few minutes before Mother started in on you know what," he said, nodding toward me.

"That's enough," Sanford said sharply.

"She should know what she's in for, what sort of family she has contracted to do business with, don't you think?" Daniel replied.

"Please," Celine pleaded. He shrugged.

"Okay, I'll be civil. Really. How do you like life here, Janet?" he asked me.

"I like it a lot," I said.

"And they put you in that snobby school?"

"Peabody is not a snobby school. It's a special school with advantages," Celine corrected.

"Did they tell you I went there but I was asked to please seek another place for my studies?"

I shook my head.

"My brother," Celine explained, "is what is generally known as a spoiled brat. No matter how much money my parents were willing to spend on him or what they were willing to do, he always managed to spoil it," she said, glaring at him.

"I always did choke on that silver spoon," he said with another shrug. "Mildred," he called when she appeared, "you've outdone yourself with this veal. It's as succulent as a virgin's lips," he said, smacking his own lips together. Mildred turned bright pink.

"Daniel!" Celine cried.

"Just trying to be complimentary," he said, "and appreciative." He leaned toward me to whisper loudly. "My sister always complains that I'm not appreciative."

I looked at Sanford, who put his silverware down a little harder than usual.

"How are things at the printing company, Daniel?" Sanford asked.

Daniel straightened in his chair and wiped his mouth with a napkin.

"Well, when I left for my vacation, we were down five percent from this period last year, which raised father's blood pressure five percent, but when I stopped by late today to pick up my mail, he told me we had been given the Glenn golf clubs account and that spiked us back to where we were, so his blood pressure improved. I swear his heart is connected to the Dow-Jones. If there's a crash, it's curtains," he said, slicing his forefinger across his Adam's apple.

"You can ridicule him all you want, Daniel, but he built a successful business for you and a comfortable life for both of us," Celine scolded.

"Yes, yes, I suppose so. I'm just having fun," he confessed to me. "Something my brother-in-law here doesn't have much of because he works too hard. All work and no play, Sanford," he warned. Then he gazed at me. "So," he said, "you're taking dance lessons, I hear."

"Yes," I said softly.

"And she's doing very well," Celine added.

"That's nice." He sat back. "I must say, sister dear, you and Mr. Glass chose a little gem here. I'm impressed, Sanford."

"We're very fond of Janet and we hope she's

growing fond of us," Sanford replied, and I was glad to see him smile.

"Are you?" Daniel asked me with that impish twinkle in his eyes.

"Yes," I said quickly.

He laughed.

"Are you sure I can't take her for a little ride on the cycle?"

"Absolutely sure," Celine said. "If you want to go out and be reckless, I can't stop you, but you won't be reckless with my daughter," she told him. "Not now," she added, "now that she's on the threshold of becoming someone very special."

"Really?" Daniel said, gazing at me across the table. He smiled. "I would have thought she was already someone special. Even before she came here," he added, dazzling me with his smile.

I couldn't help liking him even though Celine's expression and harsh words made it clear she disapproved.

After dinner Daniel and Sanford went off to the den to talk and Celine and I went to the living room, where she apologized for her brother's behavior.

"Your new uncle is really good-hearted, but he's just a bit lost at the moment. We're doing our best to help him," she said. "It's difficult. His problem is he hasn't any goals. He has no focus, and that's the most important thing to have in life, Janet, focus and determination. He doesn't want anything enough to sacrifice and suffer some pain. He's too selfish and indulgent," she continued.

She gazed up at her own portrait above the mantel and sighed.

"We came from the same home, had the same parents, but sometimes, sometimes, he seems like a stranger to me."

"Did he ever want to dance, too?" I asked.

"Daniel?" she laughed. "Daniel has two left feet and he doesn't have the attention span to learn a single exercise. But," she said sighing again, "he's my brother. I have to love him."

Then she looked at me.

"And you're my hope," she said. "I will always love you."

Knowing that Celine's eyes were always following me and that I was her hope made me try harder, but it also made me feel worse if I didn't please Madame Malisorf or make progress as fast as I was expected to make it. The day after my uncle Daniel's explosive introduction, Celine had a doctor's appointment that ran late and kept her from attending my dance lesson after school. Without her sitting there in the corner, I felt a little more at ease, and even Dimitri seemed friendlier. Toward the end of the lesson, Madame Malisorf declared that tomorrow she would start me on pointe.

"I don't understand why she's doing that," Dimitri declared after she had left for her next lesson. He was old enough to drive and had his own car. "She's the most demanding dance instructor in the area and doesn't easily put a student on pointe. Certainly never this early." He thought a moment. "She's probably just satisfying your mother. Your feet aren't even properly developed."

"They are too," I said looking down at them to see if he was right.

He wiped his face with the towel and stared at me. "I've always liked to watch young girls develop," he said suddenly.

The way he was gazing at me made me very self-conscious. My leotards were as tight as his, and for the first time I was embarrassed by how much they revealed.

"Are you developing breasts or is that just some baby fat?" he asked, jabbing his finger toward me.

My breath caught in my throat and I jumped away from his reach.

"You know, I've heard there's an avant-garde group of dancers who dance naked. Wanna try it?" he asked. After what he'd just done, I had no idea if he was kidding me or not.

"Naked?" I couldn't imagine such a thing.

"It's supposed to give you more freedom of expression. I really might try it one of these days," he said. "Well?"

"Well what?"

"You didn't answer my question, breasts or baby fat?"

"That's very personal," I mumbled.

"You shouldn't be ashamed of your body," he continued.

"I'm not ashamed."

"Do I look like I'm ashamed of mine? Am I hiding anything from you? That's right, look at me," he said, turning so he faced me fully. He smiled. "I remember how you looked at me that first day."

I started to shake my head.

"Don't deny it. Honesty is the most important characteristic for a dancer. Your honesty will be evident when you move. Madame Malisorf always says that. Breasts or baby fat?" he pursued. He stepped closer to me.

He smiled, his upper lip curling in to his now familiar sneer.

"I could make you look very bad here, you know. Madame will take you off pointe in seconds. I don't think your mother would appreciate that, do you?"

Tears clouded my vision.

"What do you want from me?" I cried.

"Let me decide for myself," he said and reached out to touch my chest. I was too frightened to stop him. "I'm still not sure. I'll tell you when I know," he added. I started to turn away from him, but he seized my leotard at the shoulder and began peeling it off before I could get away.

"Stop," I begged him.

"Ashamed?" He practically growled the word.

"No, but please, don't." I pleaded.

"If you don't let me see, I will ruin your first day on pointe," he threatened.

I swallowed down the lump in my throat and froze, my heart pounding as he continued to lower my leotard until he could reveal my chest. He stood there staring at me. Then, very slowly, his eyes narrow and strangely dark, he touched me. I jumped back as if his fingers were filled with electricity.

"Breasts," he concluded. "There, was that so difficult?" he asked and did a full pirouette, a leap, and a soft fall before heading out the studio door and leaving me behind, tears streaming down my cheeks, my heart pounding.

I pulled up my leotard and followed him out. I remained in the shadows of the hallway until I heard him leave the house.

"Is there anything wrong?" Mildred asked, seeing me cowering in a corner.

"No," I said. "I was just resting."

She tilted her head in confusion.

I hurried down the hall, away from her questioning eyes, up the stairs, and to my room, shutting the door behind me quickly. I was still embarrassed and frightened by the experience in the studio. My legs were actually trembling. What frightened me the most was the feeling of being trapped and helpless. He could have stripped me naked and I would have been afraid to stop him. Why did he do it? Why did he take such advantage of me? Why didn't I cry for help? At least Mildred could have come to help me.

I wiped away my tears and looked at myself in the mirror. No one had ever treated me as anything more than a little girl. No boy had ever thought of me sexually before as far as I knew. But now my breasts were budding. My time was coming. When Dimitri had touched me, I was terrified, but there was a strange new sensation as well. I wasn't sure if I was more afraid of him or what had happened inside me.

How lucky other girls were, girls who had mothers and sisters to talk to at a moment like this, I thought. If I mentioned to Celine what had happened, it might create havoc with my dance lessons. Madame Malisorf might even walk out on us and then what would I do?

How would I keep this a secret? What would it feel like to stand across from Dimitri tomorrow? I would be nervous enough as it was auditioning to begin on pointe. I couldn't help wondering if this was the first of many more experiences I would have to endure to please Celine.

That, as much as anything else, caused me to be afraid of what tomorrow would bring.

Eight

I tossed and turned for hours that night, and when I finally did fall asleep, I had so many nightmares, I kept waking up in a cold sweat, and by morning I was actually shivering and the back of my neck ached. I fell asleep again just before I was supposed to get up and get ready for school. A soft knock at the door woke me. Sanford looked in.

"You should be getting up, Janet," he said with a smile.

I nodded and started to sit up when the ache traveled down my spine and I groaned. Sanford grew concerned and stepped into my room.

"What's wrong?"

"I don't feel so good," I complained. "My neck aches and I'm cold," I said through chattering teeth.

He put his hand on my forehead and looked even more worried.

"You feel like you have fever. I'll get a thermometer," he said and hurried out of the room. He was back in less than a minute and put the thermometer under my tongue.

"I was afraid of this," he muttered. He paced as he waited. "You've been working too hard on your schoolwork and your dancing. You need more time to rest. You're growing, too, and all this is so new and frightening for you, I'm sure. No one listens to me, but I know I'm right about this."

He looked at the thermometer and nodded.

"A hundred and one. That's a fever. You stay right there, young lady. I'm sending Mildred up with some aspirin for you. Does your throat hurt?"

I shook my head.

"No, just my neck and shoulders ache. And the backs of my legs," I added, but they were always aching so I didn't think anything special about it.

He stared at me a moment.

"I've changed my mind. I won't give you aspirins yet. I'm taking you to the doctor," he decided. "Just throw something on, anything, I'll meet you downstairs," he added, and left the room.

I got up slowly, washed my face, and dressed in an old flannel shirt and a pair of loose-fitting jeans. As I passed Sanford and Celine's room, I could hear their muffled voices. Celine sounded very upset.

"What are you talking about?" I heard her say. "That's nonsense. People don't get sick from dancing too much."

"I didn't say that was the only cause. The child's exhausted."

"Nonsense. She's young. She has an unlimited well of energy," Celine insisted. I didn't have the strength to listen to more so I slowly made my way downstairs.

When Sanford joined me in the entryway, he offered to carry me to the car, but I wasn't in that much pain and I felt silly with him just holding my arm as if I were some old lady.

"I've already called Dr. Franklin. He's a good friend and he's coming into his office a little early just to see you first," Sanford explained.

"Is Celine angry at me?" I asked. She hadn't even come to see how I was.

"No, of course not. She's concerned, that's all," he said but quickly looked away.

The doctor examined me and concluded that I had the flu. He didn't prescribe anything more than aspirin and rest. Less than an hour later, I was back in my bed, taking aspirin and sipping some tea.

"I'll call from the factory," Sanford told Mildred. "Take her temperature in about two hours, okay?"

"Yes sir," she said with a smile.

I fell back to sleep and did have a better rest. I could have slept longer, but I sensed someone was in my room and opened my eyes to see Celine in her wheelchair at my bedside, staring at me.

"You don't feel very warm to me," she said, taking her hand from my forehead.

"I do feel a little better," I agreed, though I really still felt sore and tired.

"Good. Don't worry about the schoolwork. I've

already called and your work will be delivered to the house later this afternoon. Rest for the remainder of the day until your dance lesson," she added.

"My dance lesson? But maybe I should wait until tomorrow, Mother," I said weakly.

"No, no, you never cancel a lesson with Madame Malisorf. She cancels you. Do you have any idea how many other people are after her to work with their sons and daughters? This is a coup, a major accomplishment getting her to concentrate on you like this, and you're doing well. She told me she had decided to put you on pointe. I'm so proud of you, dear. It took me years to go on pointe. Do you know that?"

I shook my head.

"Well, it did, so you see how talented you are."

"But I'm afraid I won't do well if I don't feel well," I moaned.

"We must never let our bodies disappoint us, Janet," she insisted. "A dancer *must* be dedicated. No matter what, when it comes time to perform, you perform. I even danced on the day my grandmother died. I was very close to her. She favored me and had a lot to do with my parents' supporting my efforts to become a ballerina. I was sad but I had to dance and that was that. If I could dance on my grandmother's day of death, you can dance with a little ache and a little fever, Janet. Right? Right?" she pursued when I didn't reply quickly enough.

"Yes," I said softly. I couldn't help but wish that Sanford was home to save me.

"Good. Then it's settled. Rest until I call for you,"

she said and started to wheel herself out. "Actually, this is lucky. You were able to rest all day before starting your first lesson on pointe. See? Everything works out for the dedicated," she declared and left.

She danced on the day her grandmother died, I thought. I never had a grandmother, not even a mother, but if I had them, I would love them too much not to be too sad to do anything if they died. I could never be that dedicated. Was there something wrong with me?

Mildred came to take my temperature and told me it was under a hundred. I still had a dull ache at the back of my neck and I hadn't eaten much all day. I nibbled on some toast and jelly and a few spoonfuls of hot oatmeal. My stomach churned angrily with every morsel I swallowed and I knew if I tried to eat any more it would make me sick.

Sanford sent a message that he hoped I felt better and apologized for having to remain at the factory. Mildred told me he said he had some major problems or he would have been home earlier.

I fell asleep again and then I woke to the sound of Celine's stairway elevator chair. I waited, staring at my door. Moments later she came rolling into my room.

"Time to get up, dear," she sang as if it was first thing in the morning. "Take a hot shower to warm up your muscles and put on your leotards and your pointe shoes."

I groaned as I sat up, and when I stood, I felt a bit woozy, but I tried to hide it from her. I knew that I had no choice but to dance for her.

"Just take your shower quickly," Celine ordered.

My legs felt so tight. How could I ever dance? I had trouble walking. Nevertheless, I forced myself into the shower and stood under the water, letting it stream down my neck and back. It did make me feel a little better.

"Hurry downstairs," Celine said as she left my room. "I want you to do some warm-up exercises before Madame Malisorf arrives. Dimitri is already here. He'll coach you," she added and my heart started to pound as I thought about him and his creepy eyes inspecting my body.

It nearly exhausted me to put on my leotards and shoes, but I did it. When I descended the stairs, Mildred came out of the living room where she had been dusting and polishing furniture. She looked very surprised.

"You shouldn't be out of bed, Janet." She put her arm around me and began to turn me back toward the stairs. "Mr. Delorice left me orders and—"

"My mother wants me at my dance lesson," I said.

"She does? Oh." Her tone of voice made it clear which Delorice she was more afraid of crossing.

"Janet," Celine called sharply from upstairs.

"I'm coming," I said and hurried up to the studio.

Dimitri was at the barre stretching. As usual he was totally oblivious to everyone and everything around him. I approached, took my position, and began. Finally, he looked at me.

"Today is your big day," he said. "If you're nice to me, I'll make you look good."

He laughed and broke away to do what I had already learned were *frappés* on three-quarter pointe. He made it look as easy as walking and from the smug look on his face, I knew he was showing off. His arrogant smile was beginning to make me feel sicker than the flu.

Madame Malisorf arrived within minutes and looked pleased that I had already warmed up.

"Let me see your feet," she ordered and inspected my pointe shoes. "Excellent. Well done, Celine," she told my mother, who nodded and smiled. "Pull up," she ordered.

A ballet posture that aligns the body so you stand up straight with hips level and even, shoulders open but relaxed and centered over the hips, your pelvis straight, back straight, head up, weight centered evenly between your feet, was known as *pulled up*. Madame Malisorf told me to imagine myself suspended by a thread attached to the top of my head. She said I did it well and that I had excellent posture.

"The most important thing to remember for pointe work is proper coordination of your whole body, each part adapting correctly and without strain to any new position without losing your placement, Janet," Madame Malisorf began, her nasal voice sounding haughtier than usual.

Dimitri, at her side, demonstrated. He looked like a giant puppet to me.

"We have worked hard at developing your strength. I want your knees absolutely straight like Dimitri's. I am satisfied that your ankle joint is sufficiently flexible to form with the forefoot at a right-angle when on the demi-pointe. Do not curl or clutch your toes. Dimitri," she said and again he demonstrated.

As I began the exercises and moves she ordered, she continually yelled, "Line, posture, line. No, no, no, you're sagging. Why are you acting so weak? Again, again. Dimitri," she said with frustration. "Another demonstration. Look at him, watch him, study him," she commanded. Finally she lost her patience and seized me at the shoulders and turned me toward Dimitri. "Watch him!"

He stepped right in front of me, maybe half a foot away and began.

"See how important posture is?"

"Yes, Madame," I said.

"So? Why today are you forgetting it?"

I looked at Celine. She shook her head gently. I would be permitted no excuses. I couldn't even mention my being sick. I began again, trying harder. My body shook so much inside, it felt as if my bones were rattling, but again, I kept it all hidden.

Dimitri demonstrated the ronds de jambe en l'air, the petit and grand battements, everything with an air of superiority. The music pounded in my ears. I felt more awkward than ever, and every time I gazed at Madame Malisorf, I saw her disapproval and disappointment.

"Stop, stop, stop," she cried. "Maybe it's too soon," she muttered, shaking her head.

"No," I moaned. My ankles felt like they would

snap and my toes would probably be permanently cramped, but I could not stop. My new life depended on it.

Dimitri looked at me and then stepped up beside me.

"Let's try again, Madame," he said, putting his hands on my hips. "I'll help guide her through it."

Reluctantly, she clapped her hands and we began. Dimitri whispered in my ear, explaining how I should move and which way to lean and turn. I felt different, better and safer in his strong hands. He had great strength and was practically holding me up at times.

"Better," Madame Malisorf muttered. "Yes, that's it. Good. Keep the line. Good."

I felt like a limp dishrag when the lesson finally ended. My leotards were soaked through.

"An adequate first attempt," Madame Malisorf declared, stressing the word *adequate.*

"She'll be much better tomorrow," Celine said, wheeling up to us.

"Perhaps not tomorrow but soon after," Madame Malisorf allowed.

Dimitri was sweating almost as much as me.

"Thank you for your extra effort, Dimitri," she told him. "You should take a warm shower immediately," she added. "I don't want my prize pupil going out in the chilly air and getting sick. Celine?"

"Of course. Go up and use my shower, Dimitri. Janet, show him my room, please."

Madame Malisorf turned to Celine. "In two weeks

I'm presenting a recital with my newest students and Janet will be included."

"Oh, Janet, that's wonderful. Did you hear what she said? Thank you, Madame. Thank you," Celine said. "Your first recital. How wonderful, Janet."

"Recital?" I squeaked. "You mean with an audience and everything?"

"You will be ready," Madame Malisorf declared with a small smile, "for what you will be asked to do."

"Oh yes, she'll be ready. Whatever it is, she'll be ready," Celine assured her.

Dimitri took his bag and followed me out of the studio.

"You were awful in the beginning," he said as we reached the stairway.

"I was sick. I'm still sick. I had a fever this morning," I complained.

He laughed.

"I'm glad you didn't tell Madame that. She hates excuses," he explained. "Lead the way," he added, nodding at the steps. I started up. "You know your rear end has become quite tight and round just in the short time I've been working with you."

I was too embarrassed to say anything and continued upstairs where I showed him Celine and Sanford's bathroom. After I'd given him a clean towel I hurried away to my own room to shower and crawl back into bed. My ankles ached worse than any other part of my body and when I took off my pointe shoes, my feet were covered with red blotches.

I turned on my shower and took off my leotards, but just before I stepped into the stall, I heard Dimitri say, "Pull up."

I spun around, shocked. There he was with a towel around his waist, gazing at me.

"Pull up," he said again. "Posture, posture."

"Go away!" I cried, covering myself as best I could. He laughed.

"Come on. Pull up. Remember what I told you about that group that dances naked?" He reached for my hand. I wrapped my hands around myself tightly, but he was too strong and pulled my arm away from my chest. Then, in another motion, he undid his towel and stood naked before me. I couldn't take my eyes off him, despite my shock and terror.

He went on his toes, pulled me closer, turned me around, and lifted me in the air. Then he set me down and pressed his body against me.

"There," he said. "Didn't that feel good?"

He laughed and scooped up his towel, wrapping it around his waist as he walked out of my room.

I could barely breathe.

My head was spinning. Slowly, I sank to the floor and sat there, stunned. A moment later, I thought I was going to retch. I literally crawled over to the shower and stepped into the steamy stall.

Within minutes I got out, dried myself quickly, and crawled into bed as I had planned. Just as I closed my eyes, I heard my door open and Dimitri looked in.

"Until tomorrow. Oh. And as I said, very nice and

tight little rear end. You're going to be a dancer after all," he added with a laugh and was gone.

Not only couldn't I talk, I couldn't even think. I pressed my hands to my stomach and turned on my side. In moments I was asleep.

I'd only been asleep a few hours when I woke to the sound of bickering. I knew I had slept awhile because it was already dark outside. Sanford's and Celine's voices carried down the hallway. He couldn't believe she had forced me to take a lesson.

"She had a fever. Dr. Franklin said she has the flu, Celine. How could you put her through all that physical exertion?"

"You don't understand," she told him. "She has to understand obstacles, overcome them, build an inner strength. That's what makes the difference between a real dancer and an amateur, a child and a woman. She did well enough today to be invited to a recital. Didn't you hear what I said? A recital!"

"She's too young, Celine," Sanford insisted.

"No, you fool. She's almost too old. In a matter of weeks, she's grown years. You don't know about anything but glass and that stupid factory of yours. Stick with that and leave our daughter to me. You took away my chance, but you won't take away hers," she cried.

And then there was silence.

Nine

Despite what Celine had said at dinner, I didn't get to meet my new grandparents until the day of Madame Malisorf's recital. Twice a year she held a recital to debut her new students and showcase her older ones. The new dancers like myself were given a variety of exercises and moves to demonstrate. The older ones each performed a scene from a famous ballet. Dimitri was dancing the lead in *Romeo and Juliet.*

Because I learned and practiced in my own studio, I had never met the half dozen other beginning students. Consequently they didn't know how far I had progressed and I had no idea what they could do either. When Sanford, Celine, and I arrived at Madame Malisorf's studio, the other students and I studied each other during warm-ups as if we were gunfighters soon to be in a shoot-out. From the intense expressions on the faces of the parents, grandparents, sisters and brothers, I sensed that everyone was hoping their son or daughter or sibling would look the most impressive. I knew Celine was hoping that. All the way to the studio, she bragged about me.

"When they all find out that you not only didn't have any training before you came to live with us, but you hadn't even seen a ballet, they will be amazed. And wait until they discover how quickly Madame Malisorf put you on pointe," she added with a little laugh. "I can just imagine their faces, can't you, Sanford?"

"I still think she was rushed along a bit when it came to that, Celine," he said softly. He was the only one to notice my horrible aches and pains and asked me each night if I wanted a hot pack or a massage. Sometimes it was so bad I could barely walk the next day.

"I think Madame Malisorf is the best judge of that, Sanford. If she didn't think Janet was doing well, she wouldn't want her in the recital," she insisted.

As if I wasn't nervous enough already, Celine's words and ultra-high expectations were making me tremble. Maybe because I was so nervous, my feet ached even more. They were so swollen, I could barely lace my shoes this morning.

When we got to Madame Malisorf's studio we saw that a small crowd of spectators had already arrived, made up mostly of families of the dancers, but also, according to Celine, consisting of some ballet lovers and other teachers, even ballet producers on the lookout for potential new stars.

The studio had a small stage and a dressing area behind it. I was already wearing my tutu and pointe shoes, so I was ready for warm-ups. I had just begun when I saw Sanford wheeling Celine toward me, and an older man with a charcoal gray mustache and an older lady, tall, with her hair a tinted bluish gray and teased, walked beside them. The woman wore far too much makeup, I thought, the rouge so dark on her cheeks and the lipstick so thick on her lips it made her look like a clown.

The gentleman was in a dark blue suit and tie. He had a spry walk and a friendly smile lit by blue eyes that made him look almost as young as Sanford. The elderly lady's face was taut, her gray eyes flint cold. Even when she drew closer, she looked like someone wearing a mask.

"Janet, I want you to meet my parents, Mr. and Mrs. Westfall," Celine said.

These were the two people who would be my grandparents, I quickly thought. Before I could speak, the gentleman said, "Hello, dear."

"Hello." My voice was barely louder than a whisper.

My new grandmother gazed down at me and from head to toe I was assessed, weighed, measured.

"She is petite. Nearly thirteen, you say?" she asked Celine.

"Yes, Mother, but she moves as gracefully as a butterfly. I wouldn't want her to be any different," Celine said proudly.

"What if she doesn't grow much more?" Mrs.

Westfall asked, and as she stared down at me I noticed she was sparkling with jewelry. Around her neck she wore a dazzling diamond necklace and her fingers were covered with rings, rubies, diamonds, all in gold and platinum settings.

"Of course she'll grow," Sanford said and his indignant voice surprised me.

"I doubt it," my new grandmother muttered. "Well, where are we supposed to sit?" she said, turning and looking at the already well-filled auditorium.

"Those are our seats to the right there." Sanford nodded at some empty chairs in the first row. That appeared to please my new grandmother.

"Well, let's sit down." She headed toward the seats with a graceful gait, her head held high.

"Good luck, young lady," my new grandfather said.

"Afterward," Celine said, taking my hand, "we'll all go out for dinner and celebrate."

"Just relax and do your best," Sanford told me and gave me his special smile.

"Oh no," Celine cried when she turned in her chair. "It's my brother. Who expected he would come?"

Daniel came strutting down the aisle, a big wide grin on his face. He wore a cowboy hat, a pale yellow western shirt, jeans, and boots. Everything looked new, but because the rest of the audience was dressed as if it were really a city ballet theater, he stood out and caused an immediate wave of chatter.

"That's how you come dressed to this?" Celine said as he approached us.

"What's wrong with what I'm wearing? It cost enough," he added. "Hey, break a leg," he said to me. There wasn't a seat for him so he took a place against the wall, folded his arms, and leaned back.

Soon after Daniel arrived I left my family and joined the other performers who were at the barres exercising. Dimitri stopped and came over to me.

"Relax," he said. "You're too tight. This isn't exactly the Metropolitan Ballet, you know. It's just a bunch of proud parents mooing and gooing."

"Are your parents here?" I asked.

"Of course not," he said. "This isn't anything."

"It is to me," I admitted. He smirked. Then he smiled that arrogant smile and I was sorry that I'd let him know how important tonight was to me.

"Just pretend I'm out there with you and you'll be fine. In fact," he said leaning toward me, "imagine I'm naked."

My face instantly grew hot. He laughed and moved off to join the older students. I saw them all looking my way. He was whispering to them and they were smiling and laughing. I tried to ignore them, to concentrate on what I was doing, but my heart wouldn't stop thumping and I was having trouble catching my breath.

Finally, Madame Malisorf took the floor and the room grew so still you could hear someone clear his throat way in the back of the audience.

"Good afternoon, everyone. Thank you for coming to our semiannual recital. We will begin today with a demonstration of some of the basic, yet difficult ballet exercises, what we call the adage portion of our class, to be performed by my primary class students. You will note how well the students maintain position and balance.

"All of them, I am happy to say, are now dancing *sur les pointes* or on pointe, as we say. As some of you who have been here before know, toe dancing was developed early in the nineteenth century but did not become widely used by ballet dancers until the eighteen thirties, when the Swedish-Italian ballerina Marie Taglioni demonstrated its potential for poetic effect. Heritage, style, technique, grace, and form are what we emphasize at the Malisorf School of Ballet.

"Without further comment, then, my primary students," she announced, did a small bow, and backed away, nodding at the piano player as she did so.

We knew what we had to do as soon as the music started and all of us took position. The most difficult part of the routine as far as I was concerned was the *entrechat,* something I had just been taught. The entrechat is one of the steps of elevation. The dancer jumps straight up, beats the calves of the legs together in midair, and lands softly. Madame Malisorf wanted us to connect that with a pirouette before coming to a graceful stop, and then a bow, hopefully to applause.

I looked at my new grandparents and then at Celine, who wore a small smile on her lips. Sanford nodded at me and gave me a wider smile. Daniel looked like he was laughing at everyone. He stepped away from the wall and pretended to go on pointe and then fell back against the wall.

The music began. As I danced, I noticed every one of the primary students glancing at everyone else. I remembered how important it was to concentrate, to feel the music, to be in your own little world, and I tried to ignore them. The only face I caught a glimpse of was Dimitri's. He looked as sternly critical as Madame Malisorf.

The pain in my feet was excruciating. I might as well be in some sort of torture chamber, I thought. Why had Madame Malisorf been ignoring my agony? Was this really the way a dancer developed or was Dimitri right: she was pushing me because Celine wanted it that way?

Soon after we had begun, the girl beside me began to close the gap between us. Madame Malisorf never had us rehearse together. It was just assumed we would all remain in our own space and do what we were taught to do. I should have paid more attention to those around me because the girl came down after a turn and actually grazed the skirt of my tutu with her right hand.

It put me off balance, but I didn't realize it until I finished the entrechat and began to pirouette. I leaned too far in her direction so that when she turned and I spun, we collided and both lost our balance. I fell to the polished floor in an awkward flop that resulted in my sitting down hard on my hands. She continued to lose her balance and nearly collided with another dancer before falling on her side.

The audience roared with laughter, Daniel's laugh one of the loudest. Dimitri looked sick. Celine's mouth opened and closed and then her face filled with disbelief. Sanford looked sad, but my new grandmother kept shaking her head and smirking. My new grandfather just looked surprised.

Madame Malisorf, off to the right, gestured for us to rise quickly, and I did so. I started to perform the last steps again, but she shook her head and indicated I should simply stop and join the others in their bows.

There was loud applause. The guests appeared to have enjoyed our imperfections. Madame Malisorf took the center stage again and waited for silence.

"Well," she said, "that's why we spend most of our youth trying to do the simplest exercises and steps. Ballet is truly the dance of the gods," she added. "My primary students," she said gesturing at us and stressing the word *primary*. There was loud applause again and we all hurried off the stage. The older students approached to take our places. Dimitri glared at me.

My stomach felt as if it had filled with gravel. The girl who had collided with me came over to me immediately.

"You little idiot," she said. The others stopped to listen. "How could you be so clumsy? Why didn't you watch where you were going?"

"I did. You came too close to me," I cried.

"Everyone saw it. Whose fault was it?" she asked her friends.

"The Dwarf's," one of the boys quipped and they all laughed. The girl fired another look of hate at me and they walked away. I sat on a chair, my tears zigzagging down my cheeks and dropping off my chin.

"Hey, hey," I heard someone say and glanced up to see Sanford walking through the backstage area. "There's no reason for that. You did fine."

"I did horribly," I moaned.

"No, no. It wasn't your fault."

"Everyone thinks it was," I said, wiping my tears away with the back of my hands.

"Come on," he said. "We'll watch the rest of the recital."

I took his hand and went out to the audience. It seemed like everyone was looking at me and laughing. I kept my head down, my eyes fixed on my feet as we went around and down the side to reach the chairs. There were two empty ones. My new grandparents had left.

Celine said nothing. She sucked in her breath and stared at the stage as the scene from *Romeo and Juliet* began. Dimitri was as wonderful as he was in our studio. He danced as if he owned the stage and it was apparent, even to me, really just a beginner, that he made the others look better than they were. When their scene ended, the applause was louder, the faces of the guests full of appreciation. Madame Malisorf announced a reception in the next room where she would be serving hors d'oeuvres and wine for the adults.

"Let's just go home," Celine grumbled.

"Celine . . ." Sanford began and I knew he didn't

want to make me feel any more awkward than I already did.

"Please," she said. "Let's just go home."

He got behind her chair and started to wheel her out. Some of the people stopped to say they enjoyed my dancing.

"Don't be discouraged, little one," a red-faced man said. "It's like riding a horse. Just get up and do it again," he advised. His wife pulled him away. Celine shot him a nasty, hateful look and then turned toward the doorway. We couldn't get out of there fast enough for her.

I wondered where Daniel was and spotted him talking to one of the older ballerinas. He waved at me as we left, but I was too embarrassed to wave back. It wasn't until we were all in the car that I spoke.

"I'm sorry, Mother," I said. "I didn't know that girl was so close to me and she didn't notice me either."

"It was the other girl's fault," Sanford comforted.

Celine was so quiet, I didn't think she would speak to me again, but after a few minutes she began.

"You can't blame anything on the other dancer. You have to be aware of the other dancer. If she or he is off, you have to compensate. That's what makes you the best." Her tone left no room for argument, but still Sanford tried to defend me.

"She's just starting, Celine," Sanford reminded her. "Mistakes are something you learn from."

"Mistakes should be made in practice, not in recital," she spat. "You'll have to work harder." She was ashamed of me and didn't pretend to hide it.

"Harder? How can she work any harder than she's working, Celine? She doesn't do anything else. She hasn't had a chance to make new friends. She needs a life, too." Sanford wouldn't give up. It shocked me since he always gave in to her so easily.

"This is her life. She wants it just as much as I want it for her. Don't you, Janet? Well?"

"Yes, Mother," I said quickly.

"See? I'll speak to Madame Malisorf. Maybe we can get her to give her one more lesson a week."

"When? On the weekend? Celine, you're being unreasonable." Sanford said.

"Sanford, I'm tired of you arguing with me. And I will not have you always taking *her* side. You are my husband, Sanford; your allegiance belongs with me. Janet *will have* an extra lesson."

Sanford shook his head.

"I still think that might be too much, Celine," Sanford said, gently this time.

"Let Madame Malisorf and I decide what's too much, Sanford."

He didn't argue anymore. As we headed for home I wondered what happened to the idea of going out to dinner? What happened to my new grandparents? I was afraid to ask, and I didn't need to since Celine told me anyway.

"My mother and father were embarrassed and went straight home," she said, her voice steely.

I didn't think it was possible to feel any smaller than I was, but I wished I could just sink into the crevices between the seats and disappear. As soon as we arrived home, I ran upstairs to my room and shut the door. A short while later, I heard a soft knock. "Come in," I called out.

Sanford entered and smiled at me. I was sitting on the bed. I had cried all the tears I had stored for sad occasions. My eyes ached.

"Now I don't want you feeling so terrible," he said kindly. "You'll have many more chances to do better."

"I'll make another mistake for sure," I said. "I'm not as good as Celine thinks I am."

"Don't underestimate yourself after just one recital, Janet. Everyone, even the greatest dancers, makes mistakes." He put his hand on my shoulder, then rubbed it along my tight, aching neck.

"She hates me now," I mumbled.

"Oh no," he said. "She's just very determined. She'll relax and realize it's not the end of the world, too. You'll see," he promised. He brushed back my hair. "You were definitely the cutest dancer out there. I'm sure most people thought you were the best one on stage," he encouraged.

"They did?"

"Sure. All eyes were on you."

"Which made it worse for me," I pointed out.

He laughed.

"Now, don't you think about it anymore. Think about happy things. Isn't your real birthday next Saturday?"

"Yes, but Celine wanted to change it to the day you adopted me," I reminded him.

"That was just Celine's silly wish. Why don't you

and I plan your birthday party," he said. "I know you haven't had a chance to make new friends, but maybe you'll be able to at your party. Think of some children you'd like to invite. We'll have a good time," he promised.

"Will my grandparents come?" I asked.

His smile stiffened.

"I imagine so," he said. "Now, go on. Change and we'll all have dinner."

"Celine's really not mad at me?" I asked hopefully.

"No. Celine's had a very big disappointment in her life. It's hard for her to have any more. That's all. She'll be fine. We'll all be fine," he said.

It was meant to be a promise, but it came out more like a prayer, and most of my life, my prayers had never been answered.

Ten

Madame Malisorf refused to add another day to my weekly ballet lessons. Celine and she had the conversation three days later—the very first lesson after the recital.

"No," Madame Malisorf said. "It was partly my mistake to have rushed her along. I should never have agreed to put her on pointe. I should have listened to my own instincts. Janet has to find her own level of competence, her own capabilities. Talent is like water. If you remove the obstructions, it will rise to its highest possible level by itself."

"That's not true, Madame Malisorf," Celine declared. "We must set her limits. We must determine her capabilities. She won't strive if we don't push her. She doesn't have the inner discipline."

Madame Malisorf gazed at me warming up alongside Dimitri, who had said nothing yet about my performance at the recital.

"You must be careful. You could make her lose interest and affection for the beauty and the skills, Celine. If you overtrain an athlete, he or she starts to regress, lose muscle, skill."

"We'll take that chance. Double her training time. Money is no object," Celine insisted.

"Money has never been nor will it ever be a consideration for me," Madame Malisorf snapped back at her, holding her shoulders and head proudly.

Celine seemed to wilt in the chair.

"I know that, Madame, I just meant—"

"If I am to be the girl's teacher, Celine, I am to be in control. I will determine the schedule of lessons. More is not always better. What's better is to get more quality out of what you already have. If you think otherwise—"

"Yes, yes, you're right," Celine said quickly. "Of course, you're right, Madame Malisorf. I was just so disappointed the other day and I know you were, too."

"On the contrary, I was not," she said. Celine's head lifted. Even I had to pause in my exercises and look her way.

"You weren't?" Celine sounded skeptical.

"No. I was happy to see the child get right up and attempt to continue. *That* is stamina, determination. That comes from here," she said holding her palm against her heart.

"Yes," Celine said, looking at me. "Of course,

you're right again, Madame. I'm grateful that we have you."

"Then let's not waste the time we do have, Celine." Dismissing Celine with a flick of her wrist, Madame Malisorf approached Dimitri and me and our lesson began.

It was a good lesson. Even I felt that I had accomplished more than usual. The only mention Madame Malisorf made of the recital was when she made reference to my work on pointe. For the rest of the lesson she had Dimitri take me through a series of exercises and complimented me on my work.

Yet none of this seemed to ease Celine's concerns. She sat glumly in her chair and when the lesson ended and Dimitri and Madame Malisorf were gone, Celine wheeled up to me to say she thought Madame Malisorf was wrong.

"She just doesn't want to give up her own free time," Celine said peevishly. "In ballet more is better. If you're not obsessed with it, you won't be successful. It has to be demanding on your body and your soul. I'll practice with you on the weekend," she added. "We'll begin this Saturday."

"But this Saturday is my birthday and Sanford said we're having a party. I've invited some of my classmates," I moaned.

"Oh, *Sanford* is planning your party, is he?" The look in her eyes chilled me. "Well, the party isn't an all-day affair, is it? We'll practice in the morning and you can have your party in the afternoon, if you must have it at all," she declared, then turned her chair and wheeled herself away.

Ever since the recital, Celine had been behaving differently toward me. She was more impatient, her words harsher, her eyes more critical. She spent more time alone, sometimes just sitting and staring out the window. And any time I mentioned Sanford she narrowed her eyes and looked at me like she was trying to see inside me, see what I was thinking and feeling. Once I even found her backed into a corner, the shadows draped over her like a blanket. She was staring at the painting of herself in her dance costume.

When I mentioned my concern to Sanford, he said I should just give her time. I didn't mention that I thought Celine was upset at the time he and I spent together, though, since I was afraid he would avoid me in order to keep in Celine's good graces.

"She has her ups and downs," he explained. "Everything has been happening so fast, she just needs time to adjust."

He and I went for one of our walks on the grounds, down to the lake. It was special times like these, spending time with a daddy who loved and cared for me, that made all the hours of torture in the studio worthwhile.

"I've made all the plans for your birthday party," Sanford said when we reached the edge of the water. "We're going to have a barbecue, hot dogs and hamburgers and steaks for the adults."

"Who's coming?" I asked, hoping he would mention my new grandparents.

"Some of the people at my plant whom you've met, Mrs. Williams from Peabody, Madame Malisorf, of course, and yes," he added quickly, reading my mind, "Celine's parents and Daniel will stop by. How many people have you invited?"

"Ten," I said.

"Good. We have a nice party planned. Remember, I don't want anyone using the rowboat without an adult present, okay?"

I nodded. This was the most exciting thing in my life, even more exciting than the recital. I had never had a real birthday party. The only time I'd had a birthday cake, it was for me and two other children at the orphanage at the same time. Sharing it took away from its specialness. Birthdays aren't special without a family to help you celebrate, without a mother to remember things about your growing up and a daddy to give you that special kiss and say, "My little girl's growing up. Soon she'll have eyes for someone else beside me." Finally, I was going to have a party that really was solely my own and a big party, too!

I told Sanford that Celine wanted me to practice dance on the morning of my birthday and his eyes grew small and troubled. Later, at dinner, he mentioned it and Celine shot a look at me as if to say I had betrayed her.

"Did she go crying to you about it?" she asked. "Why is it that you've suddenly become her knight in shining armor?"

"Come on, Celine. She just mentioned it when I told her about the plans for her party. I thought we would all decorate the family room in the morning and—"

"Really, Sanford, what did you expect me to do? Climb a ladder and hang balloons?" she asked disdainfully.

"No, of course not. I just thought . . ." I could tell he was weakening.

"There are no holidays, no days off, no time to forget what is your destiny, Janet," she said, turning back to me.

"I know. I wasn't complaining," I said. I didn't want her to think I wasn't grateful.

She stared at me a moment. It was a hard look, and her eyes were full of disappointment. I had to look down at my food.

"I know you're a young girl, but as a dancer you are entering a world that requires you to become an adult faster, Janet," she continued. "It will make you stronger for everything in life. I promise."

I looked up and she smiled.

"You've come so far so fast. It wasn't long ago when you were just a lost child in that orphanage. Now you have a name and a talent. You're going to be someone. Don't give up on me," she said, her voice surprising me with its soft pleading.

"Oh, I won't do that, Mother." How could she fear that *I* would give up on *her?*

"Good. Good. Then it's settled. We'll work in the morning and then you can enjoy your party. Mildred will decorate the family room," she told Sanford.

"I'd like to help," he said.

"Yes, I suppose you would," Celine told him, and I could see her scrutinizing him as she often did me, trying to peer inside his mind.

Celine was a sterner teacher than Madame Malisorf. The morning of my birthday, she was waiting impatiently for me in the studio. I was on my way into the studio when Mildred called out to me that I had a telephone call. One of the girls at school, Betty Lowe, called to talk to me about my party and the five boys I had invited. She said everyone knew how much Josh Brown liked me. My conversation lasted longer than I realized and Celine was annoyed when I joined her in the studio, five minutes late.

"What have I told you about time and its importance when it comes to practice, Janet? I thought you understood," she snapped as soon as I entered the studio.

"I'm sorry," I said. Before I could offer any explanation, she sent me directly to the barre.

I tried but I couldn't concentrate. I couldn't help thinking about my party, about everyone getting dressed up, and about the music and the food. I just knew this party would make the kids I'd invited finally let me into their group. I didn't think I had to do anything more to impress Josh, but just in case, I would be sure to wear my prettiest dress.

As these thoughts flooded my mind, I went through the motions of my routine. Celine rolled her wheelchair over until she was only inches from me and began to criticize my form and tempo.

"You're missing your mark," she said. "No, not so fast. Listen to the music. That landing was too hard! You don't land like an elephant, you float like a butterfly. Relax your knees. No. Stop!" she screamed and covered her face with her hands.

"I'm sorry," I said when she stayed silent. "I'm trying."

"You're not trying. Your mind is elsewhere. I wish Sanford had never thought up this birthday party," she muttered, her normally pretty mouth twisted, her eyes burning with an inner rage that made me look away. "All right," she said finally. "We'll make it up later. Go get ready for your party. I know when I'm fighting a lost cause. Believe me, I know when I'm doing that," she added, still very bitter.

I apologized again, but as soon as I left her behind me in the studio and rounded the corner of the doorway, I ran through the house, up the stairs, and to my room. I wanted to try my hair in a new style and I still hadn't decided on which dress I should wear. I had decided to polish my nails, too. When my first guests arrived, I was still primping and Sanford had to come to my door to tell me it was time to come down to greet people.

The presents were piled up like Christmas gifts under a tree. Mildred had helium balloons on the ceiling with different-colored ribbons dangling. There were birthday decorations on the windows and walls, and the food was so impressive, I heard Mrs. Williams wonder aloud what Sanford and Celine would do for a wedding.

A wedding? I thought. Would I become a famous dancer and marry another famous dancer? Would I marry a rich businessman like Sanford? Would I go to college and meet some handsome young man? It was as if my life here was the key to unlocking a treasure chest of fantasies, fantasies that could actually come true!

My new grandparents were the last to arrive. I heard Celine ask about Daniel and saw her mother grimace.

"Who knows where he is?" she groaned. "That's why we're late. He was supposed to drive us."

"Happy birthday," my grandfather said when he saw me standing nearby. He was the one who handed me my present.

"Yes, happy birthday," my grandmother followed. She didn't give me much more than a passing glance before getting into a conversation with the other guests. My grandfather began a discussion with Sanford and I returned to my friends. We danced and drank punch and ate. Josh was at my side most of the time, although suddenly Billy Ross was asking me to dance as well.

Afterward, I cut the huge birthday cake. I had to blow out the candles and everyone sang "Happy Birthday" to me, everyone but my grandmother, who stood staring with a dark, unhappy expression on her face. While we ate cake I opened presents and everyone oohed and ahed over the pretty clothes, the hair dryer, the jewelry. My grandparents had bought me a pair of leather gloves that turned out to be at least two sizes too big.

I hated to see the party come to an end. Josh stayed behind and reminded me I had promised to show him our lake. I told Sanford where we were going and we left the house. It was a bit cool and overcast. I wore my new leather jacket that Sanford and Celine had bought me.

"This is a great house," Josh said. "It's twice as big as mine. And all this land, I could have my own baseball field," he continued. "You're lucky."

"I am lucky," I said. We stood at the crest of the hill, looking down at the lake.

"I'm glad you transferred into our school," Josh said. "Otherwise, I probably wouldn't have ever met you."

"No, you wouldn't have," I said, thinking about where I had come from. I was almost tempted to tell him the truth. He was so sweet, but I was afraid that the moment he heard the word *orphan,* he would back away and pretend he never knew me.

"Can we go in the rowboat?" he asked when he spotted the boat docked onshore.

"My father doesn't want me to go without an adult. I don't swim," I confessed.

"Really? How come?"

I shrugged.

"I just never learned."

His eyes grew narrow and his eyebrows nearly touched. Then he smiled.

"Maybe I'll be the one to teach you this summer."

"I'd like that," I said.

"I never gave you a birthday kiss," he said.

I didn't move and he leaned toward me slowly. I closed my eyes and there, on the crest of the hill behind my new home, I was kissed for the first time on the lips. It didn't last long. There was even a little friction shock, but I thought it was the most wonderful kiss in the world, better than any I had seen on television or in the movies. The little warm feeling that followed lingered for a moment around my heart and then trickled into my pool of memories where it would stay forever and ever.

"Janet!" We turned to see Sanford beckoning. "Josh's father is here to pick him up."

"Okay," I called back and we started for the house. Josh took my hand. Neither of us spoke. We let go before we rounded the house to greet his father, who wished me a happy birthday.

"See you in school," Josh said. I wished I could kiss him good-bye, but he looked embarrassed and hurried to get into his father's car. Moments later, he was waving good-bye and my party was over. I felt like I did when we were given some wonderful special dessert at the orphanage. When it was coming to an end, I wanted to linger and linger over the last tidbits of pleasure.

I went back inside. Mildred was busy cleaning up, but she didn't look upset about the extra work and when I offered to help her, she laughed and said not to worry. I was about to go upstairs to change out of my party dress, when I heard voices in the dining room. My grandparents were still here, having coffee and talking with Celine.

I was nervous about interrupting them, so I hesitated near the door. Just before I decided I would enter and try to get to know them a little better, I heard my grandmother say, "She'll always be a stranger to me, Celine. She's not of our blood and blood is the most important thing in a family."

"That's ridiculous, Mother, and anyway, I'm not concerned about family. I don't just want a daughter. Anyone can have a daughter. I want a dancer." My heart fell at her words. What did she mean?

"More reason to question what you are doing, Celine. I saw the girl at the recital. What in heaven's name caused you to believe she had anything special?"

"She does," Celine insisted.

"Well, if she does, she keeps it well hidden," my grandmother said. "Where is she? You would think she would show some respect. I took the time to come here."

I decided that was my cue and I entered.

"Hello," I said, my voice quavering, my stomach in knots over Celine's words. "Thank you for the present, Grandmother and Grandfather." My grandfather nodded and smiled. My grandmother tightened the corner of her mouth.

"We have to go," she said. "Your brother is a constant worry for me," she added, looking at Celine. "I'm afraid he's going to end up marrying one of those floozies and disgrace all of us one of these days," she added as she rose.

"It's your own fault," Celine said. "You spoiled him."

"I didn't spoil him. Your father spoiled him," she accused.

"He'll be all right," Sanford said. "He's just sowing his wild oats."

"Really?" my grandmother said. "Well, when do you think he'll run out of oats?"

Sanford laughed and then escorted them out. My grandfather patted me on the head as they left and mumbled something about "Many happy returns."

I remained with Celine, who sat there brooding in her chair.

"Thank you for the party," I told her. She looked up as if just realizing I was still in the room.

"Where were you?"

"I went for a walk with Josh to show him the lake," I said.

She rolled her chair around the table and came toward me.

"You've got to be careful when it comes to boys," she began.

I smiled. I was just thirteen.

"I know what you're thinking. You think you have plenty of time to worry about romance, but believe me, you don't. Not you. You're special. I don't want you to turn your brain into Jell-O with silly lovesickness. It's distracting and this morning you saw what distraction can do."

She drew closer until we were gazing into each other's eyes.

"Sex draws on your creative energies, Janet. It can drain you," she explained. "When I was dancing and approaching the peak of my development, I refrained from all sexual activities with Sanford. For a long time, we even slept in separate rooms," she added.

I didn't say anything and I didn't move. I don't think I even blinked.

"I had many boys chasing after me, especially when I was your age," she continued, "but I didn't have time to waste on schoolgirl crushes. You won't either so don't encourage any." She started to wheel herself away and stopped. "Tomorrow," she said, "we'll try to make up for today."

She left me standing there looking after her. "Make up for today?" She made it sound as if my birthday and my birthday party were a total inconvenience.

I had a grandmother who didn't really want me and a mother who only wanted me so that I could be the dancer she couldn't be.

No, Josh, I thought, maybe I'm not as lucky as you imagine.

Outside, the sky turned darker. The rain began and the drops that hit the windows looked like heaven's tears.

Eleven

Once Celine and I began working weekends on my dancing, it became a regular part of my schedule. A number of times, Sanford tried to plan family outings: day trips, shopping, movie matinees, or just a ride and dinner in a nice restaurant. Celine not only rejected his suggestions; she became annoyed and angry at him just for making them.

After my birthday party, I was invited to other girls' houses, and one night I was invited to a pajama party at Betty Lowe's. Celine always had a reason why I shouldn't go, the primary one being I would stay up too late, be too tired, and start my dance practice too late.

"Parents don't watch their children very well anymore," she told me. "I can't be sure you'll be well chaperoned, and I know what happens at these all-girl parties. Boys always sneak over and then . . . things happen. Not that I ever went to any sleepovers—I knew enough not to be distracted," she added.

I tried to explain my situation to my new friends, but after I had turned down half a dozen invitations, the invitations stopped coming and once again, I felt a gap growing between me and the other students at the school. Even Josh began to lose interest in me because we never had a chance to be alone. Once, and only because Sanford had talked Celine into permitting me to go with him to the factory after my dance lesson on a Saturday, I was able to meet Josh at the custard stand. Sanford knew that was why I wanted to go along with him and he permitted me to stay there for nearly two hours before coming around to bring me home.

"It's probably best for you not to mention this to Celine," Sanford told me. "Not that we want to keep any secrets from her. I just don't want her worrying."

I nodded, but he didn't have to ask. I wouldn't have dreamed of mentioning it.

I did my best to explain my situation to Josh, but he couldn't understand how my dancing prevented me from doing nearly everything any of the other kids could do. The crisis came when he formally asked me to the movies. His father was going to drive us. Sanford said yes but Celine said no and they got into the worst argument they had since I had arrived.

"This time it's only a night at the movies and ice cream afterward, ice cream full of fat that she doesn't need. Tomorrow it will be a whole weekend day and night. And then she'll be wanting to go on weekend jaunts with girls who have nothing but bubble gum brains and two left feet."

"She's only thirteen, Celine."

"When I was thirteen, I had performed in twelve programs and I had danced in *Sleeping Beauty* at the Albany Center for the Performing Arts. You've seen the news clippings."

"That's you. Janet's Janet."

"Janet has opportunities now she would never have had, Sanford. It's practically sinful to do anything that would frustrate or detract from them." She would not be dissuaded.

"But—"

"Haven't you done enough damage to ballet for one lifetime?" she screamed at him.

When Sanford came to my door that evening, I already knew what the decision was.

"I'm sorry," he said. "Celine thinks you're too young for this sort of thing."

He said it with his head down, his eyes on the floor.

"I'll think of something nice for us to do soon," he added, and left me crying tears into my pillow.

Josh's face dropped and actually turned ashen when I told him I couldn't go with him that Friday night. I tried to give him an explanation, but he just shook his head.

"What is it, your parents don't think I'm rich enough?" he shot back at me and then turned and left me standing alone in the school hallway before I could deny it.

I felt as if I were entering Celine's private world of shadows now. One of my girlfriends called to tease me and sang, "All work and no play make Janet a dull girl." The world that had become filled with sunshine and color began to turn shades of gray. Even when it was a clear sky, I felt as if clouds hung over me. My moodiness seeped into my performances at lessons. Madame Malisorf's eyes narrowed into slits of suspicion. Celine had made me promise never to tell Madame Malisorf how hard she and I worked on the weekends, but my master teacher was too perceptive.

"Aren't you resting your legs?" she asked me directly one afternoon. Celine was in her usual corner observing. I glanced her way. Madame Malisorf followed the shift in my eyes and turned.

"Celine, are you working this student seven days a week?" she demanded.

"On occasion, I go over something with her, Madame Malisorf. She's young and—"

"I want her to have a full twenty-four hours of rest. Those muscles need some time to rebuild. Every time we work out, we break them down. You, of all people, should know that," she said, shaking her head. "Make sure she has the rest required," she demanded.

Celine promised, but never kept her promise, and if I mentioned it, she would go into a rage and then a depression, backing herself into one of those dark corners in the house to stare sadly at the pictures of her former self. Sometimes, she simply read and reread a dance program and I'd find her asleep in her chair, the program in her lap, clutched tightly in her fingers. I didn't have the heart to put up any real resistance.

I tried to do better, to be sharp, to hit my marks. Now, without any friends calling me, I did my homework and went to bed early. I even did what she had asked me to do when I first enrolled in school. I pretended to have cramps and got myself excused from physical education class a number of times. I needed to conserve my energy. I had grown terrified of being tired or sluggish.

Summer was drawing closer and with it was the promise of attending a prestigious dance school. However, money couldn't buy someone a place in the school. Everyone had to audition and Celine's new obsession was getting me prepared for that audition. Madame Malisorf agreed to help win me a spot. She thought it was a good idea for me to go to the school because she was going to spend most of her summer in Europe as she usually did. My lessons became reviews of fundamentals. Dimitri rarely came to practice anymore. He had already been accepted to a school for dance in New York City and was preparing himself for the new training.

We had to travel to Bennington, Vermont, where the audition for the dance school was being held. I was actually excited about it because I would be spending eight weeks at the school and I had read the program and schedule and seen that there was more rest and recreation time than I now had. Of course, almost anywhere would give me more time. At the end of the school's brochure were testimonials written by former students and many of them talked about the social events, singing around the campfire, their weekly social dance, and short bus trips to museums and historic sights. Not everything had to do with dance. The school's philosophy was that a more rounded person makes a more complete artist. It was very expensive to go there and it amazed me that so many people would compete to spend so much money.

At my final lesson before the audition, Madame Malisorf put me through what she predicted would be the school's test. She stood back alongside Celine and tried to be an objective judge. At the end she and Celine spoke softly for a moment and then Madame Malisorf smiled.

"I would give you a place in my school, Janet," she said. "You've made considerable improvement and you have reached a quality of performance that would justify the investment of further time and effort," she claimed. Celine beamed.

I was happy too because I really wanted to get into the school. I think a part of me, a strong part of me, wanted to get away for a while, and not feel so guilty about every misstep. Before she left, Madame Malisorf warned Celine not to wear me out.

"She's a fragile commodity now, Celine. We've taken her far, too far too fast perhaps, but she's there. Now let's let her develop at a normal pace. Otherwise . . ." She looked at me. "We'll ruin what we've created."

"Don't worry, Madame. I will cherish her as much as I cherished myself, if not more."

Despite the hard days and the difficult lessons, despite her critical eyes and often harsh comments, I had grown to appreciate and respect Madame Malisorf. I was even a bit afraid of what would happen without her overseeing everything, but she left assuring me that my teachers at the school would be of the highest quality.

"I'll see you in September," she told me and left.

"I knew it," Celine declared once we were alone. "I knew she would come to see you as I do. We must continue to prepare. This is wonderful, wonderful," she said and for the next few days, she was as animated and excited as she had been when I first arrived.

Sanford, however, looked more troubled by it all. Problems at the factory took up more and more of his time and he continually apologized to me about it. It was as if he was sorry he was leaving me alone with Celine so much. Celine wasn't the least bit interested in the factory and didn't have the patience to listen to anything Sanford said. She was so focused on my audition, it seemed that she thought of nothing else from the moment she rose to the moment she fell asleep.

And then, the week before my audition, there was a new family crisis. Daniel had run off and married a woman he had gotten pregnant. My grandparents were overwrought. They held a family meeting at our house. I wasn't invited, but they spoke so loudly, I would have had to have been deaf not to hear.

"Both my children just go out and do impulsive

things," Grandmother cried. "Neither of you thinks about the family name anymore."

I heard them all trying to calm her, but she was beside herself. They talked about Daniel's new wife and how she came from a lower class of people.

"What sort of a child would a woman like that produce?" Grandmother asked. "We should disown them both. We should."

If they did that, what would happen to the baby? I wondered. Would he or she become an orphan like I was?

The sound of discussion turned to the sounds of sobbing. Soon afterward, my grandparents emerged, my grandmother looking distraught, her eyes bloodshot, her makeup smudged. She gazed at me, then turned and hurried out of the house.

Daniel was the main subject of conversation at the beginning of dinner that night, but Celine put a quick, sharp end to it.

"I don't want to hear his name anymore this week. I don't want anything to distract us from our objective, Sanford. Forget about him."

"But your parents . . ." he began.

"They'll get over it," she said, and turned to me to talk about the things we should sharpen in my presentation.

Finally, the day arrived. I had trouble sleeping the night before, slipping in and out of nightmares. In most I either fell or got so dizzy in my pirouette, I looked clumsy. I saw heads shaking and Celine shrinking in her wheelchair.

The moment I moved my legs to get out of bed that morning, I felt the pain in my stomach. It was as if there was a fist closing inside me and then my lower back ached so hard and deeply, it brought tears to my eyes. I crunched up and took deep breaths. The warm trickle on the inside of my thigh sent chills of terror shooting down to my feet and bouncing back up through my body to curl in my head and make my brain scream. Gingerly, inches at a time, I reached down, and when I saw the blood on my fingertips, I cried.

"No, not now, not today," I pleaded with my insistent body.

I swung my legs around, but when I put my weight on them, they crumbled and I found myself on all fours, the pain growing worse, nearly taking my breath away. I went on my side and lay there in a fetal position, trying to catch my breath. That was when my door burst open and Celine wheeled herself in, her face full of excitement as she cried, "Wake up, wake up. Today is our day. Wake . . ."

She froze, her hands glued to the top of her wheels as she stared down at me.

"What are you doing, Janet?"

"It's . . . my period, Mother," I said. "I woke up and I was bleeding. I have such cramps and my back aches. I have a terrible headache, too. Every time I lift my head a little, it feels like steel marbles are rolling around inside me."

"Why didn't you put on the protection I bought you?" she demanded. "You should always be anticipating this. I told you," she insisted when I shook my head.

"No, you never told me to do that before I went to sleep every night."

"This is ridiculous. Get up on your feet. Clean yourself and get dressed. I'll have Mildred change the sheets on your bed. Get up!" she screamed.

I heard Sanford pounding his feet on the steps as he charged up our stairway.

"What is it, Celine? Why are you shouting? What's wrong?" he cried and came through the doorway, stopping just behind her. "Janet!"

"It's nothing. She's only gotten her period."

"It hurts so much," I wailed.

"Don't be ridiculous," Celine insisted.

"If she says it hurts, Celine . . ." Sanford began.

"Of course it hurts, Sanford. It's never pleasant, but she's just being melodramatic."

"I don't know. I've heard of young girls practically being incapacitated. My sister had to be brought home from school. I remember—"

"Your sister is an idiot," Celine said and wheeled herself closer to me. "Get up this minute," she ordered.

I struggled into a sitting position and then, using the bed, started to rise. Sanford rushed to my side and helped me stand.

"You're going to ruin the rug. Get into the bathroom. Don't you have any pride?" Celine screamed.

"Stop yelling at her," Sanford urged. He helped me into the bathroom and then stepped out while I cleaned myself and found the sanitary napkins. I had to sit on the closed toilet seat to catch my breath. The pain didn't lessen.

"What are you doing in there?" Celine called. She came to the bathroom door.

I reached for the sink and pulled myself up. Every step brought more pain. I opened the door and looked out at her.

"It hurts so much," I complained.

"It will go away. Get dressed. We're leaving in an hour," she said and spun around.

I started out of the bathroom. The cramps kept me clutching my stomach and leaning over. I tried to move around the room, get my dress from the closet, put on my shoes, but the pain just got worse. The only position that brought any relief was lying on my side and pulling my legs up.

How would I ever dance today? I wondered. How could I perform those leaps and turns? Just the thought of going on pointe brought more pain to my back and stomach. My head was pounding.

"What are you doing?" I heard Celine cry. She was in my doorway. "Why aren't you dressed?"

I didn't reply. I clutched my stomach and took deep breaths.

"Janet!"

"What's happening now?" Sanford asked.

"She's not getting dressed. Look at her," Celine demanded.

"Janet," Sanford said. "Are you all right?"

"No," I groaned. "Every time I try to stand, it hurts."

"She can't possibly go today, Celine. You'll have to postpone it," he told her.

"Are you mad? You can't postpone this. There are so many girls trying out. They'll choose their quota before she has a chance to compete. We've got to go," Celine insisted.

"But she can't even stand," he protested.

"Of course she can. Stand up," Celine ordered. She wheeled toward the bed. Sanford held out his hands to stop her.

"Celine, please."

"Stand up, stand up, you ungrateful urchin. Stand up!" she screamed at the top of her lungs.

I had to try again. I rose and put my feet down. Sanford stood and watched as I made the effort. As my body straightened, the pain in my stomach shot up into my chest. I cried, folded, and fell back to the bed.

"Stand up!" Celine shouted.

Sanford forcefully turned her around in the chair.

"Stop this. She has to go. Stop it, Sanford. Stop it," she cried. He continued to wheel her forcefully out of my room.

"She probably needs some kind of medication. I'll have to take her to the doctor," he said.

"That's ridiculous. You fool. She won't get into the school. Janet!" she cried, her voice echoing in the hallway.

My body tightened. I was so frightened. I squeezed my eyes shut to clamp out the world around me. There was a buzzing in my ear and then a darkness, a comfortable, easeful darkness in which I no longer felt the pain and the agony.

I felt like I was floating. My arms had turned into paper-thin wings. I was drifting through the darkness toward a pinhole of light and it felt so wonderful, so easy. I glided and turned, dove and rose, fluttering.

Then I passed what looked like a wall of mirrors on both sides, drifting, gently raising and lowering my paper-thin wings. I looked at myself as I continued toward the light.

And amazingly, I was a butterfly.

Twelve

"What's wrong with her?" I heard a voice say. It sounded far away, like a voice at the end of a tunnel, so it was hard to recognize it.

"All of her vital signs are good. This is some sort of anxiety attack, Sanford."

"That's ridiculous," another voice snapped. The darkness began to diminish a bit. "She has nothing to make her anxious. She has more than most girls her age have."

"You don't know as much about her past as you think you do, Celine. There are many things working in the subconscious mind. And then this might all be due to the psychological trauma of having her first period," he added.

"Did you ever hear anything so ridiculous as that? Please, Doctor," Celine insisted. "Give her something."

"There's nothing to give her but a little time and then a lot of tender loving care, Celine."

"What do you think she's been getting?"

"Celine." Sanford's strong voice broke through the darkness.

"Well, he talks like we've been torturing the child," she said.

The darkness dwindled some more and the light began to grow stronger, wider. My eyelids fluttered.

"She's waking up."

I opened my eyes and looked into Dr. Franklin's face.

"Hello there," he said, smiling. "How are you doing?"

I was so confused. I closed my eyes and tried to think and then I opened them and looked around. I was still in my room. Celine was at the foot of my bed and Sanford was standing beside her with his hand on the back of her chair.

"Can you sit up?" the doctor asked.

I nodded and started to do so. I was a little dizzy, but that passed quickly and I was up. There was a dull ache in my back and my stomach felt woozy. I gazed at the clock and saw that it was midafternoon.

"There. She'll be fine," the doctor said. "Just a day's rest now. The worst is over," he added.

"Is it?" Celine asked dryly. She was shaking her head and glaring at me.

The doctor closed his bag and left the room with Sanford. Celine wheeled herself closer.

"I don't know what happened to me, Mother," I said. "I'll get dressed."

"Dressed?" She laughed a thin, bone-chilling laugh. "For what? It's over. Your chance to get into the school is over. We missed the audition."

"Can't we reschedule it?" I asked. My throat was so dry, it hurt to speak.

"No. There's no point in it," she said, her eyes small. "They went through dozens of girls and filled their openings by now."

"I'm sorry," I said.

"Me too. All this work, the hours and hours of lessons, the best shoes . . ." She shook her head, turned her chair, and wheeled out of my room.

I stepped off the bed and started for the bathroom. It felt like I was walking on a floor of balloons. My ankles wobbled at first and then I grew stronger. I splashed cold water on my face and brushed back my hair. Still feeling weak, I went to my closet and found something to wear. Mildred came to my room just as I finished dressing.

"Mr. Delorice wanted me to see if you were hungry," she said. "I'll bring you something."

"No, I can come down. Thank you, Mildred."

She said she would make me some hot soup and a toasted cheese sandwich, which I told her sounded good. When I went out into the hallway I saw the door to Celine's bedroom was open so I peeked in. She was in bed, staring up at the ceiling.

"I'm feeling better," I said. She didn't respond. "Are you all right, Mother?"

She closed her eyes. My heart began to thump. Was she so angry at me that she would pretend not to hear me? I hurried away as fast as I could and descended the stairs. Sanford was on the phone in his den talking to someone at his factory. He waved when I appeared in the doorway and indicated he would be right with me. I went into the dining room and Mildred brought me my soup and sandwich.

"Is Celine very angry at me?" I asked when Sanford appeared.

"No, no," he said. "She's disappointed, but things will look better in the morning. They always do. How are you doing?" he asked, petting my hair.

"I'm better. I feel like I just climbed a high mountain and ran miles," I told him. He smiled and nodded.

"I guess it's true when they say men have it easier. I'll just go look in on Celine," he added and left to go upstairs.

When he came down again, he looked more concerned. He flashed a quick smile at me and told me he had to go to the factory for a little while.

"Celine's resting. Try not to disturb her," he added, and left.

I went upstairs quietly, thinking again that I would just peek in on her, but Celine's door was closed. It remained closed for the rest of the day and night. I watched some television, read, and went up to bed before Sanford returned from the factory.

When I woke in the morning, I did feel better. The sun was shining brightly through my curtains. I wanted to wear something cheerful so I chose a yellow blouse with a white skirt and the light blue sneakers Celine and Sanford had bought me the first week I arrived. I fixed my hair into a ponytail. When I stepped out of my room, I saw that Celine's bedroom door was still closed, but I imagined Sanford was downstairs at the dining room table, reading his paper and waiting for me as he had been almost every morning since they brought me here from the orphanage.

When I got downstairs, however, there was no one in the dining room. Mildred came from the kitchen and told me Sanford had been up very early and was already gone.

"What about my mother?" I asked her.

"I brought her breakfast, but she didn't eat much of her dinner last night and she didn't look like she was very interested in any breakfast. She hardly spoke," she added, shaking her head. "I think she's sick."

"Maybe Sanford went for the doctor," I said.

"No," Mildred said. The way she pressed her lips shut told me she knew more. "He didn't go for the doctor."

"What is it, Mildred? What else is wrong?"

"I don't know that anything's wrong," she said. "Mr. Delorice, he was very concerned about his business this morning. Not that I listen in on his phone calls," she added quickly.

"I know you don't, Mildred. Please tell me what you do know," I pleaded.

"Something happened at the factory this week, but I don't know what. I just know it's made him very upset," she said. "I'll bring you some breakfast."

"I'm going up to see my mother first," I told her and hurried up the stairway. I knocked on Celine's door but she didn't respond. I waited a moment and then opened it slowly and peered in.

Celine was in her wheelchair staring out a window. She was still in her nightgown and her hair was unbrushed. She wore no lipstick.

"Mother?" I said coming up behind her. She didn't turn, so I spoke louder. She simply stared out the window. "Are you all right, Mother?"

Suddenly she started to laugh. It began with a low rumbling in her throat, and then her face broke into a wide smile with a wild look in her eyes and her laughter got louder, stranger. Tears began to stream out of her eyes. Her shoulders shook. She seized the wheels of her chair and rolled them forward and then backward, and forward again until she hit the wall.

"Mother, what are you doing? Why are you doing that?" I cried.

She simply laughed and continued.

I stepped away.

"Stop it," I screamed. "Please."

Her laughter grew even louder as she wheeled forward and backward, each time slamming harder into the wall.

"Mother! Stop!"

She didn't so I turned and ran from the room right into Sanford, who was coming up the stairway.

"Something's wrong with Celine," I cried. "She won't stop laughing and she keeps wheeling her chair into the wall."

"What? Oh no."

He hurried past me and into the bedroom. I heard him pleading with her to stop. Her laughter was still so loud I had to cover my ears because it was so terrifying. Mildred came to the foot of the stairway.

"What's wrong, Janet?"

"It's Celine. She won't stop laughing."

"Oh no," she said and shook her head. "She did that once before." She shook her head again and walked away.

I looked toward Celine's bedroom, my heart thumping so hard I thought my chest would just split apart.

Finally the laughter stopped. I started toward the bedroom but before I got there, Sanford closed the door. I stood there for a while and then went downstairs to wait. Mildred brought me some juice, toast, and eggs, but I couldn't eat anything. Not long afterward, I heard the doorbell and Mildred welcomed Dr. Franklin. He hurried up the stairs. I followed, but again I heard the bedroom door shut.

The doctor remained in there a long time. I went downstairs to wait and then went out front and sat on the bench under the weeping willow trees. It was such a pretty day, with only a puff of marshmallow cloud here and there. Birds were singing and fluttering all around me. A curious squirrel paused and stared at me, even when I began to speak to it. Then it scurried up a tree. On such a glorious morning, how could things be so gray and dismal in my heart?

Finally the front door opened. Sanford stood talking softly to Dr. Franklin for a few moments. They shook hands and the doctor walked to his car. I rose and he looked my way.

"And how are you feeling?" he asked.

"I'm better. How's my mother?"

"Sanford will speak to you," he said cryptically and got into his car. I watched him drive off and then I hurried into the house. Sanford was in his den on the phone again. He held his right forefinger up and then turned in his chair so his back was to me as he continued his conversation. I didn't know where to go. Suddenly I felt so lost. I felt like a stranger, an intruder. Celine's bedroom door was still shut tight. I wandered through the house, paused at the studio, and then went up to my room and sat on my bed, waiting. It seemed forever until Sanford came up.

"I'm sorry," he said. "I have a crisis at my plant. It seems my foreman was embezzling from me but luckily I found out in time. I could have been bankrupted. I've had to work things out with my business manager and accountant as well as the district attorney and that's still not over. In the middle of it all . . . well, Celine's not doing well."

"What's wrong with her?" I asked, my eyes tearing. "Is it all my fault?"

"No, no," he said. He stood there gazing at me for a moment and then he took a deep breath, looked toward the window, his own eyes glassing over, and shook his head. "It's all my fault. I put her in that chair, not you. I took away the thing that meant the most to her, that gave her a reason to be. We've just been going through the motions of living ever since," he added. "Then, she woke up one morning and thought about us adopting someone like you. I thought it was our salvation, my salvation, I should say.

"I didn't think it out properly," he continued, crossing my room to stand by the window. He spoke with his back to me. "I should have realized what you, what anyone in your shoes—pointe shoes," he corrected, turning to me with a smile, "would be put through. It wasn't fair."

"I didn't mind it," I said quickly. "It's been hard, but . . ."

"It's been cruel," he corrected, turning to me. "That's what it's been. Your childhood has been disregarded, ignored, sacrificed to satisfy an unrealistic dream. You can never be what Celine wants—you can't give her back her legs, her career, her dream. No one can, even the most talented dancer. She tried to live through you, and I am sorry to say, I let it happen because it bought me some peace and relief from my own dark, oppressive clouds of guilt." He smiled. "In a way, Janet, I have been exploiting you, too. I'm sorry."

"I don't understand," I cried.

"I know. It's too much to lay on someone your age. It's very unfair to burden you so. This family has more baggage than anyone can imagine.

"Anyway," he continued with his hands behind his back, "I can't ignore Celine's deeper problems anymore. She's going to need professional help and it will be a very long and arduous journey, one that may never end. I'm sorry," he said, "that I ever permitted you to be brought into this. You're still young enough to have another chance, a better chance for a good, healthy young life."

"What do you mean?" I asked, my heart stopping.

"I can't take care of Celine and give you the proper home life you deserve at the same time," he said. "It's better for everyone if you have another opportunity."

"Another opportunity?" He couldn't be saying what I thought he was.

"It won't be pleasant for you here, Janet, and I don't think Celine will make any improvements if she sees you and believes she's failed again. Not that I think she has. I think you've done splendidly, and anyone in a normal family situation would be proud of you. I'm proud of you. I am. But I'm also very afraid for you.

"The truth is," he said, gazing toward the window again, "I'm even afraid for myself."

He smiled at me. It was a brave smile.

"I hate to lose you. You're a delightful young lady and a pleasure to have around. This place is not going to be the same," he said. "I want you to know you mean a lot to me, Janet. You brought some real light into my life and into our home. Now it's my turn to bring light into yours."

"You're giving me back?" I finally asked, choking back the tears.

"I don't want to, but that's what's best. I've got to devote all my time to getting Celine well. I owe her that, Janet, surely you understand. There won't be anyone to look after you properly and I'm afraid Celine won't be any sort of mother to anyone.

"You've already seen what your grandparents are like. They're absorbed now in their own little crisis with Daniel. I swear he does what he does just to torment them. No," Sanford said, "this is not a happy little family at the moment and certainly no place in which to nurture a child. You deserve better."

"It's all my fault," I cried. "Because I got my period at the worst time."

"No, no, no," Sanford cajoled. "I see now that it was a blessing. I mean, just suppose you went to that audition and weren't chosen. She would have had the same reaction, and if you were chosen, you would have some other test in due time, a test that you wouldn't pass to her satisfaction. You never could because you can't be her. I think she's realized that; she's facing it and that's why she's . . . having her problems. The truth is, Janet, Celine may have to be institutionalized. This is so painful for me. I'm sorry," he said. "Please, don't blame yourself. I'll see to what has to be done. I'm sure that it won't be long before another, healthier, couple scoops you up."

He kissed me on the forehead and left. I sat there, stunned, gazing around my beautiful room. Just as fast as it had been given to me, it was going to be taken away. I wished I had never been brought here, I thought. It was worse to have seen this and lost it than never to have seen it at all. How many mommies and daddies would I lose? How many times would I have to say good-bye?

I was angry, raging inside, my emotions tossing and turning like waves in a hurricane. I felt betrayed. I was never really given the chance to love them.

At dinner Sanford told me he had made arrangements and that the child protection service wanted me to go to a group foster home where I would stay until I was adopted again.

"They said it was very nice and you would have lots of new friends."

"I made lots of new friends here," I said.

He nodded, his eyes sad.

"I'm sorry, Janet. It breaks my heart. It really does," he said and turned away, but not before I saw the tears in his eyes.

I believed him, but it didn't make any of it easier. In fact, it made it harder.

There was a flurry of activity the following morning. A special-duty nurse arrived to help with Celine, and soon after, the Westfalls visited. Celine's mother gave me little more than a passing glance before she went upstairs to see Celine. Afterward, Sanford and his father-in-law went into Sanford's office to discuss the events at the glass factory. When they were leaving, my grandmother looked in at me in the living room, turned to Sanford, and said, "Celine wasted precious energy to make a silk purse out of a sow's ear."

I wasn't sure what it all meant, but I sensed that she was blaming me.

Later in the day, Sanford sent Mildred up to my room to help me pack my things. I still had not seen Celine because she hadn't come out of her room and her door was always shut, but I couldn't leave without at least speaking to her one more time. I went to the door and knocked. The nurse opened it.

"I have to say good-bye," I told her. She wasn't going to let me in, but Sanford had come up for me and told her it was okay. She stepped aside and I entered.

Celine was in her wheelchair at the window, just gazing out at the front yard. I put my hand on hers and she turned very slowly.

"I'm sorry, Celine. I wanted you to be my mother. I wanted to dance for you."

She simply stared at me as if I were a total stranger.

"I hope you get better real soon. Thank you for trying to make me a prima ballerina."

She blinked.

"It's time," Sanford said from the doorway.

I nodded, leaned over, and kissed Celine on the cheek.

"Good-bye," I whispered.

As I turned, she seized my hand.

"Are there a lot of people out there? Is it a big audience?" she asked.

"What?"

She smiled.

"I'm just warming up. Tell Madame Malisorf I'll be right there and tell her I'm ready. Tell her I've already begun to hear the music. She likes that. Will you tell her?"

"Yes, Celine, of course." I had no idea what she was talking about.

"Thank you," she said and turned back to the window.

For a moment I thought I did hear the music. I remembered what she had told me when we had first met. "When you're good, and you will be good, you will lose yourself in the music, Janet. It will carry you off. . . ."

It was carrying me off now.

I looked back at her once and then left her home forever.

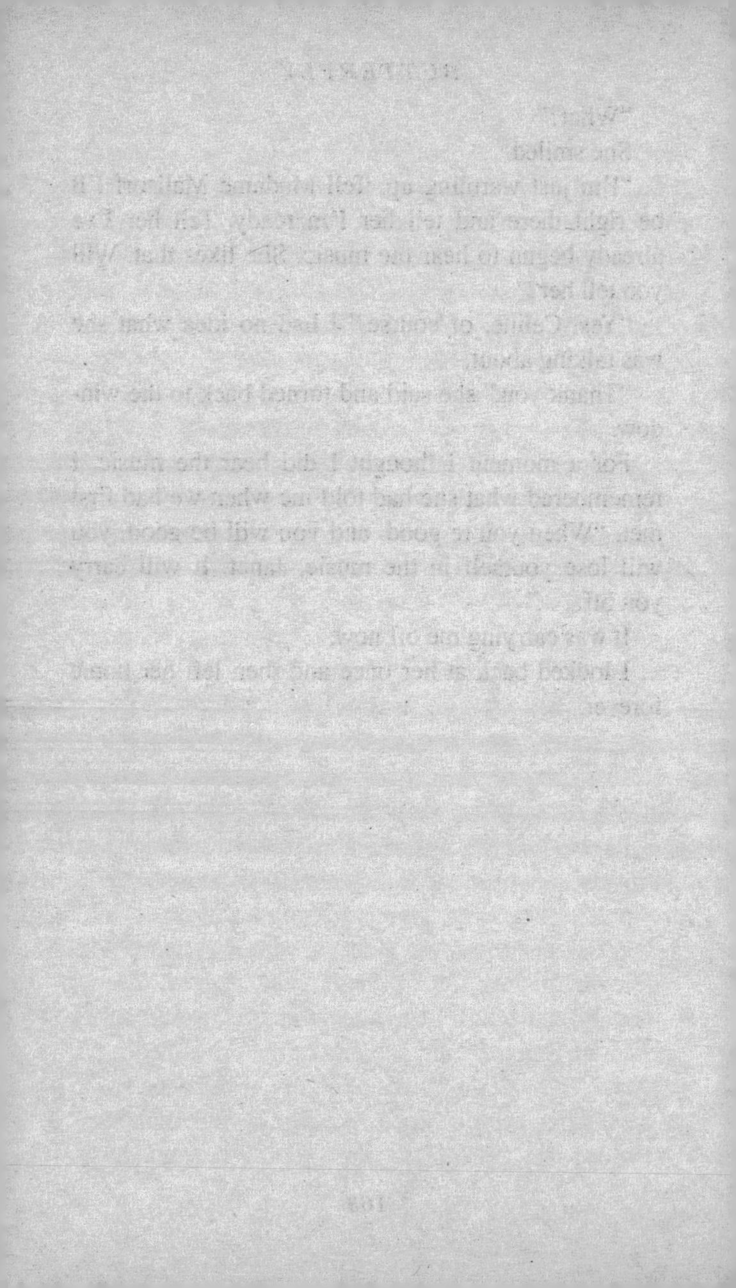

Epilogue

When we drove away from the house, I did not look back. I felt as if I was leaving a storybook and the covers were being closed behind me. I didn't want to see my story end. I wanted to remember it forever as it was: bright, warm, full of the magic of flowers and birds, rabbits and squirrels, a fantasy house, my land of Oz.

I sat in the rear of the big car. In the trunk were two suitcases full of my new clothes, shoes, and ballet costumes, as well as my wonderful pointe shoes. At first I didn't want to take anything. I wanted to leave with little more than I had when I had arrived. Then I thought, if I didn't have these things, I would surely wake up one morning and think I had dreamed it all, all the faces, all the voices, even my birthday party.

"I hope you'll keep up with your dancing," Sanford said. "You really were getting very good."

I didn't say anything. I sat quietly and gazed out the side window watching the scenery drift by. It felt as if the world were on a ribbon that unraveled and floated behind us. Every once in a while, Sanford would say something else. I saw him gazing at me in the rearview mirror. His eyes were full of sadness and guilt.

"I hope Celine gets better," I told him.

"Thank you." And again I saw tears in his eyes.

We were going to the group foster home, a place called The Lakewood House. Sanford explained that it was run by a couple, Gordon and Louise Tooey, who used to run it as a tourist rooming house. It was a little under a two-hour drive.

"It will only be temporary for you, I'm sure," he said.

On the way he wanted to stop to get me something to eat, but I told him I wasn't hungry. The faster we got there and I started my new life, the better, I thought. At the moment I truly felt in limbo.

Sanford followed written directions but he got lost once and had to pull into a garage for new directions. Finally we were on the road that led to the group house.

"There it is," Sanford declared.

Ahead of us was a very large, gray two-story house. It had as much if not more grounds than Sanford and Celine's home. I saw four young girls walking together toward what looked like a ball field. Two teenage boys were mowing grass and a tall, muscular man with a shock of dark brown hair and a chiseled face was shouting at some other children who were raking up the cut grass.

"Looks nice," Sanford commented.

After we parked he got out my suitcases. A tall brunette with shoulder-length hair pinned back burst out of the front entrance. She looked about fifty and I thought her best feature was her startling blue eyes.

"This must be Janet. I've been expecting you all day, sweetheart," she declared, coming right up to me. "What a pretty little girl you are."

"Yes, she is," Sanford said sadly.

"Welcome to The Lakewood House, honey. My name is Louise. I'll show you to your room. Right now, she has a room all to herself," she told Sanford, "but we're expecting new children soon."

He smiled and nodded.

"Gordon!" Louise shouted. "Gordon."

"What is it?" he called back.

"The new girl's arrived."

"Wonderful. I gotta look after these kids, they never get the lawn right," he said. He looked very grouchy to me.

"Gordon takes pride in how we keep up the place," Louise explained. "All of us help, but you'll see. It's fun," she said. "Come on in. Please," she added, putting her hand on my shoulder and guiding me up the stairs to the front door.

There was a small entryway and then a large room filled with old furniture.

"The Lakewood was one of the most desirable tourist houses in its day," Louise told Sanford. She went on to explain how the resort business had died and how she and her husband, Gordon, had decided to use the property as a group foster home. She didn't have any children of her own, "but I always consider my wards my own," she added.

We went upstairs and stopped at a room that was half the size of my room at the Delorice residence.

"I just cleaned it thoroughly. The girls share the bathroom across the hall," Louise explained. "Co-operation is the key word here," she told Sanford. "It prepares them for life."

Sanford smiled again. He set my suitcases down.

"Well," Louise said, looking at him and then at me. "Why don't I give you two time to say good-bye and then I'll show Janet around the house."

"Thank you," Sanford said.

She left us and I sat on what was to be my bunk. He stood there silently for a moment.

"Oh, I wanted you to have some money," he began, and dug into his pocket to produce a billfold and pulled out some large bills. I started to shake my head. "No, please, take it and hide it," he insisted. "First chance you get, put it in the bank. Having a little money of your own will give you some independence, Janet." He forced the money into my hand. "You won't be here long," he said, looking around. "You're a very talented, beautiful child."

I didn't know what to say to him.

"Well, maybe I'll look in on you from time to time. Would you like that?"

I shook my head and he looked surprised.

"You wouldn't? Why not?"

"When you get old, you lose your memory," I said, "so you won't remember what you can't have any-more."

He stared at me and smiled.

"Who told you that?"

I shrugged. "Nobody. I thought it up one day."

"You're probably right. It's nature's way. But I hope you don't forget me, Janet. I won't forget you."

"Celine's already forgotten me," I said.

"She's just mixed you up with memories of her-self," he said.

"Then it's better she forgets."

He looked like he was going to cry. All he had ever done before was kiss me softly on the forehead and hold my hand crossing streets. He went to his knees this time and embraced me, holding me to him for a moment.

"I wanted a daughter like you, more than anything," he whispered. Then he kissed me on the cheek and stood up quickly, turned, and walked out of the room. I listened to his footsteps descending the stairway.

For a long moment I just sat there staring at the floor. Finally I went to the window and looked down and saw his car disappear down the road. I started to cry, the first tear exploding in a hot drop to trickle down my cheek, when suddenly a beautiful butterfly landed on the windowsill. It lingered for a moment and then lifted into the wind. I watched it flutter away and I thought, someday, that will be me.

Crystal

Prologue

One night Mr. Philips forgot his keys. It was as simple as that. Even though I was just a little over eleven, I had been helping in the administrative office as usual, filing purchase orders, receipts, and repair orders. I had left Molly Stuart's watch in Mr. Philips's bathroom when I had taken it off to wash my hands. I didn't have a watch, and she let me borrow hers once in a while. When she saw I didn't have it on my wrist, she asked me about it, and I remembered. This was after supper, when we were all in our rooms doing homework. I told her not to worry. I knew where it was. She fumed and fumed until blood flooded her face. She was positive someone would have stolen it by now because Mr. Philips's office door was never locked. So I left my room and hurried downstairs. I entered, put on the lights, and looked in the bathroom. There it was on the sink where I had left it.

I turned to leave, and that was when I saw Mr. Philips's keys on his desk. I knew they were the keys to the secret files, the files that held information about each of us. Other kids were always asking me if I had ever seen the files out while I was working there. I never had.

My heart skipped a beat. I looked at the door and back at those magical keys. It was close to impossible for an orphan to learn about his or her biological past, at least until he or she turned eighteen. All I had ever been told was that my mother had been too sick to keep me and that I had no father.

I had never done a dishonest thing in my life, but this was different, I thought. This was not stealing. This was merely taking something that really belonged to me: knowledge about my own past. Quietly, I closed the front door, and then I went to the desk, picked up the keys, and found the one that would open the drawers containing the secret files.

Funny, how I stood there, afraid to touch the file that had my name on its tab. Was I afraid to break a rule or afraid to learn about myself? Finally, I got up enough nerve and pulled out my file. It was thicker than I had imagined it could be. I turned off the office lights so I wouldn't attract any attention and sat on the floor by the bathroom with the door only slightly ajar. A thin shaft of light escaped and provided enough illumination for me to read the pages.

The first few were filled with information I already knew about myself: medical history, school records. But the bottom stack of pages opened the dark doors of my past and revealed information that both surprised and frightened me.

According to what I read, my mother, Amanda Perry, had been diagnosed as a manic-depressive when she was only in her mid-teens. She was institutionalized at seventeen after repeated efforts to commit suicide, once cutting her wrists and twice trying to overdose with sleeping pills.

I read on and learned that while my mother was in a mental facility, she was impregnated by an attendant. Apparently, they never knew which attendant, so I realized that some degenerate out there was my father, unless I wanted to believe that my mother and this attendant had the most romantic and wonderful love affair between her drug therapies, cold baths, and electric shock treatments.

Anyway, when they realized my mother was pregnant, someone made the official decision not to abort me. After I was born, obviously neither my paternal nor my maternal grandparents wanted anything to do with me, and Mr. Degenerate Attendant wasn't going to come out and claim me, so I was immediately made a ward of the state. My reports didn't say who had named me Crystal. I like to think it was the one and only thing my poor mother had been able to give me. I had nothing else, not even the slightest idea who I was, until I managed to sneak into these files.

I saw a simple statement about my mother's death at the age of twenty-two. Her last attempt at taking her own life was a successful one. I would never meet her, even years from now when I was on my own.

I remember the revelations made my hands shake and gave me a hollow feeling at the base of my stomach. Would I inherit my mother's mental problems? Would I inherit my father's evil ways? After I put the file back, locked up the cabinet, returned the keys to the desk, and left, I had to go right to the bathroom because I felt as if I had to throw up.

I managed to keep my supper down but washed my face with cold water just to calm myself. When I looked in the mirror then, I studied myself, searching my eyes, my mouth, looking for some sign of evil. I felt like Dr. Jekyll searching for a glimpse of Mr. Hyde. From that day forward, I've had nightmares about it. In them I see myself become mentally ill and so sick that I would be put in some clinic and locked away forever.

I suppose it was just natural that any psychologist who knew about my past would wonder if I shared any characteristics with my parents. From what I had read, I understood that my mother apparently acted out in school often and was a very difficult student for all the teachers. She was constantly in trouble. I've never been like that, but I recently read that this sort of behavior is considered a call for help, just as attempting suicide is.

With all these calls for help, the world seemed like a great big ocean with many people drowning and lifeguards whimsically choosing to help this one or that one. Naturally, the richer ones always were saved or at least tossed a lifeline. Those like me were shoved into mental institutions, group foster homes, orphanages, and prisons. We were swept under the rug with so many others. It made me wonder how anyone could walk on it.

I never told anyone what I had learned, of course, but I began to understand why it was that few prospective parents ever showed interest in me. They probably were given information about my past and decided not to take a chance on someone like me.

Once, when I was at a different orphanage, I was sitting outside and reading *The Diary of Anne Frank.* (I was always two or three reading grade levels above other kids my age.) Suddenly, I felt a shadow move over me, and I looked up to see a balloon drifting in the wind, the string dangling like a tail. Some little child had loosened his or her grip, and it had escaped. Now, however, it drifted aimlessly, attached to no one, doomed never to return to its owner. It disappeared over a rim of treetops, and I thought, that's what we're all like here, balloons that someone released willingly or unwillingly, poor souls lost and sailing into the wind, waiting and hoping for another hand to take hold of us and bring us back to earth.

Three more years went by without my being adopted or given a foster home. I was still helping Mr. Philips in his office, and about a year ago, he started calling me Little Miss Efficiency. I didn't mind it, even when he used me to rankle his assistants. He always said things like, "Why can't you be as responsible or as careful as Crystal?" He even said that occasionally to his secretary, Mrs. Mills.

Mrs. Mills always looked as if she were drowning

in carbon copies. Her fingers were usually blue or black because of ribbons, ink cartridges, and toner she had to change. In the morning, she came to work looking as well put together as a work of classical art, not a strand of her blue-gray hair out of place, her makeup perfect, her clothing clean and unwrinkled, but by the end of the day, her bangs were always dangling over her eyes, her blouse usually had a smudge somewhere on it, maybe two, her lipstick had somehow spread onto a cheek, and she had become a work of abstract art. I know she's one person who never resented me. She was always happy to greet me and appreciated the work I did, work she would probably have had to do otherwise.

For someone my age, I know a lot about human psychology. I got interested in it after I read about my mother. Now I'm thinking I might be a doctor someday, and anyway, it's good to know as much as you can about psychology. It comes in handy, especially around orphanages.

But it's not always an asset to be smarter than other people or more responsible. This is especially true for orphans. The more helpless you seem, the better your chances are for being adopted. If you look as if you can take care of yourself, who wants you? At least, that's another one of my theories for why I was a prisoner of the system for as long as I was. Prospective adoption parents don't like feeling inferior to the child they might adopt. I've seen it firsthand.

There was this couple who asked specifically for me. They wanted a child who was older. The woman, whose name was Chastity, had a silly little grin on her face. Her husband called her Chas, and she called him Arn, short for Arnold. I suppose they would have ended up calling me Crys. Completing words was difficult for them. They had the same problem with sentences, always leaving a part dangling, like when Chas asked me, "What do you want to be when you . . ."

"When I what?" I forced her to say.

"Get older. Graduate from . . ."

"College or high school or the armed services or secretarial school or computer training?" I cataloged. I had taken an immediate dislike to them. She giggled too much, and he looked as if he wanted to be someplace else the moment he walked into the room.

"Yes," she said, giggling.

"I suppose I want to be a doctor, but I might want to be a writer. I'm not absolutely sure. What do you want to be?" I asked her, and she batted her eyelashes with a smile of utter confusion.

"What?"

"When you . . ." I looked at Arn, and he smirked.

Her smile wilted like a flower and gradually evaporated completely. Her eyes were forbidding and soon filled with a nervous energy. I couldn't count how many times she gazed longingly at the door.

They looked quite relieved when the interview ended. I didn't have another interview until just a week ago, but I was happy to meet Thelma and Karl Morris. Apparently, my background didn't frighten them, nor did my being precocious annoy them. In fact, afterward, Mr. Philips told me I was exactly what they wanted: an adolescent who promised to be no problem, who wouldn't make a major demand on their lives, who had some independence, and who was in good health.

Thelma seemed convinced that whatever damage she believed I'd suffered as an orphan would be corrected after a few weeks of life in her and Karl's home. I loved her cockeyed optimism. She was a small woman in her late twenties with very curly light brown hair and hazel eyes that were as bright and innocent as a six-year-old's.

Karl was only a few inches taller, with thin dark brown hair and dull brown eyes. He looked much older but was only in his early thirties. He had a soft, friendly smile that settled in his pudgy face like berries in cream. He was stout. His hands were small, but his fingers were thick.

He was an accountant, and she said she was a housewife, but they had long ago decided that was a job, too, and she should be paid a salary for it. She had even gotten raises when they had good years. They couldn't stop talking about themselves. It was as if they wanted to get out their entire lives in one meeting.

The best thing I could say about them was that there was absolutely nothing subtle, contrived, or threatening about them. What you saw was what you got. I liked that. It made me feel at ease. At times during the interview, it was more as if I was there to decide if *I* would adopt *them.*

"Everything is just too serious here," Thelma told me toward the end of our session. She grimaced, fold-ing her mouth into a disapproving frown. "It's just too serious a place for a young person to think of as any sort of home. I don't hear any laughter. I don't see any smiles."

Then she suddenly grew very serious herself and leaned toward me to whisper. "You don't have a boyfriend yet, do you? I'd hate to break up a budding romance."

"Hardly," I told her. "Most of the boys here are quite immature." She liked that and was immediately relieved.

"Good," she said. "Then it's settled. You'll come home with us, and we'll never speak of anything unpleasant again. We don't believe in sadness—if you don't think about the bad things in life, you'll find they all just go away. You'll see."

I should have known what that meant, but for once in my short life, I decided to stop analyzing everyone and just enjoy the company of someone, especially someone who wanted to be my mother.

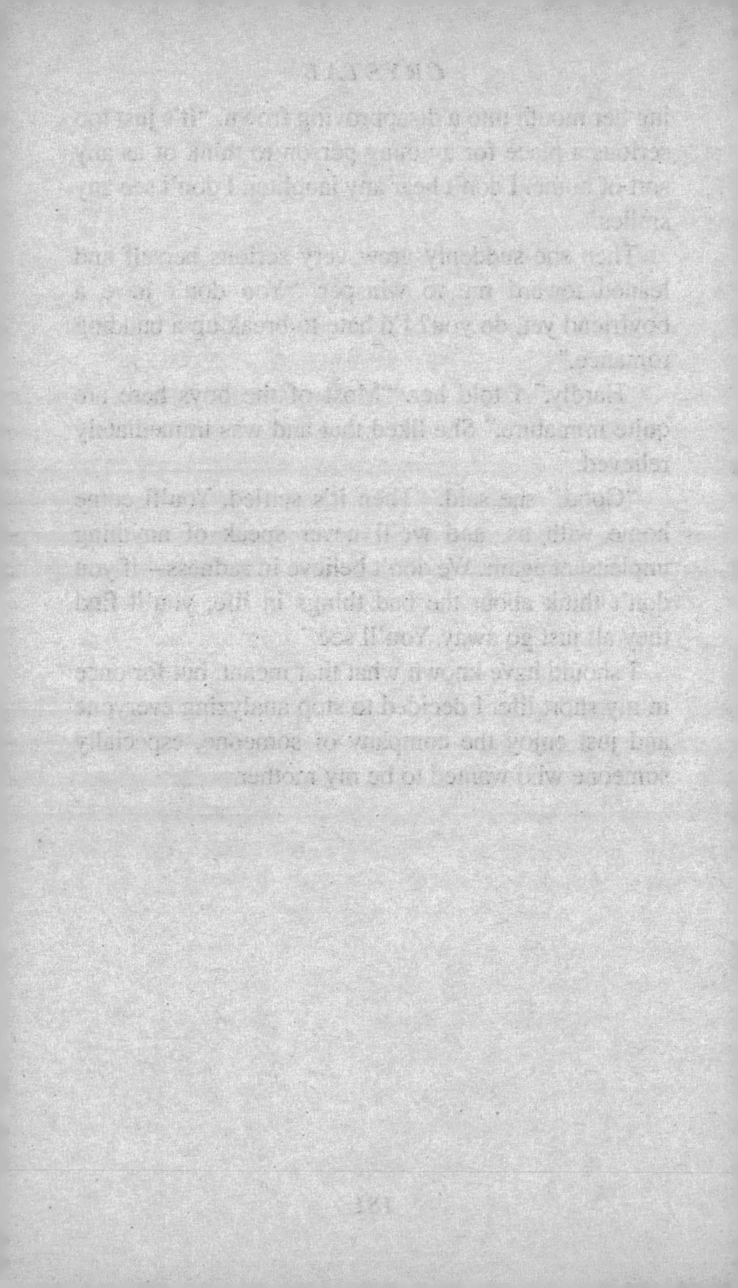

1

A New Beginning

Going home with the Morrises was like taking a guided tour of their lives on a sightseeing bus. They drove a moderately priced sedan chosen, Karl said, for its gas efficiency and for its high rating in Consumer Reports.

"Karl makes the decisions about everything we buy," Thelma explained with a light laugh that punctuated most of what she said. "He says an informed consumer is a protected consumer. You can't believe in advertisements. Advertisements, especially commercials, are just full of a lot of misinformation, right, Karl?"

"Yes, dear," Karl agreed.

I sat in the rear, and Thelma remained turned on an angle so she could talk to me all the way to their home—my new home—in Wappingers Falls, New York.

"Karl and I were childhood sweethearts. Did I tell you that?"

She continued before I could tell her she had.

"We started to go together in the tenth grade, and when Karl went to college, I remained faithful to him, and he remained faithful to me. After he graduated and was appointed to his position at IBM, we planned our wedding. Karl helped my parents make all the arrangements, right down to the best place to go for flowers, right, Karl?"

"That's true," he said, nodding. He didn't take his eyes off the road.

"Ordinarily, Karl doesn't like to have long conversations in the car when he's driving," Thelma explained, gazing at him and smiling. "He says people forget how driving a car is something that requires their full attention."

"Especially nowadays," Karl elaborated, "with so many more cars on the road, so many more teenage drivers and older drivers. Those two age groups account for more than sixty percent of all accidents."

"Karl has all sorts of statistics like that floating around his mind," Thelma said proudly. "Just last week, I was thinking about replacing our gas stove with a new electric range, and Karl converted BTUs . . . is that it, Karl? BTUs?"

"Yes."

"BTUs into pennies of cost and showed me how the gas stove was more efficient. Isn't it wonderful to have a husband like Karl who can keep you from making the wrong decisions?"

I smiled and gazed out the windows. The orphanage wasn't much more than fifty or so miles from where my new parents lived, but I had never traveled this far north. Other than some school field trips, I hadn't been to many places at all. Just leaving the orphanage and going twenty miles by car was an adventure.

It was late summer, and the cooler autumn winds had already begun to descend from the north. Leaves were turning rust and orange, and when I could see far into the distance and look over the heavily wooded mountains, I thought the ripple of colors was breathtakingly beautiful. This was a bright, sunny day, too. The sky was a deep, rich blue, and the clouds that flowed across it in a stream of wind stretched themselves until they became as thin as gauze. Way off to the south, an airplane turned into a silver dot and then disappeared into the clouds.

I was happy and full of hope. I would have a home, a place to call my own, and someone else to care about besides myself, as well as, I hoped, someone to care about me. How simple that was and how taken for granted by most people, but how wonderful and new and precious it was for orphans like myself.

"Karl is the oldest of three brothers and the only one married. His middle brother, Stuart, is a salesman for an air-conditioner manufacturer in Albany, and his younger brother, Gary, has graduated from a culinary institute in Poughkeepsie, where Karl's father lives. Gary was hired to cook on a cruise ship, so we don't hear from him or see him much at all.

"Karl and his brothers are not far apart in age, but they're not all that close. No one is in Karl's family, right, Karl?"

Karl nearly turned to look at her. His head started to move and then stopped when an automobile about fifty yards in front of us emerged from a driveway and he had to slow down.

"If they didn't speak to each other on the phone occasionally, they wouldn't know who still existed in the family and who didn't. Karl's father is still alive, but his mother passed away, what, two years ago, Karl?"

"A year and eleven months tomorrow," Karl said mechanically.

"A year and eleven months," she repeated like a translator.

So I have two uncles and a grandfather on Karl's side, I thought. Before I could ask about her side, she volunteered the information.

"I don't have any brothers or sisters," Thelma said. "My mother wasn't supposed to have any children. She had breast cancer when she was only seventeen, and the doctors advised her not to have children. Then, late in life, when she was in her early thirties, she became pregnant with me. My father was forty-one at the time. Now my mother is fifty-eight and my father is sixty-nine.

"I bet you're wondering why we don't have any children of our own. Before you, I mean," she added quickly.

"It's none of my business," I said.

"Oh, sure it is. Everything that's our business is your business now. We're going to be a family, so we have to share and be honest with each other, right, Karl?"

"Absolutely," he said, signaling to change lanes and pass the car ahead of us.

"Karl's sperm count is too low," she said with a smile, as if she were delighted about it.

"I don't know if we should talk about *that,* Thelma." The back of Karl's neck turned pink with embarrassment.

"Oh, of course we can. She's old enough and probably knows everything there is to know. Kids today are very advanced. How can they not help it, with all that's on television? Do you watch television much, Crystal?"

"No," I answered.

"Oh," she said, the excitement fading in her face for the first time since we had met. Her eyes looked like tiny flashlights with weakened batteries. Then she thought of something and smiled again. "Well, that's probably because you didn't have much opportunity in a home with so many other children. Anyway, we did try to have children. As soon as Karl determined it was financially sensible for us, we tried, right, Karl?"

He nodded.

"Nothing happened no matter how we planned it. I used a thermometer to take my temperature, plotted the days on my calendar, even planned some romantic evenings," she said, blushing. She shrugged. "Nothing happened. We just thought we were missing," she continued. "Take better aim, I used to tell him, didn't I, Karl?"

"Thelma, you're embarrassing me," he said.

"Oh, fiddledy-doo. We're a family. We can't be embarrassed," she emphasized.

The simplicity and honesty with which she talked about the most intimate details of her life fascinated me.

"Anyway," she continued, turning back to me, "Karl read up on it and learned that he should keep his scrotum cool. He avoided wearing anything tight, refrained from taking hot baths, and tried to keep himself cool, especially before we were going to make a baby. We even waited longer between times because periods of sexual restraint usually increase the volume and potency of sperm, right, Karl?"

"You don't have to get into the nitty-gritty details, Thelma."

"Oh, sure I do. I want Crystal to understand. I was reading a magazine the other day, *Modern Parent* or something like that, and the article said mothers and daughters especially should be honest and open about everything so they can build trust.

"Where was I?" she asked. "Oh, volume and potency of sperm. So, when that didn't work, we went to a doctor. You know that the average male produces anywhere from 120 million to 600 million sperm in a single ejaculation?"

"You have trouble with so many other facts and statistics, Thelma. How come you don't forget that one?" Karl asked gently.

"I don't know. It's not easy to forget, I guess," she said, shrugging. "Anyway, we found out that Karl was way below that and it didn't matter what he did. We still tried and tried, of course, and then we finally decided to adopt. Actually, I got the idea from *Throbs of the Heart* by Torch Summers, and then I discussed it with Karl and he agreed it would be a good idea.

"However, taking care of a baby is not an easy job. You have to wake up at night, and then you're too tired to do anything the next day, even watch television. So, that's how come we went looking for an older child and found you," she concluded.

"Our baby-making problem is not that unusual," Karl interjected during the first quiet moment. "Infertility used to be thought mainly a woman's problem, but the problem lies with the man in thirty-five percent of the cases."

"Karl feels sorry, but I don't blame him," Thelma said in a voice a little above a whisper. "It's like what happens in *Love's Second Chance* by Amanda Fairchild. Did you ever read that one? I know you read a lot."

"No," I said. "I've never heard of it."

"Oh. Well, I think it was number one on the romance chart for four months last year. Anyway, April's lover has Karl's problem, only he doesn't know it until after April gets pregnant, obviously with someone else's child. It's so sad at the end when April dies in childbirth."

Thelma's eyes actually teared over. Then she jumped in her seat and smiled.

"Let's not think of sad things today. Today's a big day for all of us. We're going to a restaurant for dinner tonight, right, Karl?"

"Yes. I thought we'd go to the Sea Shell. Do you like seafood, Crystal?" he asked.

"I haven't eaten much of it, but yes," I said.

"Ordinarily, we don't go out to eat. It's not practical," Thelma said. "But Karl believes the Sea Shell gives you the best value for your dollar."

"Lobster and shrimp are expensive in restaurants especially, but they give you a good combination plate and plenty of salad and bread. I like their combination dinners. Good value," he pointed out. "You'll like their choice of desserts, too. I bet you like chocolate cake."

"It's my favorite," I admitted. All this talk of food was making my stomach growl.

"We have so much to learn about each other," Thelma said. "I want to know all your favorite things, like your favorite colors, favorite movie stars, favorite everything. I hope we have a lot of the same favorites, but even if we don't, it won't matter," she assured me, nodding so firmly it looked as if she was assuring herself just as much.

A little more than an hour later, we drove up a residential street and pulled into the driveway of a small ranch-style house with light gray aluminum siding, black aluminum window shutters, a sidewalk between two patches of lawn, hedges along the sidewalk and in front of the house, and a red maple tree off to the left. A large, plain aluminum mailbox in front was labeled MORRIS and had the address printed under it.

"Home sweet home," Thelma said as the garage door went up.

We pulled into the garage, a garage that looked neater than some of the rooms in the orphanage. It had shelves on the rear wall, and everything on them was labeled and organized. The floor of the garage even had a carpet over it.

Karl helped with my luggage and my box of books. I followed them through a door that led right into the kitchen.

"Karl designed our house," Thelma explained. "He thought it was practical to come directly from the garage into the kitchen, so we could get our groceries easily out of the car and into their proper cabinets."

It was a small but very neat and clean-looking kitchen. There was a breakfast nook on the right with a bay window that looked out on a fenced-in backyard. There wasn't much more lawn in the rear of the house than there was in the front.

Above the table was a cork board with notes pinned to it and a calendar with dates circled. The front of the refrigerator had a magnetic board with a list of foods that had to be replaced.

"Right this way," Karl said.

We left the kitchen and walked through a small corridor that led first to the living room and front door. There was a short entryway with a closet for coats just inside it. There was a den off the entryway that had walls of bookcases, sofas, and chairs, all facing the large television set. Just past that was the dining room. The furniture was all colonial.

My room wasn't much larger than my room at the orphanage, but it had bright, flowery wallpaper, filmy white cotton curtains, a desk with a large cupboard above it, and a twin-size bed with pink and white pillows and comforter. There was a closet on the left and a smaller one on the right.

"You can use this smaller closet for storing things other than clothes," Karl explained.

I paused at the desk and opened the cupboard to see a computer all set up inside.

"Surprise!" Thelma cried, clapping. "We got that just for you only two days ago. Karl priced them and found the best deal."

"It's very updated," Karl said. "I have you connected to the Internet also, so you can get your research done right in your room when you start school in a few weeks."

"Thank you," I said, overwhelmed. No one had ever bought me anything expensive. For a moment, it took my breath away, and I just ran the tips of my fingers over the keys to check that it was real.

"Now, don't you get like some of those other children we hear about," Thelma warned, "and spend all your time alone staring at the computer screen. We want to be a family and spend time together at dinner and watching television."

"Me, too," I said, nodding. I was really too excited to listen to anything she said. "Thank you."

"It's our pleasure," Karl said.

"I'll help you unpack your clothes, and we'll see what new things you'll need right away. We'll make a list, and Karl will tell us where it's best to go, right, Karl?"

"Absolutely," he said.

"Oh, dear. Oh, dear, no!" Thelma said, suddenly putting her hand to her heart.

Mine skipped a beat. Had I done something wrong already?

"What's the matter?" Karl asked her.

"Look at the time," she said, nodding at the small clock on my computer desk. "It's a little past three. I'm missing *Hearts and Flowers,* and today Ariel learns if Todd is the father of her child. Do you watch that one?" she asked me. I looked at Karl for help. I had no idea what she was talking about.

"She means her soap opera. How can she follow that one, Thelma? She would probably be coming home from school or still be in school when that one is on."

"Oh, I forgot that. Well, you know what I do when I have to miss a show. I videotape it. Only, with all the excitement, I forgot to set up the videotape machine. Do you mind waiting a little, dear? I'll help you unpack as soon as the show's over."

"That's all right," I said, putting my first suitcase on the bed and snapping it open. "There isn't much for me to do."

"No, no, no, Crystal, sweetheart." She reached for my hand. "You come with me. We'll watch the show together," she said, "and then we'll take care of your room."

I glanced at Karl, hoping he would rescue me as Thelma pulled me toward the door.

"Thelma, remember we have to get ready precisely at five to go to the restaurant," he said.

"Okay, Karl," she said. She was really tugging me. I practically flew out of the room.

"Welcome to our happy home," Karl called after me.

2
Another World

One of the biggest fears any of us orphans has is that when we do become part of a family, we won't be able to adjust to their style of life. We won't know how to behave at their dinner table, how to behave in front of the other relatives, how to keep our rooms and spend our time. In short, we won't know how to please our new parents. For us it would always be like an audition. We'd feel their eyes following us everywhere we went, hear their whispers, wonder what they really thought. Were they happy they had taken us into their lives, or were they sorry and looking for a graceful way to give us back?

It was easy to adapt to life with my new parents, to know what they expected, liked, and disliked. There was nothing unpredictable about Karl. He was the most organized person I had ever met. He rose at precisely the same time every day, weekend or not.

"People make a mistake sleeping later on the weekends," he told me. "It confuses their body clock."

He also ate the same thing for breakfast every weekday, a combination of cold cereals, mixing the correct formula of fibers and grains with fruit. On weekends, he made himself an omelet with egg whites, or he had oatmeal and raisins. Although he was chubby, he paid attention to nutrition and wanted me to do the same.

What he didn't do was exercise. He admitted that this was a fault, but he made little effort to correct it, the closest thing being his purchase of a treadmill, after what he described as months and months of comparison shopping. I commented that it looked brand-new, and he confessed that he still had to develop a regular schedule for its use.

"Maybe now that you're here to remind me," he said, "I'll pay more attention to those things."

I didn't think he needed my reminders for anything. All of his things were organized and inventoried. He knew exactly how many socks he had, how many white shirts, how many pairs of pants and jackets, how many ties. He could even tell me how much each item had cost. What was even more impressive was he knew just how many times he had worn what and knew when something had to be cleaned and pressed. He serviced his clothes the way people service their cars, and when something had been worn, cleaned, or washed a certain number of times, he retired it to a bag marked "To be donated."

Karl continued his organized, regimented existence

throughout his day, always eating at the same hour in the evening, watching his news program, reading his newspapers and his magazines, and going to sleep at exactly ten P.M. every night, even on weekends, unless they had plans for an evening out.

If Thelma indicated she wanted to see a movie, Karl would research the reviews and report to her first, deciding whether or not it was a waste of money. If there was any doubt, he would suggest the matinee show because it was discounted and wasn't as great a risk.

"Balance, Crystal," he explained. "That's what makes life truly comfortable, maintaining balance. Assets on one side, liabilities on the other. Everything you do, everyone you meet has assets and liabilities. Learn what they are, and you'll know how to proceed."

He often lectured to me like that, and I listened respectfully, even though many times I thought he was being obsessive about it. Not everything in life could be measured on a profit-and-loss statement, I thought.

In a way, Thelma's life was almost as regimented and organized as Karl's, only hers was determined by the television scheduling of her soap operas and other programs. If she left the house for any reason during the day, she scheduled her appointments and errands around what was on TV that day. Although she could videotape shows, she said it wasn't the same as being there when they were actually on.

"It's like watching history being made rather than watching it later on the news," she told me.

She had reading time reserved, as well, and sat on her rocker with a lace shawl around her shoulders, reading whatever had come in that month from her romance novels club. Pots could boil over, phones could ring, someone might come to the door. It didn't matter once she was engrossed in her story; she didn't care. She truly left one world for another.

Nevertheless, she was as devoted to Karl and his needs as any wife could be. On Sundays, Karl would plan the week's menu, carefully selecting foods that could be utilized in different ways so as to justify buying them in larger quantities or make use of left-overs. Thelma would then develop that menu, following it to a T. If something wasn't just the way Karl had planned it, she treated it like a major crisis. One morning, I had to go with her to another super-market nearly twenty miles away because the one she shopped at didn't have the brand of canned peaches Karl wanted.

Whereas Karl was a quiet, careful driver, Thelma talked so much from the moment she sat behind the wheel that my ears were ringing. Her attention was often distracted, and twice I jumped so high I nearly bumped my head on the roof when she crossed lanes abruptly and drivers honked their horns.

A week after I arrived, we took a ride to visit Karl's father. He lived alone in a small Cape Cod–style house, the same house he had lived in for nearly forty years. It was in a very quiet, old residential neighbor-hood of single-family homes, most as old as Karl's father's.

Karl's father was taller and considerably thinner than his son, with a face that reminded me of Abraham Lincoln, long and chiseled. From the pictures I saw on the table in the living room, I concluded Karl took after his mother more. His brothers, on the other hand, resembled their father, both being taller and leaner than Karl.

Papa Morris, as he was introduced to me, was a feisty old man who had worked for the city water department. He was content to live on his pension and social security, socialize with his retired friends, play cards, visit the local bar, and read his newspapers. Karl had arranged for a woman to come and clean twice a week, but Karl's father wouldn't permit anyone to cook for him.

"When I can't take care of myself, I'll know it," he muttered after Karl had made the suggestion again.

However, the kitchen wasn't very clean. Pots were caked with beans and rice, and some dishes were piled up, waiting for the cleaning lady. Thelma went right to work when we arrived. I helped her, and we got the kitchen into some order while Karl and his father talked. Then we all sat in the living room and had fresh lemonade.

Papa Morris stared at me with interest while Thelma described what a wonderful beginning we had all had together since I had come to live with her and Karl. Papa Morris's large, glassy brown eyes narrowed with suspicion.

"You like livin' with these two?" he asked me skeptically.

"Yes, sir," I answered quickly.

"Yes, sir?" he muttered, and looked at Karl, who sat with his hands in his lap.

"She's a very polite young lady," Thelma said. "A lot like Whelma Matthews on *Days in the Sun,*" she added, looking at me proudly.

"You don't have to call me sir, Missy. No one's ever called me sir. I don't wear no airs. I'm just a pensioner."

"She's very smart, Pa. All A's in school," Thelma continued.

"That's good." He nodded at me, his face softening some. "My Lily always wanted grandchildren, but none of my boys gave her any. Grandchildren are sort of a return on your investment," he muttered.

"Speaking of investments," he continued, turning to Karl, "what's been happening with that mutual fund you had me put my CD into, Karl?"

"You're up twenty-two percent, Dad."

"Good. Smart boy, Karl," he said, and reached into his top pocket for some chewing tobacco.

"You should give that up, Dad. It's been known to cause mouth cancer," Karl said. "I was just reading an article about that yesterday."

"I've been doing it for fifty years. No point in stopping something I enjoy now, right, Thelma?"

She looked at Karl apprehensively. "Well, I . . ."

"Of course you should, and of course there's a point to stopping, Dad. Why cause yourself unnecessary suffering?" Karl insisted.

"I'm not suffering. I'm enjoying. I don't know who's a worse nag, you or that woman you send around here. All she does is complain about the work I make for her. How much you paying her?"

"Ten dollars an hour," Karl said.

"Ten dollars! You know," he said, looking at me, "once that was enough to feed the family for a week."

"There have been many reasons for inflation since then," I said.

"That so? You an economic genius like Karl?" he asked me.

"No, sir. I just read a little."

"Oh, she reads a lot, Pa. She reads more than I do," Thelma said.

"Lily liked to read," he said, and thought a moment. Then he slapped his hand down hard on the arm of his chair. Thelma and I jumped in our seats.

"Well now, you bring this polite young lady around more often," he said, rising.

"We can stay a little longer, Pa," Thelma said.

"Well, I can't," he said. "I've got to meet Charlie, Richard, and Marty at Gordon's for our regular game of pinochle," he told her sternly.

Thelma looked to Karl.

"Well, we just came by to introduce you to Crystal and see how you were doing, Dad," Karl said, standing.

"I'm doing as good as I can with what I got," he said, looking toward me.

We all rose.

"Pleased to have met you," he said to me. He held out his hand, and I shook it. He had long, rough fingers with fingernails that were yellow and thick and two years past when they should have been trimmed.

On the way home, I thought about him and about what I'd always imagined my grandparents to be like. Never in any of my dreams did I imagine myself shaking hands with them. I thought they would be full of hugs and kisses, gloating over me and bragging about me just the way they did in movies and books. Maybe Thelma's mother and father would be more like that, I hoped.

And they were.

Thelma's mother was a small woman like her, actually smaller, birdlike and very thin with wrists that looked as if they might crack if she lifted a full cup of coffee, but she had a big smile and the loveliest blue-green eyes. She kept her hair its natural gray and styled neatly. Thelma's father was tall and lean but much warmer than Karl's father. They insisted I call them Grandpa and Grandma immediately, and Grandma hugged and kissed me as soon as we were all introduced.

"I'm so happy there'll be someone young in this house. Now it will be a real home. You make sure you spoil this child, Karl Morris," she warned, shaking her right forefinger in his face. "None of that thinking like an accountant when it comes to her. That's what parents are supposed to do, and if you don't, we will," she added with a mock threat.

Before they left that day, they even gave me twenty dollars. Grandma said, "Buy whatever Karl doesn't want you to have, whatever he thinks is a waste of money." She laughed and kissed me again. I liked her a lot and looked forward to the next time I would see her.

Of all that had happened since I had come to live with Karl and Thelma, this was the best, I thought. My grandparents had finally made me feel part of a real family. Life with Karl and Thelma had started on such a formal and organized note, I had yet to think of them as parents. Karl was more like an adviser, and Thelma was so wrapped up in her books and programs that I felt more like a guest she had invited to share her fantasies.

I was looking forward to the start of school, making new friends, and being challenged by new subjects and teachers. Thelma took me to registration. Because of my record, I was put in an advanced class, and she bragged about it all throughout dinner that night. As always, however, she found a fictional character with whom to compare me.

"Brenda's daughter in *Thunder in My Heart* is just like you, Crystal. She's such a whiz kid, too. Maybe she'll be president someday."

"How can Brenda's daughter be president someday, Thelma?" Karl asked her. "She's in a book you've read, right?"

"Oh, but there's a sequel coming, Karl. There's always a sequel," she said, smiling.

"I see," he said, nodding and looking at me.

"Crystal's smarter, though," Thelma said. "You should hear some of the things she says, Karl. She can figure out what's going to happen on my soaps before it happens."

"They're pretty predictable," I commented.

"What's that mean?" Thelma asked, batting her eyelashes.

"It means they're not hard to figure out," Karl said. "They're simple."

"Oh." She laughed her thin laugh. "They're hard for me," she said.

Karl gazed at me, and we talked about something else. I felt bad about it and afterward apologized.

"I didn't mean to make fun of your programs, Thelma," I said.

"Oh, did you make fun of them? I didn't think you did. How could you make fun of them? They're so full of excitement and romance. Don't you like that?"

"I like good stories, yes," I said.

"There, then. I knew you would. Don't forget, tomorrow we'll learn about November's ex-husband. Do you think he still loves her?"

"I don't remember him," I admitted. She looked at me as if I had said the silliest thing.

"You can't forget Edmond. He's soooo handsome. If he came to my front door, I'd swoon," she told me, following with her little, thin laugh.

I wondered if everyone who watched soap operas was as committed to them and as involved with them as Thelma was. A few days later, one of her favorite characters died on *Days in the Sun.* I came in on the show just as it happened, and she began to sob so hard, I got frightened. She started to shout at the television set.

"He can't be dead. He can't be. How can he die? Please don't let him die. Oh, Crystal, he's dead! Grant's dead! How can he be dead?"

"People die in real life, Mom," I said, "so they have to have some die in the shows, don't they?"

"No," she insisted, her face filled with more anger than I had seen up until now. "It's not fair. They got us to love him, and now they've killed him. It's not fair!" she cried.

She went into a deep depression afterward, and nothing I could say or do changed it. She was still that way when Karl came home and we all sat down to dinner. He asked why she was so sad, and she told him and then burst into tears again. He looked at me, and I looked down at my plate. My heart was thumping. I didn't know what to say.

"You're frightening your daughter," Karl remarked.

She looked at me and swallowed back her sobs.

"Oh. I didn't mean to frighten you, Crystal. It's just so sad."

"It's only a show, Mom," I said. "Tomorrow, something new will happen, and you'll feel better."

"Yes, yes, I will. That's right. See Karl, see how smart she is?"

"That I do," Karl said.

We finished our meal, but afterward, I found Thelma in her rocker just staring at the floor.

"I'm going upstairs to read and sleep now," I said.

"What? Oh, yes, good night, dear. Try to think good thoughts. Poor Grant," she said. "It makes me think of how it was when Karl's mother died."

I stared at her. How could the death of a real person be the same as the death of a soap opera character?

"He's an actor, Mom. He'll be back on another show," I said softly.

"Who is?"

"Grant."

"No, silly," she said. "Grant's not an actor. Grant was a person who died. I don't think of them as actors," she admitted. She started rocking again and stared at the floor. "Everyone will be so sad tomorrow on the show, so sad."

"Maybe you shouldn't watch it, then," I suggested. She looked up at me as if what I had said was blasphemous.

"I've got to watch it, Crystal. I care about them all. They're my friends," she said. She made it seem as if they knew she was watching and they depended on her.

She looked at the floor again instead of kissing me good night as she had done from the first day I had arrived. I hurried upstairs to sleep. I didn't know exactly why, but for the first time since I had come to live there, I felt a little trepidation. I lay there wondering why. I guess I was afraid that my new mother would always care more about her characters than she would about me.

I had found a home full of family pictures, talk about relatives, promises for upcoming holidays and trips. I had grandparents, and I would soon be in a new school. I had my own room, and I had begun a whole new life.

But what if I woke up in the morning and found that someone had turned a dial and I was back in the orphanage?

3
Peas in a Pod

Two days before school began, I was sitting outside and reading. Thelma wanted me to watch Emergency Care with her. It was a new late-morning series about an ER at a big-city hospital. She tried to get me to watch it with her by telling me I would learn a lot of medical information.

"And you do think you want to be a doctor someday, Crystal," she emphasized. "So you'll learn a lot."

"I'll learn more from reading," I told her. I saw it made her unhappy, but I felt as if I was overdosed on soap operas and television in general. At the orphanage, if I watched two shows a week, that was a lot. I knew most of the other kids my age thought I was weird because I'd rather read a book or work on the computer than watch their favorite nighttime shows, but that's how I was.

It was also a beautiful day, and I couldn't see myself wasting it closed up in the living room with the glow of a television screen on my eyes. This was actually my favorite time of the year. Summer was fading fast, and the air had the feel of the soon-to-be crisp autumn days. It smelled fresher, looked clearer. Without the humidity and high temperatures, I felt more energetic. I was even restless sitting and reading.

"Hi," I heard someone say, and looked up to see a girl about my age with long, sunflower-yellow hair standing at our front gate. She wore a pair of baggy shorts and a T-shirt with half moons all over it. A pair of long silver earrings with tiny blue and green stones dangled from her ears. "I live over there," she said, pointing to a house across the street.

"Hi," I said, and tried to remember if I'd seen her around the neighborhood.

"You just moved in with Karl and Thelma, right? I heard about it," she said before I could respond. She tossed some strands of her hair back over her shoulder as if she were tossing away a candy wrapper. "My name's Helga. I think we're going to be in the same class. You're going into tenth?"

"Yes. I'm Crystal," I said.

"Helga and Crystal. They'll think we're sisters." She giggled. She put all her weight on her right leg. From where I was sitting, it looked as if she was leaning against an imaginary wall. "What are you reading?"

"*Lord of the Flies.* It's on our English reading list this year," I said.

"How do you know that?"

"I asked when I registered, and they gave me the list," I told her.

She grimaced, bounced her weight to her left leg and then back to her right, which I would discover later was something she habitually did when she was confused or annoyed.

"You're doing schoolwork already?" she whined.

"Why not?" I shrugged. "I like being ahead."

"You must be a good student," she said, lingering at the gate. She sounded disappointed.

"Aren't you?" I asked.

She shrugged.

"I get C's and sometimes B's. As long as I don't get D's and F's, my parents don't bug me. Did you live with some other family last year?" she followed quickly.

"No," I said.

She stared at me as if she was building the courage to ask another question.

"I lived in an orphanage," I explained.

"Oh. Did you have any brothers or sisters you had to leave behind or who got adopted into other families?"

"No," I said, "but I've seen that happen, and it's not pleasant."

She smiled. "I hope you don't mind me being nosy. My mother says it's a family character trait. As soon as we hear or see something that's not really our business, we perk up and stick our ears out. She says our family was the inspiration for the first spies."

I laughed.

"You want to go for a walk? I'll show you the neighborhood," she said.

"Okay," I said, standing. I paused for a moment and looked back at the front door.

"What's wrong?" she asked.

"I'm just wondering if I should tell my mother."

"Your mother? Oh, they make you check in and out?"

"No."

"So? We're just going down the street."

I nodded. Since I didn't expect to be away long, I decided not to interrupt her soap opera.

It wasn't until I walked up to Helga that I realized she was at least three inches taller than I was. She had patches of tiny freckles over the crests of her cheeks, and it looked as if someone had dotted them with a ballpoint pen in light brown ink.

"Those are pretty thick glasses you're wearing," she said.

"I have astigmatism."

"Bummer," she said. "You oughtta go with me to the mall one day and get nicer frames. Maybe prescription sunglasses, too. You'll look better."

"I don't wear them for looks. I wear them to help me see and read," I said.

She laughed. "Sure. Until someone like Tom MacNamara looks your way. He's so cool, but he's a senior this year and probably won't even look at us. He also happens to be captain of the football team."

"I probably wouldn't be interested in him anyway," I said, and she stopped walking.

"Sure you wouldn't." She bounced her weight from one leg to the other. "Did you have a boyfriend at the orphanage?"

"No. I have never really had a boyfriend," I admitted.

She stared a moment and then started walking again.

"Me, neither," she confessed. "Oh, I pretended to like Jack Martin one year just so it looked like I had a boyfriend, but I never even kissed him, and when he went to kiss me, I turned my head so he kissed my cheek like an uncle or someone. You see this big house?" she said, pausing. "Clara Seymour lives here. She's a senior this year and will probably be senior prom queen. Her father's a heart doctor, a cardio-something."

"Cardiologist," I said.

"Yes, I think that's it." She tilted her head and squinted at me. "You are smart."

"I'm thinking of becoming a doctor myself someday."

"A doctor!" she said. "It costs a lot, I heard."

"I hope to win scholarships, too," I added.

"I'll be glad just to get my diploma. I haven't the slightest idea what I'll do. I was thinking I might become an actress, but I didn't even make the junior play."

"What do you like to do?"

"Party," she said, laughing, "and watch television.

Oh!" She stopped and took my arm. "Watch out for the dog at this house," she said, nodding at a small A-frame. "Old Lady Potter lives there, and she has a mean rottweiler for protection. Last year, he bit a UPS delivery driver and there was a big commotion with the police and everything."

"I'll definitely stay out of that yard." I laughed. "Thanks for the advice."

"If you turn right at the corner and go two blocks, you reach the Quick Shop where you can get magazines, gum, and stuff. We're not far from the school, only about two miles. You going to take the bus?"

"I guess so," I said. "I don't think Karl wants to drive me every day, especially since there is a bus."

"You call him Karl?" she asked quickly.

"Right now I do," I said, looking away.

"But Thelma you call Mom?"

"She wanted it that way from the start," I said. "You know what? You're right."

"What?"

"You *are* nosy."

She laughed. "Come on, I'll introduce you to Bernie Felder. I have a feeling you two will get along real well. Bernie's a genius, too."

"I'm not a genius," I corrected.

"Whatever." She sped up, and we walked to another ranch-style house with a brick facade. It looked like an expensive house. The landscaping was more elaborate than most, and the house was almost twice the size of Karl and Thelma's.

"What do Bernie's parents do?" I asked.

"His father owns a big tire store that services trucks," she said. "Bernie's an only child, like you."

"What about you?"

"I have a younger brother I ignore," she said. "My parents named him William, but they call him Buster."

"Buster?"

"When you see him, you'll see why. He looks like a Buster, and he's always busting things," she added. "Come on." She headed for the front door.

"Maybe we should call first," I said, but she pushed the door buzzer.

"I'd rather be unexpected," she said. "It's more fun."

A maid answered the door, and Helga asked for Bernie. A few moments later, a boy about my height with straggly red hair and light green eyes appeared. He wore a T-shirt that looked two sizes too big and a pair of jeans with sneakers and no socks. His face was pale with full red lips and a cleft chin.

"Hi, Bernie," Helga said.

He grimaced. "What do you want?" he demanded.

"That's not a very nice way to say hello," she remarked.

"I was in the middle of something," he said apologetically.

"You're not making bombs, are you? My mother always thinks Bernie's making bombs," she told me.

When she turned to me, Bernie finally looked my way, and his face filled with interest. "Who's this?"

"Our new neighbor, Bernie. If you hadn't jumped

down my throat, I would have been able to introduce you."

"I'm sorry," he said, turning to me. "Hello."

"Hello. I'm sorry we interrupted you, but . . ."

"It's all right." He looked embarrassed.

"Of course it's all right. What could Bernie be doing that can't be interrupted?" Helga asked.

"Whatever it is, it's important to him," I remarked dryly. She smirked, but Bernie's face softened.

"You just moved here?" he asked.

"If you didn't have your nose in a test tube all the time, you would have known about her," Helga said. "Her name is Crystal, and the Morrises adopted her."

"Oh?" he said, his lips forming a little circle as he gazed at me with even more interest.

"She was an orphan," Helga added. She stepped back to look at me. They both stared a moment, neither speaking.

"That's orphan, not alien," I said, and Bernie smiled.

"She reads a lot, and she's very smart," Helga continued. "Maybe even smarter than you, Bernie. That's why I thought you two should meet."

"Really?" he said, his interest in me growing even more.

"This was her idea. I'm sorry we bothered you." I started to turn away.

"Hey. That's okay," he called. "Come on in."

"Bernie's inviting us in," Helga said, raising her eyebrows. "You going to show us your laboratory, Bernie?"

"I don't have a laboratory," he snapped at her. She laughed. He turned to me. "Helga and her friends are always making stuff up about me."

"No, we don't, Bernie," she said. "Anyway, if we do, you should be honored we talk about you."

"Some honor," Bernie said. He stepped back, and Helga gestured emphatically for me to follow her into the house. I did.

Right away, I saw that Bernie's parents had a lot of money. There were paintings all over the walls, and the rooms were very big and full of expensive-looking furnishings. In the hallway to his room was a glass case filled with figurines. The floors were all covered with carpet so soft I felt as if I were walking on marshmallows.

Bernie's room was twice, maybe three times as big as mine. He had a large desk, a computer, and all sorts of hardware. I recognized a scanner and two printers. He even had his own fax machine. One wall was covered with charts that included the anatomy of the human body, a breakdown of the planets and some galaxies, an evolution time line, and a historical summary of American presidents and vice presidents with a listing of major events during their terms.

On the right were shelves that held a microscope, slides, scales, and even a Bunsen burner. I saw chemistry sets and shelves and shelves of reference books. What didn't he have? I wondered.

"You see?" Helga said. "He has a laboratory in his room."

"It's not a laboratory. I have a few things to develop my interests," he said defensively. "I want to get into genetic research someday."

"I don't even know what that means," Helga said.

He frowned and shook his head. "You know what this is?" he asked me, pointing to what looked like a Tinker Toy.

"Yes," I said. "It's a model of DNA."

"Right!" he said, his face becoming more animated than it had been since we met.

"What's DNA?" Helga asked.

"It has to do with genetics," Bernie said quickly. "You want to look at this? I put this together myself," he told me, and I drew closer.

"Don't you have a CD player or something in here?" Helga asked.

"No," he said quickly.

"Well, how do you listen to music?" she demanded.

"I listen on my computer when I want to listen to music," he said, and turned his back on her.

"This is like being back in school," she complained. "Not one movie poster, not one rock star poster, just all this . . . this educational stuff."

"It's very good," I said, nodding at his model. He beamed with pride.

"Come on, Crystal," Helga said. "I'll show you the rest of the neighborhood. Maybe Fern Peabody is home. She's going steady with Gary Lakewood, and she always has good stories to tell."

"I've got some interesting slides," Bernie said, ignoring her. "I just got them yesterday. They're from human embryos."

"Really?" I said.

"Ugh," Helga said. "Do they smell?"

"Of course not," Bernie snapped. "You should pay more attention in science class."

"Boring," she sang. "I'm going," she threatened.

Bernie held his hand on his microscope and looked at me.

"I'm staying," I said. I knew I should probably go with her to meet more of the neighborhood kids, but Bernie's projects really intrigued me.

"I knew it," Helga said. "Peas in a pod. I'll talk to you later," she threw back at me as she left Bernie's room.

He smiled. Then he brought his microscope to the desk and hurriedly set things up. "Sit right there," he said, pointing to his chair.

He slipped in the slides and began to talk about them as I gazed through the microscope. It really was like being at a class lecture, but I didn't mind. Some of it I knew, but most of it I didn't. He was so excited about having an audience, he went on and on and then brought out some other slides. I got so involved I didn't realize the time until I glanced at the clock by his bed.

"Oh, no," I said. "I'd better get home. I didn't tell my mother I was leaving. I didn't think I'd be away this long, and it's ten minutes past dinner."

"Right," he said with disappointment. He looked at the clock. "I don't eat dinner at any set time. I eat when I'm hungry."

"What about your parents?"

"They usually go out or eat at different times," he said.

"You never eat together?"

"Sometimes," he said as he put away his slides.

"Thanks for showing me everything," I told him as I walked to the door.

"Sure," he said.

He followed me out and down the hall.

"Maybe I'll see you again," I said, turning back to him just before leaving.

"Okay," he said. "Any time you want."

"Thank you," I said, and started away.

"Oh," he began.

I paused. "Yes?"

"I forgot. What's your name again?"

"It's Crystal," I said.

"I'm Bernie," he said.

I wanted to say, "I know, I remember your name. How could I not remember your name?" But he closed the door before I could add a word.

I hurried down the sidewalk. When I reached the house, I saw that my book was missing from the arm of the chair. It put a small panic in me because I realized Thelma had come looking for me. I quickened my steps and practically ran into the house.

"There," Karl said, hearing the door close and stepping out of the living room. "She's back, and she's all right."

I looked in and saw Thelma, her eyes bloodshot, her face pale. She was clutching her skirt and twisting the material anxiously.

"Oh, Crystal. I was sure something terrible had happened to you. When I walked out there to call you in for dinner and all I found was your book . . ."

"I'm sorry," I said both to Karl and to her. "A girl came by to introduce herself, and then we went for a walk and it took longer than I thought it would. We stopped to visit Bernie Felder and . . ."

"When I saw that book and the empty chair," Thelma continued, not listening to my explanation, "all I could think of was *Heart Shell* by Amanda Glass. That's the story about the little girl who was kidnapped and brought up by another family. There's a scene just like this. They find her children's book on the grass by her little chair. It's not until she's a young woman that she returns to her real parents."

I just stared.

"Well, she wasn't kidnapped," Karl said calmly, "so put all that horror out of your mind, Thelma."

He turned to me. "Next time, Crystal, please let us know where you are going," he chastised firmly.

"I'm sorry. I didn't think I'd be that long. I got too involved with Bernie Felder's slides. I never saw so much stuff in someone's house and . . ."

"It's all right. Dinner is a little late, but it's all right. Let's forget about it, Thelma, okay?" He looked at his watch. "There's no sense in wasting any more time over it."

"Right," she said, taking a deep breath. "It's all right." She smiled. "I'm just happy you're back," she said, as if I had been away for ages. "That's what the mother said in *Heart Shell.* I'm just happy you're back."

She hugged me as if she was afraid that if she ever let go, I'd disappear. I felt very confused. I was happy that someone cared so much about me, that someone could be sad and distraught just with the fear of my being gone, and yet I had to wonder. When Thelma looked at me, whom did she really see?

Me or the girl in *Heart Shell?*

4
Casting Call

Thelma felt better at dinner after she started to tell me about her soap opera. Because I was still feeling guilty for what I had done, I pretended to be interested in the story and the characters. However, it seemed silly to me that people fell in and out of such passionate love affairs so easily, that people betrayed each other despite how long they had known and trusted each other, and that children could despise their parents so much. For Thelma, however, what happened on the soaps was gospel. It was as if some biblical prophet wrote the scripts.

To some extent, I couldn't blame her. Most of the leading men seemed godlike, perfect. The women were glamorous even when they woke in the morning. When I innocently asked if we were to believe they went to sleep wearing makeup, Thelma said when someone is that beautiful, she always looks as if she's wearing makeup.

"I never met anyone that beautiful," I remarked, and she laughed in such a way it made me feel as though I were the uninformed one.

"That's why they're my special people," she said. "See why I like to watch my soaps?"

I suppose it was all right to watch them, I thought, as long as we remembered that life wasn't really like a soap opera. Our lives weren't filled with dramatic events, and people rarely felt as passionate about anything as they constantly did on that small screen.

"What happened between Nevada and Johnny Lee touched my heart," she exclaimed toward the end of dinner. She smiled, and tears filled the deep furrows around her eyes. Then she looked at Karl and reached for his hand.

Karl glanced at me when she put her hand over his. He looked uncomfortable, but he didn't stop her or pull away, and I wondered what sort of love life my new parents shared. In all of the pictures of them that were in the house, they looked so formal, Karl always standing stiffly, Thelma always looking as if she was afraid she would make a terrible social mistake.

Later in the evening, I discovered just what sort of a romantic life they had. I had gone up to bed before them as usual. When I left them in the living room, Karl was reading *Business Weekly* and Thelma was watching a videotape she had made of a recent soap she had to miss so she could keep a dentist appointment. I finished reading my book and felt a little tired. Once again, I apologized to Thelma for giving her a scare earlier, and I promised I would never do anything like that again.

"You're so sweet to say that, dear. Karl and I knew from the moment we set eyes on you that you were a responsible young lady and things like this wouldn't happen often, if at all. All is forgiven," she said with an unexpected, theatrical air, her voice rising, her arms sweeping the air in an over-the-top dramatic gesture. Even Karl lowered his magazine and gazed at her with concern for a moment.

She held her arms out for me, and I went to her so she could embrace me, rocking back and forth as she spoke in a chantlike voice. "We must be good to each other, kind and considerate and loving. You have suffered so much, my little darling, and my life has been so empty without you. The love we all have for each other is almost holy. Always, forever and ever, always fit us into the corners of your life. Do you promise, Crystal? Do you?"

"Yes," I said, not sure what it was I was promising to do.

She sighed deeply but still held on to me.

"Thelma," Karl said gently, "the child is tired and wants to go to bed."

"Yes, to bed," she said. "Good night, dear. Good night, good night, good night," she sang in my ear, and kissed me on the top of my head.

"Good night," I told them, and went upstairs.

Could it be, I wondered, that someone really did need me more than I needed her? No one had ever held me like that, much less held me that long, and although female staff members at the orphanages had kissed me occasionally, those kisses were quick smacks of their lips, almost like little pats on my cheeks and forehead. I felt nothing, no love, no deep concern. No, I thought, despite all her faults, Thelma did make me feel wanted, and what was more important than that?

I had just closed my eyes and tucked the blanket under my chin when I heard soft footsteps in the hallway. Then, in a voice I almost didn't recognize, I heard Thelma calling. It was confusing. I had to sit up to listen harder.

"Johnny Lee," I heard. "Please, please forgive me. Please, don't hate me."

At first, I thought she was simply repeating lines she loved from the show she had seen, but then I heard Karl say, "I don't hate you. I could never hate you, Nevada."

"I want to give myself to you," she said. "I want to give myself to you like I have never given myself to anyone, Johnny Lee."

"I know. I want you, too," Karl said.

There was a silence and then the soft sound of footsteps. I went to the door and opened it a crack to peek out. There they were in the hallway, kissing fully on the lips. I was mesmerized. Karl put his left hand under Thelma's blouse.

"No," she said, pulling back.

"Why not?" he asked, raising his voice.

"It doesn't happen like that. Nothing like that happens until she cries," Thelma said.

He pulled his hand out from under her blouse and held her hips.

"Okay, okay," he said. "I forgot."

"You're ruining it," she accused.

"I said I forgot."

"Start over," she commanded.

"What? Why?"

"You've got to start over," she insisted.

"That's silly, Thelma."

"Don't call me Thelma!" she exclaimed. "You're ruining it!"

"All right, all right. I'm sorry. I'll start over."

He turned from her, and I closed the door softly so neither of them would see me spying. My heart was pounding so hard, however, I was afraid they would hear the thumping in my chest. I listened.

Karl went down the hallway and closed a door. Then he opened it.

"Nevada," he called.

I opened my door again. Thelma was standing with her back to me now. She turned slowly, her face so different. She really looked as if she was on some sort of stage.

"Johnny Lee," she said, and wiped her cheeks. I could see she was crying real tears. "Please, please forgive me. Please, don't hate me."

"I don't hate you. I could never hate you, Nevada."

"I want to give myself to you," she repeated. "I want to give myself to you like I have never given myself to anyone, Johnny Lee."

"I know. I want you, too," Karl repeated his lines just as he'd said them before.

He stepped up to her, and they embraced but did not kiss. This time, he kept his hands on her hips. She started to cry, her whole body shaking. He embraced her and held her against his chest, kissing her hair, her cheeks, and then holding her head up softly so he could kiss her lips.

Then his hand returned to the bottom of her blouse and moved up over her breast again. She moaned.

"Will it be different tonight, Johnny Lee? Will it be going to the moon and back?"

"Just like I promised," Karl said. He lowered his right arm around her waist, and they turned toward their bedroom. Thelma laid her head on his shoulder as they walked toward their room. I watched until they disappeared inside, the door closing softly behind them.

I didn't want to eavesdrop on them, but curiosity was like a magnet drawing me toward the wall between our two bedrooms. I put the tips of my fingers against it. Their voices were muffled, as were Thelma's sobs. I brought my ear to the wall and closed my eyes.

"Oh, Johnny Lee," she said. "Touch me everywhere this time. Do what you promised you would do. Make my body sing."

"I will."

They were quiet, but I heard the distinct sound of the bedsprings. Her moans grew louder, longer. There was a combination of moans and cries that made me even more curious. Was lovemaking painful as well as pleasureful? Why wasn't he crying out, too?

Finally, after a long, loud cry, everything grew silent. I listened for a while longer and then retreated to my own bed. Was that the way it was supposed to be? I knew every scientific detail. I could describe the hormones, the movement of blood, even the nerve impulses, but the emotions were so confusing. Sex was one thing, but sex with love was supposed to be another.

Suddenly, I heard a door open and some more whispering. I got out of bed and went to my own door again.

"Good night, good night, parting is such sweet sorrow . . ."

They both laughed.

Karl was in the hallway looking back at their bedroom. He blew a kiss. He was fully dressed.

"I wish you could stay," Thelma said.

"So do I."

"Someday."

"Someday," he said, and turned. I stepped back as he walked past my bedroom. I heard Thelma close her door.

I wish you could stay? Where was he going? What did this mean?

For a long moment, it was very quiet. Then Karl's footsteps echoed down the hallway as if he was deliberately trying to be loud. I opened the door again and watched him walk past to their bedroom. When he opened the door, I heard him say, "You still up, Thelma?"

"I couldn't sleep," she replied, "so I decided to read a little, but I'm tired now."

"Good. It's bedtime," he said, and entered the bedroom, closing the door.

I put my ear to the wall and listened. I heard water running in their bathroom sink and a toilet flush. Neither of them spoke for the longest time, and then I heard Karl say, "Good night, Thelma."

"Good night, Karl."

All was quiet. I returned to my bed, but I didn't fall asleep for quite a while. How could adults be like children, playing games and pretending? What would love be like for me if it ever happened to me? What sort of a man would find me attractive, or would no man find me attractive and I would be forced to imagine a life, too?

How I wished I had a big sister or a close friend, someone in whom I would be unafraid to confide, someone I could trust with my deepest hidden secrets. That was what was truly wonderful about family, I thought. When you had one, you didn't have to keep all of your troubled feelings and fears simmering under a pot. You could go to them and be unafraid to lift the lid. You could help each other and keep each other from being afraid.

Wasn't that the most important thing?

Of course, the next morning, I said nothing about what I had seen and heard Thelma and Karl do the night before. I felt guilty for spying on them anyway. Karl had made plans to return home from work early so he, Thelma, and I could go shopping for things I would need at the start of school the next day. At first, he was just going to tell Thelma where the best places were and have us go ourselves, but she complained that this was a family thing and he should be a part of it. He thought about it and agreed.

"You have to forgive me," he told me. "I'm not used to thinking like a parent. Of course I'll be here. Of course I want to be part of everything important."

I know he tried to relax and make it seem like fun, but it just wasn't in his nature to treat purchasing as anything less than a serious project. Thelma had made a list of clothing, and I had made a list of school supplies. Karl took our lists and researched everything. He knew exactly where the best prices were for every item. Colors, fashions, and styles played the least role. Our shopping was planned efficiently, down to where we would eat dinner and even what was the best food value.

"A family," Karl explained as we ate, "is really a small enterprise, a business venture, a partnership. The more that's planned, the better it will be."

"Karl even planned our wedding and honeymoon so as to take advantage of some good specials, didn't you, Karl?" Thelma said proudly.

"Yes. It was off-season, after Labor Day, the best time to find good values."

"But was it someplace you wanted to go?" I asked.

"If it's a good value for the dollar, it's where I want to be," Karl replied. "People pay more for the things they want and need because they don't do the necessary research and planning."

"Karl has even bought our final resting places and has our funerals arranged, don't you, Karl?" Thelma said. "He did it shortly after we got married."

"That soon?" I asked innocently.

"Having family members make final arrangements is one of the biggest rip-offs. You need to make your arrangements when you're alive. Don't be afraid to think ahead, Crystal. Never let anyone intimidate you into thinking you're being too practical. You can never be too practical," he instructed.

Thelma's parents had asked us to stop over at their house when we were finished shopping for my school things. They said they had something they wanted to give me. As we drove there, Karl reminded Thelma of the time and how long he wanted us to stay.

My new grandparents had a small but cozy ranch-style home. Thelma said that Karl had found it for them shortly after her father retired.

"It fit their new budget perfectly," he said with pride. "That's another thing you can't think about too soon: your retirement. Most people don't put away enough and suffer because of it."

"But not us," Thelma chimed.

"No, not us," Karl agreed with a smile.

What my grandparents had for me was a brown leather briefcase with my name embroidered in gold letters on the outside. I was more pleased with it than anything else I had gotten that day.

"It wasn't necessary to buy real leather, Martha," Karl told my grandmother.

"Of course it was," she replied, and smiled at me. "Why shouldn't she have the nicest things?"

We had tea, and Grandma served her homemade sugar cookies, which I thought were delicious. Then she told stories about her days at school. She had attended a smaller, rural school. She talked about how she had to walk almost a mile and a half to get there.

"Even in the snow!"

"Even in the snow because we didn't have schoolbuses like you do now."

Grandpa tried to match her stories with his own, and she kept correcting him and saying he was exaggerating. They were both funny and delightful. I was really beginning to enjoy myself when Karl announced it was time to go home.

"Tomorrow's her first day at a new school," he declared when my grandmother complained we hadn't even been there an hour. "She needs an early night."

"Well, you call me as soon as you can afterward and tell me all about your first day, Crystal," Grandma said.

"I will. Thank you again for the briefcase," I said.

She hugged me. "Our pleasure. We don't have much to spend our money on these days but medicines and such."

"You've got the best health plan," Karl said.

"Oh, I don't want to talk about that," Grandma said quickly. "Now that we have a granddaughter, I don't want to talk about my ailments."

We said good night and left.

"If they didn't have the plan I got them," Karl muttered when we got into the car, "she would be bankrupt paying for that heart medicine. Those prescriptions are very expensive."

"She knows," Thelma said. "She's just excited about Crystal. As we all are," she added. "I wish I could attend class with you tomorrow, Crystal. I wish I was starting over again."

"It's not easy to change schools," Karl said. "It's nothing to envy."

"I know. Did you ever read *Love on Wheels,* about that family that lives in a motor home and has to go from place to place, town to town, following farm work?"

"No," I replied.

"Just when Stacy finds the love of her life, she has to leave him. I'll give it to you," Thelma promised. "In fact, you should read all my books. Then we could talk about them, about all my special people. Wouldn't that be nice?"

I didn't answer fast enough.

"She'll have too much to do now that school's starting," Karl said, coming to my rescue.

"She has to have time off, doesn't she? What's a better way to spend it than reading?" Thelma countered.

How funny, I thought. I would get assignments at school and assignments at home. There was no doubt in my mind which ones my mother thought were more important.

Once I got home and put all my new things away, I realized Karl wasn't so wrong. I did need to get to bed.

I was so nervous about the next day and what it would bring, sleep was as hard to grasp and hold as an icicle. He was right about another thing, too. It wasn't easy to change schools, to make new friends, to get used to different teachers and rules.

It was almost like losing your memory and starting over as a different person.

And wasn't that exactly what I was, a new person with a new last name and a new family?

My old self curled up in some dark corner, shivering, naked, and alone.

"What will become of me?" she asked.

"In time," I told her, "you will disappear."

It was a cruel thought, but it was what I hoped would happen, wasn't it?

It was also what made me cower in my own new corner of the world, just as naked and just as frightened about tomorrow.

5
A New Friend

To my surprise, Karl decided he would take me to school every morning, but I had to come home on the bus. It wasn't a problem, because the route was just a few minutes out of his way to work. Nevertheless, it was really Thelma who had suggested it.

"It will give you two more time to get to know each other," she said. I was waiting for her to add the name of a book and the names of characters in a similar situation, but she didn't. Karl considered and decided she was right.

Karl and I hadn't spent all that much time together without Thelma. She was always the one who began conversations or asked questions. When Karl and I drove off that first morning, I remembered he didn't like being distracted from his driving, so I didn't say anything. For a while, we drove in complete silence, interrupted occasionally by his describing the route we were taking.

"What is your favorite subject?" he finally asked.

"Science, especially biology," I replied. He nodded, his eyes fixed firmly on the car ahead of us.

"I enjoyed science, but math was always my favorite. I never told anyone," he said, flashing a small smile at me before whipping his head back to watch the road, "but to me numbers are living things. They resemble one-, two-, and multicelled animals, depending on the combinations, formulas, and so on."

"That's interesting," I said. He liked that, and I was glad. Talking to him had taken the edge off my nervousness. I was distracted enough not to worry about my imminent entrance to a new school full of strangers.

"I feel like I'm creating something when I work out my accounts and balance sheets. Everything has a way of relating to everything else. I bet you can understand what I'm saying," he added.

"I think so," I said, even though I wasn't sure I did, and he gave me a wider smile.

"When we were trying to make a baby, I was hoping he or she would grow up to be someone I could talk to, someone who was bright enough to understand. That's why I was so happy when Thelma said she liked you, too. Most kids have fluff in their heads today," he continued, his eyes darkening. "They don't get serious about life until it's almost too late or, in many cases, too late. There are too many distractions. Don't tell Thelma I said this, but I think it's good that you don't want to spend all your free time staring into a light bulb."

"A light bulb?"

"That's all television is to me, a light bulb with idiotic stuff on its surface," he muttered. "I don't even like the way they report the news. The news is a comic book these days."

I was surprised at how forcefully he condemned television. I could see him rushing into people's homes and smashing screens with a sledge hammer, yet when it came to his own home, he sat silently reading his magazines while Thelma sat entranced.

"Thelma really loves her programs," I said.

"I know. And I appreciate how you humor her," he added with a smile.

"Did she always spend so much time watching them?"

He was quiet, concentrating on his driving. We stopped at a traffic light, and he took a deep breath. "She didn't tell you everything about our attempt to have a baby of our own," he confessed. "We tried in vitro fertilization. You know what that is?"

"Yes," I said. "Taking out a woman's egg, inserting sperm into it in a Petri dish, and placing it back in the woman's womb."

"You are smart. Yes. Well, it didn't work for her. She miscarried. She was very depressed afterward. Very depressed," he emphasized, raising his eyebrows and widening his eyes. "It was then that she began to watch television. Getting involved in the stories was the only thing that excited her. I couldn't oppose it." He paused and then glanced at me quickly. "I didn't want to tell you this so soon," he continued, "but you're my big hope."

"Me? How?"

"I'm hoping she'll become so involved with you and real-life things that she'll start to drift away from the make-believe world. I was holding my breath when you first came to our home, waiting to see if you were going to get sucked into those soap operas with her. You don't know how glad I am that you haven't been," he said.

"I like a good story," I confessed.

"Sure, who doesn't? But it can't become your whole life. It does for people who have nothing but popcorn in their heads. You're not one of them. You're a serious young lady. You're going to be someone, and I want to be there when they hand you your first diploma."

I smiled. He sounded proud already, and I hadn't done a thing. In fact, it was the first time I felt he sounded like a real father.

"I hope you're there too," I told him.

He seemed to relax in his seat and soften his grip around the steering wheel. We really were getting to know each other better. Thelma had made a good suggestion.

"I'll tell you another one of my secrets," he offered. "I even view people in terms of numbers."

"How do you do that?" I asked.

"Easy." He paused as if he wasn't going to say any more, but he had a small smile on his lips again. "Some people are positive numbers, and many are negative. Didn't you ever hear someone say, 'He's a complete zero'? Well, that's how I group people in my mind, only I have categories in the negatives, too." He laughed. "My immediate superior is a minus ten. He used to be a minus five, but he's gotten worse."

"I've heard about women being rated like that," I said. "A beautiful woman is supposed to be a ten."

"Yeah, but that's a stupid use of numbers," he said angrily. It was as if numbers were his province and no one else had a right to use them. "You don't measure someone solely on the way he or she looks. It's what's going on in here," he said, stabbing his temple with his forefinger so hard I imagined the pain, "that counts. Counts, get it?" he said, smiling.

I nodded.

"There she blows," he cried, nodding ahead of us. I saw the school building down the street. Arriving buses were emptying their passengers. Old friends were hugging and talking excitedly to one another. They all had that first-day-of-school look, the clean and crisp appearance their parents most likely imposed on them.

"You know the number of the bus that takes you home?" Karl asked.

"Yes."

"Okay, have a great first day," he said, pulling to the curb. He looked at me as if he wanted to give me a kiss good-bye. I waited a moment expecting it, but he just smiled and nodded again, squirming in his seat as if he was uncomfortable. We were still orbiting each other like strangers, waiting for something that would make us truly father and daughter. Why was it so much harder for me than it was for all those young people laughing and shouting in front of the school? What wonderful things had they done to deserve their families, their mommies and daddies? What terrible thing had I done to be born alone?

" 'Bye," I cried, and hopped out of the car. I turned to wave, but he was pulling away, his attention locked on the driveway in front of him.

First days of school always had a special feeling to them. The desks, the blackboards, the hallways, the bathrooms, windows, and floors were squeaky clean. You could still smell the detergents, wood polish, glass cleaner, and fresh paint. Voices, footsteps, and bells all had a deeper, longer echo. There was an electricity of expectation and anticipation in the air, as well as some mystery. What was going to be required of us? How well would we get along with our new teachers? How well would we get along with one another? Those who had been here before studied one another to discover the changes a summer of fun or work or both had effected on their bodies, their faces, and, most of all, their personalities.

Girls and boys alike were exploring new styles, wore their hair differently, dressed more maturely. Those who were more insecure about themselves held themselves back toward the rear, in the shadows, out of the direct flow of conversations and attention, while the confident strutted with their heads high, seeking to reclaim their turf quickly and eyeing every possible contender with suspicion.

New kids were interesting and yet threatening. I

could almost hear their suspicion when they looked at me. The girl who was expected to win the lead in the school play wondered if I would try out and take her part away. The students who were at the top of their classes, racing toward the awards and honors, wondered if I would be real competition. Girls who were leaders of their little cliques feared I might be more sophisticated and win away their loyal followers. Girls and even boys who fell outside the circle of social life hoped I might be another one of them, a friend, a buoy to cling to in the sea of turmoil adults called the teenage years, adolescence.

I was here. I had landed, and I was living with a family now. No one could fix the label of orphan on my forehead like the mark of Cain and make me feel so different that I saw curiosity and rejection in the eyes of those who were supposed to be friends. At least, that was what I hoped.

The moment I spotted Helga talking and laughing with a group of girls near the girls' room, I felt a dark foreboding take hold of my heart. She saw me and nudged someone, and they all grew quiet and looked my way.

"Hi," she called, waving me toward her.

"Hi."

"You didn't take the bus this morning, so I didn't know whether or not you were still living with Karl and Thelma," she said.

"Why wouldn't I be?" I shot back.

She looked at her friends and then at me and shrugged.

"I just wondered," she said, shifting her weight from one leg to the other and smiling again. "I introduced Crystal to Bernie Felder. We went over to his house, and she didn't want to leave. How long did you stay?"

"A while," I said. So that was it, I thought. I was being punished for not doing exactly what she had wanted, for defying her and staying with Bernie.

"Crystal's a genius, too," she said with an ugly twist in her lips.

"I'm far from a genius, but I am polite," I said. I turned to the others. "My name is Crystal Morris."

They stared a moment, and then a short brunette with a face like a little doll, her features small and perfect, stuck out her hand.

"I'm Alicia."

"I'm Mona," said another girl, with a rounder face, straight light brown hair, and brown eyes. Her fingers were short and stubby.

"My name is Rachael Peterson," a girl almost as tall as Helga said in a very formal voice. She didn't offer her hand, but she looked at my briefcase. "Is that real leather?" she asked.

"Yes."

"Very nice," she said.

"Thank you. My grandparents gave it to me."

"Grandparents? How can you have grandparents?" Helga asked quickly.

"Thelma's parents are my grandparents," I said dryly. "That's how it works."

"So how did you get to school this morning?"

Helga asked, ignoring my sarcasm. "You didn't come with Bernie, did you?"

"Karl took me on the way to work. He's going to take me every morning, but I'll go home on the bus," I explained.

"Still calling him Karl, I see," Helga said, shifting her eyes to her friends. She smiled wryly, her lips twisting again.

"Well, I wasn't as lucky as the rest of you. I wasn't born into a family," I said. I saw Alicia's eyebrows lift. Mona's eyes filled with confusion.

"I told you she was very intelligent," Helga said quickly.

Alicia and Mona nodded, but Rachael continued just to stare down at me.

"It doesn't take a lot of intelligence to know not to say things that will embarrass someone who is new and a stranger to the school," I said. "That usually shows a lack of it." I turned and walked toward my homeroom just as the bell rang.

Bernie Felder was in my homeroom. He nodded when he saw me, his eyes softening as if they saw my distress at being new and unsure of myself, but he didn't sit near me. He took the last seat in the first row, as if that seat had been waiting for him all summer. Our homeroom teacher didn't seem to care where anyone sat, so I sat up front and opened my briefcase.

Homeroom was extended on the first day so all the school's rules could be explained. Most of the students paid little attention. Even our homeroom teacher seemed bored with it and looked relieved when the bell for passing to the first class rang.

I did make some friends during the course of the school day: a pair of redheaded twins named Rea and Zoe, who told me their parents deliberately had looked for names with the same number of letters, a heavy black girl named Haley Thomas, and a tall, very thin boy named Randal Wolfe who was the school's chess champion. There was another girl named Ashley who remained in the background, too shy to say anything. The twins wore matching dresses and had their hair styled in a similar fashion. They told me they enjoyed playing tricks on people and even their teachers by pretending to be each other from time to time.

"When we get married, we'll do it to our husbands, too," Rea said, laughing.

We all sat at the same table and ate lunch together. I looked for Bernie, but he wasn't in the cafeteria. Later, when I saw him in the hallway, I asked him where he had been. He looked embarrassed and very nervous because I had stopped him to talk. His eyes shifted from side to side, and then he looked down at the floor when he replied.

"I eat lunch in the bio lab. Mr. Friedman lets me. I get work done and sometimes help him set up his equipment for his classes. He lets me run some of my own experiments from time to time, usually after school," he added, and looked up. "How do you like your first day so far?"

"It's okay. I really like my English teacher and our math teacher," I said. Bernie was in my math class.

He nodded.

"Mr. Albert is the best one to have for geometry. We're lucky. I gotta go to gym," he said, moving away. "I'm always late for gym."

I watched him walk quickly down the hallway, and then I went to the library for my study period. I didn't see him again until the end of the school day when I stepped onto the bus. Helga was up front with Alicia. She smiled at me.

"Bernie's in the back," she said.

"You're not funny," I told her, but she laughed anyway.

I made my way back, passing Ashley, who sat alone looking as if she wanted to ask me to sit with her. Bernie glanced up at me and then looked at the textbook he had opened. I sat across from him and gazed out the window.

"Your friend Helga's been saying things about us," I heard him say, and turned.

"What did you say?"

"Some of the guys in my gym class were saying things about us," he told me.

"First, she's not my friend. I met her for the first time when I met you. And second, I don't think I could be friends with her. She's not very nice."

He didn't move his lips, but his eyes smiled.

"I wondered how you could be friends with her," he said, and then looked at his book again.

We rode in silence all the way back to our neighborhood. My stop was before his. I said good-bye, and he nodded and looked at his book again. Helga had already gotten off. She was waiting for me on the sidewalk.

"I'm not trying to be mean," she said. "I was just teasing you. I'd really like to be friends."

"Why?" I asked her.

"Why?"

"Yes, why do you want to be friends with me?"

"I don't know. Why does anyone become friends with anyone?" she replied.

"Usually because they have something in common, they like the same things, they want to do the same things," I said.

"So?"

"So when you think of something you and I might like to do together, let me know," I said, and walked away. Maybe I was being unforgiving; maybe I just didn't trust her. Whatever the reason, it felt good.

I heard the television set when I entered the house and knew what soap Thelma was watching and how important it was to her, but I remembered what Karl had said to me in the morning and how much he was hoping I would help bring Thelma back to reality.

"Hi," I said, and she looked up.

"Oh, Crystal, you're back from school. I want to hear all about your first day. Just a minute, and there will be a commercial," she said.

"I'll go change first," I said.

She nodded, her eyes already drawn back to the screen. When I returned, the television was turned off and Thelma was sitting quietly in the rocking chair, moving back and forth slightly and staring down at the floor.

"Mom?" I said, and she looked up, her eyes blank for a moment and then suddenly coming on like a pair of tiny lamps.

"Oh, Crystal. I'm stunned. Just at the end, Brock told his mother he's gay, and all this time I thought he was in love with Megan. I mean, I never would have known." She shook her head. "What's her mother going to say?"

"Um, I'm not sure," I said, not knowing how to answer her. I decided instead to tell her about my day. "I like my new school."

"What? Oh, yes, the school. How was your first day?"

"It was good. I like most of my teachers."

"Did you make any friends?" she asked, as if that was the main reason for school.

"A few," I said. "I ate lunch with a pair of twins."

"A pair of twins? Isn't that something? Girls?"

"Yes, Rea and Zoe. They're very nice."

"Rea? Where did I hear that name before? Rea? Oh, yes, *Yesterday's Children*. Rea was Lindsey's lost sister."

"This Rea is real, Mom. I can call her on the phone and speak with her. I can go places with her. I can study with her. I can touch her. She's real."

Thelma stared at me as if I had lost my mind. "That's nice, dear. Oh, I better get started on dinner. Would you like to set the table?"

"Of course," I said, feeling frustrated.

When Karl came home, he asked me many more questions about school. In fact, we had one of the longest conversations we had had since I arrived. Every once in a while, both of us would look at Thelma. She would simply smile.

"It's so nice to have real family conversations around the dinner table," she finally said.

Karl beamed and then winked at me. I felt as if he and I were co-conspirators.

Right after dinner, the phone rang and Karl called to me. "It's for you," he said.

"Oh, good," Thelma said. "She's making friends quickly."

I couldn't imagine who it could be. I hoped it wasn't Helga.

"Hello," I said hesitantly.

"I got my new slides today, cross sections of human heart tissue. I thought you might be interested," Bernie said without saying hello.

"Yes, I would be interested," I replied.

"Can you come over?"

"Now?"

He didn't answer.

"I suppose so," I said. I held my hand over the mouthpiece and asked Karl and Thelma, telling them what Bernie had to show me.

"As long as you don't stay out too late," Karl said. Thelma just smiled.

"I'll be there as soon as I finish helping clean up our dinner dishes," I told Bernie. He hung up without saying good-bye.

"You don't have to help me," Thelma said. "It's not much. Go on."

"Are you sure, Mom?"

"Of course."

I went to my room and got my light jacket. When I started out, Thelma was at the door.

"You're going to go look at cross sections of a human heart?" she asked.

"That's what he says."

She shook her head. "I'm sure that's interesting. Is he a good-looking boy?"

"He's all right," I said. "I'm really more interested in the slides."

She tilted her head like a puppy when it hears a totally confusing noise. Then she smiled, laughed, and said, "Wouldn't it be something if you could see love under a microscope, too? Then we'd know if someone was really heartsick." She laughed again. "Have a good time," she called back as she returned to the kitchen.

I shook my head and laughed myself. It would be something if we could see feelings and know if they were honest and true.

Then everyone would know if I really was more interested in the slides.

6
My Tutor

Bernie answered the door himself. The house was dark and quiet.

"Maid's night off," he muttered, and stepped back.

"Where are your parents?" I asked as I entered. After having lived all my life in orphanages and now living with Thelma, who kept the television on the way some people kept on lights, it seemed strange to enter a home that was so silent.

"Out," he said. "At a meeting or a dinner or something. They left numbers in the kitchen, but I didn't look at them. Come on," he said, leading the way down the hall to his room.

He had the microscope out and the new slides beside it. Next to that was a plastic replica of the human heart.

"These cells come from heart muscle," he said, and

glanced into the microscope. He had yet to look at me directly.

I stepped up beside him and waited, and then he moved to the side.

"Go on, take a look," he said.

I sat and looked through the eyepiece. I had to adjust the focus to fit my vision, but it soon came in clear, and I was amazed at the detail I could see.

"This came with it," he explained, and read from a sheet of printed material.

" 'We studied cardiac explants and autopsy hearts of patients with chronic congestive heart failure caused by either a dilated cardiomyopathy or ischemic heart disease and compared them with normal hearts. In control hearts, endothelial cells rarely were positive for PAL-E. In hearts of patients with ischemic cardiomyopathies, there was distinct staining with this marker.

" 'Conclusions: A phenotypic shift in endothelial antigen expression of the coronary microvasculature occurs in both ischemic hearts and hearts with dilated cardiomyopathies, as revealed by PAL-E, compared with control hearts. The change may relate to compensatory mechanisms in long-standing chronic heart failure.' "

He put the paper down as if he assumed I understood any or all of it. I shook my head. "Where did you get all this?"

"A friend of my father's works at a cardiovascular research lab in Minnesota. He sent it. My father tells everyone I'm some sort of scientific genius, and they send me things." He gazed at the sheet. "This is heavy research."

"Let me see it," I said, and he handed me the paper. I reread most of what he had read aloud. "No way could I understand it." I shook my head. "This might as well be in a foreign language. I mean, I know what some of the words mean, but putting it all together . . . I guess they've found a way to diagnose a heart problem."

"Right," he said. He looked relieved that I didn't know much more than he did.

I gazed at the cell under the microscope again.

"It is interesting to know that this was once part of a human being," I said.

"I didn't show you half of it before. I've got cells from all sorts of human organs," he said with more excitement in his voice. He went to his special small file cabinet and opened a drawer. Gazing in, he read from the labels. "Liver, kidney, lungs, ovaries, the prostate, even some brain cells."

It was almost as if I had gone shopping at a department store for human cells and he was the salesman. I couldn't help but smile.

"What's so funny?" he asked sharply.

"Nothing," I said, not wanting to make him feel bad. "It's just unusual to see someone have all that in his room."

He slammed the drawer closed. "I thought you would be interested and even excited about it," he said.

"I am! Really, Bernie, I am," I cried.

He looked at me sideways, his eyes narrow with suspicion.

"I mean it. I'm sorry," I said.

He hesitated and then opened the drawer again. "You want to see anything else?" he asked.

"I'd like to see a brain cell."

He brought it over and set it up in the microscope. Then he stepped back, and I looked.

"You know there are about ten billion of those in your brain," he said as I studied the cell. "The brain controls every vital function of our bodies and even controls our emotions like hate, anger, love."

This time, I did laugh.

"What?"

"My mother, Thelma," I said, looking up at him, "asked if we could see love in the heart cell."

"That's an old medieval belief that love is centered in the heart. I told you. It's all in the brain," he corrected. "And you can't see feelings."

"I know. It was just a silly little idea."

"Right. It is silly," he said. He started to put away the slides. "Do you know what you want to be?" he asked me.

"Maybe a doctor. I like writing, too. I might even be a teacher," I said, and he grimaced. "You wouldn't want to be a teacher?" I asked.

"Hardly," he said, turning back to me. "I couldn't put up with giggly girls and jocks and all their problems."

"But good teachers are important," I said.

"I'm not going to do that," he insisted. "Pure

research is what I want to do. I don't want to put up with stupid people."

"But why do it if you don't care about people?" I asked.

"I care. I just don't want to be . . . interrupted and annoyed."

"Not everyone will be annoying," I insisted.

He stared at me. "You like to argue, don't you?"

"No, but I don't mind having a discussion," I said. He finally smiled, a small twitch of his lips in the corners and a brighter light in his green eyes.

"You hungry?"

"No. I just finished supper, remember? Didn't you eat your supper?"

"No. I got too involved with my new slides and forgot. The maid left me something to warm up. You want to watch me eat?" he asked.

"Is it as much fun as looking at the slides?"

He laughed. "You're the first girl I've met who's easy to talk to," he said.

"Thanks, I guess."

"Come on," he said, and I followed him to the kitchen. It was three times the size of ours and had appliances that looked as if they belonged in a space station.

"What is that?" I asked, pointing at a machine on the counter.

"That? A cappuccino machine. My mother likes her cappuccino after dinner. Whenever she eats at home," he added. He opened the giant refrigerator and took out a covered plate. "Lasagna," he said. "I just have to put it in the microwave for a couple of minutes."

I watched him do so.

"How about something to drink? Lemonade, iced tea, soda, milk, beer?"

"Beer!"

"You never had it?" he asked skeptically.

"Not really," I said. "I'll have whatever you have."

He poured us both some iced tea. There was a place setting all ready for him at the dining-room table. It was a large, oval, dark oak table with thick legs. There were twelve captain's chairs set around the table, and above us a large chandelier dangled on a gold chain. Behind us, the wall was all mirror. Against the far wall was a grand hutch with matching wood, filled with dishes and glasses that all looked very expensive.

Bernie brought his food out and set it down. "Our maid is a good cook. Otherwise I'd starve," he quipped.

"Your mother doesn't cook?"

"My mother? She couldn't boil water without burning it," he said.

"You can't burn water."

"It's a joke. At least, it was supposed to be."

"How often do you eat alone like this?" I asked.

He paused and thought, as if I had given him a difficult question to answer. "On the average, I'd say four times a week."

"Four!"

"I said average, so you know that there are weeks when it's more," he lectured.

"You should be a teacher," I said. "You like pointing things out, and I bet you love correcting people."

He gazed at me a moment and then smiled. "You want to do our math homework after I eat?" he asked.

"I did it before dinner," I said.

"I did it on the bus," he countered.

"So why did you ask?"

He shrugged. "I thought I'd help you."

"Maybe I would have helped you."

He laughed again and then grew serious, his eyes small and fixed on me intently. Bernie had a way of looking at people as if they were under his microscope. It made me a little uncomfortable.

"What?" I said.

"I was wondering what it was like for you, living in an orphanage," he said.

"Here I go again." I moaned.

"What?"

"That's all anyone wants to know."

"I was just curious, from a scientific point of view," he added.

"You really want to know? I'll tell you, it was hard," I fired at him. "I didn't feel like I was anyone. I felt like I was dangling, waiting for my life to start. Everyone is jealous of whatever lucky thing happens to anyone else. Counselors, social workers, adults who come around to choose a child make you feel like you're . . ."

"Under a microscope?"

"Yes, exactly. And it's no fun. You're afraid to make friends with someone because he or she might be gone the next month."

"What about your real parents?" he asked.

"What about them?"

"Why did they give you up?"

"My mother had me out of wedlock," I said. "She was too sick to take care of me. I don't know who my father is, and I don't care."

"Why not?"

"I just don't," I said, tears burning under my eyelids. "So, to answer your question, it wasn't pleasant," I concluded in a tone that was much sharper than I intended.

Bernie didn't wince or look away. He just nodded. "I understand," he said.

"Really? I don't see how you could unless you were an orphan, too," I replied, not in a very generous mood.

He looked around the room and then at me. "I *am* an orphan," he said nonchalantly, as if it was an obvious fact. "An orphan with parents. It's always been like this. My mother treats me as if I was some sort of space creature. She had a difficult pregnancy with me, and she had to have a cesarean delivery. You know what that is, right?"

"Of course."

"So she never had any more children, and if she could have, she probably would have aborted me. Once, when she was angry at me for something, she said that," he added hotly.

"How terrible," I said, shaking my head.

"My father is disappointed that I'm not a jock. He tries to get me to go down to his place and work with his mechanics, to build myself or, as he puts it, to build character. He thinks character comes from sweat."

He dropped his fork onto the plate with a clang that nearly made me jump in my seat.

"Sorry," he said. "I know you don't want to hear this garbage."

"That's all right. I'm just surprised, that's all," I said.

"You're surprised? You can imagine how surprised I am. Well," he said, pushing back from the table, "they leave me alone and buy me whatever I ask for. You know what I think." His eyes were now looking glassy with tears. "I think my own mother is afraid of me. She hates coming into my room. She says she can't stand looking at those specimens I have in jars and that it smells. Does my room smell?"

"No," I answered honestly.

"All she wants to do is buy me what's fashionable in clothes. That's practically the only time I go anywhere with her."

I looked down. How strange it was to hear someone with parents sound more unhappy than I was without them. Maybe he was right; maybe there were more orphans out there than I could have imagined.

"Did you ever have a boyfriend at the orphanage?" he asked softly.

I looked up and shook my head. "Everyone I meet wants to know that, too. Even Thelma asked me that," I said.

"I just wondered what kind of boys you liked," he said.

"I like boys who are honest and intelligent and caring about someone else's feelings as much as they are about their own."

"What about looks?"

"It helps if they don't have a wart on the tip of their nose or an eye in the middle of their forehead," I said, and he laughed.

"I think you're nice," he said. "I think you're nicer than most girls I know who aren't orphans. You must have good genes," he concluded. "Your mother must have been nice, too."

I looked away.

"What did she die of?" he asked. I was silent. "What was her sickness?"

"She was a manic-depressive," I shot back at him, and stood up. "She died in a mental hospital. I'd appreciate it if you wouldn't tell anyone. So, you see, my genes are not so good after all. I've got to go home," I said. "I told them I wouldn't be here that long."

"I'm sorry. I didn't mean . . ."

"It doesn't matter. Thanks for showing me your slides," I said, and headed for the door.

He came after me and took my arm to stop me before I opened the door. "I'm sorry," he said. "I didn't mean to ask so many personal questions."

"It's all right. I've got to learn how to deal with it," I said. "I'm just afraid, that's all, afraid of becoming her."

"You won't," he assured me.

"I won't? What about your belief about genes?"

"You have your father's genes, too."

"He was worse," I said, without going into it.

"Well, you have grandparents. There are lots of combinations and influences on who we are."

"When do we find out?" I asked him, my tears now bubbling at the lids.

"Find out what?"

"Who we are."

"We're always making discoveries about that," he said.

I opened the door.

"Hey," he said, stepping out alongside me.

"What?"

"Thanks for coming over." He leaned in before I could react and kissed me quickly on the cheek.

"Why did you do that?"

He shrugged. "My genes, I guess," he said, and laughed as he stepped back inside and closed the door.

I stood there for a moment with my hand on my cheek where he had kissed it. It had happened so fast, too fast. I was disappointed.

That's the first time a boy ever did that to me, I thought as I started for home. I tried to understand the excitement that made my heart thump and brought a heat to my face. There was a movement of feelings through my body, a current that rushed in waves from my legs, through my stomach, and up around my heart, sending trickles of electricity down to the very tips of my fingers. Was this love, my first love?

My eyes were filled with his green eyes. His smile fit like a glove over mine. My brain of ten billion cells was a kaleidoscope of emotions. I felt sorry for him living like an orphan in that big, beautiful, expensive house. I wanted to go back and be with him. I wanted to hold him in my arms and tell him how to overcome the loneliness, a loneliness so strong that even all the money in the world, buying all the things he could fancy, wouldn't stop it from making his heart ache. I wanted to kiss his cheek, and then I wanted our lips to touch.

I wanted more, and what I wanted frightened me.

I closed my eyes but quickened my steps. When I opened them, I was standing in front of my new home.

I started to laugh.

It was funny. When I had left, Thelma had asked if I could see love under the microscope.

Maybe I had.

7
Seeing Stars

Falling asleep was harder than ever after I returned from Bernie's house. Thelma kept me busy with chatter about a new nighttime serial she had watched for the first time. She described the entire first episode in detail, including its settings and all its major characters. My mind wandered even as she spoke. I could hear her droning on, and I watched her animated face go through all the emotions, plucking a sigh from here, a laugh from there, and then loading up on smiles and tears before she finished with the declaration, "This is the best evening program I've seen."

I promised to watch it with her next time and then went to my room to finish my homework and organize my notebook. My stomach felt as if it had a mad bumblebee buzzing around inside. I couldn't concentrate on anything and found myself gazing out the window at the stars. I was hypnotized by the glitter and twinkle of the jeweled sky, and when I did think, I realized I had rarely spent time looking at the night sky when I lived at an orphanage. I always felt shut up, contained, and chained by bureaucratic rules and paperwork that left me feeling small and alone, just another number in some official's logbook, just another problem for society. It was better to remain unnoticed, to fold up in some corner, swallow back my tears, hide my face in books, and close the shades on my windows. There was no place for stars or for dreams in that world.

But now, after just one day at my new school, meeting new people, feeling like someone, I saw myself as reborn. I unfolded like a flower that had been stuck between the pages of the child welfare system's books. I was free to grow, to feel, to cry, and to laugh. I had a home. I had a name. I had a right to be alive and to be heard.

I couldn't help feeling like a fish out of water, however. Expressing emotions, having an opinion, and being confident around other kids my age was so new it all made me anxious and even a little afraid. Now, more than ever, I didn't want to fail. I couldn't be a disappointment to people who had invested their faith in me. I would be the best possible student, I thought. Karl would be very proud. I would help Thelma forget the ugliness and disappointments in her past, and I would give her as well as myself a reason to face a new day.

And then I would permit myself to grow into a woman. This frightened me most of all. As long as I was still seen as a little girl, I was safe, even in the orphanage. I lived in some neutral place without sex, unnoticed and unremarkable, especially by boys.

Bernie's kiss had suddenly changed all that. I felt like Sleeping Beauty. Of course, I had thoughts about sex and romance before, but somehow I never thought of myself as potentially someone's lover. I was still an observer, the little girl who sits beside the older, far more sophisticated girls and listens with wide eyes and interest to the intimate stories describing events and experiences that were still more like fantasy or science fiction but never something that would happen to me.

Now it could happen to me. I touched the place on my cheek where Bernie had kissed me, and then I rose and gazed at myself in the mirror. Was my face more mature? Would anyone look at me now and think that's a pretty young woman?

I laid out my nightgown on the bed and then went to the bathroom, brushed my teeth, took off my clothes, and returned, but I didn't put on my nightgown. Naked, I stood before the mirror and studied my body, noting the shape of my blossoming breasts. When I turned on an angle, I saw how my body was taking shape, how the curves were softening and filling out.

My heart pounded as I looked at myself this way. I felt as if I had nudged some part of my inner self that had been hibernating. It lifted its head and smiled, welcoming my curiosity. Yes, I could hear it whisper from within, I am here, I am ready to take you on a new journey full of exciting feelings and emotions. The biological streams flowing inside will join and rush over every dry part of you. Anyone looking at your lips, your eyes, or touching your hand will see the heat and the hunger. I will make you a woman. My body was filled with the promise.

I put on my nightgown and crawled under the covers until I was snug. The soft, plush pillow was a cloud beneath my head. I was floating over the lightning and thunder of excitement I had aroused in myself, but still I tossed and turned for hours until I finally settled into a warm pocket of sleep, exhausted.

The sound of doors closing, the quick, heavy beat of footsteps, the cries coming from Thelma jerked me out of the darkness. I listened. Either Karl or Thelma rushed up the stairs and back to the bedroom. Thelma was crying. I rose quickly and went to my door.

She was standing in the hallway with her coat on. She saw me and wiped away the tears that were streaming down her cheeks so hard they actually dripped from her chin.

"Oh, Crystal, you're up. I'm sorry we woke you, but maybe it's better."

Karl came out of the bedroom wearing his coat, too.

"What's wrong?" I asked.

"It's my mother!" Thelma cried. "She was just rushed to the emergency room. We have to go. My father is so upset he could have a stroke."

"Should I get dressed?" I asked.

"No, no," Karl said. "This could be hours and

hours. You go back to sleep, and tomorrow morning, if we're not back in time, you take the bus to school. We'll be fine." He put his arm around Thelma's waist.

She reached for me and held me against her for a moment. Then the two of them hurried on.

"Isn't there anything I can do?" I called to them.

"No, no, just go back to sleep," Karl replied.

Their footsteps died away as they turned and headed for the garage.

I went to the window in my room and gazed out to watch them drive off. The street was otherwise deserted, the small patches of illumination from the lights creating a quilt of yellowish white in the darkness all the way to the corner and beyond where Karl's car turned and disappeared into the night.

The house was deadly quiet. It had all happened so fast, I felt as if I had dreamed it, especially after I crawled back under my covers and closed my eyes. It was far more difficult now to fall asleep, but shortly before the first light of day, I did. The alarm woke me. Otherwise, I would have slept through most of the morning.

I took a long shower and made myself some oatmeal. As I ate my breakfast, I looked toward the phone, hoping Karl would call before the bus came, but he didn't. I was tempted to get myself to the hospital instead of going to school, but I thought it might upset them more, so I finished getting dressed, gathered my books, and went out to wait for the bus.

Helga was already standing at the bus stop with Ashley Raymond, whose mother, Vera, was practically the only neighbor Thelma spoke to, and only because Vera was into watching soap operas, too.

"Isn't Karl taking you to school today?" Helga sang.

Ashley was about my height with light brown hair and a pair of large blue eyes too big for her small mouth and nose. She gazed at me. She always looked like a frightened doe to me. I had said about four words to her before this.

"Something happened to my grandmother last night, and he and Thelma had to rush to the hospital. They're still there," I explained.

If there was any sympathy in Helga, it was down so deep in her heart it would take an oil rig two weeks to find it. She smirked and nudged Ashley.

"Bernie will be happy. He'll have someone to sit with," she said.

"What's wrong with your grandmother?" Ashley asked quietly.

"I don't know. They rushed out too fast for me to ask questions," I said.

"I know her. She's a nice lady," Ashley said.

"Yes, she is."

"How many times did you actually even meet her?" Helga fired at me, as if I had no right to comment.

"It doesn't take long for me to know who is nice and who isn't," I said, fixing my angry eyes on her. She had to look away, but with a short, little laugh.

The bus arrived, and we boarded. I made my way to the rear, where Bernie was sitting and reading. He didn't even realize I was there until I sat beside him.

"What are you doing on the bus?" he asked with surprise.

I told him, and he shook his head.

"That's too bad."

"I hope she'll be all right," I said.

"Me, too. My mother's terrified of becoming old," he said after a moment, "but not because she might die. She's afraid of wrinkles and dry skin and gray hairs. She's had two cosmetic surgeries this year alone and"—he lowered his voice to a whisper—"a tummy tuck. You look tired." He studied me harder.

"I am."

We heard loud laughter and looked up front, where Helga and some of the other kids were talking and gazing back at us.

"When I first met Helga, I thought it would be nice to have a friend. I never really had a close friend," I said. "I almost made a big mistake."

"The woods are full of wolves," he muttered, staring at them. Then he turned to me. "I'll be your close friend if you like."

I smiled. "Okay," I said.

He went back to his reading as if looking at me was painful now. I sat with my eyes closed and shut out the chatter and the laughter until we reached the school and the beginning of my second day.

It was nearly impossible to concentrate in class. I couldn't help wondering and worrying. At lunchtime, Bernie escorted me to the pay phone and waited as I called home. The phone rang and rang until Karl's voice came on from the answering machine, asking the caller to leave a name and number, time of call, and a brief statement of the call's purpose. It sounded more like the message at an office than at a house. I left my name.

"No one's home yet," I told Bernie.

He thought a moment. "Well, that's good. Whatever's being done for her is still being done."

Bernie was a little reluctant about returning to the cafeteria to have lunch with me, but he agreed, and we sat together at a small table toward the rear. From this position, we could see that many other students were looking at us and talking about us.

"It feels like we're in a fishbowl," Bernie quipped. He ate and read his science book, pausing occasionally to talk about something from our class work.

I began to wonder if his kissing me was something I had imagined. He showed so little interest in me and actually jumped in his seat when our arms grazed each other. Other girls who had boyfriends sat closer to them, some practically on their laps, laughing and talking to each other as if there were no one else in the cafeteria. When the bell rang to end the lunch hour, they walked off holding hands. Bernie and I walked side by side but clutching our books as if they were life vests and we were on the deck of a sinking ship. I saw from the way some of the other girls looked at us, whispering and giggling, that we were already the subject of very nasty jokes.

My next class was nearly half over when the speaker on the wall clicked and a voice requested that my teacher send me to the principal's office. Everyone looked at me as I rose and left the room. The principal's secretary told me to take a seat and wait. A few minutes later, the door opened, and there was Karl with Mr. Nissen. I didn't need to hear any words. The expressions on their faces told all.

"I didn't want to take you out of school, Crystal, but Thelma is asking for you and thinks you should come right home with me," he said.

"Of course." I didn't know what else to say.

"Don't worry about your homework. I'll see to it that your assignments are sent to the house," Mr. Nissen said.

"She won't be out that long," Karl assured him.

"Take whatever time she needs," Mr. Nissen said. "Please give Mrs. Morris my sympathies."

I realized I had left my briefcase, books, and notebooks on my desk and had to hurry back to get them. Everyone turned my way when I entered and went to my desk. Our teacher paused. I gathered up my books and put them into the briefcase quickly.

"What are you doing, Crystal?" Mr. Saddler asked.

I went up to him. It wasn't the sort of thing I wanted to shout out. "I'm sorry, Mr. Saddler, but I have to go right home. My grandmother has died."

"Oh," he said. He looked awkward and confused, like someone who had stepped onto ice. "Of course. I'm sorry."

He waited for me to leave before he started the class again. As I walked toward the door, I looked over at Bernie. He nodded at me, his face as tight and as serious as a doctor giving his patient's loved ones hard news. I left quickly, the door closing behind me softly, and then I hurried down the corridor to where Karl was waiting. We walked out together, neither of us saying a word until we were in his car.

"What happened?" I finally asked.

"The doctor said she didn't have much more than fifteen percent of her heart muscle working by the time she was brought in. They did the best they could. She lasted longer than they thought she would. Thelma says that was because of you."

"Me?"

"She says her mother wanted to stay with us longer so she could see you grow up in our family. It's what she believes, and it's what makes it sadder for her," he said. "I'm sorry that you've had such a hard beginning with us," he added.

"How's Grandpa?" I asked.

Karl shook his head. "Fragile. I don't know how he is going to last alone. As sick as she was, Thelma's mother took good care of him," he said.

"What's going to happen to him?"

"As soon as I can, I'll start looking for a good adult residency for him. We can't take him in with us. We don't have the room," he added.

If I hadn't come to live with them, they would have the room, I thought. I felt just terrible about it. Would Grandpa resent me? Would Thelma?

"I could share my room with him," I suggested.

"Of course you can't," Karl said. "Besides, we can't give him the attention he's going to need.

Thelma's not good at looking after sick folk. If I get a cold, she panics. Don't you get sick," he warned. "Those damn shows put all sorts of ideas in her head about this illness and that. Mention a pain, and she'll give you an episode on *Community Hospital* that fits it. No, don't worry about Grandpa. I'll see to him," Karl promised. "With his insurance and retirement pension, he can afford something decent."

That didn't make me feel any better about it, but I didn't say anything else. When we entered the house, I saw a glow coming from the television set, yet as we drew closer, I didn't hear anything.

"We're back," Karl called, and stopped in the doorway.

Thelma was sitting in her favorite chair, staring at the silent television screen, her face streaked with tears. She looked up at me, and her shoulders shook.

"Poor Grandma," she said. "She wanted to have a grandchild so much, and just when she had one, she goes and dies. It's so unfair. It's like . . . like the electricity going off just at an important part in one of my programs."

"I'm sorry," I said, certain that her mother's death meant more to her than a power outage. She was just upset. "She was very nice. I was hoping to get to know her a lot more."

"You poor dear. Now you have no grandmother," she cried.

I didn't know whether or not I should run to her side and hug her. She turned from me and stared at the television screen.

"Do you want something to eat, Thelma?" Karl asked. He turned to me. "She hasn't eaten a thing all day."

"I'll make you something, Mom."

She smiled through her tears. "Maybe just some tea and toast with a little jelly," she said. "And then come and sit beside me for a while."

Karl and I went to the kitchen and got her tea and toast together on a tray that I started to bring back to her.

"Do you think you'll be all right here?" he asked me before I returned to Thelma. "I have to stop at the office for a few minutes."

"Yes, we'll be fine," I said.

He told Thelma what he was doing, but she didn't respond. She didn't turn from the silent screen until I brought the tray to her and set it up on the coffee table. I watched her nibble the toast and sip the tea, her eyes shifting with the movements of the actors on the surface of the picture tube. Keeping the sound off appeared to be her gesture of mourning.

"The funeral is the day after tomorrow," she said during the commercial. Her eyes still remained fixed on the screen, as if she was afraid that if she didn't keep looking at it she would fall apart. "Karl has everything arranged."

"Where's Grandpa?" I asked.

"He's home with some of their friends. People about their age. He's more comfortable at home," she continued. She nibbled some more of her toast and sipped her tea. "When you lose someone you love, you're better off being where everything is familiar, doing the things you're accustomed to doing. Grandma wouldn't want me to miss my show," she added when the program continued.

I stared at her, and then I looked at the set. The characters were obviously screaming at each other in an argument of some kind. What good was it watching with the sound off? Thelma shook her head as if she could hear the words anyway.

"Isn't it better if we just talk, Mom?" I asked softly.

"Talk? About what? Not about Grandma," she said, shaking her head vigorously. "I don't want to talk about her dying. She wasn't supposed to die," she said firmly, as if someone had rewritten a script. "She wanted to watch her granddaughter grow up. I told Karl we should adopt a child a long time ago. We shouldn't have waited to get you. Now look at what's happened. It doesn't fit," she said. "It all doesn't fit."

"We can't plan our lives like a soap opera is planned, Mom. We don't have that power." I wanted to add "yet," because I believed that someday science would crack all the mysteries of genetics and a great deal about our lives would be predetermined, but this wasn't the time to bring that up, I thought.

She shook her head. "I don't want to talk about it," she said. "It's too sad." She looked at the television set. "You're never home for this one. I told you about it, though. This is the one with the daughter who has AIDS. Her parents are blaming each other. See?"

I looked down at the floor. I was far from an expert

on mourning the death of a loved one. Until now, I had no loved ones. No death had ever touched me deeply. Even when I read about my real mother, it was more like reading a story about someone else. I didn't have her face in my mind, her voice in my memory. I couldn't recall her touching me, kissing me, speaking to me. I had no father, no grandparents, no relatives' deaths to mourn. I never even had a close friend or someone at one of the orphanages with whom I had grown so close that I was saddened by their passing or departure.

Being alone had its advantages, I thought. I could only mourn myself. I need only be sorry about myself.

Helga was right in a sense. I hadn't known my new grandmother long enough to feel as deeply about her death as most grandchildren would feel about the deaths of their beloved grandparents. Shouldn't I be crying? Shouldn't I be in a corner somewhere, sobbing? I wasn't sure about my own feelings and actions. I wasn't even sure I should be criticizing Thelma for what she was doing. Maybe it was wrong to take away her distractions. Maybe it was wrong to force her to face the reality of her mother's death.

She finished her toast and smiled at me. "I'm glad you're here with me," she said. "I'm sorry you're missing class, though."

"It's all right. I'll get the work sent home. Bernie will probably bring it over later," I conjectured.

"That's nice. You can sit closer to me," she suggested.

I moved closer, and she reached out and took my

hand. Then she turned back to the silent television screen. I watched her face. The shadows and the light bounced off it, leaving her with a smile and then with a look of pity or disgust. Occasionally, she sighed or smacked her lips in criticism. I widened my eyes in astonishment. It was truly as though she knew what they were saying.

I wanted to ask her how she could watch the show this way. I wanted to point out that the sound was off, but I couldn't get myself to do it. It was like telling someone what they saw wasn't real, that it was only make-believe.

Thelma needed make-believe, I thought. Who was I to tell her she couldn't have it or she shouldn't believe?

I let her hold my hand tighter and sat beside her in silence.

It was the way Karl found us when he returned.

8
Truth or Dare

After dinner, Ashley and her mother, Vera, came to offer condolences to Thelma. Ashley had all the homework I had missed at the end of the day, even from the classes Bernie and I shared. She told me he had given it to her on the bus. I felt let down because I had hoped he would bring it over himself. Sometimes my eyes were like windows with the shades up. Ashley took one look at me and saw the disappointment.

"Bernie's really very shy," she said. "I'm probably one of the few people he speaks to once in a while, and that's only because I never make fun of him. I think he's brilliant."

"He *is* brilliant," I said. I took Ashley to my room while her mother visited with Thelma and Karl.

"What was it like living in an orphanage?" she asked as soon as we were alone. Was there anyone who looked at me and didn't wonder about that? "Were the adults cruel to you?"

"It's not like an orphanage in a Dickens novel," I said.

"What's a Dickens novel?"

"Charles Dickens? *A Christmas Carol? Tale of Two Cities? Hard Times?* Doesn't any of that ring a bell?" I followed with a frown.

"Oh yeah," she said, but she still had a blank look on her face.

"What I mean is, it isn't like living with your own family, having your own room, but you're not made to shovel coal or wash floors, and you don't have to wear rags and eat gruel."

"Gruel? Ugh."

"You don't have to eat it," I emphasized. "I wasn't happy there, but I wasn't being tortured."

She nodded. "Helga says girls who live in orphanages lose their virginity faster," she commented.

"What? Where does she get the right to make such a stupid statement? How does she know about girls who live in orphanages?" I demanded.

Ashley shrugged. "It's just what she says."

"Well, for your information and for hers, it isn't so." I saw the way Ashley was staring at me. "I haven't lost mine," I added. "It sounds to me like Helga's lost hers."

Ashley laughed. "Sometimes I think she wishes she did. The way she chases after some of the boys, I mean. She told me she would let Todd Philips do anything he wanted if he took her out."

"She said that?"

"Uh-huh." Ashley nodded, those big eyes even bigger.

"She might be disappointed," I muttered.

"Why?" Ashley asked quickly. "I thought that was the most wonderful thing that could happen."

"Who told you that?"

She shrugged again. "I just listen to what the others say, especially those who've had sex and brag about it in the girls' room. They make it sound wonderful."

"Well, I wouldn't really know . . . I've never . . ." I was about to tell Ashley I'd never even been kissed, but I didn't really trust that she would keep that information to herself. "I've never been one to kiss and tell," I said instead.

We talked a while about movie star kisses and who we thought kissed best, and I could tell that Ashley was as curious about what it would be like to kiss a boy as I was.

After Ashley left, I began my homework, eager to think about something other than boys. Before Thelma and Karl went to sleep, he returned to my room.

"Maybe you should go to school tomorrow, Crystal. There's really no point in your sitting around here all day."

"Won't Thelma need me?" I asked.

He thought a moment. "She'll sleep a lot," he said.

"Just the same, I think I'll stay nearby," I offered.

He smiled. "Okay. You're probably right. It's nice to have someone else in the house who cares about her," he added. I thought he might come farther into my room and kiss me good night, but he stood there, nodding a moment longer, and then he said good night and closed the door.

It takes time to become father and daughter, I thought, and with some it takes a lot longer.

Thelma didn't rise as early as she ordinarily did the next morning. Karl brought her some breakfast and then asked me to look in on her after a while. He said he was off to check on Grandpa before going to work. I offered to go along, but he said he would have to bring me home afterward and that would add too much time to his being away from his office.

"You'd be surprised how the work piles up on me," he said.

"Won't they understand at the company?" I asked him.

"No one supervises me more than I supervise myself," Karl replied. He nodded, his eyes intense. "That's the secret to being successful, Crystal: demand more of yourself than others do. You're your own best critic, understand?"

"Yes," I said.

He left, and I sat quietly, reading ahead in my history book, imagining what the next assignment would be. A little over an hour later, Thelma appeared in the living-room doorway. Her hair was disheveled, her eyes bloodshot. Her skin was ashen. She looked as if she had aged years in one night. She had a half dozen tissues clutched in her hand. Still in her nightgown, she shuffled across the room in what looked like

Karl's slippers and plopped with a deep sigh into her favorite chair.

"Would you like something, Mom?" I asked.

She shook her head. "I don't like thinking about my mother," she said softly. "It hurts. I wanted to go to the phone to call her this morning like I usually do before *Shadows at Dawn.* I actually lifted the receiver before I remembered she was gone."

She sniffled and wiped her eyes. "What can I do?" she cried.

"We could talk, Mom. Sometimes it feels better when you talk about what's bothering you," I said. My counselors always used that line on me when I was at the orphanages. There really was some truth to it, however.

Thelma stared at me a moment. "I can't," she said, shaking her head. "Every time I think about her, I start to cry. I can't. It's better not to think." She snapped up the television remote as if it were a bottle of pills promising relief.

She turned on the television set and flipped through the channels until she found a program she liked. This time, she left the sound on, too. She began to react to what she was watching, smiling, laughing, looking concerned. I had begun to read again when I suddenly heard her say, "I dread going to the funeral tomorrow. Why do we have to have funerals?"

"It's our last chance to say good-bye," I said, even though I had never been to a funeral before and the very thought of going put almost as much apprehension in me.

"I don't want to say good-bye." She moaned. "I hate good-byes. I wish I could just sit here and watch it on television. That way, if it got too sad, I could turn it off, turn to something else."

"My psychologist at the orphanage always told me it's worse to avoid your problems, Mom. It's better to face them and deal with them," I said softly.

She stared at me a moment and then smiled. "You're so smart," she said. "We're lucky to have you. I will have something to eat. Could you make me some scrambled eggs and toast?"

"Sure," I said, getting up quickly.

"And some coffee," she called as I started out. Then she turned back to her program.

Thelma remained there most of the day, getting up only to go to the bathroom. I made her lunch as well. She didn't talk unless she had a comment to make about something she was watching. The highlight of her day began when her first soap was on. After that, I might as well have gone to school. Karl called to see how she was and to tell me that he had someone taking care of Grandpa. I told him what Thelma was doing.

"Maybe she's better off," he said.

"I'm not doing much," I complained. I wanted to add that he'd been right. I should have gone to school.

"You're there. That's something," he said. "She probably wouldn't eat anything otherwise."

He was right about that, but I still felt more like a maid than a daughter. I wanted to talk. I wanted to hear Thelma tell stories about her mother, about what it was like being her daughter, the things they had shared, their precious moments, all that she would miss. I wanted to feel that I was part of a family and not back in the orphanage with strangers.

When Thelma started to cry about what was happening to a character on her program, I got up and went to my room. How could she care so much more about make-believe people? Was it because it felt safer? The program ended, and you didn't have to think about them anymore? Was that it? But Thelma seemed to think about the characters constantly, not just when the show was on. I couldn't make any sense of it.

A little while later, the doorbell rang. It was Ashley and her mother again, only this time Bernie was with them.

"Hi," I said, smiling mostly for Bernie's benefit.

"How's she doing?" Mrs. Raymond asked.

"She's been watching television, trying not to think about it," I said.

"I don't blame her," Mrs. Raymond said.

"We brought all your homework," Ashley said. "And Bernie came along to help explain anything new."

"Thanks."

I stepped back, and everyone entered. Mrs. Raymond went to see Thelma, and I took Ashley and Bernie to my room. Bernie opened the math book and began to talk about the new problems immediately. I listened and nodded when he asked if I understood.

Ashley sat on my bed and watched us work. When his explanations ended, Bernie sat at my computer.

"So when is the funeral?" he asked.

"In the morning. There won't be many people there. Karl's father isn't able to travel, and his brother in Albany can't get away. His younger brother is at sea. None of Thelma's cousins are coming. Some of my grandparents' older friends will be there."

"And my mother will be there," Ashley said quickly. "She won't let me. She says I have to go to school."

"She's right," Bernie said. "School is more important. Funerals are really unnecessary."

"Unnecessary? How can you say that?" Ashley asked.

"When someone dies, it's over. There's no point in wasting any more time about it."

"That's a horrible thing to say," Ashley declared. "You have to pay respect."

"To what? The person's gone. You're better off saying good-bye to a picture," he remarked. "I hated going to my grandfather's funeral. There was a big party afterward, full of people who really never knew him. It was just an excuse for a party."

"We're not having anything afterward," I said.

"Good," Bernie said.

"That's cruel, Bernie Felder," Ashley charged.

"I'm just being realistic," he said. "When you die, you return to some form of energy, and that energy goes into something else. That's it."

"What else?" Ashley asked, her eyebrows hoisted so high they were practically in the middle of her forehead.

"I don't know. Maybe . . . a plant or a bug."

"A bug! Crystal, you don't believe that, do you?"

"I don't know what I believe," I said. "Sometimes I imagine my real mother is with me, her spirit, but then I think that's silly."

"It's not silly. It's beautiful," Ashley said. "I'm not going to be any bug, Bernie Felder. Maybe you are."

"Maybe," Bernie said casually.

"You don't care?"

"Why should I care? I won't know anything different," he said, and Ashley groaned.

"I swear," she said. "Scientists are the most boring people. I hate the subject, especially experiments with all those smelly chemicals and dead worms. Experiments make me sick."

"I bet I can think of an experiment you'd like. How about an experiment to find out what kind of kisses we like best?" I asked her, thinking she'd call my bluff.

"Crystal!" she said, shifting her eyes to Bernie.

"What kind of experiment?" he asked excitedly.

I made up an experiment that was almost like a contest—judging the best kiss. He listened and nodded without laughing. Ashley's face turned pink when I turned to ask if she was willing to join in.

"Interesting," Bernie said. "I don't see how it's really scientific . . ." He thought a moment and then nodded at me. "But I'd like to be part of it."

"Good," I said.

"What?" Ashley cried. "Crystal, I thought you were just kidding!"

"Don't be chicken, Ashley," Bernie said. "It's not like we're doing anything serious—just kissing."

"But I don't want to be judged against Crystal . . . I've never kissed a boy before!" she cried, turning to me for help.

I wanted to make Ashley feel better and tell her I'd never kissed a boy, either, but I wanted to keep my inexperience from Bernie. "You'll have to swear to keep this a secret. You know what someone like Helga would do if she found out."

Ashley looked at Bernie and then at me apprehensively.

"You're not going to get pregnant or anything like that," Bernie promised. "You're just going to discover more about yourself, and it will be knowledge that will make you wiser, stronger. That's the purpose and power of knowledge."

"He's right," I said. "Okay?"

"Maybe," Ashley said. "I'll see," she added cautiously, but I could tell she was almost as intrigued about it as we were.

Bernie volunteered to set up what he called the control procedures. He said we would be more secure if we met at his house. With some reluctance, Ashley agreed.

"This is like playing doctor," she whispered to me when we left my room.

"Did you ever do that?" I asked. She shifted her eyes to Bernie and then to me.

"No," she said. "Did you?"

"No, but I wanted to," I admitted.

She took a small breath and said, "Me, too."

Then she hurried to join her mother and leave, frightened by her own confession.

The funeral the next day was simple and took less time than I expected, probably because Karl had everything so well organized. After the church service, the undertaker's car took us to the cemetery. Grandpa looked very fragile, clinging to the arm of a special-duty nurse Karl had hired. Thelma seemed like someone drugged, right from the moment she woke and dressed. Whenever I looked at her, her eyes were unfocused and distant. It was as if they were open but shut off, and she was not seeing or listening to anything that went on around her. She had retreated into her own mind. Maybe she was replaying one of her television programs.

Karl led her about, moving everyone along gracefully and efficiently. Some of the people from his office attended the church service, but at the cemetery, there were only two other elderly couples who had been friends with Thelma's mother, her father and the nurse, Thelma, Karl, me, Ashley's mother, and the minister.

It really wasn't a good day for a funeral. It was too warm and bright with a nearly cloudless sky, the blue more like turquoise. At the cemetery, the air was filled with the aroma of freshly cut grass. Birds flitted from tree to tree, and squirrels frolicked about the tombstones as if the entire cemetery had been created for their sole pleasure.

I couldn't help wondering what my real mother's funeral must have been like. I imagined myself finding out where she was buried and going to visit her grave someday. What would I say? Who would hear it, anyway? Was Bernie right? Was there nothing left of us afterward, or did something precious linger, something we didn't understand, couldn't understand?

On the way home, Thelma finally spoke. She said, "Poor Mom. I hope she's not alone."

That was what Thelma was most afraid of, I thought, being alone. For years, her television programs had provided her with the families and friends she never had in real life. They had filled her life with distraction and kept her from thinking about her own loneliness. Karl thought adopting me would help, but I still didn't feel I was giving them much, and I certainly didn't feel we were a family. At least, not what I thought a family would be like.

Grandpa came home with us to eat, but he fell asleep in his chair after having only a few bites. He looked as if he had shrunken and withered with his sorrow. I hoped in my secret heart that someday, somehow, I would find someone who loved me as much. That, I thought, was the true antidote to loneliness, the best cure of all.

Two days later, Grandpa had a stroke and was taken to the hospital. He didn't die, but he was so incapacitated Karl had to arrange for him to be placed in permanent institutional care. Thelma couldn't stand the thought of visiting him in such surroundings.

"Why do we have to grow old?" She moaned. "It's

not fair. Elena doesn't look a day older than she did when I first started to watch *Shadows of Forever.* We should all live inside a television program."

Karl shook his head helplessly and went back to his business magazine. I returned to my homework, and our lives continued as if we were three shadows searching for a way to become whole again.

We visited Karl's father, but it wasn't any more successful a visit than the first one. He grew impatient with Thelma's sad demeanor and Karl's criticism of his lifestyle and went off to be with his friends. A few days later, Karl's brother Stuart finally drove over from Albany to meet me and offer his sympathies to Thelma. He was taller and thinner than Karl, but he had colder eyes and a hard, chiseled face on which a smile settled only fleetingly. He asked me questions about school but seemed uncomfortable when I spoke to him and looked at him. I noticed he avoided my eyes and didn't look directly at me when he spoke to me.

After Stuart left, Karl revealed that his brother had almost become a monk. He said it was still possible that one day he would.

"People make him nervous," he said. "He cherishes solitude."

"How does he work as a salesman, then?" I asked. "Salesmen have to meet people."

"He does most of his work over the telephone. He's a telemarketer."

I was disappointed. I had been hoping my uncle would be friendlier and more fun. I had even imagined going to visit him in Albany. I complained about it to Bernie and Ashley the day after.

Ever since we had decided to be part of an experiment, Ashley began to hang around with me, and consequently with Bernie, more at school. She sat with us at lunch.

"My biggest hope was that I would become part of a real family," I said, "and have relatives with parties and birthdays, anniversaries and weddings. All of it. Sometimes I feel more alone than I was at the orphanage."

Ashley looked very sad for me, her eyes full of pain, but Bernie sat musing for a moment as if I had brought up a topic from science class.

"Family is overrated," he suddenly declared with that confident, really arrogant air in which he answered questions and made statements in class. "It's a myth created by greeting-card companies. People are too into themselves to be that sort of thing anymore."

"That's terrible. My family isn't into themselves," Ashley protested.

Bernie's eyebrows nearly touched as he creased his lips. "Your father is always traveling. You told us that yourself a few days ago, and your mother is terrified of becoming old, just like mine. Face it," he said, nodding at me, "we're not so much different from Crystal. No one really listens to us. Usually, we're in the way. At best, we're a mild annoyance."

"I'm not!"

"We're all orphans," Bernie muttered. "We're all searching for something that's not there."

"That's not true. You don't believe that, Crystal, do you?"

"I don't know," I said. "I don't want to believe that, but I don't know."

Ashley looked terribly distraught, ready to get up and run away. Then Bernie leaned in to whisper. "Let's not worry about all that. Let's get to our experiment. I'm ready," he said. "My house tonight, about seven-thirty. Okay?"

I looked at Ashley. Her face suddenly changed from dark to light, her eyes shifting nervously as she looked at me and then at Bernie.

"Fine," I said. "Ashley?"

"Okay," she said in a small voice. "But I'm not an orphan."

Bernie laughed. I hadn't heard him laugh that hard before. It brought a smile to my face, and that made Ashley smile, too.

Across the cafeteria, the other students who had been looking at us with disdain were now suddenly full of curiosity about us.

But nowhere near as much as we were about ourselves.

9
In the Name of Science

"This is a graph," Bernie began, holding up a grid. "There's one for each of us."

Ashley and I sat on two chairs in his room while he stood and lectured. Ashley said it felt as if she were back in school. I asked her to be patient.

"This will be session one," he continued, closing and opening his eyes with annoyance. "We will do the same things each session and rate our reactions to them on a scale of one to ten, ten being the most intense. Our objective is to determine how kissing affects us, which kisses we like best, and so on. Understand?" he asked. He did sound and look like Mr. Friedman, our science teacher.

"No," Ashley said, shaking her head. "It sounds like gobbledygook. What does a graph have to do with kissing?"

"The graph doesn't have anything to do with it. It's

just a way of recording reactions scientifically." Bernie sighed with frustration. He looked at me. "You see why I could never be a teacher?"

Bernie shook his head, took a deep breath, and returned to his chart.

"We'll meet here every night over the next week or so," he said.

"I still don't understand what we're doing," Ashley whined.

"Ultimately, we're going to see which kinds of kisses we like best, dry, quick pecks or long, wet ones," Bernie said a bit cruelly. "You have thought about kissing a boy before, right? Just pretend I'm whatever boy you're in love with this week, and plant one on me."

Ashley sucked in her breath and held it. She looked as if she might explode. Her eyes bulged. She looked from me to Bernie and then started to shake her head.

"I won't do that," she said. She kept shaking her head.

"You're not going to sit there and tell us you've never thought about kissing a boy?" He was getting exasperated. "It's natural to think about it."

She couldn't get any redder, I thought, and I felt myself blushing as well. All this talk about kissing was making me as nervous as Ashley.

"It's very important that we're honest with one another," Bernie emphasized. "In science, honesty is essential. We can't hide truth, and we can't pretend. No one here is going to laugh or make fun of anyone else, either. We're serious, and we're going to be adult about it, right, Crystal?"

"Yes," I said, surprised myself at how clinical Bernie made it all seem. It didn't even sound sexy or mysterious. Which is how I always dreamed it would be.

"Why is he the one telling us everything we have to do?" Ashley complained.

"You asked me to help with this experiment, and I've done it," Bernie said.

"I didn't ask. Crystal and I were curious about kissing, and you butted in, right, Crystal?"

"Yes, but we need Bernie's help."

"You're going to do this?" she asked.

"Yes," I said, looking at Bernie, who seemed more determined and purposeful than ever. "I'm very interested, and I know we'll learn a lot more about ourselves."

She glued her huge eyes to my face for a moment.

"Well?" Bernie demanded.

"All right," Ashley said. "If Crystal's going to do it, I'll try."

"Good," Bernie said. He walked over to his door and locked it. Then he went to the windows and closed all the blinds tightly. Ashley's eyes followed his every move. He handed each of us a graph.

"The numbers at the side correspond to the activities," he explained. "It will be easier if we just refer to them by their numbers. On the top as you see are the dates, beginning with today. As long as we keep this scientific, we'll do fine," he added.

He went to a cabinet under his wall of shelves and opened it.

"What's that?" Ashley asked before he had a chance to explain.

"It's a digital blood-pressure cup, and it also records pulse."

"Where did you get that?" she asked, as if it were some forbidden fruit.

"You can get these anywhere, Ashley. They sell them in drugstores. It's no big deal," Bernie said. "Now, when you're aroused," he continued in his scientist's voice, "your blood pressure should rise and your pulse, of course, will quicken. Let's take our blood pressures and pulses right now before we do anything else, so we'll know what to consider normal and what not, okay? Who's first?"

"I'll start," I said, and Bernie fit the cup around my arm. When I was done, he measured Ashley.

"You must be a little nervous," he said. "I wouldn't expect your pressure to be this high."

He did his own, which was as low as mine.

"How come you two are so calm?" Ashley asked suspiciously. "Aren't you nervous, Crystal?"

"No." It was true. Now that we were ready to begin, I was more anxious than nervous to find out what it felt like to be kissed.

She looked skeptical. "Now what?" she asked.

Bernie sat across from us, crossed his legs, and gazed at his notes.

"Now, we should kiss. Ashley, you want to go first?" he asked.

Ashley popped up from her chair like a jack-in-the-box. She fumbled with the door lock and ran out before Bernie could ask her what she was doing. Moments later, we heard the front door slam.

Bernie and I looked at each other.

"I don't think she was quite ready for this," he said with a smile.

"I think you did all that just to get rid of her," I said, finally beginning to understand why he had been so clinical.

His eyes met mine as he tried to hide the truth.

"I knew she wouldn't be ready. Why waste time with her?"

"Why did you want to do this?" I asked. "Remember," I quickly followed, "honesty is essential in science."

He started to smile and stopped to put on his serious face again. "I've had different feelings about you, different from what I've felt about other girls, and I wanted to understand why," he explained.

"So this is still an experiment?"

"Yes," he said. "What else could it be?"

I wanted to say it could be love; it could be romance. I wanted to say that maybe we shouldn't dissect our feelings, that maybe that would destroy them, but I didn't say anything. I didn't want to drive him away, and there was an excitement that started as a small trembling in my legs and moved up my spine until my heartbeat quickened.

"Should we get on with this?" Bernie asked. His eyes were full of anticipation and hope.

Once, at the orphanage, I had caught a girl named Marsha Benjamin in a very passionate embrace with a boy much older than she. His name was Glen Fraser, and I remember being afraid of him, afraid of the way he looked at me. I was too young to understand why at the time, but when I saw him and Marsha kissing, his hand under her skirt, his body moving roughly against hers, forcing her to turn so that he could move between her legs, I gasped first in fear and then in astonishment. I started to run away but stopped, unable to shut my curious eyes. The truth was, I was fascinated with Marsha's face, with the way she let her head fall back, with her small moans, and especially with her hands, first trying to stop it all from happening and then, suddenly, apparently filled with uncontrollable excitement, pulling her hand away from his to hold him behind his neck as if she were clinging to him for dear life.

He turned and saw me standing there, watching them. He didn't get angry. He smiled coolly and said, "There's room for one more."

I ran. I ran so hard and fast someone would have thought I was being pursued by a monster. Years later, I would think the monster was inside me. I wanted to conquer it, to be unafraid, and I thought that would never happen until I was fulfilled and loved by someone I could feel good about. Now I wondered if Bernie could be that person.

"Yes," I replied finally, "let's go on with it."

Bernie smiled, and then, as if he read my thoughts, he said, "We'll go slowly, of course, and if either of us is uncomfortable, we'll stop immediately. That would only ruin the experiment, anyway."

"Fine," I said, swallowing back the lump of nervousness that tried to rise in my throat.

Bernie walked over and began to kiss me. I closed my eyes and let my mind drift, but I could feel my heart pounding crazily, and I worried that Bernie could feel it, too. I pulled away, and Bernie slowly dropped his hands from my shoulders.

Bernie lifted his eyes slowly and gazed at me.

"How do you feel?" he asked.

"Very nervous," I said.

"You're the bravest girl I ever met. I didn't think you would do this," he confessed, and I thought I heard a faint quiver of nervousness in his voice.

"I told you," I said, trying to sound brave, "I'm as interested as you."

He nodded.

"What do we do next?" I asked.

"Why don't we try a French kiss? You know, with our tongues?" he said. "You tell me everything that's happening to you, and I'll do the same, okay?"

I nodded. I began to wish I'd left with Ashley, but I knew it was too late to turn back now. Besides, I was curious about Bernie and the way his kiss had made me feel.

"Ready?"

"Yes," I said. I looked up at the ceiling and then at him, and we both stood there.

His eyes drank me in from head to toe. I had never had a boy look at me the way Bernie was doing. It made my head swim.

"My heart is pounding," he said. He began to walk

around me. "I'm nervous, and I'm afraid I might do something wrong," he admitted. He sounded like someone reporting from outer space—as if I weren't in the same room as him, experiencing the same feelings and emotions.

"Me, too." I wanted to be honest about my reactions, for the sake of the experiment, of course.

"What?"

"Everything you said," I said, my voice cracking, my eyes closing as he walked around me. I could feel his breath on my neck. A moment later, he was in front of me again, only inches away.

"I'm going to close my eyes," he said, "and then I'm going to try this French kiss thing, okay?"

He closed his eyes and kissed me.

I wasn't too sure I liked this kind of kiss. I felt as if I could tell what Bernie had had for dinner. I'd seen kids kiss in school like this, and they seemed to enjoy it, so I decided to try to like it. After a while, my heart began pounding stronger, and my hands started to feel sweaty. This time, though, it was Bernie who stopped our kiss.

"Wow." He shook his head as if he were trying to clear the fog out. "*Now* I see what all the hype is for."

"Um . . . yeah, me, too." I couldn't help but wonder if kissing all boys felt this nice.

"I think we should stop for tonight, but I definitely want to try this again. As long as we keep it experimental, of course," he added.

"Experimental . . . of course," I answered, trying to keep the disappointment out of my voice. I was never one of those girls who got all dreamy when they talked about boys and kissing, but I never thought it would be cold or clinical, either.

"I wonder if Ashley's going to tell her other friends about this," he said.

"I'll make sure she doesn't."

"They'll make up stories about us anyway," he said, holding his eyes on mine. "They probably already have."

"Probably," I agreed.

There was a long moment of silence between us. To me, it was as if we had fantasized the kisses we'd shared. It had all been so fast it was one blurry memory. Only the graph in my hands with my comments confirmed that I hadn't been dreaming.

"I'd better get home," I said.

"I'll walk you." He smiled at my surprise. "I don't think I could do any reading, concentrate on anything, or go to sleep for a while anyway," he explained.

I laughed to hide what I was feeling, the same excitement still echoing in my body.

He opened the door, and we started out. We were almost to the door when we heard someone call from the living room.

"My mother," Bernie said under his breath.

A very elegant-looking woman, dressed as if she was on her way to an important ball or just returning from one, came toward us, her long diamond-studded earrings swinging from her lobes. Her styled hair was nearly platinum, the strands so perfectly shaped I wondered if she was wearing a wig. She was tall, with an hourglass figure that seemed held together by wires and pins. When she stepped out of the shadows and drew closer, I saw that her face was so free of wrinkles it looked like a mask. Her temples were stiff, pulling back on her eyes as if her skin had shrunk. Her nose was small, but the nostrils were a little too large. The puffiness in her lips made her smile seem painful. It was more of a grimace.

The fingers of her left hand were full of rings. She looked like a walking jewelry store with her diamond necklace, hairpin, and bracelets. I thought she might have taken a bath in expensive perfume. The scent arrived days before she did.

"Who's this, Bernard?" she asked.

"A friend," he said quickly.

"Why don't you introduce me? You've never had a friend over before, and especially not a female friend," she said, her eyes fixed on me.

"This is Crystal," he said. "Crystal, my mother."

"Hello," I said quickly.

"Crystal who?" she asked without replying.

"Crystal Morris," Bernie said. "She was just going home."

"Morris? Which Morris is that? Charlie Morris from the advertisement agency?"

"No," Bernie said. "I'm walking her home." He practically lunged at the front door and opened it.

"It's nice to meet you," his mother said as I started after him. "It's about time Bernie brought someone home," she added. She looked as if she could shatter her face by changing expression too rapidly. I gazed back at her once and then hurried to catch up to Bernie, who was already out of the house.

He closed the door behind me and nearly jogged down the walkway.

"Maybe we shouldn't have run out like that, Bernie," I said, catching up. He walked faster.

"All she wants me to do is have girlfriends, listen to rock music, and dress like some teenage movie or television star," he muttered. "Look at her," he said, stopping and gazing back at his house. "If that was your mother, would you want anyone to meet her? She just likes to embarrass me." He started walking again. " 'It's about time you brought someone home,' " he mimicked. " 'Especially a female friend.' "

"She's probably just worried about you," I offered.

"No, she's not. She's worried about herself, about what it will look like if I'm not a so-called normal young man. Let's not talk about it. It just gets me angry," he said.

We walked silently until we reached my house. It was an overcast night, and there was a chill in the air. Our breath could be seen in vague little puffs. Neither of us was really dressed warmly enough.

"You hold onto these," he said at the door. He handed me the graphs. I hadn't noticed them clutched in his hand.

"We should probably just leave them in your room," I said.

He shook his head. "Sometimes, when I'm in school, she goes into my room and searches it, looking for something bizarre. I deliberately left a dissected frog reeking from formaldehyde on the table one morning, and she stayed away for a while, but she still spies on me from time to time. I don't want her finding these papers," he said. "She would never understand."

"Okay," I said, taking them. I was certain Karl and Thelma wouldn't understand, either, but I wasn't ready for our experiments to end.

"Good night." He hesitated. "I really enjoyed our experiment," he said. "I'm looking forward to tomorrow." He turned to leave and then stepped back to kiss me quickly on the cheek again.

I stood there with my hand on my cheek, watching him disappear up the sidewalk. Then I went inside, my brain whirling, a potpourri of emotions making me dizzy. Karl was still up, but Thelma had gone to bed.

"She was very tired tonight. She kept falling asleep in her chair, so I got her to go to bed," he explained. "How are you doing?"

"Okay," I said.

"Good. Well, the worst is over," he declared. "Now we'll return to a normal life."

What is a normal life? I wanted to ask. Was it a life full of loneliness and fear? Was it a life in which we ignored each other? Thelma wasn't all that different from the day I had arrived. Instead of returning to the real world because of me, she continued to work at getting me to join her in make-believe. Karl remained steadfast and loyal to his organized schedule. I had met many new kids my age, but many of them seemed even more troubled than I was, and they had always had families!

"I'm going to sleep, too," I said. "Good night."

"Good night. See you in the morning," he called, his eyes still following the words on the page of the magazine in his hand.

I went to my room and got ready for bed. After I slipped under the covers, I leaned back on my pillow and reached for the graphs. I knew what I had written on mine, but I didn't know what was on Bernie's.

His numbers were as high as mine, but what he wrote on the bottom drew my interest.

I have never been strongly attracted to anyone this way before. I wonder if this means Crystal is special or if it is a natural reaction to kissing a pretty girl.

Most everyone else, I thought, would think what he wrote was very strange, but I knew this was the only way Bernie could say "I love you."

For now, it would have to do.

I had great hope for tomorrow.

Tonight, for once, it was easy to close my eyes, dream, and fall asleep.

10
Heart's Desire

Ashley looked frightened when I confronted her at school the next day. Bernie had been afraid that she would go around spreading stories about us, but instead, she was afraid we would spread stories about her.

"Did you stay?" she asked me in a whisper when we met at our lockers in the hallway. She checked to be sure no one could overhear our conversation.

"Yes," I said.

"And did you do it?" she quickly followed.

"Of course," I said, slamming my locker shut and starting for homeroom. She trailed along like a puppy tugged on an invisible leash.

"What happened?" she gasped.

I stopped and spun on her. "If you want to know so much, why didn't you stay?"

"I couldn't," she said, her face looking as if she would break into hysterical sobs any moment.

"Did you tell anyone? Helga, for example?"

She shook her head so vigorously I thought her eyes would rattle.

"Good," I said, continuing on to homeroom. She remained beside me, step for step, until she saw Bernie, and then she lowered her head and went to her seat.

Bernie looked at her and then at me, his eyes full of questions. I indicated it was all right, and he relaxed his shoulders. He didn't speak to me until we were passing to our first class. When he approached, Ashley stepped away again.

"I can't meet you for lunch today," he said. "I promised to help Mr. Friedman set up his equipment."

"Okay," I said quickly.

"Is everything all right?"

"Yes," I replied.

"Then you'll be at my house the same time tonight?"

I paused, and he searched anxiously for the answer in my eyes.

"We'll move on down the chart," he added.

"I'll be there," I said. We walked on to class. At lunch, Ashley couldn't wait to join me.

"Are you going to tell me what happened?" she asked as soon as she put her tray on the table and slipped into the chair beside me.

"We only kissed twice," I remarked, my voice as coldly factual as could be.

"Only two? Why just two?"

"It's hard to explain it to someone who wasn't

there," I said, "but it was all very scientific. Nothing bad happened."

She actually looked disappointed. "Did you like kissing him?"

"No. I mean yes. I mean . . . listen, I can't talk about it like this," I said sharply. "It makes it sound dirty."

She nodded as if she understood. "I'm not trying to make fun of you, Crystal. It's different for you and Bernie," she said sadly. "You're both so smart. I felt like I didn't belong there with you two, and I was frightened. If you ever want to tell me anything, I promise I'll listen and keep it all to myself."

I saw that although she couldn't be part of our experiments, she wanted to feel as though she was special, as though she was in on it and had clearance to know top-secret things. Ashley is still a little girl, I told myself. For her, this is all still a game, like "you show me yours, and I'll show you mine." However, if I drove her away, she could turn on us and might spread stories.

"Okay," I promised. "I'll tell you stuff when there's something to tell, when there are real, scientific conclusions."

She smiled. "Can you come over to my house Friday night and have dinner with me and my mother?" she asked. "My father is still away on a business trip," she added before I could ask. From the way she spoke about him, I understood that he was away almost as much as he was there. "Maybe you can help me with my math for the big test next week."

"I'll ask my parents," I promised. She beamed.

I understood that Ashley wasn't very popular and was rarely invited to anything. The other girls treated her as though she was socially below them, an outsider because of her size and timidity. Despite what had occurred at Bernie's house, I was rapidly becoming her best friend. She looked up to me and liked the fact that although the other girls weren't necessarily friendly, they were not anxious to challenge me head on, either. Years of institutionalized life had hardened my outer shell, perhaps. I was certainly unafraid of girls like Helga, back-stabbers who gossiped about you in the girls' room but shut right up when you were face-to-face with them. They had so many misconceptions about orphans. If they wanted to believe I was capable of scratching their eyes out, let them, I thought. Long ago, I learned that if I couldn't have another girl or boy like me for who I was, it was better they feared me. At least then I was safe.

As the school day drew to a close, I felt excitement building inside me like distant thunder on the horizon. Every once in a while, a small jolt of electricity shot through my heart. My stomach sizzled and didn't stop. I could barely eat dinner. How far would we go on Bernie's chart? When I gazed at the pages alone in my room, they felt like fire in my hands. The heat traveled up my arms and swirled around my heart. Looking at myself in the mirror, I saw how flushed my cheeks were and how charged my eyes appeared. Would Karl take one look at me and understand? Would Thelma, whose daily dose of passion through the television set could choke Venus?

"Are you feeling all right tonight, Crystal?" Karl did ask at dinner.

Thelma looked up anxiously.

"Yes," I said. "I'm just a little concerned about my first math exam."

"Oh," Thelma said with a laugh. "You'll probably get a hundred. Won't she, Karl?"

"She'll do well," he agreed. "Being nervous about your tests is all right as long as it doesn't interfere with your performance. It's the students who don't worry about their tests who do the worst. You're a truly self-motivated young lady, Crystal. We're very proud of that, aren't we, Thelma?"

"What? Oh, yes, we are, dear. The other parents are going to be so jealous of us," she added happily. "Your school grades were one of the first things Karl considered, right, Karl?"

"Yes, they were," he admitted.

I gazed at both of them and thought for a moment. If I had received C's instead of A's, they wouldn't have adopted me. It didn't seem right somehow to base so much on test results, certainly not when it came to making someone your daughter. If my grades fell off, would they give me back?

"Ashley Raymond asked me if I would have dinner with her and her mother this Friday," I said. "Would that be all right?"

"Actually," Karl said, "that would be perfect. I don't think we'll be back in time for dinner. I was going to have Thelma prepare something for you to heat up."

"Back in time? Where are we going, Karl?" Thelma sounded confused.

"Don't you remember, Thelma?" he asked softly. "We have an appointment with the doctors and administrator at the clinic concerning your father's condition. He's going to have to be moved to another facility where he can get more round-the-clock attention."

"I hate doing those things," she muttered. "Can't we just phone them?"

"No, dear. There are papers to sign. It won't take that long." He smiled at me. "Thelma doesn't like to remember sad things. With the time it takes to go to the home and back, I didn't want you waiting on us for dinner, Crystal."

"Maybe she can go with us, Karl?"

"You just heard her say Ashley invited her to dinner, Thelma. Let her get to know other children her age," Karl declared. "You want her to have friends, don't you?"

"Yes," she said in a small voice. Ever since her mother's death, she seemed to be even more withdrawn and afraid of real life. I thought if she could crawl right into the television set or into a book, she would.

"That's settled, then," Karl said.

Thelma started to eat again and then stopped.

"You know what's on tonight, Crystal? *Romance Theater*, and it's a brand-new story," she said.

"I'm studying for my math test with Bernie

Felder," I said. It wasn't a total lie. I expected Bernie and I were going to do some of that.

"Oh. Well," she said, thinking, "maybe I'll tape it for you to watch with me later this weekend, okay?"

"That would be nice," I said, and she looked satisfied.

Karl stared at me with troubled eyes. I avoided his gaze and finished my dinner. After helping Thelma with the dishes, I went to my room, gathered my books, and stuck our graphs into my notebook. Thelma was already involved in a television program. Karl was settled in his chair, reading the *Wall Street Journal.*

"Don't be too late," he called when I went to the front door.

"I won't." I took a deep breath and went out.

It was a clear evening, the stars looking somehow bigger, brighter. The street was quiet, but the shadows looked deeper and longer, and my heart filled my ears with a thumping so loud I didn't hear any cars go by. When I reached Bernie's front door, I felt as if I had floated to it. My finger trembled against the door button. I heard it ding inside, and moments later, Bernie opened it.

"Hi," he said.

"Hi." I stepped in, half expecting to see his mother, too, but as usual, his house was quiet.

"No one's home," he said quickly, and followed that with a conspiratorial smile. "Don't worry. We're not going to be interrupted."

"I thought we might study a little for the math test, too," I said.

"Sure, but it's going to be easy. Mr. Albert's first tests always are. He likes to give everyone the feeling they can do well. False hope," he quipped as we walked to his room. As soon as we entered, he closed the door and then turned to me. "Did you bring the graphs back?"

"Yes," I said, taking them out of the notebook and handing them to him.

He gazed down at them as if he had forgotten what was written.

"Good," he said, and looked at me. "Are you ready?" I hesitated, and he looked worried. "You still want to go on with the experiment, don't you?"

"Sure, sure I do." I wanted to tell him how much I'd been thinking about our kisses, but I was afraid he wouldn't want to continue if I wasn't serious about the experiment.

I couldn't help but hope that for Bernie too, our experiment was more than just a scientific test.

Bernie's kiss started off sweet like the first time, but soon he became more insistent, forcing me to kiss him deeper and longer. These sorts of kisses made me nervous, but not in the good, special way I'd felt before. As Bernie pressed his lips and then his body against mine, I couldn't help but feel that he wanted to do more than just kiss.

Pushing him away, I took a step backward.

"Bernie, stop, we need to take breaks to write down our results." I hoped I sounded calm; inside I felt as if my heart would break from beating so quickly.

"Aw, come on, Crystal, it was just starting to get

interesting." He stepped toward me and reached out to put his hands on my shoulder.

"Bernie, no, I'm not comfortable with this." I turned away and walked toward his desk. I grabbed my chart and started to write down my results, but my hands were shaking so badly I couldn't do much more than scrawl.

"Crystal, I don't understand. Did I do something wrong? Don't you want to continue with the experiment?" Bernie sounded hurt, and although I knew we had to stop this, I didn't want him to think I didn't like him.

"No, Bernie, it's nothing like that. It's just that . . . this is starting to feel like more than an experiment . . . and I don't think I'm ready for that." I hoped he would appreciate my honesty.

"Well, fine, Crystal. I guess you're just like Ashley . . . too scared to do anything adult, even in the name of science!" He stormed to the bedroom door. "I can't believe you're acting like this is something . . . something wrong or dirty or whatever. You're obviously way younger than I thought. I think you'd better leave, Crystal. And don't bother coming back."

As I ran out of Bernie's house, tears streaming down my face, I couldn't help but feel I was wrong to have ended our experiment. I wanted to be able to return. Bernie was my friend. I didn't mean to make him feel we'd done something dirty. In fact, I was beginning to think there was something special between us, that what we were doing meant something. And I hoped maybe Bernie thought that, too. Now I guess I'd never find out how he really felt about me. If his thoughts were of me when we were kissing . . . or if he was really only thinking of charts and graphs.

Maybe Thelma was right—it was much easier to be involved in someone else's life on TV than it was to be involved in your own real life.

At my house, I stopped and sat on a lawn chair to catch my breath. I didn't want to go inside looking and feeling as I did. They would wonder why I was home so soon, anyway. Before Bernie, I thought, I had never had a boy even try to kiss me.

The night air chilled me. I embraced myself and rocked back and forth. I couldn't throw off the bad feelings.

How hard it was to get someone to love you in a way that made you happy, I thought, but how desperately we wanted it and needed it. Suddenly, Thelma didn't seem as silly and distracted to me as I had believed. She only wanted to be loved as much as the characters on her soap operas were loved.

Karl and Thelma looked up when I entered.

"Home so soon?" Karl asked.

"There wasn't much to study." I gazed at the television set. "So I thought I would come home and watch the program with Mom."

"Really?" she cried.

Karl looked at me suspiciously, his eyes narrowing.

"Everything all right?" he asked.

"Yes."

"Why wouldn't everything be all right?" Thelma

demanded. "She's home to watch the show with me. That's all."

She absolutely glowed. Her eyes were bright with happiness.

"Yes," I said. "Yes, I am."

"You're just in time," she said, and made a place for me beside her.

11
Shattered Dreams

Bernie was waiting by my locker in the morning. I glanced at him and went right to unlocking my combination lock.

"I'm sorry," he said. "I think we just went too fast on the chart. Can't we try again?"

"No. I think we were right yesterday. Let's wait and see what happens naturally." I hoped I sounded more sure of myself than I felt.

"You're the only person I would have ever done this with," he said sadly, turned, and walked away.

Ashley was watching from across the hall. She hurried over to me.

"My parents said I could come to your house for dinner Friday night," I said. Her eyes brightened like Christmas tree lights. "Don't ask me any other questions," I said sharply. "Not a single one."

She took one look at my face and nodded. Bernie

wasn't there at lunch, and he avoided looking at me in class. I put all my concentration into my schoolwork, driving every other thought from my mind. Ashley was so afraid of my demeanor, she walked and sat quietly beside me all day, becoming talkative only after the final bell, when we were on our way to the bus.

"I'll tell my mother you're coming. After we eat and study our math, maybe we can listen to some music. I bought two new CDs this week. Do you like Timmy and the Grasshoppers?"

"I never heard of them." I turned to look at her. "I rarely listen to rock music."

"Oh," she said softly.

I sighed deeply. "But maybe I should be brought up to date. Sure," I said. "We'll listen to some music."

"Great."

She bounced ahead of me onto the bus. Bernie was in the rear in his usual seat already. He kept his eyes on his book. I took a seat in the middle, and Ashley got in beside me.

"Aren't you two becoming the cozy ones?" Helga quipped as she walked past.

"Jealous?" I asked with a cold smile.

"Of what?" she shot back, glancing at her friends for the applause she expected in their eyes.

"Of intelligence, personality, charm, wit, in short, everything you're missing," I fired back.

Her mouth opened and closed as she searched for some proper response, but the kids behind her in the aisle shouted for her to move along, and she just twisted her shoulder and tossed back her hair.

"You're not afraid of anyone, are you?" Ashley asked with a voice full of admiration.

I thought. "Yes," I said.

"Who?" she wanted to know.

"Myself," I said.

Of course, I knew she wouldn't understand. It would be years before she would.

The next two days were much the same. I put most of my attention and energy into my schoolwork, my first term paper, my first big set of exams. At night, I took some time to watch television with Thelma, and she and I began to talk about other things. I learned more and more about her own childhood, her dreams and disappointments. Karl looked pleased and came up with the plan for us to take a weekend holiday in Montreal, in Canada, in two weeks. That made Thelma even happier, and I began to believe that maybe we could be a real family after all.

On Friday, after school, I returned home, changed, did some of the schoolwork I wanted out of the way, and then walked over to Ashley's house. Her mother was very happy to see me. I was actually embarrassed by all the attention. No one, not even Thelma, was so attentive, fawned over me so much, and worried that I wouldn't like what she was preparing for dinner, concerned that she had what I liked to drink and what I liked for dessert.

"How often is your father away like this?" I asked Ashley when we were alone in her room after dinner. The empty chair at the head of the table was conspicuous. It gave me an eerie feeling, as if a ghost were sitting there. Whether out of habit or just to keep the table looking balanced, Ashley's mother placed a setting at the head of the table.

"Almost every other week these days. They fight a lot about it," Ashley revealed. "Last week, my mother accused him of having another family."

"Does he have to work like that?"

"He says he does," she replied sadly. "I feel sorry for her. She's alone so much."

I nodded sympathetically. So many of the kids I had met in school who had families were just as lonely as I had been. In various ways, their homes and lives were shattered and held together by the weakest glue, and although they didn't live in an institutional setting as I had, they often wore the faces of orphans, faces that revealed their loneliness, a longing for more affection and love, their eyes searching the faces of their friends, looking to see if anyone had more.

I went to Ashley's math book and helped her understand our newest assignments. She seemed to understand.

"You should be a teacher," she said. "You're better than Mr. Albert."

"Hardly." I laughed.

We were about to listen to music when we heard the phone ring. Ashley paused. I could see she was hoping it was her father calling from wherever he was. She was practically holding her breath. That was why we both heard her mother cry out so clearly.

"Oh, no! When?" she screamed.

Ashley's eyes were flooded quickly with fear. Moments later, her mother came to the door of Ashley's bedroom. I glanced at Ashley's face. She was nearly in tears, anticipating the worst.

"Crystal," Mrs. Raymond said, turning to me instead. "There's been a terrible accident. Do you know your uncle Stuart's number in Albany?"

"I'm sure it's in my father's Rolodex," I said. "I'll go look it up." I ran from the room before she could tell me another thing. My heart was pounding so hard that my legs felt like rubber. I nearly tripped at the front door. Outside, I broke into a trot. Tears were already blurring my vision. What sort of an accident? What did it mean?

I charged into my house and down the hall to Karl's den. After I found Uncle Stuart's telephone number, I took a deep breath, unable to swallow down a lump in my throat that threatened to choke off my air.

Nevertheless, I ran out again and back to Ashley's house. I went in and thrust the telephone number at her mother as if I were a relay runner passing the wand. She took it slowly, her eyes on me, filled with tears. She told us she'd explain after she'd talked with Uncle Stuart and asked us to wait in the living room. I left the room with Ashley but lingered outside in the hall. I just couldn't wait any longer to hear what had happened.

Ashley looked scared but moved down the hallway to be near me. We looked at each other and then turned as Mrs. Raymond began to speak.

"Stuart," she said, "this is Vera Raymond, Thelma's friend. Yes, yes, I'm fine. Stuart, a friend of my husband's in the police department here just called me. There's been a terrible accident. A car accident. Karl and Thelma . . . both of them have been killed, Stuart. I'm so sorry," she said.

Ashley stifled a cry with her fist in her mouth. I shook my head at her.

No, that's not true, I thought. Karl's too good a driver. He's the most careful driver in the world. They're too young to die.

"Yes, it happened today, just a few hours ago. A drunk driver in a pickup truck crossed the median to their side of the highway. They had no chance. I'm sorry."

Pickup truck? A drunk driver? For a moment, it was like eavesdropping on someone else's life. I felt I was watching and listening to one of Thelma's shows. It was make-believe, fantasy, some serial show. Boy, is Thelma going to be angry about this one, I thought. Just when she got so attached to the characters, they write them out of the show. I shook my head.

Ashley was staring at me in the strangest way. She looked frozen in time, a wax figure of fear.

"Yes," Mrs. Raymond said quietly. "She's with us. What do you want to do?"

There was a silence, and my mind raced with what Stuart could be telling her. What would happen to me? Would I be sent back to the orphanage?

"I understand, Stuart, but what do you want me to do in the interim? Really? All right. I'll find out and take care of it," she said. "I'm very sorry, Stuart. It's hit me so hard, I'm having trouble absorbing it myself. I'm sorry."

She hung up and slowly walked out into the hallway. From the look on her face, I could tell that she was startled to see me standing there but also a little relieved that she didn't have to explain the tragedy all over again.

"I'm sorry, Crystal," she said. "It's so horrible. I'm sorry, honey."

"I've got to go home now," I said. "I promised my mother I wouldn't stay out too late. They like me to be there when they return."

"No, honey, listen to me."

"Thank you so much for dinner, Mrs. Raymond. Thanks, Ashley. I'll call you. Thanks," I said, and rushed to the door.

"Crystal!" Mrs. Raymond shouted, but I was out the door again, running hard this time until I was gasping for breath at my front door. I charged through and shouted.

"I'm home!"

The silence greeted me. It was like being in Bernie's house. I stood there with my hand on my side, breathing hard, listening.

That was just some show, I kept telling myself. Ashley's mother is like Thelma. She loves her shows, too. I bet I know which one it was, I thought. I laughed. Sure, I told myself, I bet I know.

When the doorbell rang, I was sitting in Thelma's chair watching television. I ignored it, and it rang again and again. Someone started to pound on it. A voice threatened to break it down. The doorbell rang again. There was more pounding. When the commercial came on, I rose and went to the door.

A man and a woman were standing there. The man was in a suit and tie. He wore glasses and carried a small briefcase. The woman was short and wide in the hips. She had dark brown hair cut in a short, straight style. I could smell the child welfare agency on them. They had the look.

"Hello, Crystal. My name's Mr. Kolton, and this is Ms. Thacker. We're here to help you," he said.

"I can't go anywhere yet," I said. "My show is still on."

"What?" he asked.

"I'm watching something on television, something Thelma would watch and want to know about later when she returns. She forgot to set up the video recorder."

They looked at each other, and the woman shook her head.

"You're going to be all right," the man said with an institutional smile. To me, it looked as if they were both wearing familiar masks, masks I had seen all my life.

"I don't know that yet," I said. "We have to wait for the ending."

I left them standing in the doorway and returned to the television set. They came in. The woman sat with me while the man made some calls. A few hours later, I was in the rear of their car, heading back to the lair of the monster, the system, the only real mother and father I had ever known.

Epilogue

"This is going to be a lot better than the orphanage, Crystal," Ms. Thacker promised as we approached the driveway of the Lakewood House.

Ahead of us was a very large two-story house of gray clapboard with a wraparound porch. There were maple and weeping willow trees in front and lots of green lawn. As we drew closer, I saw there was a lake in the rear.

"Louise Tooey is probably the best foster mother we have. She treats all her wards as though they were her very own children. All of them say so," Ms. Thacker continued.

"This actually was once a resort," Mr. Kolton added. "And a very popular one at that. There's a rather big dining room, a nice lobby, ballfields."

"Beautiful grounds," Ms. Thacker emphasized.

"Maybe you would like to move in with me," I said dryly.

She just glanced at me and then smiled with that syrupy look of understanding I hated and continued to look out the window.

"There are other girls your age here, and the school system you'll attend is one of the best," Mr. Kolton said.

"How do you know that?" I queried. He glanced back at me and kept driving without replying.

"Crystal does well wherever she goes to school," Ms. Thacker said. Mr. Kolton laughed. "She'll probably end up tutoring the other kids here, won't you, Crystal?"

I didn't reply. I stared out the window, but I wasn't looking at my new home. My thoughts were back at the funeral I had just attended. Ironically, Karl had been right in planning it all before his and Thelma's deaths. The agency had decided I could attend the service even though Karl and Thelma had not completed the adoption process. Their family members all offered me their condolences and then guiltily explained that they had no place for me. Karl's brothers couldn't take me in. His father and Thelma's father were incapable of being guardians, and Thelma had no relatives who were interested.

Ashley and her mother were at the funeral, as were Uncle Stuart and some people from Karl's office. Before the ceremony ended, I looked back and saw Bernie standing near a tree, watching. After the final prayers were said, I headed toward the car with Mr. Kolton and Ms. Thacker. Ashley ran up to hug me and to promise she would write me if I would write her. I nodded. I hated promises. They were like those balloons I had seen drifting in the wind. They had shape until the air escaped, and then everyone forgot them.

Bernie stepped out from the tree, and I stopped.

"I thought you didn't approve of funerals," I said.

"I don't, but I wanted to be here for you."

"What's that, step seven?" I asked.

He looked down.

"I'm sorry," I said. He looked up at me. "We were both wrong. We both should have just said what we felt and not used any disguises."

He nodded.

"I guess we did learn something important, then," he said.

"Yes. I guess we did."

I got into the car. He stood there and waved as we drove off.

I could still see him standing there now. I blinked and woke to the present as Mr. Kolton brought the car to a stop in front of the big house. They got out my things, and we walked inside. A boy and a girl, not older than ten or eleven, were playing a board game on a big table. They looked up with curiosity. A door opened at the rear of the hall, and a tall woman with her shoulder-length brown hair swinging loosely about her face came hurrying out to greet us. Although she had a pretty face and bright blue eyes, the wrinkles in her forehead and at the corners of her eyes were deep enough to cause me to think she was older than she first appeared.

"Hello," she cried with excitement. "I was in the kitchen and didn't hear you drive up. I suppose this is Crystal. Hi, Crystal. Welcome to the Lakewood. This is going to be a real home. You'll see. You have a nice roommate, too. Her name is Janet, and she's the sweetest little girl. She's shy, but I bet you'll get her to be more outgoing. They tell me you're very smart," she said. "We sure could use some help in that department," she told Mr. Kolton. He smiled. I thought she would never stop talking. "Although my kids usually do well. We insist they do their homework before anything else. There are rules here, but good rules. Oh, I forgot to introduce myself. I'm Louise Tooey," she said, holding out her hand.

I took it to shake, but she held onto mine and patted it.

"I know you're a little frightened about being in a new place, but this is a special place. It was once one of the most popular tourist houses. It's really a very warm place, full of fun. You'll see. Anyway . . ."

"Go on!" we heard someone shout.

A boy about fourteen came charging down the stairway. His face was full of fear. Above him, a tall man with a wooden face towered above us all. He had thick shoulders and long, muscular arms, one of which had a tattoo on the forearm.

"Gordon," Louise said, nodding at Mr. Kolton and Ms. Thacker. "The agency is here with a new girl."

His threatening posture relaxed, and the face that

had looked so dangerous moments before softened.

"Well, hello there," he said. He glanced at the boy. "Go on and do your chores, Billy," he said sternly. Then he smiled at Mr. Kolton. "Got to maintain discipline around here."

"Of course," Mr. Kolton said. The boy hurried out of the building.

"This is Crystal. Crystal, this is my husband, Gordon."

"Welcome," Gordon said. There was something in his eyes that frightened me, an animal look. I glanced at Mr. Kolton and Ms. Thacker to see if they saw it, too, but they seemed oblivious to everything but the task at hand, which was to hand me over and leave.

"Why don't I show Crystal her room and have her meet Janet? Gordon, you can take her suitcases, right?"

"Sure," he said, practically seizing them.

"We'll just be a minute," she told Mr. Kolton.

"Fine. Good luck, Crystal," he called to me as I started for the steps.

"Yes, good luck, honey." Ms. Thacker followed. I didn't look back.

Louise talked a continuous stream as we ascended, describing the house, its history, and how much she enjoyed having foster children.

"You're all precious to us, right, Gordon?" she said.

"Yeah," he muttered. "Precious."

She paused at a door and knocked before opening it. A small girl with a face as perfect as a cherub's looked up at us. She lay curled up on her bed. She wore what looked like a tutu and a pair of pointe shoes.

"Janet, you're not sick again, are you, dear?" Louise asked quickly.

She shook her head.

"Just tired from practicing your ballet?"

She nodded, her eyes on me and full of terror.

"This is your new roommate, Crystal. Crystal, this is Janet. I just know you two will get along well. Janet's not a bad student, either, are you, Janet?"

She shook her head.

"Maybe now that you have a roommate, you won't stay to yourself so much," Louise said.

Gordon slapped the suitcases on the floor. "I got things to do," he grunted.

"Fine, dear," Louise said.

"Yeah, fine," he muttered.

"Gordon growls a lot," Louise said when he left, "but he's a pussycat at heart. Well, I'm going to let you two get acquainted while I go down and finish up the business with the agency people. Feel free to roam about and explore your new home," Louise added. "Welcome again, dear," she said, and left us.

I looked at Janet. She seemed so fragile, but her legs did look firm and muscular.

"You study ballet?" I asked. She nodded.

She's as shy as a butterfly, I thought, and went to my suitcases. She watched me for a few moments and then sat up.

"I don't study it anymore. I don't have any teacher," she said.

I looked back at her. "If you like doing it, just keep doing it. Maybe someday you'll get another teacher," I said.

She smiled. It was a pretty smile, a smile hungry to shine on someone who would give her love. I liked her. Maybe it was good that she was so shy and fragile. Maybe it was good that I would have someone else to look after besides myself, I thought.

I went to the window and looked out toward the lake. "It is pretty here," I said.

In the falling, purplish light of the failing day, the stars began to emerge, each like the tip of a magic wand, full of promises.

Janet and I sat by the window and looked up. I was pleasantly surprised when her hand found mine. We sat silently for a moment. Maybe there wasn't a family out there waiting for us. Maybe the only family we would have was each other. Maybe the only promises we would fulfill were the promises we made to each other. We had no wealth, no currency, nothing to offer each other but trust.

Afterward, she showed me pictures of herself in a ballet costume and began to tell me about her life. It didn't come fast. She had been wounded in love as I had, and she was afraid to confide in anyone. The secrets of our hearts would have to be unraveled like a ball of string, a little at a time. We would weave our pasts, our pains, and our dreams around each other until we were safely in each other's cocoon.

Only then could we go back into the world.

I looked back at her. "If you are doing it just [illegible], maybe the modeling, you'll get another [illegible]," I said.

She smiled. It was a funny smile, a smile hungry to hold on to someone who would give her love. I liked it. Maybe it was [illegible] pictures of myself and [illegible] it. Maybe it was so good that I would have something else to look at besides myself, I thought.

I went to the window and looked out toward the lake. "It's pretty here," I said.

In the [illegible] purplish light of the falling day, the stars began to emerge, each like the tip of a magic wand, full of promise.

Janet and I sat by the window and looked up. I was [illegible] surprised when her hand found mine. We [illegible] already [illegible]. Maybe those were [illegible] out there waiting for us. Maybe the only family we would have was each other. Maybe the only promises [illegible] would [illegible] the promises we made to each other. We had no [illegible] polishing each other [illegible].

Afterward, she showed me pictures of herself in a ballet costume and began to tell me about her life. I didn't know that she had been [illegible] as I had, and she was afraid to [illegible]. [illegible] would [illegible] a [illegible]. We would [illegible] our [illegible], and our dreams around [illegible] until we were safely in each other's cocoon.

Only then could we go back into the world.

Brooke

Prologue

When I first set eyes on Pamela Thompson, I thought she was a movie star. I was twelve, and I had shoulder-length hair the color of wheat. Most of the time, I kept it tied with the faded pink ribbon my mother had tied around it just before she dropped me off at the children's protection service and disappeared from my life. I wasn't quite two years old at the time, so I can't really remember her, but I often think of myself then as a top, spinning and spinning until I finally stopped and found myself lost in the child welfare system that had passed me from institution to institution until I wound up one morning staring wide-eyed at this tall, glamorous woman with dazzling blue eyes and hair woven out of gold.

Her husband, Peter, tall and as distinguished as a president, stood beside her with his arms folded under his camelhair overcoat and smiled down at me. It was the middle of April, and we were in a suburban New York community, Monroe, but Peter was as tanned as someone in California or Florida. They were the most attractive couple I had ever met. Even the social worker, Mrs. Talbot, who didn't seem to think much of anyone, looked impressed.

What did two such glamorous-looking people want with me? I wondered.

"She has perfect posture, Peter. Look how she stands with her shoulders back," Pamela said.

"Perfect," he agreed, smiling and nodding as he gazed at me. His soft green eyes had a friendly twinkle in them. His hair was rust colored and was as shiny and healthy as his wife's.

Pamela squatted down beside me so her face was next to mine. "Look at us side by side, Peter."

"I see it," he said, laughing. "Amazing."

"We have the same shaped nose and mouth, don't we?"

"Identical," he agreed. I thought he must have poor eyesight. I didn't look at all like her.

"What about her eyes?"

"Well," he said, "they're blue, but yours are a little bit more aqua."

"That's what it always says in my write-ups," Pamela told Mrs. Talbot. "Aqua eyes. Still," she said to Peter, "they're close."

"Close," he admitted.

She took my hand in hers and studied my fingers. "You can tell a great deal about someone's potential beauty by looking at her fingers. That's what Miss

America told me last year, and I agree. These are beautiful fingers, Peter. The knuckles don't stick up. Brooke, you've been biting your nails, haven't you?" she asked me, and pursed her lips to indicate a no-no.

I looked at Mrs. Talbot. "I don't bite my nails," I said.

"Well, whoever cuts them doesn't do a very good job."

"She cuts her own nails, Mrs. Thompson. The girls don't have any sort of beauty care here," Mrs. Talbot said sternly.

Pamela smiled at her as though Mrs. Talbot didn't know what she was talking about, and then she sprang back to her full height. "We'll take her," she declared. "Won't we, Peter?"

"Absolutely," he said.

I felt as if I had been bought. I looked at Mrs. Talbot. She wore a very disapproving frown. "Someone will be out to interview you in a week or so, Mrs. Thompson," she said. "If you'll step back into my office and complete the paperwork . . ."

"A week or so! Peter?" she whined.

"Mrs. Talbot," Peter said, stepping up to her. "May I use your telephone, please?"

She stared at him.

"I think I can cut to the chase," he said, "and I know how eager you people are to find proper homes for these children. We're on the same side," he added with a smile, and I suddenly realized that he could be very slick when he wanted to be.

Mrs. Talbot stiffened. "We're not taking sides, Mr. Thompson. We're merely following procedures."

"Precisely," he said. "May I use your phone?"

"Very well," she said. "Go ahead."

"Thank you."

Mrs. Talbot stepped back, and Peter went into her inner office.

"I'm so excited about you," Pamela told me while Peter was in the office on the phone. "You take good care of your teeth, I see."

"I brush them twice a day," I said. I didn't think I was doing anything special.

"Some people just have naturally good teeth," she told Mrs. Talbot, whose teeth were somewhat crooked and gray. "I always had good teeth. Your teeth and your smile are your trademark," she recited. "Don't ever neglect them," she warned. "Don't ever neglect anything, your hair, your skin, your hands. How old do you think I am? Go on, take a guess."

Again, I looked to Mrs. Talbot for help, but she simply looked toward the window and tapped her fingers on the table in the conference room.

"Twenty-five," I said.

"There, you see? Twenty-five. I happen to be thirty-two years old. I wouldn't tell everyone that, of course, but I wanted to make a point."

She looked at Mrs. Talbot.

"And what point would that be, Mrs. Thompson?" Mrs. Talbot asked.

"What point? Why, simply that you don't have to grow old before your time if you take good care of yourself. Do you sing or dance or do anything creative, Brooke?" she asked me.

"No," I answered hesitantly. I wondered if I should make something up.

"She happens to be the best female athlete at the orphanage, and I dare say, she's tops at her school," Mrs. Talbot bragged.

"Athlete?" Pamela laughed. "This girl is not going to be some athlete hidden on the back pages of sports magazines. She's going to be on the cover of fashion magazines. Look at that face, those features, the perfection. If I had given birth to a daughter, Brooke, she would look exactly like you. Peter?" she said when he appeared. He smiled.

"There's someone on the phone waiting to speak with you, Mrs. Talbot," he said, and winked at Pamela.

She put her hand on my shoulder and pulled me closer to her. "Darling, Brooke," she cried, "you're coming home with us."

When you're brought up in an institutional world, full of bureaucracy, you can't help but be very impressed by people who have the power to snap their fingers and get what they want. It's exciting. It's as if you're suddenly whisked away on a magic carpet and the world that you thought was reserved only for the lucky chosen few will now be yours, too.

Who would blame me for rushing into their arms?

1
A Whole New Ball Game

In my most secret dreams, the sort you keep buried under your pillow and hope to find waiting in the darkness for you as soon as you close your eyes, I saw my real mother coming to the orphanage, and she was nothing like the Thompsons. I don't mean to say that my mother wasn't beautiful, too, wasn't just as beautiful as Pamela, because she was. And in my dream she never looked any older than Pamela, either.

The mother in my dreams really had my color hair and my eyes. She was, I suppose, what I thought I would look like when I grew up. She was beautiful inside and out and was especially good at making people smile. The moment sad people saw her, they forgot their unhappiness. With my mother beside me, I, too, would forget what it was like to be unhappy.

In my dream, she always picked me out from the other orphans immediately, and when I looked at her standing there in the doorway, I knew instantly who she was. She held her arms open, and I ran to them. She covered my face with kisses and mumbled a string of apologies. I didn't care about apologies. I was too happy.

"I'll just be a few minutes," she would tell me and go into the administrative offices to sign all the papers. Before I knew it, I would be walking out of the orphanage, holding her hand, getting into her car, and driving off with her to start my new life. We would have so much to say, so many things to catch up on, that both of us would babble incessantly right up to the moment she put me to bed with a kiss and a promise to be there for me always.

Of course, it was just a dream, and she never came. I never talked about her, nor did I ever ask anyone at the orphanage any questions about her. All I knew was she had left me because she was too young to take care of me, but in the deepest places in my heart, I couldn't help but harbor the hope that she had always planned to come back for me when she was old enough to take care of me. Surely, she woke many nights as I did and lay there wondering about me, wondering what I looked like, if I was lonely or afraid.

We orphans didn't go to very many places other than to school, but once in a while there was a school field trip to New York City to go to a museum, an exhibition, or a show. Whenever we entered the city, I pressed my face to the bus window and studied the people who hurried up and down the sidewalks, hoping to catch sight of a young woman who could be my mother. I knew I had as much chance of doing that as I had of winning the lottery, but it was a secret wish, and after all, wishes and dreams were really what nourished us orphans the most. Without them, we would truly be the lost and forgotten.

I can't say I ever even imagined a couple like Pamela and Peter Thompson would want to become my foster parents and then adopt me and make me part of their family forever. People as rich and as important as they were had other ways to get children than coming to an ordinary orphanage like this. Surely, they didn't go searching themselves. They had someone to do that sort of thing for them.

So I did feel as if I had won the lottery that day, the day I left the orphanage with them. I was wearing a pair of jeans, sneakers, and a New York Yankees T-shirt. I had traded a *Party of Five* poster for it. Pamela saw what the rest of my wardrobe was like and told Peter, "Just leave it. Leave everything from her past behind, Peter."

I didn't know what to say. I didn't have many important possessions. In fact, the only one that was important to me was a faded pink ribbon that I was supposedly wearing the day my mother left me. I managed to shove it into the pocket of my jeans.

"Our first stop," Pamela told me, "is going to be Bloomingdale's."

Peter brought his Rolls-Royce up to the front of the orphanage, and though I had heard of them, I had never actually seen one of them before. It looked gold-plated. I was too awestruck to ask if it was real gold.

The interior smelled brand-new, and the leather felt so soft, I couldn't imagine what it must have cost. Some of the other kids were gazing out the windows, their faces pressed to the glass. They looked as if they were trapped in a fishbowl. I waved and then got in. When we drove away, it did feel as if I was being swept away on a magic carpet.

I didn't think Pamela literally meant we'd be going straight to Bloomingdale's, but that is exactly where Peter drove us. Everyone knew Pamela at the department store. As soon as we stepped onto the juniors floor, the salesgirls came rushing toward us like sharks. Pamela rattled off requests with a wave of her hand and paraded down the aisles pointing at this and that. We were there trying on clothes for hours.

As I tried on different outfits, blouses, skirts, jackets, even hats, Pamela and Peter sat like members of an audience at a fashion show. I had never tried on so many different articles of clothing, much less seen them. Pamela was just as concerned about how I wore the clothes as she was about how they fit. Soon I did feel as if I were modeling.

"Slowly, Brooke, walk slowly. Keep your head high and your shoulders back. Don't forget your good posture now, now that you're wearing clothes that can enhance your appearance. When you turn, just pause for a moment. That's it. You're wearing that skirt too high in the waist." She laughed. "You act like you hardly ever wear a skirt."

"I hardly do," I said. "I'm more comfortable in jeans."

"Jeans. That's ridiculous. There are no feminine lines in jeans. I didn't know the hems were that high this year, Millie," she said to the salesgirl helping me.

"Oh, yes, Mrs. Thompson. These are the latest fashions."

"The latest fashions? Hardly," Pamela said. "For the latest fashions, you would have to go to Paris. Whatever we have in our stores now is already months behind. Don't hold your arms like that, Brooke. You look too stiff. You look," she said, laughing, "like you're about to catch a baseball. Doesn't she, Peter?"

"Yes," he said, laughing along.

She actually got up to show me how to walk, to hold my arms, to turn and hold my head. Why was it so important to know all that when I was trying on clothes? I wondered. She anticipated the question.

"We really can't tell how good these garments will look on you unless you wear them correctly, Brooke. Posture and poise, the two sisters of style, will help you make anything you wear look special, understand?"

I nodded, and she smiled.

"You've been so good, I think you deserve something special. Doesn't she, Peter?"

"I was thinking the same thing, Pamela. What would you suggest?"

"She needs a good watch for that precious little wrist. I was thinking one of those new Cartier watches I spotted on the way into the store."

"You're absolutely right. As usual," Peter said with a laugh.

When I saw the price of what Pamela called a good watch, I couldn't speak. The salesman took it out and put it on my wrist. It felt hot. I was terrified of breaking or losing it. The diamonds glittered in the face.

"It just needs a little adjustment in the band to fit her," Pamela said, holding my hand higher so Peter could see the watch on my wrist.

He nodded. "Looks good on her," he said.

"It's so much money," I whispered. If Pamela heard me, she chose to pretend she hadn't.

"We'll take it," Peter said quickly.

What was Christmas going to be like? I wondered. I was actually dizzy from being swept along on a buying rampage that took no note of cost. How rich were my new parents?

I couldn't believe my eyes when I saw the house Pamela and Peter called home. It wasn't a house; it was a mansion, like Tara in *Gone with the Wind,* or maybe like the White House. It was taller and wider than the orphanage, with tall columns and what looked like marble front steps that led to a marble portico. There was a smaller upstairs porch as well.

The lawn that rolled out in front of the house was bigger than two baseball fields side by side, I thought. I saw fountains and benches. Two older men in white pants and white shirts pruned a flower bed that looked as wide and as long as an Olympic swimming pool. When we turned into the circular driveway, I saw that there was a swimming pool behind the house, and what looked like cabanas.

"How do you like it?" Pamela asked expectantly.

"Just you two live here?" I asked, and they both laughed.

"We have servants who live in a part of the house, but yes, until now, just Peter and I lived here."

"It's so big," I said.

"As you know, Peter is an attorney. He practices corporate law and happens to be active in state politics, too. That's why we were able to bring you home so soon," she explained. "And you already know that I was nearly Miss America," she added. "For many years, I was a runway model. That's why I know so much about style and appearance," she added without a tidbit of modesty.

"I think we've overwhelmed her, Pamela," Peter said.

"That's all right. We have so much to do. We don't have time to spoon-feed our lives to her, Peter. She's going to get right into the swing of things, aren't you, sweetheart?"

"I guess," I said, still gawking as we came to a stop.

Instantly, the front door opened, and a tall, thin man with two puffs of gray hair over his ears came hurrying out, followed by a short brunette in a blue maid's uniform with a lace white apron over the skirt.

"Hello, Sacket," Peter called when he stepped out of the car.

"Sir," Sacket replied. He looked to be in his fifties or early sixties. He had small, dark eyes and a long nose that looked as if it was still growing down toward his thin mouth and sharply cut jaw. The paleness in his face made the color in his lips look like lipstick.

"Welcome back, Mr. Thompson," he said in a voice much deeper than I had anticipated. It seemed to start in his stomach and echo through his mouth with the resonance of a church organ.

The maid flitted about the car like a moth, nervously waiting for Pamela to give her orders. She didn't look much older than thirty herself, but she was very plain, no makeup, her nose too small for her wide, thick mouth. Her nervous brown eyes blinked rapidly. She wiped her hands on her apron and stood back when Pamela stepped out of the car.

"Start bringing the packages in the trunk up to Brooke's room, Joline."

"Yes, ma'am," she said. She glanced at me quickly and moved around the vehicle to join Sacket at the rear. They began to load their arms with my packages.

"Peter, could you show Brooke the house while I freshen up?" Pamela asked him. She turned to me. "Traveling and shopping can make your skin so dry, especially when you go into those department stores with their centralized air. All that dust, too," she added.

"No problem, dear," Peter said. "Brooke," he said, holding out his arm. At first, I didn't understand. He brought it closer, and I put my arm through. "Shall we tour your new home?" he said, smiling.

I looked at the servants rushing up with my packages, the grounds people pruning and manicuring the flowers, hedges, and lawn, the vastness of the property, and my head began to spin. It all made me feel faint.

My new home?

All my life, I had lived in rooms no bigger than a closet, sometimes even sharing the space with another orphaned girl. I shared the bathroom with a half dozen other children most of the time. I ate in a cafeteria, fought to watch what I wanted to watch on our one television set, and protected my small space like a mother bear protecting her cubs.

Then, in almost the blink of an eye, I was brought to what looked like a palace. I couldn't speak. The lump in my throat was so hard, I felt as if I had swallowed an apple. I leaned on Peter's arm for real, and he led me up the stairs to the grand front door through which Pamela hurried as if the house were a sanctuary from the evil forces that would steal away her beauty.

"*Voilà,*" he said, standing back so I could step inside.

Once within the long entryway with tile floors that resembled chocolate and vanilla swirled ice cream, I turned in slow circles, gaping at the big oil paintings that looked as if they were taken from some European museum. I gazed at the large gold chandelier above us and the grand tapestry on the wall above the hallway, beside the semicircular stairway with steps covered in thick eggshell-white carpet that looked as fluffy as rabbit fur.

"That's a scene from *Romeo and Juliet,*" Peter said, nodding at the tapestry. "The masked ball. You haven't read that yet, I suppose?"

I shook my head.

"But I bet you know the story, huh?"

"A little," I said.

"What do you think so far?" he asked.

"I don't know what to say. It's so big in here." I gasped, and he laughed.

"Close to ten thousand square feet," he bragged. "Come along."

At his side, I viewed the enormous living room with its white grand piano.

"Neither of us plays, I'm afraid. Do you?"

I shook my head.

"Well, maybe we should think about getting you lessons. Would you like that?" he asked.

"I don't know," I replied. I really didn't know. I had never had a desire to play the piano. Of course, I would never have had an opportunity to learn, anyway.

"There are probably many new things you will find yourself wanting to do," Peter remarked thoughtfully. "When things seem so impossible, I imagine you don't give them a second thought, huh?"

I nodded. That made sense. He was smart. He had to be smart to have earned enough money for all of this, I thought.

There were many more expensive-looking paintings, very expensive-looking vases and crystal, and all of the furniture was spotless, the wooden arms and legs polished until they glittered, the sofas and chairs looking as if no one had ever sat on them.

"We don't spend enough time in here," Peter said as if he could read my thoughts. "It's one of those showpiece rooms. We're usually in the den, where we have our television set. Maybe now that you're here, we'll have some quality family time sitting and talking. It's a good room for talking, isn't it?" he asked with a smile.

"It makes me feel like I should whisper. It's like a room in a famous house or something," I said, and he laughed.

"I love to see the faces of those who view my home for the first time, because, through them, I can see it freshly myself," he said.

We continued down a hallway lined with mirrors in gilded, scrolled frames, small tables with vases full of fresh flowers, and paintings wherever there was free space.

"You have so many paintings," I said, as I stopped to study a beautiful seascape.

"Art's a good investment these days," Peter said. "You enjoy the beauty while it grows in value. That's better than some boring old corporate bond, huh?"

I shrugged. It was all a foreign language to me. He laughed.

"Pamela has about the same level of interest. She's one of those women who just want the machine to keep producing but don't care to know anything about the machine, which is all right," he added quickly. "I handle that part of our lives, and she . . . well, she's beautiful and makes me look good. Know what I mean?" he said with a wink.

Again, I had no idea, so I just smiled.

"Pamela is convinced you're going to be just as

beautiful as she is. You know, she really did almost make it to the Miss America pageant," he said.

"Really?"

"Uh-huh. First, she was prom queen, homecoming queen, Miss Aluminum Siding, something like that. Then, she was Miss Chesapeake Bay and a finalist for Miss Delaware, which would have taken her to the pageant. She lost out to the daughter of a very wealthy racehorse owner. The old fix was in there, I imagine," he said.

We stopped at the dining room. You had to have servants to eat a meal there, I thought. The oval dark cherry-wood table looked big enough to seat all the children in the orphanage, the administrators, cooks, custodians, and even some visitors. It had a dozen settings with goblets and wine glasses and more silverware than I saw in our whole cafeteria. There was a large matching hutch filled with glasses and dishes on one side and serving tables, highback chairs, a wall mirror, and two chandeliers as well.

"Dinner and all formal meals are served here, of course," Peter said with a sweep of his hand. "Pamela supervises everything in the house," he explained. "Her parents sent her to a finishing school, what some people call a charm school. She knows all there is to know about etiquette. You'll learn a lot from her. I swear," he said with a laugh, "she should have been born into royalty. She could live in that world. Our den or family room, as some refer to it," he continued, stopping at the next door on our right.

The furniture was black leather, and the television

looked as big as some movie theater screens. Red velvet drapes were opened to reveal the pool and the cabana through large panel windows. A whole section of the room had its walls devoted to pictures of Pamela. I was drawn to them.

"There she is!" Peter cried. "Winning beauty contests, representing companies, riding in parades, meeting celebrities and important politicians, modeling designer clothes, which is how I met her."

I gaped. My new mother knew all these famous people?

Peter came to stand beside me. "Impressive, huh?"

"Yes," I said.

"I got lucky when she fell in love with me. She's a constant surprise. Pamela has her own kind of rare beauty, and she knows what beauty can do and cannot do," he said, nodding at me. "You're going to learn a lot of information that's practical for an attractive female," he promised. The way he spoke made it seem as if Pamela and now I, which I didn't believe for a moment, were citizens of a different country or part of a different species because of our looks. "She can be innocent and childlike when she has to and sharp, seductive, sophisticated, and keen when she has to, and she knows when to be which. Few women I know do, and that includes the brainy ones who work at my firm, the Ms. this and the Ms. thats," he said with some bitterness.

He seemed to become aware that he was getting too serious and smiled.

"That's a state-of-the-art digital sound system," he

pointed out, "with Surround Sound. Few people have it, the technology is so new. Comfortable room, huh?"

I was listening with half an ear, part of me still awed at the luxuriousness in this overwhelming house. He continued the tour, showing me the two downstairs baths, servants' quarters, the kitchen, which looked big enough to handle a restaurant full of people, and the library, his office at home, which was dark and baronial with hundreds of leather-bound books.

"I'm afraid I'm unreasonable when it comes to my office. I don't permit anyone in here without me being present. Too many important documents and private papers," he explained. I saw a machine rolling out printed matter. "I get things faxed directly here sometimes. Well, now let's go upstairs and see your room."

I returned with him to the stairway and began to ascend. We heard what sounded like opera coming from a set of closed double doors at the end of the hallway.

"Pamela likes to listen to operettas while she's in her boudoir." When I made a face, he laughed. "You'll see."

We stopped at a tall door, and he glanced at me with that impish glitter in his eyes just before he opened it. This time, I couldn't swallow back my gasp.

The room, my room, was four times the size of what my room had been at the orphanage, and my bed was big enough to be a trampoline! It had four light pink posts and a headboard with a long-stemmed rose embossed on it. There was a milk-white desk with drawers and across the room a long counter with mirrors and a vanity table. The table was covered with brushes, containers of makeup, eyeliner, tubes of lipstick, a hair dryer, and an ivory box full of barrettes and hair ties.

All of my new clothes were put away in the dressers and large walk-in closet, and still there was room for lots and lots more. In the closet were mirrors and even a small table and chair.

On both sides of the bed were large windows draped in white and pink gingham curtains. My room looked out on a view of the countryside, and in the distance I could see a small lake.

Peter opened a cabinet across from the bed to show me a small television set. He then opened the bottom cabinet to reveal the sound system.

"We'll get you some music this weekend," he promised. "Pamela already has the next few days planned out, and shopping is a large part of it. So?" he said, standing there with his hands on his hips. "Are you happy?"

I shook my head. Happy just wasn't a big enough word. I turned around and then touched things to be sure they were all really there and this wasn't a dream.

"This is my room?" I finally had to ask.

He laughed. "Of course. Why don't you rest and then shower or bathe and dress for dinner, our first together. Pamela has had something special prepared. She's determined to spoil you rotten. She says a beautiful woman has to be spoiled. She must be right. After all, who can deny I have spoiled her?" he said.

There was a knock on the door, and we turned to see Joline.

"Mrs. Thompson sent me to see if Miss Brooke would like me to run her bath now," she said.

Miss Brooke? I thought.

"See," Peter said, "how Pamela is always thinking ahead. Well?"

"Well what?" I asked.

"Would you like Joline to run your bath now?"

"Run my bath?"

"Get it ready for you?" Peter explained.

I gazed at the large, round tub in the sparkling bathroom. What was so hard about getting a bath ready?

"I can do that," I said.

"Of course you can," he said, "but from now on, someone else will do it for you. It's what Pamela wants. She wants you to be just like her."

Something nudged me deep down inside where all my dreams and secret thoughts were kept. It was like a tiny alarm. An alarm I didn't quite understand.

I gazed at my new clothes, my expensive watch, my whole new world, so much more privileged and safe than the orphanage.

What could possibly be the danger here?

2
Out with the Old

When Pamela had sent Joline to run my bath, she didn't mean simply to turn on the water. She instructed her on just how much of each of the bath powders and oils to mix as well. I stood by, watching her measure it all out with the precision of a chemist.

"What is all that?" I asked.

"These are things Mrs. Thompson says will keep your skin soft and silky and keep you from aging."

"Aging? I don't think I have to worry about aging. I'm not even thirteen," I said.

She smiled at me as if I had said something very stupid and then turned on the water. After that, she set out big fluffy bath towels and my robe and slippers.

"Is there anything else you need?" she asked me.

"No," I said. I couldn't imagine anything else to ask for.

"Have a nice bath," she said, and left.

Have a nice bath? I looked at the tub. At the orphanage, we usually took quick showers, and whenever we took a bath, that was in and out, too. Other people always needed to use the bathroom. What was I supposed to do in a bath except wash and get out?

I took off my clothes and folded my T-shirt over my jeans neatly, placing them on the counter by the sinks. Even though my clothes were old and worn, it seemed I should treat them special just because they were now here in a bathroom fit for a princess. I had two sinks! Why would one room have two sinks in its bathroom, and what was that bowl next to the toilet?

The rich marble tiles felt cool beneath my naked feet. I shut off the water. Bubbles had risen so high they threatened to spill over the edge of the tub. I stepped in and lowered myself gingerly. I don't know how she did it, but Joline got the water just right for me, not too hot, not too cold. It did feel good, and I had to laugh at myself reflected in the mirrors around the tub. There I was with only my head emerging from the small sea of bubbles.

Instead of a wash cloth, there was a sponge on a handle dangling from the shower rack. I ran it over my legs and sat back to rest my head against the soft, cushioned pillow attached to the bathtub. The soapy water snapped and crackled around me.

Could it be that fairy tales do come true? How much happier was Cinderella?

"There you are, a perfect fit," Pamela said as she came into my bathroom. She had her hair tied under a small towel and wore a long red silk bathrobe with

Japanese letters drawn across the front. There was what looked like layers of thin mud over her cheeks and forehead. "How does it feel?"

"Very nice," I said, trying not to stare at her.

"Joline put in a little too much bubble bath, I see, but that's all right. We were born to indulge ourselves, you and I. Your indulgence was put on hold for a while, but that's over," she declared with the confidence of a queen. "Peter says you like your new home."

"It's a palace," I said.

She laughed. "Why not? We're a pair of princesses, aren't we? Don't you want to try the jets?"

"Jets?"

She bent down and pushed a brass button at the foot of the tub, and suddenly the water began to circulate madly, streams of it striking me in the legs and back. I screamed with delight, and she laughed. The bubbles grew bigger and bigger until I had to wipe them aside to see her standing there. She pressed the button again, and the jets stopped.

"I'll have to be sure to tell Joline she used too much bubble bath so she gets it right tomorrow night," she said.

"Tomorrow night?" Was I to take a bath like this every night?

"Of course. You have to cleanse the pores of your skin every day and rid them of the poisons. These gels and powders," she continued, pointing to the bottles and containers Joline had used, "are chosen with expert care. I have one of the best dermatologists in the country advising me on skin care. You're not going to get any of those ugly blemishes teenagers get," she vowed with such vengeance that my heart rose and fell. "Not my daughter, not the daughter of Pamela Thompson."

She pushed aside some of the bubbles and studied my hair.

"There's a lot of work to be done," she remarked as her fingers tested the strands. "Your hair feels like straw when it should feel like silk, and it needs to be thickened. I'll give you your first shampoo." She went to the counter to choose one. "We'll start with this," she decided. "Get your head wet."

I dipped myself down until my head went under water and then came up into her waiting hands. She poured the shampoo over me and began to scrub it in. I felt the ends of her long fingernails scratch at my scalp. A few times she hurt me, but I didn't complain. When she was done, she told me to dunk under the water again. I was surprised when her hands followed and continued to massage my scalp under the water, keeping me there until my lungs began to burn. I came up with a gasp.

She turned on a shower head attached to a short hose and rinsed me off. Then she returned to the counter to choose a conditioner. She worked that in and told me to let it set for a while.

"I've never really spent so long washing my hair before," I confessed. It seemed like a lot of work, anyway, and I couldn't imagine why it was important that your hair feel like silk instead of straw, but I didn't say that.

"You've got to do it every day from now on. You

should try not to miss a day, even if you're sick. Beauty like ours can never be taken for granted, Brooke. Did you ever hear of antitoxins?"

I shook my head.

"Toxins age you, but there are antitoxins to battle them and keep us from getting old too fast. I intend never to look my age, even if I have to fight it with plastic surgery. I know what you're thinking," she said before I uttered a sound. "You're thinking I already have had plastic surgery, right?"

I shook my head.

"How else could I look like a teenager or a woman just twenty, right?"

"I don't even know what plastic surgery does," I confessed.

She wasn't listening. "Plastic surgery is the artificial last resort," she lectured. "It's for the lazy. If you watch your diet, exercise, and nurture your skin the way you and I do, there is no reason to go under the knife."

"Should I get out now?" I asked. I didn't want to interrupt her, but the water was getting cold.

"What?"

"Should I get out of the bathtub?"

"Oh, first we want to rinse out your conditioner," she said, and went to the small hose again. "From now on, you'll be able to do this yourself, and if you're too tired, you can have Joline do it."

"This is the first time anyone's washed my hair that I can remember," I said. "I imagine they did when I was a baby."

"You're always a baby when it comes to being pampered, especially by men. Never, never let them believe they've made you happy," she advised.

"Why not?"

"They'll think they've done enough. They can never do enough. That's our motto. Okay, step out," she said, and I rose.

"Just as I thought. You have a perky little figure, not an ounce of baby fat," she remarked. "Actually," she said, letting me stand there naked and not handing me my towel, "you're a bit more muscular than I expected. We don't want to be too hard," she warned as she pinched the muscle in my thigh. "Men like their women to feel like women," she said.

She handed me the towel finally, and I wrapped it around myself quickly, drying my body as she studied me. She looked at my pile of clothes.

"Weren't you wearing a bra?" she asked.

"No."

"Your breasts are forming. It's never too early for a woman to worry about sagging," she declared. "First thing we do tomorrow is buy you more underthings. Sit at the table, and I'll dry and brush out your hair."

"Thank you," I said, and sat with the towel still wrapped around me.

She started the blow dryer and ran the brush through my hair. "It's nice having someone else to nurture and develop. It's as if I'm starting over. Of course, I couldn't do this with just anyone. I had to have a young girl who had promise. I'm just surprised at the size of your shoulders," she muttered. "I wonder why I never noticed they were so broad."

"My shoulders?"

"How did you get them to be so . . . manly? You don't do those exercises with weights, do you?"

I shook my head. What was wrong with strong shoulders?

"I suppose it's just something that happened. I'm sure it will change as your hormones do. And we can help them along," she whispered in my ear.

"We can what?"

"Make our female hormones more efficient. I have some pills, some nutritional supplements my nutritionalist has provided. I'll tell you all about it. Oh, there's so much to do. Isn't this fun?" she said. "See how much nicer your hair feels? Go on, touch it," she said, and I did. It did feel softer. I nodded.

"You're going to be a contestant faster than you think," she said.

"A contestant?"

"For the beauty pageants." She laughed. "Maybe I'll enter you in Miss Teenage New York this year. Yes, I will," she decided instantly. "And you'll win, too. Think of what they will say." She stepped back. The headlines flashed across her eyes as she envisioned them and drew them in the air with the brush. " 'Pamela Thompson's daughter declared Miss Teenage New York.' I love it."

I stared at her reflection in the mirror. She was still fantasizing some scene on a beauty pageant stage. My eyes went to the toilet again. "What's that?" I asked.

"What?" She looked. "Oh, that's a bidet. Don't you know what that is?" I shook my head. "You poor thing. That's to keep us clean in our private place," she said. "You have to do it every day, too. Women don't realize how they can . . . smell."

I looked at it, my eyes wide.

"It feels good, too," she said. She laughed. "Men want that to be the healthiest place on our bodies, but I bet you know all about that, don't you?" she asked guardedly.

"No," I said, "not really."

"Not really?" She stared at me a moment. "You're a virgin?"

"Uh-huh," I said, amazed that she would even ask.

"What a wonderful idea," she declared, "to be virginal until you win your first big pageant. I love it. You must promise me you'll not give yourself to just any old boy, Brooke. Sex is your treasure," she advised. "You must guard it like a dragon who guards the pots of gold in its cave, okay? We'll talk a lot more about this. That's what mothers are for. I'm a mother," she declared, gazing at herself in the mirror. "Who in his right mind would look at me and think, even for a moment, that I was old enough?" She laughed, and then her gaze went to my clothes again.

"We've got to get rid of those. I'm sorry you brought them in here," she said.

"What?" I asked.

She picked up my T-shirt and jeans as if they were diseased.

"Ugh. They still reek of that horrible place. I hate jeans on a girl, anyway."

She opened a drawer and took out a pair of scissors. Before I could utter a protest, she jabbed the scissors into the seat of my jeans and tore a gash through them. Then she pulled them apart and threw them and my T-shirt on the floor.

"Just leave it there for Joline to put in the garbage," she said.

She washed her hands as if she had been handling contaminated clothing and then smiled at my shocked face.

"Time to pick out something to wear to dinner," she said. "We want to look beautiful together when we enter and Peter looks up from the table. We want to take his breath away. From now on, every time we walk into a room together, we want to captivate our audience. That," she declared with a sharp nod, "is what we were placed on earth to do."

Before I followed her out to the bedroom, I went to my jeans and took out my hair ribbon, thankful to see that it hadn't been cut in two. I clutched it tightly in my hand, and as she sifted through all my new clothes, I shoved it into a dresser drawer. I was afraid she might want to throw that out, too.

"No, no, no, maybe, yes," she declared, and plucked the blue dress off its hanger. "Try this," she said, handing it to me, and stood back.

Why did she have to see it on me again? I wondered. She had seen it on me in the store. She knew what it looked like.

"Don't you think you should put on a pair of panties first?" she asked with a smile when I dropped the towel and reached for the dress.

I nodded and went to the dresser drawer. After I put the panties on, I slipped the dress over my head and pulled it down. It fit a little snugly and had wide straps and a U-shaped collar. I turned to face her, and she grimaced.

"I don't know why I didn't notice it before, but your shoulders and arms are so . . ."

"What?" I asked.

"Manly," she repeated. "I'll have to speak to my doctor about you. There must be a way to get you to look softer," she decided. "Now you see why clothes are like living things."

I shook my head.

"They take on different personalities in different environments. Back at the department store, under those harsh lights, colors were washed out, and the garments appeared one way, but here, in a warmer setting, in a bedroom or in a dining room, they're different. I wouldn't have bought this one," she concluded. "From now on, I'm going to have them bring your clothing here to try on."

"Bring them here? You mean to my room?"

"Of course," she said. "We were all just in too big a rush. But"—she recovered with a smile—"no harm done. We'll buy some more. That's all. I have a blue dress to wear, too. How experienced are you with makeup?" she asked.

"I put on lipstick sometimes," I said.

"Lipstick?" She laughed. "Sit at your table. Go on. Quickly. I have my own hair to style and my own makeup to do yet."

Why were we getting so dressed up for dinner? I wondered. Were there more people coming? Was it going to be like a party?

I sat, and she came up behind me. She turned on the magnifying mirror, and the light washed away any shadows on my face. Then she pressed her palms against my cheeks and turned my head from side to side, studying me.

She nodded. "Now that I have you under the light, I see where we have to make your nose look smaller. I want to highlight your eyes and thicken your lip line just a little."

She began to work on me as if I were being made up for a ball. The surprise in my face was easy to see. I was never very good at disguising my feelings. Whenever I thought something was stupid, the corners of my mouth turned up in a smirk that gave my feelings away. One of my grade-school teachers, Mrs. Carden, once told me that my forehead was as good as a blackboard on which my thoughts appeared in bright, white, chalky letters.

"Every time you go out of this room, and especially every time you leave this house," Pamela lectured, "you have to remember you are onstage. A woman, a real woman, is always performing, Brooke. Every man who looks at you is your audience. Whether we like it or not, we're attractive, and that means men's eyes are like little spotlights always turned on our faces and bodies.

"And even if you're married for ages or going with some beau for months, you still have to surprise him with your elegance and beauty every time he sets eyes on you, understand?"

"Why?" I asked.

"Why?" She stopped working and put her hands on her hips. "Why? Because if we didn't, they would look elsewhere, for one, and because we want to be the center of their attention always. Wait, just wait," she continued, returning to the makeup, "until you're out there, competing. You'll see. It's a cutthroat, ruthless world when it comes to winning the affections of men. Every woman, whether she wants to admit it or not, is competing with every other woman. When I walk into a room, who do you think looks at me first? The men? No. Their wives look at me and tremble.

"I have the feeling," she concluded, "that I found you just in time. You're still young enough to develop good habits. Press your lips together. There," she said. "Let's look at you now."

She turned my head toward the mirror and stood behind me again, her hands moving me so that she could get a profile.

"See the difference? You walked in here a child, and now you look like a young woman, which is what I'm going to make you into."

I stared at myself. With the eyeliner, the rouge, the lipstick, I did look entirely different, but I wasn't sure I liked it. I felt clownish. I was afraid to utter a word, and I was terrified that my blackboard of a forehead would write out my disapproval. If it did, she didn't notice, maybe because she had covered it in makeup.

"Don't think you have to spend a lot of time in the sun to get your skin this shade, Brooke. The sunlight is devastating. Those horrible ultraviolet rays age us. We don't need it with this makeup, anyway. Well now, you look ready. Come along and talk to me while I get dressed."

I rose and started after her.

"Wait," she said with a harshness I hadn't heard before. "You weren't planning on walking around *barefoot,* were you?" The way she said *barefoot* made it sound like a sin.

"What? Oh," I said, looking down.

"Put on the shoes that match the dress," she ordered sternly.

I went to the closet and stared at the dozens of pairs she had bought me.

"The pair second from the right," she said impatiently. "You have so much to learn. Thank goodness I came along."

I put on my shoes and followed her out, glancing through my bathroom doors at my torn jeans and my T-shirt lying on the floor where she had thrown them. It was like saying good-bye to an old friend. Dressed in my expensive clothes, my hair styled, my face made up, I felt as if I had betrayed someone. Myself?

"Come on," she urged when I hesitated. "Peter is already downstairs. Of course, we must always keep men waiting. That's a golden rule. Never be on time, and never, never, never be early. The longer they are made to wait, the more their anticipation builds, and the louder the applause in their eyes," she said. "Now, get moving. I need time to make myself more beautiful, too."

I hurried after her, and when she opened the double doors to the master bedroom, I felt the breath spiral up from my lungs and get caught in my throat like a giant soap bubble. It wasn't a bedroom; it was a separate house!

There was a long carpeted landing that led to two steps. On the right was a living room with furniture and a television set. On the left was a bedroom that surely was fit for a queen. It was round and had its own white marble fireplace, but what was astounding to me was the bed, because it, too, was round with big, fluffy pillows. Above it was a ceiling of mirrors. There were mirrors everywhere. I gaped.

Pamela saw my amazement and laughed.

"Maybe now you'll understand what I meant when I said we were always on the stage, always performing, Brooke." She looked at the bed and then up at the ceiling. "You know what it's like?" she asked, her voice softer but full of passion.

I shook my head.

"It's like we're in our own movie, and you know what?"

I waited, afraid to breathe.

"We're always the stars," she said, and laughed.

3
All the World's a Stage

Pamela had me sit beside her at her vanity table. It was designed so that the mirrors weren't only in front of her. They followed the curve of the wall and surrounded her. She could glance to the right or left and see her profile without moving her head. She said it was important that she know how she appeared from every angle, every side, and especially the rear. "When they see how fabulous I look from behind," she explained, "they'll be dying to see my face."

She spoke to me in the mirror instead of turning to look at me directly. It was as if we were looking at each other through windows.

"Always call me Pamela," she told me. "It's nice to have a daughter, and I want to be known as your mother, but I'd rather people thought we looked more like sisters, wouldn't you?" she asked.

I nodded even though I wasn't sure. I had friends at

the orphanage, girls who were so much like me we could have been sisters. We shared clothes, did schoolwork together, sometimes talked about boys and other girls at school who often snubbed us because we were from the orphanage. Together we battled, and together we suffered. For the first time, I thought of the life I'd left behind and how I would miss it.

But what I never had was someone older, someone motherly to whom I felt I could turn, not with complaints but with questions, more intimate questions, questions I didn't feel comfortable asking my counselors or teachers. Not being able to have someone like that left me feeling even more alone, listening to the echo of my own thoughts.

"These women who have children early get to look so matronly even when they're barely out of their twenties. It's all about attitude, and attitude is very important, Brooke. It will have a direct effect on your appearance. If you think of yourself as older, you'll look older. I think of myself as becoming even more beautiful, just blossoming," she said, smiling at her image in the mirror. She looked at me.

"I don't want you to think I didn't want children. I just couldn't have them while I was in competition and while I was a model. Having children changes your shape. Now," she said, smiling, "I still have my shape, *and* I have a daughter."

She wiped the thin layer of brown facial mud off gingerly with a dampened sponge and then stared harder for a moment and leaned in toward the glass.

Her right forefinger shot up to the crest of her left cheek as if she had just been bitten by a bug. She touched it and then turned to me.

"Do you see a small redness here?" she said, pointing to the spot.

I looked. "No," I said.

She returned to the mirror, studied herself again, and then nodded.

"It's not something an untrained eye would see," she said, "but there's a dry spot here. Every time I go out of this house, I come home with something bad."

She looked over the rows of jars filled with skin creams and lotions. Her eyes turned a bit frantic when she lifted one and realized it was empty.

"Damn that girl. I told her to keep this table stocked, to check every day and replace anything that was empty or even near empty," she said, rising. She went to the closet on her right and opened the door.

When she stepped to the side, I saw the shelves and shelves filled with cosmetic supplies. It looked as if she had her own drugstore. She plucked a jar off a shelf and returned to her table.

"This has special herbal ingredients," she began. "It replenishes the body's natural oils." She dipped her fingers into the jar and smeared the gooey-looking, chalky fluid over her cheek, gently rubbing it into her skin. Then she wiped off the residue and looked at herself again.

"There," she said, turning to me. "See the difference?"

I saw no changes, but I nodded anyway.

"Your skin is very sensitive to atmospheric changes, my dermatologist says. It was so hot in that orphanage, for example, and then we went to that air-conditioned department store, but they don't filter their air conditioners enough, and there are particles floating around that stick to your skin and begin to break down the texture.

"The water in this house is specially filtered," she continued. "Harsh minerals are removed so you don't have to worry about baths and showers."

It had never occurred to me ever to worry about such a thing, anyway.

"Our air conditioners, heaters, everything is filtered. Other people's homes are filled with dust. Sometimes I feel like wearing a surgical mask when we're invited to someone's house, even Peter's wealthiest clients. They just don't know, or they just don't care about the beauty regimen," she railed.

She sighed as she began to brush out her hair.

"These ends are splitting again. I told my stylist he wasn't trimming it right. Damn," she said, and then stopped. "See that, see?" she said, pointing at her face. "Whenever I get upset, that persistent wrinkle shows itself just under my right eye. There, see?"

There was a very tiny crease in her skin, but I would never call it a wrinkle.

She took a deep breath, closed her eyes, and sat there quietly for a moment. I waited until she opened her eyes again.

"Anxiety, aggravation, worry, and stress hasten the aging process. My meditation instructor has taught me how to prevent it. I must chant and tell myself I will not be upset. But it's so hard sometimes," she moaned.

She stared at me.

"You shouldn't squint like that, Brooke. See how your forehead wrinkles? It's never too early to think about it. Do you need glasses?"

"I don't think so," I said.

"Don't worry about it if you do. We'll get you the best contact lenses. Peter wears contact lenses."

"He does?"

"He's a good-looking man, your new father, isn't he?" she asked with a proud smile. "I didn't just marry for money and position. I married a handsome man."

"Yes, he is handsome," I agreed.

"And he's a good lover, too, a considerate lover. He won't even think of kissing me until he's shaven. A man's beard can play havoc with your complexion. If a man is selfish, if all he cares about is his own sexual gratification, you'll feel used. I'm nobody's possession. I'm nobody's toy," she declared hotly as if someone had just accused her of being so. Whenever anger flashed across her face, her nostrils widened and her eyes looked as if tiny candle flames were burning behind them.

She paused and looked at me hard again. "How much do you know about sex? I know you're a virgin. You told me so, and I believe you. I hope we'll never lie to each other," she added firmly. "How close have you come? Did you have one steady boyfriend?" She fired her questions in shotgun fashion.

"I've never had a boyfriend," I said.

Disbelief filled her face. "From what I saw, the living quarters were quite close. Boys and girls shared so much, and there wasn't all that much supervision, was there? I mean, there must have been plenty of opportunities for hanky-panky. You can be honest with me, Brooke. I'm your mother now, or your mentor, I mean," she quickly corrected.

"I never had a boyfriend. Really," I said.

"But you know things, don't you?" she asked, nodding. "You know what they want, what they always want, no matter how they present themselves or what they promise. Men see you as one thing and one thing only, whether you're a prom queen or a member of the Supreme Court, Brooke, and you know what that is?"

I shook my head.

"A vessel of pleasure into which they can dip."

She returned to her makeup. "Satisfying their little telescopes," she muttered.

"Their what?"

She laughed. "Telescopes." She looked at me. "Don't tell me you've never seen one of those."

"I've seen them," I said, recalling different occasions when I had caught sight of one of the boys in the bathroom.

"So you know they come out like a telescope when they are aroused. At least, that's how I always think of them," she said, laughing. "Oh"—she squealed with delight—"isn't it going to be fun for me to experience everything again through you? That," she said, growing serious, "is why it's so important you do everything I tell you and benefit from my knowledge, especially when it comes to men. What else is more important, anyway?" She shrugged. She gazed at her large, rich surroundings. "After all, my knowledge got all this.

"And," she added, turning back to me, this time with her eyes so intense she scared me, "with my help, you will get everything, too."

Peter was sitting quietly in the dining room, waiting for us. The moment we came through the door, he rose, his face lighting up with happiness.

"You can do wonders, Pamela," he declared. "Look at her. She really is a younger version of you."

Pamela's look of satisfaction grew icy instantly. "Not so much younger, Peter," she admonished.

"No, no, of course not. It's just that she came into the house a little girl, and you've turned her into a young lady in a matter of hours," he quickly explained. He hurried to pull the chair out for her, and she sat. Then he did the same for me. I sat across from Pamela on Peter's left, and she sat on his right. There was still so much table left, I felt silly.

"I have a lot to teach her," Pamela explained.

"I told her so, and I told her there was no better woman for the job, didn't I?" he asked me. I nodded.

Pamela seemed placated. She relaxed and smiled. Seemingly out of the walls, music flowed, soft, pleasant sounds. Sacket came in with a bottle of champagne in a bucket of ice and set it down beside Peter.

"Have you ever had champagne before, Brooke?" Peter asked me.

"No," I said. "I had a sip of beer once."

He laughed.

Pamela made a small smile with her lips. She looked as if she could orchestrate every tiny movement in her face, every feature to move independently of the others.

Peter nodded at Sacket, and he poured just as much in my glass as he did in Peter's and Pamela's. Then he placed it back in the bucket and left. Peter raised his glass slowly.

"Shall we make a toast, Pamela?"

"Yes," she said.

"To our new daughter, our new family, and the beautiful women in my life," he added.

We all touched our glasses. I had seen this only in the movies, so I was very excited. I sipped my champagne a little too fast and started to cough.

"You took in too much," Pamela said. "Just let your lips touch the liquid, and permit only the tiniest amounts into your mouth. Everything you do from now on must be feminine, and to be feminine you need to be dainty, graceful."

I crunched the napkin in my hand and wiped my mouth.

"No, no, no," she cried. "You dab your mouth, Brooke. This isn't a hot dog stand, and even if it was, you wouldn't do that. It looks too manly, gross." She shook her head to rid herself of the feeling. "Go on," she insisted. "I want to see you do it right. That's it," she said when I dabbed my lips so gently I hardly touched the napkin. "Perfect. See?" She looked at Peter.

"Yes," he said. "She's going to do just fine. How do you like your champagne?" he asked me.

I shrugged. "I thought it would be sweeter."

"It's not a Coke," Pamela said. "Besides, sugar is terrible for your complexion. You'll see that we have no candy in our house and that our desserts are all gourmet when we have them. We're both very conscious of calories normally, but tonight, being it's so special, we're indulging ourselves," Pamela explained.

Joline came in with our salad. I watched Pamela to see which fork to use because there were three. Peter saw how I was studying their every move and smiled.

"Every moment of your life in this house will be a learning experience," he promised. "Just follow Pamela's instructions, and you'll do fine."

Our salad was followed by a lobster dinner. Sacket brought out wine, and I was permitted some of that as well. Everything was delicious. The dessert was something called crème brûlée. I hadn't even heard of it, much less ever tasted it, but it was wonderful. Everything was.

Afterward, we went into the family room to talk, but Pamela seemed very fidgety. She excused herself and went upstairs. I wondered what was wrong, and when Peter was called to the phone, I decided to look in on her. I hurried up the stairs and knocked on her door. She didn't answer, but I heard what sounded like someone vomiting. I opened the door and looked in.

"Pamela?" I called. "Are you all right?"

The sounds of regurgitating grew louder and then

stopped abruptly. I heard water running, and a moment later, she stepped out of the bathroom. Her face was crimson.

"Are you all right?"

"What's wrong?" she asked.

"I thought I heard you being sick."

"I'm fine," she said. "Did Peter send you up?"

"No."

"I'm fine," she insisted. "Just go back downstairs and continue to enjoy your evening. I'll be right there. Go on," she ordered.

I left, closing the door quietly behind me.

If she was sick, why was she so ashamed? I wondered.

Minutes later, she rejoined Peter and me, and she looked as perfect as she had when she had come downstairs for dinner. She was certainly not sick, I thought, not the way I knew sick people to be. Peter didn't notice anything wrong, either.

He asked me lots of questions about my life at the orphanage. Pamela was more interested in what I remembered about my mother.

"Nothing, really," I said. "All I have is a faded pink ribbon that I was told was in my hair when she left me."

"You still have it? Where? I didn't see it when you came here," Pamela said quickly. She looked at Peter fearfully.

"It was in the pocket of my jeans," I said. "I put it in my dresser drawer."

"Why would you want to keep something like that?"

"I don't know," I said, near tears.

"It's nothing, Pamela. A memory," Peter said, shrugging. She looked unhappy about it and settled back in her chair slowly.

"There are all these horror stories about families who have taken in a child, and years later, the biological mother, a woman who had nothing to do with raising the child, comes around and demands her rights," Pamela muttered.

"That can't happen here," Peter assured her. "She doesn't even remember her face. Do you, Brooke?"

I shook my head. "No."

"You shouldn't hold onto anything, not even a ribbon," Pamela said angrily. "The woman got rid of you like . . . like some unwanted puppy."

"You're upsetting her, Pamela," Peter said gently.

She looked at me and relaxed again. "I'm just concerned about you. I want you to be happy with us," she explained.

I tried to smile. This whole day was so overwhelming, so full of surprises and excitement, I couldn't keep my eyes open. Peter laughed and suggested I get a good night's rest.

"It's all just starting for you now, Brooke. This has only been a taste of what's to come," he promised.

"I'll come up with you and show you the proper way to take off your makeup," Pamela said, "and then give you something to put on your face."

"Put on? But I'm going to sleep," I said, confused.

"That's when your body is best able to replenish itself," she explained. "You want to wake up looking beautiful, don't you?"

Peter laughed. "Just listen to Pamela," he said. "You can see she knows what she's talking about."

Put on makeup every day, wash with special soaps, filter your air, eat a special diet, avoid being upset, chant, meditate, put something special on while you slept. It seemed like so much effort. If this is what I had to do to be beautiful, I thought, I think I'd rather be plain old me.

But I would never say so, not if I wanted Pamela to love me like a daughter or even a sister.

I knew that much, but what I didn't know was that what I knew was not enough, not hardly enough.

4

Secrets

For the next few days, Pamela took over my life as if I had nothing more to say about it. She set schedules for almost every waking moment and left nothing to chance. The plan was to enroll me in the Agnes Fodor School for Girls, a private school designed only for those born with silver spoons in their mouths. However, before I could be brought to the school for registration, Pamela wanted me to learn enough about poise, etiquette, and style to "fool any of the blue bloods."

"Blue bloods," she explained, "are those who are born into wealth and position, whose family lineage goes back to the most respectable and important people in our social and political history. They are taught from day one how to behave and conduct themselves, and that is how I want you to appear, as well."

"But I'm not a blue blood," I pointed out.

"You are now," she said. "Peter and I come from

the best stock, and you will carry our name. Most important, when someone looks at you, they'll be looking at me. Understand?"

I nodded, but I didn't like it. I didn't like becoming an instant blue blood. I needed more time to get used to having servants at my beck and call and more time to learn my way about a house that resembled a palace. I didn't like Joline drawing my bath every night and laying out my nightgown and slippers. I felt like an invalid. Pamela decided what colors I would wear and how I should brush my hair. When I said I had never worn nail polish, she looked at me as if I was some sort of alien creature.

"Never? I just can't believe that," she said.

When I laughed at the idea of polishing my toenails, she grew angry. "It's not funny. It's as serious as any other part of your body," she insisted.

"But who will see them?" I asked.

"It's not important who else sees them. You must understand. We're beautiful first for ourselves, to make ourselves feel special, and then, when we feel special, others will see it and think of us as special, too."

"I don't understand why we would be so special," I muttered.

"Your clothes, your coiffure, your makeup, your walk, and your smile, everything about you must coordinate, must work together. Women like us," she taught me, "are truly works of art, Brooke. That's what makes us special. Now do you understand?" she asked.

I didn't, but I saw that if I didn't look as if I did, she would grow angry.

The one time she did get very angry with me occurred three days after I had arrived, when I asked if I could call someone at the orphanage. I wanted to talk to Brenda Francis, my one close friend. I knew she missed me. I was practically the only one she spoke to, and I wanted to see how she was doing. I had left so quickly, we never really had time to say good-bye.

"Absolutely not!" Pamela said forbiddingly. "You must drive that place and everyone in it out of your memory forever.

"Very soon," she continued, "you will completely forget that you were ever an orphan." She clenched her teeth and grimaced as if pronouncing the word *orphan* filled her mouth with castor oil.

Deep inside my heart, I worried that if my new mother found orphans so distasteful, how could she ever come to love me? Maybe she was worried about that, too, and that was why she was so intent on my becoming a new person as soon as possible. For both our sakes, I thought I would try.

The first thing we did after Pamela instructed me on my morning makeup was go to the shopping mall to buy more clothes for me. In the lingerie department, she chose a padded bra. I felt foolish trying it on and even more silly when I gazed at my exaggerated figure in the mirror. I looked years older just with that cosmetic change and complained that I didn't look like the real me.

"That's exactly what I want for you," she insisted. "I know these contest judges. When you're in a Miss Teen this or that contest and you look older, they're impressed, especially the men."

I was still so surprised that she really believed I could be in any such contest. What did she see in my face that I couldn't see, that no one else saw? I thought I was plain-looking, even with the appearance of bigger breasts. Moving with the bra on reminded me of wearing a baseball catcher's chest protector. I felt bulky and thought everyone was looking at me because my bosom didn't fit the rest of me.

Before we left the store, she bought me a half dozen more skirt-and-blouse outfits, three more pairs of shoes to complete the outfits, a necklace, three pairs of earrings, and a beautiful pinky ring—a gold band with a variety of baguettes. She then made an appointment for me to have my hair trimmed and styled by her beautician the day before she would enroll me at Agnes Fodor.

When we returned home, my charm lessons began, although she told me that every moment I spent with her would be like being in charm school. She was right.

As we rode in the limousine, she instructed me on how I was to sit. She demonstrated her posture, the way she held her head, and how she kept her legs either pressed tightly together or crossed properly.

"We're going to meet many different people over the next few days, Brooke. Whenever I introduce you to someone, don't say 'Hi.' I know young people today always use that, but you want to sound cultured.

Always respond with 'Hello. I'm glad to meet you.' And always look at the person, have direct eye contact so the person feels you are paying attention to him or her and not looking over their shoulder at some gorgeous man. You can shake hands. It's proper, but you will be introduced to some of our European acquaintances as well, and they have the habit of kissing cheeks. For now, follow my lead. If I do it, you'll do it. First, put your right cheek to the right cheek of the person you're greeting, and then pull back slightly and do it again with your left cheek. Most of them like to do what is called air kissing."

"Air kissing?"

"Yes, you really don't press your lips to someone's face. You kiss the air, smacking your lips loudly enough to sound like a kiss. You'll get the hang of it," she promised with a smile.

It all sounded so silly to me. Actually, it reminded me of some of the rules Billy Tompson had come up with when I was ten and we were forming our secret club at the orphanage. He had a specially designed handshake that started with the pressing of thumbs, and he also had secret passwords. Maybe cultured, sophisticated people simply had their own club.

"I hate 'okays,' too, another big teenage word these days. When someone says, 'How are you?' you reply, 'Very well, thank you,' or 'Fine, thank you.'

"All this," she explained, "is really going to be important when the judges do their little interviews. They'll be judging you on poise and charm."

"What judges?"

"The contest judges. Aren't you listening?" she asked with irritation in her voice.

"I'm listening, but when will I be in a contest?"

"Well, of course, I don't want to enter you in anything before you're ready, but I think in about six months," she replied.

"Six months! What contest is that?"

"It's not one of the most prestigious, but it's a good one to cut your teeth on," she said. "It's the Miss New York Teenage Tourist Pageant held in Albany. The winner gets awarded scholarship money, not that you need that, and represents the state in a number of advertising promotions, print displays, and even a video. I'd like you to win," she said firmly.

Win? I wouldn't have the nerve to set foot in the door, much less go up on a stage, but Pamela had that determined look on her face that I had already come to recognize, and when that look came over her, it was better not to contradict her.

My education in what I now thought of as Proper Behavior for Blue Bloods continued as soon as we arrived home each day. The first afternoon was set aside for table etiquette. Suddenly, the dining room became a classroom.

"Sit straight," she instructed, and demonstrated. "You can lean slightly against the back of the chair. Keep your hands in your lap when you're not actually eating so you don't fidget with silverware. I hate that, especially when people tap forks on plates or the table. Rude, rude, rude. You may, as I'm doing now, rest your hand or your wrist on the table, but not your whole forearm. Don't, absolutely don't, put your hands through your hair. Hairs often float off and settle on dishes and food.

"If you have to lean forward to hear someone's conversation, you can put your elbows on the table. In fact, as you see when I do it, it looks more graceful than just leaning over stupidly. See?"

"Yes," I said, and then she made me do everything she had instructed.

"Teenagers," she said, again pronouncing the word as if we were primitive animals, "often tip their chairs back. Never do that. Of course, you know to put your napkin on your lap, but you should, out of courtesy, wait for the hostess to put hers there first. Since I'm the hostess of this house, at any of our dinners, wait for me. Understood?"

I nodded.

"Don't flap it out, either. I hate that. Some of Peter's friends wave their napkins so hard over their plates that they blow out the candle flames. They're so crude.

"Just like with the napkin," she said when Joline began serving our food, "you don't begin eating until the hostess begins.

"The first day you were here, you didn't know which piece of silverware to use first. Always start with the implement of each type that is farthest from the plate.

"Now, watch how I cut my meat, how I use my fork, and how I chew my food. Don't cut too big a piece. Chew with your mouth closed, and never talk with food in your mouth. If someone asks you a question while you're chewing, finish chewing and then reply. If your dinner partner is sophisticated, they will know to wait.

"At Agnes Fodor, you will see that the girls follow these rules of etiquette, Brooke. I don't want you to feel inferior in the school dining room. If you make a mistake, don't dwell on it, understand?"

"Yes," I said. I was never so nervous eating. In fact, my nerves were so frazzled, the food bubbled in my stomach, and I didn't remember tasting anything.

At dinner, I was to perform for Peter's benefit. I shifted my eyes to Pamela after every move, almost after every bite, to see whether she was pleased or not. Usually, she nodded slightly or raised her eyebrows if something wasn't right.

"You're doing wonders with her," Peter declared. "I told you that you were in the hands of an expert when it comes to style and beauty, didn't I, Brooke?"

"Yes," I admitted.

"I almost didn't recognize this girl," he told Pamela. "Is this the same poor waif we brought home to be our new daughter?" he joked. "Pamela, you're a master at this."

Pamela gloated in the light of Peter's compliments. Afterward, when she and I were alone, she began what she considered the second stage of my development: how to handle men.

"Do you see how often Peter gives me a compliment?" she asked. I nodded, because I did, and I wondered if all husbands were like that. "Well, it doesn't happen by accident. If you let a man know that you expect him to show his appreciation, he will fall all over himself doing just that. I'm a professional woman," she explained. "I've made femininity my profession, and I don't mean I'm one of those women's liberation creatures you see in magazines and on television news complaining. They think they'll get what they want by demanding and protesting.

"There's only one sure way to get what you want from a man," she declared. "Make him think that you believe he is someone special and that you'll always treat him that way if he treats you as someone special. Make him believe he is your protector. Be fragile, dainty. You need his strength. He'll go mad trying to protect you, to keep you happy, and *voilà,*" she said with a wide gesture, "you'll always get what you want.

"It's easier than protesting, and you enjoy yourself at the same time. Who wants to be marching with placards in the hot sun, screaming and burning bras? And who wants to look like that? Some of them wouldn't be caught dead wearing lipstick, even though they look so pale you'd think they were dead.

"I hope you understand what I'm saying, Brooke. It's very important."

I did and I didn't. Men and boys were still a big mystery to me. I felt more comfortable and secure standing up to them, since I was as strong as they were, as fast on the ball field, and never acted as if I were a weak sister. I knew they respected me, because they often chose me to be on their teams before they chose some of their male friends, but I realized this was not something Pamela would want to hear.

"Did you see the way I batted my eyelashes at Peter? Did you hear me laugh, and did you catch the movement of my eyes and shoulders? Observe me at all times," she instructed.

I was really shocked. Did Pamela actually plan every gesture, every turn of her shoulders, every movement of her eyes and mouth? And if she did, was that right? It seemed to me that she was conniving against Peter, fooling and manipulating him, and I wondered if that was something you did with someone you loved. I had to ask.

"But wouldn't Peter do anything for you, anyway, because he loves you?"

She laughed. "How do you think you get someone to love you, Brooke? You think it's like the movies or in those romance novels? You think someone looks at you like in that old song, across a crowded room, and thunderbolts strike? It's work getting someone to love you. And anyway, men don't know what they want half the time. You have to show them what they want.

"Most men think a beautiful woman is someone with big breasts whose hips swing like the pendulum in a grandfather's clock, but a beautiful woman is far more than that, Brooke. You have to nurture and develop your beauty, just as I'm showing you. And then," she said, pulling her shoulders back, "you will know, and all the men who look at you will know, you are special.

"When you're special," she concluded, "they all

fall in love with you, and you have your pick of the crowd. That," she said, "is what happened to me and what will happen to you if you do what I say."

Was winning a man the only reason for our existence and our only purpose for being? I wanted to ask, but like so many thoughts and questions tickling the tip of my tongue, I swallowed them back and stored them for some other time rather than risk her anger and disapproval.

Despite the way she talked and thought, I wanted her to love me as a mother. I wanted Peter to be my father. I wanted us to be a family. I wanted to laugh and have fun, to do things I saw other girls my age do with their families. It's only natural for Pamela to want me to be like her, I thought. That way, she would feel she really had a daughter.

What did surprise and even frighten me a bit, however, were her instructions to me on our way to enroll me at the Agnes Fodor school. She wanted me to start my new life with a big lie.

"Except for Mrs. Harper, the principal, Brooke, I don't want anyone else to know you came from an orphanage."

"What? What do you mean?" I asked.

"Mrs. Harper understands why I would like it that way. Believe me," she said, "you will feel more comfortable, especially in the company of the other girls, if that little detail was forgotten."

Forgotten? Little detail? All my life, I'd been an orphan. I had no other experiences. How could I pretend to be someone else?

"But what will I say?" I asked. "What will I tell people about myself?"

"Tell them you're our daughter. Tell them we decided to send you to Agnes Fodor because your public school has degenerated. A new group of lower-class students has gradually become the majority at the public school, and there was a lot of trouble. Your parents became concerned about your safety as well as your education. Most of the girls will understand, because most of them have had that experience. Their parents enrolled them in Agnes Fodor to get them away from inferior public education and bad influences.

"If you behave as I've been teaching you how to behave, everyone will believe you are who you say you are. At least, you won't be ashamed to invite them to your home, will you?" she asked. "I really don't think you'll have any problems," she added with a smile of confidence. "When in doubt, just keep silent until you confer with me.

"Or you can talk about me," she continued. "Tell them about my modeling, my titles. Most of their mothers are nowhere near as attractive, and they'll be jealous of you immediately."

She smiled. "I'm so excited for you. I remember when I first enrolled in charm school. I'm sure Peter and I will be very proud of you very soon," she added.

I looked out the car window. When I lived in the orphanage and I had nothing of any real value, not even a name, I didn't have to lie. Now that I was rich, now that I lived in a palace and had more clothes in my closet than ten girls all together had at the orphanage, now that I had servants and rode in a limousine, I had to pretend I was someone else.

The road to happiness was long and winding, full of traps and illusions. When I said good-bye to the girl I was when I lived at the orphanage, I never dreamed I would want her back, but for a moment, on our way to this wonderful new school for the rich and privileged, I longed to return to who I was, who I had been, just as you sometimes wish you could put on clothes that were comfortable, broken in, part of your personality, even if they were out of style and too old.

"There it is," Pamela declared. "Agnes Fodor. It doesn't even look like a school, does it?"

I gazed at the large cobblestone building set in a small valley and surrounded by greenery, beautiful trees, and a small pond in the rear. Everything was clean and perfect. And so quiet. She was right. It didn't look like a school. It looked like an old-age home.

I took a deep breath. What Pamela really should have taught me was acting. I was very uneasy. I didn't wear lies well. Surely, anyone who spoke to me would see right through my stories and answers, and then, then, it would be even worse. With a pounding heart and feet that felt as if they were plodding through mud, I entered the new school to become a new person.

5

A Shining Star

With suspicious, cold gray eyes, Mrs. Harper stared across her desk at me. I was quite overwhelmed by the school. The lobby had a mural that reached from the floor to the ceiling. It was a painting of cherubs looking up devoutly at a burning lamp. The marble floors glistened around the sofas, chairs, and tables. A girl of about fifteen greeted us as soon as we entered. She introduced herself as Hiliary Lindsey and told us she was on duty as school receptionist. She carried herself, spoke, and offered her hand to me just the way Pamela had described and instructed me to greet people. As Hiliary led us down the corridor to Mrs. Harper's office, Pamela shifted her eyes to me and gave me a nod and smile as if to say, "That's how you are to behave, see?"

I was even more nervous. The outer office was as neat and spotless as the lobby. Mrs. Harper's secretary, Miss Randall, was a short, buxom, red-haired woman with strains of gray invading the hair at her temples and the hair at the top of her wide forehead, which formed rows of thick folds when she saw us enter.

Hiliary introduced us to her and then glanced at me to give me a small smile before she left us. Moments later, the inner office door opened, and Mrs. Harper asked us to come in. She was tall with very narrow hips and a small bosom barely visible under her loose, dark blue, ankle-length dress. I couldn't guess her age. Her hair was dark brown, her eyes hazel. She had a very pointed nose and a small mouth. Her cheeks were flat, which made her face seem more narrow, but she had the kind of skin and complexion I knew Pamela admired, not a wrinkle, not even a crease in her forehead.

Everything on her desk was organized, the dark mahagony looking as polished and clean as everything else I had seen so far. Before her on the desk was a folder with my name on it.

"Agnes Fodor," she began, with her eyes still fixed on me, "is a highly regarded, prestigious, and exceptional institution. My girls all have the highest-quality behavior. You will immediately notice vast differences between Agnes Fodor and your average public school," she said. Nothing in her face moved but her small, thin lips.

"For one thing, our classes are very small. We believe in giving the students personalized instruction," she added, turning to Pamela. "For another, our students are all on what we call the honor system. We don't expect our teachers to be concerned with behavioral problems. Everyone knows the rules we live under and respects them. If a girl violates a rule, she confesses her violation. Not that any do," she added quickly. "It is not unusual for a teacher to leave his or her classroom during the administration of an exam. Our girls don't cheat. You will notice that our lockers don't have locks on them. Our girls don't steal. You will notice that our bathrooms are spotless. There are no disgusting cigarette butts in the toilets and sinks. Our girls don't smoke in school, and most don't out of school, either."

"Smoking is the worst thing for your complexion," Pamela said.

Mrs. Harper looked at her almost as hard as she was looking at me for a moment and then turned back to me with a little bounce of her head on her neck. It bobbed like a puppet's head.

"You will notice that there are no pieces of paper, no refuse of any kind on the floors in our classrooms or in our hallways. Our girls don't litter. You will never find gum stuck under chairs. We don't permit the chewing of gum.

"After lunch in our cafeteria, there is very little for the custodian to do. Our girls clean up after themselves, and that even means wiping up the tables if need be.

"During the passing between classes, no one raises her voice. Our girls don't shout to each other. Never, never in the history of Agnes Fodor, has there been any sort of violent behavior. If two girls have a disagreement, they are encouraged to bring it to the judicial committee, which is made up of girls who are elected to the position. We have a very productive and active student government organization, and we have great faith in it. The girls police themselves. If anyone should violate one of our rules, she is brought before a committee of her peers and judged and punished accordingly."

"But I thought no one violated the rules," I said. I really just said it because I was a little confused, but Mrs. Harper's stone eyes suddenly became hot coals. Her face actually blanched, and the veins in her neck stretched until they were embossed under her skin.

"I meant they rarely violate the rules, so rarely that last year, the judicial committee met only twice," she said. "All year long.

"It is," she continued, turning to Pamela, "very unusual for Agnes Fodor to admit a student who hasn't had a history of proper breeding, but given your and your husband's position in the community, we have confidence Brooke will quickly adapt to our high standards."

It started sounding like a compliment and ended up sounding like a threat, I thought. Pamela smiled.

"Oh we're sure of that," she replied.

"Very good," Mrs. Harper said, and opened my folder. She gazed at it a moment and then looked up at me again. "You haven't been exactly what we would call a good student. However, we usually find that our students experience an immediate improvement on their work here. We will expect no less from you, despite your unfortunate background.

"As your mother has requested," she continued, nodding at Pamela, "nothing about your past will leave this office. This folder remains in my files for my eyes only."

"Thank you," Pamela said.

"However," Mrs. Harper continued as if Pamela had not spoken, "you know that I know, and you know what I expect of you. Do you have any questions?"

I shook my head.

She stared, her eyes sweeping over me like tiny spotlights searching for an imperfection. I squirmed in my chair under such intense observation. Finally, she closed my folder and stood up.

"Come with me," she ordered.

I rose and followed.

Pamela stepped up to touch my arm when I reached the door.

"Good luck," she said, smiling. I nodded and continued to follow Mrs. Harper. At the entrance to the principal's office, Mrs. Harper turned to Pamela.

"We'll be right back, Mrs. Thompson," she said, gazing at me and motioning for me to continue along with her.

She walked quickly, taking surprisingly long strides. I actually had to skip a step or two to catch up with her.

"This is Mr. Rudley's class, English. He'll be your homeroom teacher as well, so he has your schedule card," she explained as she opened the door.

Mr. Rudley, a tall man of about fifty with hair a shade darker than ash, looked up from the textbook in his hands. He was sitting on the edge of the front of his desk and jumped into a standing position as soon as he saw Mrs. Harper. The class, consisting of six girls, all turned and immediately stood. They gazed at me with interest.

"This is the new student I told you would be arriving today, Mr. Rudley," Mrs. Harper said. "Her name is Brooke Thompson."

"Very good, Mrs. Harper. Welcome, Brooke. You can sit right here," he said, nodding at an empty desk to his right.

I quickly crossed the room and waited to take my seat. Mrs. Harper remained in the doorway.

"I would take it as a personal favor if you girls would help Brooke feel at home at our school. She has transferred in from a public school," she added, turning down the corners of her mouth in obvious disapproval.

The girls looked at me. One of them, a thin blonde with blue eyes and freckles sprinkled over her cheekbones, stared at me the most intently. I couldn't quite tell if it was a look of welcome or of warning.

"You'll see to it that she receives her schedule card, Mr. Rudley," Mrs. Harper said before stepping out and closing the door.

There was a moment of silence. Mr. Rudley nodded, and we all sat down. Then he went to his desk and found my card.

"Let's introduce ourselves, girls," he said to the class. "Margaret?"

"I'm Margaret Wilson. Pleased to meet you."

Before I could respond, the shorter, dark-haired girl behind her continued. "I'm Heather Harper, Mrs. Harper's niece," she added somewhat smugly.

"I'm Lisa Donald," said a girl with hair the color of rust and the greenest eyes I had ever seen. She looked older than everyone else because she had a bosom even fuller-looking than my fake one, as well as a more knowing, more sophisticated glint in her eyes.

"I'm Eva Jensen," a Scandinavian-looking blond girl said. Her face had hard, sharp features, and she was very thin.

"My name is Rosemary Gillian," said a girl with brown hair. She had a dimple in her cheek and a slightly cleft chin under thick, full lips. I thought she had an impish gleam in her eyes, especially the way she smiled at the other girls after she spoke.

"Helen Baldwin," said the girl who had first looked at me with great interest.

"Okay, that's it," Mr. Rudley said. He handed me a textbook. "I don't know what you did at your other school, but we're just starting *Romeo and Juliet*. Everyone reads a part. Some are reading two or three because there are only seven of us."

"Eight now," Rosemary pointed out.

"Exactly," Mr. Rudley said. "So, why don't you pick up the part of . . ."

"She can be Romeo," Heather Harper said. "I'm not comfortable being a man."

"He's just a boy, remember?" Lisa Donald corrected. "Mr. Rudley told us."

"That's correct. Romeo and Juliet are meant to be not much older than you people," he said.

"And anyway, Mr. Rudley told us a boy played Juliet in Shakespeare's days," Lisa continued, "so who reads what part isn't important."

"I think it is," Heather insisted. "I'd rather read Juliet. Why don't you read Romeo, then? Why should you be the one reading Juliet?"

"Mr. Rudley told me to read it," Lisa countered.

"All right, girls. Brooke?"

"I don't mind reading Romeo," I said. I looked at the others. Heather had a smirk on her face.

"Fine. Then let's get back to the play," Mr. Rudley said.

When the bell rang, Eva Jensen and Helen Baldwin came over to me first and offered to show me around. I half expected we would have more students with us at my next class, but our group of seven stayed together for the remainder of the day. The passing between classes was just as Mrs. Harper had described: orderly and subdued. Other students were introduced to me, but there was little time until lunch for me to have any real conversations. Naturally, everyone wanted to know where I had gone to school and what it was like. Only Heather Harper looked as if she didn't think much of my answers.

"Do you have any brothers or sisters?" she asked.

"No."

"Are your parents very rich?" she followed. The other girls seemed to step back to let her take over the conversation.

"Yes," I said. "My father is a very important lawyer."

"So's mine," Heather said. "How rich are you?"

"I don't know," I said. "I mean, I don't know how much money we have, exactly."

"I do," she bragged, "but I don't tell people."

"So why did you ask her to tell you?" Eva Jensen said.

"Just to see if she would," Heather said. Then she laughed. "Anyway, I could find out if I wanted to. My aunt knows just how much money everyone has. Our parents had to fill out a financial statement to qualify for the school."

"She won't tell you," Rosemary Gillian said. "And if she knew you had even said such a thing, she'd throw you out herself."

Heather seemed to wither in her chair. "I'm just kidding. Everyone's just trying to impress you, Brooke," she accused, her eyes hot. "That's what they always do when a new girl comes. So what do you think of the place?" she followed, back to her cross-examiner's attitude.

"It's beautiful," I said. "I mean, I can't believe it's a school."

The others smiled.

"Neither can we," Heather said dryly.

"I'm glad you like it here," Eva said with warm eyes. "We can always use new friends."

"What do you mean, new friends?" Heather quipped. "You mean any friends, don't you?"

The others laughed. Eva looked as if she would cry.

"I need friends, yes. You can never have enough friends," I said, and looked at Heather. "Real friends, that is."

No one spoke a moment, and then Heather laughed. "*Touché,*" she said. "You know what that means?"

I wasn't sure, but I nodded. The bell rang, and we all rose. I saw how each girl made sure her place at the table was clean. I did the same and followed them out to our next class.

Heather came up beside me. "You don't seem like you come from a rich family," she said.

"Why not?" I asked.

"You're too grateful," she replied, and smiled at what she thought was her own cleverness.

Everyone laughed, even Eva. They looked at me, and I thought, why not get right aboard their silly little ship? I laughed, too, and that made everyone, even Heather, feel better about me. Maybe I could do this, I thought. Maybe I could be someone I'm not.

Physical education class was the last class of the day for us. Our class was combined with four others that included ninth, tenth, and even eleventh graders. Altogether, we had enough for two softball teams. Our teacher, Mrs. Grossbard, was a former Olympic runner who had been on the team that won a bronze medal. She looked at me with interest when I came out in our school physical education uniform, a white blouse with the Agnes Fodor logo on the left breast and a pair of dark blue shorts. The school also provided us with sneakers and socks.

"You play this at your last school?" Mrs. Grossbard asked me.

"Yes, ma'am," I said.

"Call me coach," she said. "I have the wonderful distinction of being the school's softball coach, swimming coach, relay coach, and basketball coach. I also have the distinction of never having a winning season in any of these sports, but," she said with a sigh, "I try. I do the best I can with girls who are afraid to break a fingernail." She looked at me. "Take shortstop on the blue team and bat fifth," she ordered.

I took the field with my team. Eva played first base, probably because of her height and reach. Heather was in the outfield, sitting on the grass immediately. The other girls were on the white team.

It felt so good being outdoors, stretching my limbs and using my muscles. We had a beautiful day for a softball game. The sky was a light blue with milk-white clouds splattered here and there. The light breeze on my face was refreshing. The sun was far enough behind the trees not to get in our eyes, and the scent of freshly cut grass was intoxicating.

Unfortunately, our pitcher had trouble reaching the plate. Her first three tosses bounced in front of the batter. Mrs. Grossbard told the pitcher to move closer, and she did so. Her next pitch was too high for anyone to reach, and the one after that nearly hit the batter.

"Wait a minute," Mrs. Grossbard said. She put her hands over her eyes as if she didn't want to look at her class for a moment or as if she were speaking to herself and then took the ball and threw it at me. I caught it easily. "Throw it back," she ordered. I did. "Change places with Louise."

"Why?" Louise, our pitcher, whined.

"Oh, I don't know. I thought we'd try to get in more than one inning today," Mrs. Grossbard replied sarcastically.

Louise glared angrily at me as we passed each other.

"Warm up," Mrs. Grossbard ordered, and I threw in a half dozen pitches, all pretty much over the plate. "Play ball," she cried, her eyes brighter.

The first batter returned to the plate and swung at my first pitch. It was a blooper only about three feet in front of her. I rushed toward her and caught the ball at my waist. My team cheered. Mrs. Grossbard, who was leaning against the backstop, stood up.

The next batter took her place at the plate and struck out on three pitches. The third batter hit a dribbler down to third, and my third baseman, an eleventh grader named Stacey, made a fine pickup, which was followed by a throw good enough to beat the runner out at first base.

We went in to bat.

"You've pitched before?" Mrs. Grossbard asked me.

"Yes," I said.

"Why didn't you tell me that was your usual position?"

"I don't know," I replied.

"Usually, my girls don't hesitate to tell me what

they *think* they're good at," she remarked. "Modesty here is as rare as poverty."

I wasn't sure what she meant, but I smiled and nodded and took my seat on the bench.

Our first batter hit a weak fly ball that fell just behind the shortstop, who happened to be Lisa Donald. She fell reaching for the ball, and we had a runner on base. Our second batter struck out, but our third batter hit a hard drive between first and second. We had girls on first and third when our cleanup hitter, a chunky girl named Cora Munsen, swung and hit a hard line drive right into the hands of the second baseman, who dropped it. We had the bases loaded, and I came to bat for the first time in my new school.

All eyes were on me, some hoping I would look foolish, most just curious. I saw Mrs. Grossbard's nod of approval at the way I held the bat and took my stance. My heart was pounding. I had to step out of the box for a moment to catch my breath, collect myself, and step back.

The first pitch was too low and the second too wide, but the third was slow and down the middle, my favorite pitch. I timed it just right and hit the ball hard. It rose and rose and went over the center fielder's head. The school's baseball field was bordered in the back by a small hill. The ball hit the crest of the hill and began to roll down, but it was so far away from the center fielder, she could never get a throw back to relay another before I had rounded the bases.

My first time up, I had hit a grand-slam home run.

And Mrs. Grossbard cheered as hard as anyone I had ever had cheer for me at my public school.

Afterward, everyone was talking about my hit. Girls were coming over to introduce themselves in the locker room, and by the time we all left the gym area to board our small, plush school buses, there was hardly a student at Agnes Fodor who hadn't heard about the longest home-run ball ever hit at the field. By the end of the day, talk about my hit was so exaggerated that the story going around school was that my home run had cleared the hill.

Mrs. Grossbard came out to speak to me before I boarded the bus.

"Tomorrow," she said, "you sign up for the softball team, okay?"

"Sure," I said.

"Heck," she said, "we might even win a game."

Bursting with excitement, I hurried onto the bus, eager to brag to my new parents about my first day.

6
I Need to Be Me

Still filled with excitement, I charged up to the front door of my new house and entered, hardly able to contain myself. I was about to run up the stairs to my room to change my clothes, when Pamela stepped out of the living room.

"Good. You're home on time. Come right in here," she said, indicating the living room.

"I was just going to put my books away and change," I said. "I wanted to tell you all about . . ."

"Just step right in here now," she said with a firmer voice. "You can do that later. There is someone here I want you to meet immediately."

Obediently, I walked down the hall and entered the living room. A short, bald man with a face as round as a penny stood there gaping at me with big, watery gray eyes. He had a dark brown blotch on his otherwise shiny skull. It looked as if someone had splattered beef gravy on him because it spread in thin lines toward the back of his head and his temples.

"This is Professor Wertzman, Brooke. I've hired him to start you on piano lessons. Contestants need to show some talent, and the professor will teach you how to play well enough so you could perform something," she declared. It sounded more as if she had ordained it and it would be.

"But I don't have any musical talent. I never even tried to play the piano," I said weakly.

"That's because you never had one to play. What lessons were you ever offered at the orphanage?" she asked with a cold smile. "Now you have all the finer things in life at your beck and call. Professor Wertzman is a highly regarded piano instructor. It took a great deal to get him to free up some time for you, but he knows how important this is to me," she added, eyeing him with her icy glare.

When he smiled, his chin quivered and his nostrils went in and out like a rabbit's.

"It's an honor for me to be able to do you and Mr. Thompson a favor," he said.

"See? Everyone's trying to help you, Brooke. Beginning today, you'll have a lesson every day after school, so come right home," she commanded.

"But . . ."

"But what?" She looked at the professor, who widened his smile, and then they both looked at me.

"The coach, Mrs. Grossbard, asked me to join the school's softball team. I hit a home run in class today, a grand-slam home run my first time up at bat! I have to stay after school for practice every day."

For a moment, Pamela simply stared at me and blinked her eyes. The professor was uncomfortable standing in the long moment of silence. He cleared his throat and rocked on his heels with his hands behind his back.

"Have you any idea of the cost and the effort it took to get Professor Wertzman here?" she began softly. "Do you know that the professor tutors most of the pianists from finer families in our community? He has assured me he can get you ready to perform a piece in six months. No one else can make such a promise. You are a very lucky young lady." The way she said *lucky* made me think I was anything but.

"I don't care," I snapped. "I don't want to learn piano. I was never interested in piano. I hit a home run," I repeated, backing away. "I'm good at softball. I want to be on the team."

"Brooke!"

"No! You don't care about me at all, you just want to turn me into you!" I cried, and turned toward the stairway.

"You get right back here this instant. Brooke!"

I ran up the stairway and into my room, the tears flying from my cheeks. Then I sprawled on my bed and buried my face in my pillow.

She didn't have a right to do this, to make plans like this without asking me first. I don't care what she does, I thought. I don't care if she sends me back. I stopped sobbing, wiped my face, and sat hugging my knees, waiting for her to come angrily after me. I listened hard in anticipation of her footsteps in the hallway, but I heard nothing. Finally, I changed into what Pamela called a more casual outfit, a pair of slacks and a blouse that didn't make me feel any more comfortable than the clothes I wore to school. How I missed my jeans, T-shirts, and sweatshirts, I thought.

I was still afraid to go downstairs, so I opened my books and started my homework. It was nearly an hour and a half later when I heard a knock on my door. I hadn't heard any footsteps, and I never expected Pamela would knock. She always just walked right in.

"Yes?"

The door opened. It was Peter. He was wearing one of his expensive-looking blue suits and looked as fresh and alert as he would if he had just begun his day.

"Mind if I come in?" he asked.

"No," I said.

He smiled and closed the door softly behind him. "So," he began, "it looks like we're having our first family crisis."

"I don't have any musical talent," I moaned.

"How do you know that?"

"I don't, but I don't want to play piano," I insisted.

"Well," he said calmly before sitting on the edge of my bed, "you're too young to really know what you want and don't want. It's like someone who's never tasted caviar saying, 'I don't want to eat caviar. I don't like it.' Right?" he asked in a soft, soothing voice.

"I suppose." I sniffled. I didn't want to start crying again, but I could feel hot tears building behind my eyes.

"Well, you don't know if you want to play piano until you try. You might find the experience wonderful, and you might make such progress so quickly, you'll get excited about it yourself," he reasoned. "You're a very intelligent young lady, Brooke. I'm sure you can understand my point."

I was silent a moment, and then I caught my breath and turned to him, the tears still burning beneath my eyelids.

"I hit a home run in gym class today," I said. "It was a grand slam."

"Really?" he said, his eyes widening. "A grand slammer?"

"Uh-huh. And it was my first time at bat ever at the new school. The coach asked me to be on the team. She needs a pitcher, and I always used to be the pitcher at my old school," I told him.

"Is that right?"

"The team practices every day after school. The next game is only a week away. Every practice is important for me."

"I see. And you told Pamela this?" he asked, his eyebrows lifting as his eyes filled with concern.

"Yes."

"Now I understand," he said, nodding. He rose and walked to the window, paused there for a moment, and then turned and walked toward the door. "What if I could arrange for your piano lessons early in the evening after dinner? Do you think you could manage all that and your homework, too?"

"Yes," I said quickly, even though I had no idea if I could.

"It would only have to be this way until softball season ends," he explained, and I could tell he was still figuring out how to make it sound good to Pamela.

"But I thought the professor was doing us a favor and was only available after school," I said.

Peter winked. "We'll negotiate," he answered. "It's what I do for a living. The secret is never to panic but to step back, take a breath, and look for new doors through which you can enter the same house. This way, you get to be on the team, Pamela is satisfied that she is doing the best for you, and the professor is happier, too. I'll make sure of that. Sound good?"

I nodded. "Great. Then don't worry about it. Most of the time, we make our problems seem bigger than they are. When we look at them calmly, we realize that most of our dragons are created in our own imaginations. I want to hear more about that home run later," he said at the door. He gave me a big smile again and left.

I sighed with relief. I was lucky having someone like him for a father, I thought. No wonder he is so successful. He thinks of solutions and ideas so fast. He could probably even be president of the United States.

At dinnertime, however, I was still very nervous. Pamela sat with her lips firm, her back straight and stiff. I took my seat quietly, afraid to look at her, because when I did, she shot angry glances at me.

"Everything's arranged with Professor Wertzman," Peter said happily.

"I'm still owed an apology for poor behavior," Pamela muttered, her eyes lifting to focus on me. "Especially poor behavior in front of someone like Professor Wertzman. He goes from one important family home to another, and I wouldn't want him speaking poorly of us."

"He knows better than to do that, Pamela," Peter said.

"That's not the point."

"I'm sorry," I said. "I was just upset. It came as such a surprise."

"Here I am trying to do the best things for you," she whined, "and you make me look like a fool."

"I'm sorry," I said again.

"Everything's fine now," Peter said. "Let's just enjoy a great dinner and hear about Brooke's first day at Agnes Fodor."

"She could have had her first lesson today," Pamela said in a lower voice, retreating like a car engine puttering to a stop.

"She'll make up for it, I'm sure," Peter said. "Tell us about the school, Brooke."

I described my classes, teachers, and some of the students. Pamela was most interested in whom I was making friends with. She wanted to know about their families, but I didn't know much about anyone else's family, and I couldn't give her the information she wanted.

"You should ask more questions," she told me.

"Show that you're interested in them. Even if you don't really listen," she added.

Peter laughed. "Pamela is an expert when it comes to small talk. Everyone wants to talk to her, but at the end of the evening, she can't tell me half of what they said. No one ever seems to catch on, though, so I suppose they don't mind," he concluded with a laugh.

Why wouldn't anyone mind if you didn't really listen? What kind of people were at these grand, important parties?

"Now, tell us about your home run," he finally said. Pamela smirked and started eating while I described the teams and my hit and the aftermath.

"Girls' sports are a much bigger thing than when you were her age, Pamela," Peter explained. Somehow, I think that just made her angry again.

"When they add tennis, golf, baseball, or basketball to the Miss America contest, tell me," she quipped. Peter laughed, but he stopped talking about it.

The days that followed were harder than I ever imagined. There was so much schoolwork to catch up on besides the day-to-day work I had to do. Softball practice was the only thing I really looked forward to, and my enthusiasm put happy smiles on Coach Grossbard's face. However, it was physically demanding. Very quickly, Coach Grossbard determined that I would be the starting pitcher and bat cleanup. The only girl who seemed dissatisfied about it was Cora Munsen, who had been the team's cleanup hitter.

"You just had one lucky hit," she told me in the locker room. "You're not any better than I am at bat."

I didn't want her to hate me, so I agreed. "I'll do whatever the coach wants," I said. "It's the team that's important."

"Sure," she said. "Like you really care. You're just like the others. You want all the glory."

"That's not true, Cora."

She shook her head and walked away.

Most of the girls made fun of her because she was so big, but none of them ever said anything to her face. She looked as if she could sweep them off their feet with one swing of her heavy arms. I learned they had nicknamed her Cora Munching because she ate so much. She even sneaked food between classes. I thought that if she lost weight, she could be very pretty, but I was afraid to tell her.

After my softball practice, I had to hurry home to get ready for dinner and try to get in some homework. Occasionally, I didn't have time to shower before I sat for my piano lesson. Professor Wertzman didn't seem to care. He had a strange odor himself, an odor that nearly turned my stomach because he sat so close to me on the piano bench. I tried to turn away or hold my breath, but it was difficult not to inhale that stale, clammy, sour smell. I noticed he wore the same shirt all week, and by Friday, the collar would be yellowish brown where it touched his neck.

When he gave me instructions, he had a way of closing his eyes so that they became slits. Sometimes, when he got very excited about a mistake I had made, he would spray the piano with spit and then wipe it off with the sleeve of his left arm quickly. Often, Pamela came in to watch, and when she was in the room, his expression suddenly took on softness, his gentle, considerate teacher's voice returning. When we were alone, he spoke abruptly, had little patience, and complained continually about the difficulty he had turning a pebble into a pearl. It was always on the tip of my tongue to tell him I never asked him to perform any miracles, but I swallowed back my pride and let him lash me with ridicule and criticism.

One night, when Peter was sitting alone in the living room and reading, I stopped in to talk to him.

"I tasted caviar," I said, "and I hate it."

"What?" He looked at me, and then he smiled. "Oh. Right." He nodded.

"I'm never going to be good on the piano," I said. "Even the professor says my fingers aren't right. He says I'm too forceful and that I'd be better at drums or carpentry work."

"Is that what he said?" Peter laughed. "Well, just put up with it awhile longer until I get Pamela to think of something better."

"I don't want to be in beauty contests," I added.

"It can't hurt you to do it once or twice," he told me. "Look at it as a new experience."

"No one else at the school is going to be in any beauty contests, and there are girls in school who are really a lot prettier than I am. They're going to laugh at me and make fun of me," I warned him.

"Maybe you'll win. Then they won't laugh." The way he said it made me believe I really had a chance. Maybe Pamela *was* right about me.

"Will you and Pamela come to the home game this Saturday?" I asked. I had been mentioning it all week, but Pamela pretended she didn't hear me.

"Sure," he said. He thought a moment. "I ought to get myself a video camera, too." He looked at me. "Don't expect me to become one of those crazy Little League parents, though."

I laughed.

When he brought up the game himself at dinner that evening, Pamela refused to go.

"Do you know what damage is done to your skin sitting out there under that horrible sunlight and letting all that dust come settling on you? When you come home," she said, turning to me, "you make sure you go right into a bathtub and clean all the pollution out of your pores and wash your hair."

She thought intently for a moment and then suddenly rose and came around the table.

"Let me see your hands," she ordered. I raised my palms, and she grabbed them and ran her fingers over them.

"Just as I thought," she said to Peter. "Her skin is getting rough. Soon she'll have calluses!"

"Really?" he asked. He sounded amused, and I could see he was trying not to smile.

"Come over here and feel them. Come on."

"I believe you."

"This is just ridiculous. A daughter with hands like a ditch digger. I want you to come up to my room after dinner. I have a hand lotion you'll have to use continually. You rub it in four or five times a day."

"Four times a day? You mean even while I'm at school?" I asked.

"Of course. How much longer will this baseball nonsense continue?" She was beginning to pout.

"We only have a few games left," I said. "I came on late in the season."

"Good," she muttered, and returned to her chair.

I was afraid to tell her that I had already agreed to try out for the girls' basketball team. The coach saw me shooting baskets with some seniors and asked me to come to tryouts next week. Besides that, Coach Grossbard believed I might get chosen for the all-star game this year and have to go to a special practice after the end of our softball season. Sports were the one thing I *knew* I was good at—and I didn't intend to give them up.

Peter decided that he would drive me to my game on Saturday. I was dressed in my uniform when I came bouncing down the stairs. Pamela was expecting her masseuse, but she was still downstairs giving Joline some instructions about a new juice drink that included herbs which she claimed retarded the aging process. As soon as she saw me come down the stairs, she began a stream of complaints.

"Is that their uniform? You're dressed like a boy. Why don't you wear a skirt, at least?"

"They can't wear skirts, Pamela," Peter said, laughing.

"Why not?"

"They might have to slide into base. They have to wear something practical."

"Why don't they wear some decent color combination, then?" she followed.

"These are the school colors," I explained.

"Whoever picked them out is not very creative. Remember what I said you're to do as soon as you come home," she told me, and continued up the stairs, mumbling under her breath.

"She's really very proud of you," Peter tried to assure me. "It's just that sports have never been important to her."

On the way to the game, he talked about his own interest in sports and how he followed football and tennis.

"I play a mean game of tennis," he bragged. "One of these days, I'll take you to the club, and we'll hit a few. Would you like that?"

"Yes," I said. "I've always wanted to play tennis, but we never had anyplace to play. My old school didn't have tennis courts, but Agnes Fodor does."

"Great. Now, that's a sport I might get Pamela interested in. She likes the outfits," he told me.

The outfits? I thought. They had the least to do with why I would want to play or watch a sport. I began to wonder if Pamela and I would ever understand each other. And wasn't that important? Having a mother who understood your dreams and desires, your hopes and wishes?

As Peter and I neared the school, I thought about the team we would play today—they were undefeated. The girls on their team did look tougher, stronger, and hungrier. Their leadoff hitter was a tall African-

American girl who looked as if she could drive the ball through anyone in the infield. I saw how the girls on my team stepped back when I started to pitch, anticipating a line drive. However, I took advantage of her height and kept my pitches low. She went for two bad ones and missed, and the third was a foul that our first baseman was able to catch. My team cheered, and the nervousness they had come to the field with settled.

I grew stronger with every pitch. Once in a while, I gazed at the bleachers and saw Peter smiling at me. He had brought his new video camera and was filming the game. I had three hits that day, one a triple with two girls on base. It drove in what was to be the winning run.

The other team looked stunned. My team gathered around me and cheered as if they had won the World Series. As we left the field, I heard the other coach ask Coach Grossbard where she had gotten the ringer.

Peter was really excited all the way home. "Wait until I play the tape for Pamela. That last hit of yours was a beaut, right between the right fielder and the center fielder. How'd you do it?"

"My coach at my last school showed me how to turn my feet to place the ball," I explained. Peter was very impressed, and for the first time since I had moved in with him and Pamela, I felt proud of myself and confident that they could be proud of me.

When we arrived home, Pamela was still soaking in her milk bath, something she did after every massage. Peter hurried in to tell her about the game. I showered, washed my hair, and changed. Peter wanted to take us to a fancy restaurant to celebrate. But first, he wanted to show Pamela some of the highlights from the game.

I waited downstairs in the family room. The two of them finally appeared, Pamela looking radiant and beautiful. Peter put the tape in the machine and turned on the television set.

"Did you wash your hair with that shampoo I bought you?" Pamela asked me—it was obvious she didn't care about how well I'd done in the game.

"Yes, I did."

She put her fingers through my hair and nodded. "You don't realize the damage the sun can do to your hair."

"I wore a hat," I said.

"It doesn't cover your whole head, does it?"

"Here she is. Watch this, Pamela!" Peter cried. It was when I had my first hit, a strong single to left.

She nodded. "Did you rub the skin lotion into your hands?"

I had forgotten, but I nodded. She narrowed her eyes with suspicion and felt my hands.

"They're very dry."

"Here's where she strikes out their best hitter. Watch these three pitches. Look at that."

"You should go up and rub in the lotion," she said.

"I will."

"Here it comes, Pamela, the triple. Watch this. There. Wow! That was the winning run."

"She's developing muscles," Pamela said with a grimace. "What girl her age has muscles? Sports will make you too masculine," she warned. "Why do you insist on pursuing these silly sports?"

I felt my heart sink. I had hoped that once she saw how good I was, she would not be so down on my participation in sports, but nothing Peter showed her on the tape seemed to impress her.

"I'm hungry, Peter," she whined.

"Fine. We're ready. So what do you think?" he asked. "We got a little Babe Ruth, huh?"

"I'd rather have a little Cindy Crawford," she quipped. "Hurry upstairs and do your hands, Brooke," she ordered.

I looked at Peter and then left the room. They were both waiting in the car when I returned.

"Watch your posture," Pamela complained from the car window as I approached. "You're hunching over too much. It's your shoulders. They're getting too big, probably from swinging that heavy stick of wood."

"It's called a bat," I muttered as I got in.

She shot me a fiery look of irritation and then caught sight of herself reflected in the glass and worried about a redness in her right cheek all the way to the restaurant.

Not another word was said about my softball game. For all she cared, I could have struck out every time at bat.

Even Mrs. Talbot back at the orphanage had been prouder of me.

Before dinner ended, I looked at Pamela and asked, "Did you ever play softball, Pamela?"

"Me? Of course not." She sniffed. "Hardly."

"Then how do you know you don't like it?" I followed.

"What?"

"It's like if you never tasted caviar but said you don't like it."

She looked at Peter. "Whatever is she saying?"

Peter smiled, but I didn't smile back. And then, for the first time, I saw a dark shadow in his eyes when he glanced at Pamela and then at me.

I looked away and thought about the wonderful feeling that had traveled through me when I connected at the plate and that ball went sailing. All the lotions, herbs, vitamins, and shampoos couldn't make me feel better about myself than I had at that moment. What would happen if Pamela made me stop playing? Would I ever feel good about myself again?

7
Trial by Fire

Despite my lack of enthusiasm and my dislike of Professor Wertzman, I was able to play a crude rendition of "When the Saints Come Marching In" five weeks after I had begun my lessons. Pamela thought this proved I was talented enough to perform at the first pageant. As the reality of my actually participating in that event grew, she decided to begin instructing me on how to do what she called the Runway Walk.

"The only difference is that instead of presenting some designer's new fashion, you're really presenting yourself," she explained.

We used the long downstairs corridor in our house, and she immediately criticized the size of my steps.

"You're plodding along like a robot, not walking. You've got to glide over that stage, float. Think of yourself as made of air. That's how I was taught. Soft, soft, feminine, soft," she chanted as I repeated the journey from the front door to the dining room. "Glide. Don't move your arms so much, relax. Open your hands. You can't walk out with your fists clenched! You're not smiling, Brooke. Smile. Stop!"

She thought a moment. "You can't look bored or uncomfortable, Brooke. Beauty must be ignited with enthusiasm. This is the motto I was taught, and you must learn and live it as well."

"I feel silly," I grumbled.

"You must get over that. What you're doing is not silly. It's professional. The judges must sense that you have self-confidence."

"But I don't belong in a beauty pageant. I'm not beautiful," I insisted.

She raised her eyes to the ceiling and looked as if she was counting to ten. "All right," she said in a softer voice. "Come with me now."

She walked briskly to the stairway and waited for me to catch up. Then she caught my hand in hers and took me up to her bedroom.

"Sit," she said, pointing at her vanity table. I did so. "Look at yourself in that mirror. What do you think are your worst features?"

"All of them," I moaned.

"Wrong. You have a great deal of raw beauty. Now, do as I say," she ordered, and pulled out her lip pencils. "Bold lips are back. Not every young woman can wear bold eye shadow, but most can easily wear a bold lip color.

"If you knew anything about makeup and faces, you would know you don't have what we call bee-stung lips, so you should stay away from dark, matte shades. You need colors with more intensity. Dark colors will make your mouth look smaller. First, open your mouth." She demonstrated. "I want to line your lips fully."

I did what she said, and she began.

"Good," she said, stepping back and scrutinizing me. "I like to mix and match my lipsticks. In the morning, I'll begin with a matte lipstick. Then, later, rather than add more of that, which might look cakey, I'll smooth on either a clear gloss or lip balm. Sometimes I try a sheer moisturizing lipstick or colored gloss," she lectured as she worked.

She had my face turned to her so I didn't see everything she was doing, but she worked like an artist and then said, "There."

I turned and looked with surprise at my face. My lips were prominent now.

"My mouth looks so different," I said. She laughed.

"Audrey Hepburn, who had thin lips, used to outline just lightly over the lip line like that. Everyone has her own little tricks."

She studied my image in the mirror a moment. "You can wear a dark eye liner, I think," she said. She continued to make up my face, powdering, working on my eyes, until she had what she wanted and told me to look at myself again.

"Well?" she asked.

"I look so . . ."

"Pretty?"

I was afraid to use that word. Did I dare think it? "Different. Am I pretty?"

"I've been telling you that ever since I set eyes on you. Now that you are made up and see what you can look like, you should feel more comfortable and confident about yourself. I want you to do more in the way of makeup every day so you get used to it, Brooke."

"You mean put on makeup for school?"

"Of course. That's why I bought all this for you and had it here before you arrived. Every day from now on, I want you to prepare your face as if you were entering a beauty contest. That's what life is for us, anyway, a continually running beauty pageant."

"But none of the other girls wear makeup yet. They'll think I'm trying to look older and fit in with the older girls," I complained.

"Let them think what they want. They don't have half the beauty I . . . I mean *you* do. Let's go," she said. "Back downstairs to practice the runway walk now."

She paraded me back and forth in the hallway for nearly another hour, using music, showing me how to turn, to pause, to look out at the audience, to make myself look seductive or innocent.

"Every contestant, every model, is really an actress, Brooke. You have to assume a persona. Think of yourself as someone special, and be that person for a while. Sometimes I imagined myself like Marilyn Monroe, and sometimes I was more subtle, an Ingrid Bergman or a Deborah Kerr. Nowadays, all the girls your age are trying to be like one of those dreadful Spice Girls, but you will be someone unique. You will be . . . me," she declared, and laughed. "Just keep studying me all the time, and it will come."

Pamela's words scared me—she really did want to make me into her, and my talents and wants just didn't matter. I didn't understand—why couldn't Pamela like me for me? And, if she wouldn't even like me, how would she ever come to love me?

The next day, I began to feel a little better when I realized at least the kids at school liked me for the real me. On the bus that morning, everyone wanted to sit next to me and talk about the game. In homeroom, Mr. Rudley, who admitted he had yet to attend a school sports event, said he heard he had better show up at the next softball game. The school had a star. I knew I was blushing all over. When I looked at the others, I saw Heather staring at me. She looked so furious, it made my heart thump.

At lunch, I received all sorts of invitations. I was asked to girls' houses, told about upcoming parties and events, and invited to join clubs. Lisa Donald, who was one of the school's best tennis players, volunteered to give me instructions at her family's tennis court.

"You could come over next weekend," she said. "I'm having a few friends over, including some boys from Brandon Pierce." I knew that was an all-boys school nearby.

"Whom do you know at Brandon Pierce?" Heather challenged.

"My cousin Harrison, who's bringing a friend. We might play doubles," she told me.

All the girls looked envious. I had to admit that I had never played tennis before, ever.

"Never? How come?" Heather demanded. "Don't your parents have a court?" She made a tennis court sound as common as a bathroom.

"Yes," I said.

"So?"

"I just never played."

"Why wouldn't you play if you had a court?" she countered, stepping forward to put her face right up to mine.

"What's the difference?" Lisa demanded. "She'll learn now with a good teacher, me."

The girls laughed, but Heather just stared at me with those small, beady eyes. Helen Baldwin pushed in front of her to ask me something about our social studies homework, and then Helen started to talk about Lisa's cousin Harrison.

"He's a sex maniac," she declared. Everyone paid attention after she blurted that. "Right, Lisa?"

"It's on his mind more than it is on other boys' minds, I guess. When we were both seven and eight, he only wanted to play doctor whenever he came over."

"Did you play?" Eva asked.

"No, but once he chased me all around the property trying to get me to take off my panties."

"I wouldn't mind him taking off mine," Rosemary said. The girls giggled.

"Yes, you would," Heather charged. "Stop trying to sound like a big shot."

"He's good-looking. You said so yourself, Heather. You said you wished he would look at you," Lisa told her.

"I did not. Liar."

"What *did* you say, then?" Lisa questioned.

Heather looked at the rest of us. "I said he was wasting his time with that Paula Dworkins, that's all," Heather insisted.

"I bet he'll like Brooke," Rosemary said. The girls turned to me.

"Why should he like me?" I asked.

"He likes anyone new for a day or so," she replied. "But once he sees you swing your bat, he'll fall head over heels in love," she added.

"Yeah, and with all that makeup you're wearing, you'll be an easy target," Heather sniped at me.

The girls cackled, Heather the loudest.

"She's joking," Lisa said, "but he does like girls who are into sports. I know. He told me." They grew quiet. "That's why you want to learn tennis quickly," she said. "I imagine it won't take you long."

"It seems very strange that your father would never teach you," Heather insisted. "Don't you get along with him?"

"Mind your own business," Helen said.

"Of course we get along," I said. "He's just very busy." I was glad to turn the conversation away from the awful makeup Pamela had made me wear that morning.

Heather smirked. "That's exactly what my father says every time I ask him to do something with me," she remarked.

"The only difference is that Brooke's father's not lying," Eva said, and the girls laughed hard again. I had to smile. Heather gazed at me. If her eyes could throw darts, I'd have been full of holes.

The rest of the week went smoothly. Everyone was more excited than ever at softball practice. I did well on two tests, and my teachers gave me compliments on my efforts. Mrs. Harper actually stopped me in the hall to tell me I was making a very good transition.

"Just stay on course," she told me. Her eyes were so fierce, it sounded like a warning. I thanked her and quickly moved on.

At home, I performed my piano lessons with an attitude of resignation. I had come to the conclusion it was something I had to do, like going to the bathroom. Professor Wertzman didn't think any better of my playing, but he didn't criticize and complain as much as he usually did.

Peter was away most of the week on a big case that took him to New York City. The conversations about school and other interesting things that were happening in the world disappeared from dinner. Pamela continued to use the meal as a classroom, developing my education in proper mealtime manners. She was impressed that I had been invited to Lisa Donald's house for lunch and tennis. On her own, she had found out that Lisa's father was one of the Donalds who owned the local department store.

"I just knew you would make friends with people of quality," she said.

What did that mean, people of quality? What gave one person higher quality than another? Was it just money? I hadn't found the girls at Agnes Fodor to be any nicer than the girls I knew at my public school. They had the same hangups, problems, worries, and complaints.

Despite Mrs. Harper's resounding flattery and compliments, I discovered that her girls, her perfect girls, were not so perfect after all. They were just more subtle, more sneaky about the things they did. When the teacher left the room, they cheated. They passed notes, and they smoked in the girls' room, but they did it by the window so they could blow the smoke outside. Afterward, they always flushed the butts down the toilet. As far as graffiti went, someone wrote "Brooke wears a jock strap" on my gym locker, and Coach Grossbard had to get the janitor to find some strong detergent to wash it off. No one told Mrs. Harper. It was as if she had to be protected from any news of wrongdoing so she could continue to believe her girls were perfect.

Peter returned from New York on Friday night, and Pamela had me do the runway walk for him. She made him sit in the high-back antique chair in the hallway and watch like a judge at a beauty contest. I half expected him to burst out laughing when I began, but the look that came over him was different—I'd never seen him look at me so intently before.

"Well?" Pamela asked as soon as I made my last turn.

"Amazing. You've done amazing work, Pamela. She looks . . . older."

"Of course she does. She's more mature, more

sophisticated and confident. She's been invited to the Donalds' for lunch tomorrow," she told him.

I didn't think it was a very big deal, but she made me describe the invitation, Lisa's offer to teach me tennis, and the rich boys who were joining us for lunch and tennis. Peter wore this serious look on his face, but he gazed at me with amusement in his eyes.

"You don't have a game this Saturday?" he asked.

"It wouldn't matter if she did. She would still go to the Donalds'," Pamela interjected.

Of course I wouldn't, but I let her believe what she wanted.

"No. Our next game is at home the following Saturday," I told him. "Will you come?"

"I'll try," he said, withholding a promise. "The way this Jacobi matter is playing out, I don't know when I'll have free time this month. We thought they'd settle, but they've decided to play their hand, it seems."

Pamela didn't ask him to explain more. I realized that all the time I had been living with them, she never asked him about his work or showed any interest in any of his cases unless there was a client who interested her, and then she was more curious about the person than the case, anyway.

"What's the matter with Jacobi?" I asked.

"It's not what's the matter with him," he explained. "It's his matter, the case."

"Oh," I said, feeling stupid.

To make me feel better, he started to talk about the case, but Pamela interrupted to ask if he had gotten me the sponsor.

"What does that mean? Why do I need a sponsor?" I asked.

"For the beauty pageant. Each girl has to be sponsored, and not by her own family," Pamela said. "The company will pay all your expenses, not that we need them to. It's just the way it's done."

"Who would sponsor me?" I wondered aloud.

"A number of companies," she declared irritably. "Peter?"

"I'll talk to Gerry Lawson tomorrow. He already gave me a preliminary approval. Don't worry," he urged her, and she relaxed.

Was this really going to happen? Was I really going to participate in a beauty contest? Me? I felt as if something was in my chest tickling my heart with a feather, but I was afraid to utter the least bit of reluctance, as it would put Pamela into a horribly mean mood.

Saturday, Peter drove me to Lisa's home. Pamela stood over me at my vanity table to make sure I did my makeup right.

"Who knows who you'll meet?" she said.

Pamela came along with Peter and me so she could see the Donalds' house. It turned out to be even larger than ours, which I didn't think possible. They had more grounds, a bigger pool, a guest house, and two clay tennis courts. Pamela said the house was a Greek Revival, and she was envious of the recessed front door.

"I wanted that," she moaned. "We should redo our front."

"There's nothing wrong with our entrance, Pamela," Peter insisted. She pouted, but when I stepped out, she brightened up to warn me to behave myself and remember all the manners she had taught me.

"Especially when you eat," she called. I waved and hurried to the front door.

Lisa answered the bell herself. She was already in a tennis outfit.

"Good, you're a little early. Come on," she said before I could say hello. She took my hand and pulled me through the large house. I could only get glimpses of the large rooms, the expensive-looking furnishings and paintings. I did realize the decor was different from ours, more antique-looking.

We burst out a side door and headed for the tennis court. There was a machine set up on one side.

"What's that?"

"Daddy bought that for us to practice returning serves. You'll see," she said.

She gave me a racquet and told me it was one of the best. Then she showed me how to hold it and went through the motions of how to swing. She was so excited about teaching me.

"I never met anyone who had never even held a tennis racquet before," she declared, but she didn't cross-examine me as Heather would.

Despite practically growing up with a tennis racquet in her hand, Lisa wasn't very good. It didn't take me long to master the basic motion, and after a dozen or so practice swings, I began to develop a passable serve. I didn't think I was hitting the ball that hard, but she had difficulty returning my serve. I quickly discovered that all I had to do was hit the ball to one side and then return it to the other a little harder to defeat her. I held back, because I saw she was getting annoyed.

"You're so damn athletic," she complained. Then she stopped and looked at me suspiciously. "Were you lying? Have you played tennis before?"

"No," I said, shaking my head. "I really never have."

"It does seem strange, especially now that I see how you play."

I realized that she wasn't going to believe me. "I really haven't played," I said. "Honest."

She accepted that, and anyway, there wasn't time to talk about it anymore. Harrison and his friend shouted to us from the front of the house and started down the lawn toward the tennis courts.

The girls at school had been right: Harrison was a very good-looking dark-haired boy. He was tall, with long, slender legs jutting out of a pair of milk white tennis shorts. He wore a white polo shirt with black trim on the sleeves and collar. As they drew closer, I saw Harrison had thick, dark eyebrows. His eyes were almost black and set in a narrow face with sharp cheekbones and a strong mouth. He wore an impish smile on those firm lips and carried himself with an arrogant air, just the way a boy who knew he was good-looking and rich would.

His partner was shorter, stout, and light-haired, with a round face and blue eyes. His bottom lip looked thicker than the top, and there was a softness in his cheeks and chin that made him look more childish than handsome.

"This is your Mickey Mantle?" Harrison asked with a laugh. His friend looked as if his face was made of putty and someone had stamped a smile on it.

"Brooke, my cousin Harrison," Lisa said.

"Hi," he said. "This is Brody Taylor. You know my cousin Lisa."

"Yes, I do," Brody said.

"Are you as good at tennis as you are at softball?" Harrison asked me.

"No. I just got my first lesson."

"From Lisa?" He laughed. "That's like the blind teaching the blind."

"Really?" Lisa looked at me and smiled. "Why don't we start with boys against girls?"

"It won't even be a contest," Harrison bragged.

"We'll chance it."

"What's the bet?"

"What do you want to bet?"

"Virginity?" he quipped.

Lisa turned beet red, and Brody laughed, a sort of sniffle laugh with the air being pushed out of his nose and his body shaking.

"You're still a virgin?" I countered. It was as if we were playing tennis with words.

This time, Harrison turned crimson. "Okay, let's bet twenty dollars," he suggested.

"Fine," Lisa replied.

"Twenty dollars! I don't have any money with me," I cried.

"Don't worry about it," Lisa said. "You could always pay me back in school if we should lose."

"What do you mean, if you should lose? You mean *when* you lose," Harrison said. Brody laughed again.

"I don't even know the rules," I whispered to Lisa.

"Just keep the ball within the inside lines," she advised. She turned to Harrison. "Why don't you two warm up, then?"

"We don't need a warmup, do we, Brody?"

He shrugged. Harrison removed his racquet from his case, and Brody did the same. They took their positions on the other side of the net.

"I'll serve first," Lisa told me.

My heart was thumping. Twenty dollars! They talked about it as if it were small change.

We began to play. Harrison was good, but Brody was slow. I saw the way he positioned himself and discovered quickly that he was usually off balance. There were things that were common to all sports: posture, poise, conditioning, and timing. All I had to do was return the ball at Brody with some speed, and he usually hit it out of bounds or into the net. As we won set after set, Harrison's temper flared. He directed his fury at Brody, which only made him play worse. When Lisa and I won, Harrison threw his racquet across the lawn.

"You lied," he said, pointing at Lisa.

"What?"

"You didn't just teach her how to play. No one just learns and hits the ball like that."

"I didn't lie!" Lisa screamed, her hands on her hips. "That's what she told me. Right, Brooke?"

"It's true," I said, but he didn't look any more satisfied. "Let's forget the money," I added.

"Who cares about the money?" he muttered. "Brody, give them twenty bucks," he ordered.

"All twenty? Why do I have to give them all of it?" he whined.

"Because you let a couple of girls from Agnes Fodor make us look like fools, that's why."

Brody dug into his pocket and came up with a wad of bills. He peeled off two tens and handed them to Lisa, who took the money with a fat smile on her face. She handed me a ten.

"I don't want it," I said.

"Because you lied, right?" Harrison shot at me.

"No, because I don't need money and because I played because I wanted to play for the fun of it."

"Right," he said. "Let's get something to eat," he told Lisa.

She couldn't stop smiling. Harrison retrieved his racquet, and we all went up to the house where a lunch had been set up for us. It looked lavish enough to be a wedding reception to me, but to them it was just another meal. There were so many choices—meats, breads, salads, and different potatoes.

"Where are your parents?" Harrison asked Lisa. We sat at a patio table that had a tablecloth on it. Servants moved inconspicuously around us, cleaning up dishes, arranging foods.

"Golf club," she said between bites.

The food was delicious. I tried to remember my mealtime etiquette, but I was too hungry and started to eat too fast.

"Starving or something?" Harrison asked me.

"I forgot to eat breakfast," I said, even though I hadn't. It was something Lisa or one of the other girls would say. He accepted it.

"What took you so long to get here?" he inquired.

"Pardon?" I looked at Lisa.

"He means attending Agnes Fodor."

"Oh. I don't know. I just . . . my parents just decided I belonged there," I said.

He stared at me and then smiled. "Those real?" he asked.

"What?" I asked.

"Those boobs, they real?"

"Harrison!" Lisa squealed.

"Just asking. Nothing wrong with asking, is there, Brody?"

Brody, who had his face buried in the lobster salad, looked up and shook his head. His cheeks bulged with food.

"Well?" Harrison pursued.

"It's none of your business," I said.

He laughed. "That usually means, no, right, Brody?"

Brody nodded emphatically.

"What is he, your puppet?" I shot at him.

Harrison laughed. "She's all right, Lisa. Better than those other snot noses you call your friends," he said. He leaned over the table toward me. "Maybe I'll invite you to my house for a little one-on-one."

"What?"

"Tennis." He sat back, smiling. "Or did you want to do something else?"

"I don't want to do anything with you," I said.

"What's the matter, worried about your virginity?" he quipped. Brody started to laugh.

"No," I said. "My reputation."

Brody paused and then laughed harder.

"Shut up," Harrison snapped at him.

Harrison turned and glared at me. "I don't ask every girl to my house," he said.

"That surprises me," I replied.

Brody had to bite down on his lip to stop another laugh. Harrison caught it out of the corner of his eyes.

"Want to go listen to some music?" Lisa asked, growing nervous. "Harrison?"

He turned to her, a look of annoyance on his face. "What for?" he asked. "I'm not interested in wasting any more of my time." He stood up. "Maybe I'll come watch you play your next ball game," he said to me.

"Fine."

"Don't strike out," he said with a self-satisfied smile, "or I'll have my puppet here laugh."

"I can't think of a better reason not to," I said, and looked at Brody, who wiped his mouth, thanked Lisa for the lunch, and ran off to catch up with Harrison.

We watched them in silence, and then Lisa turned to me.

"Wow," she said. "No one's ever put Harrison down like that. Most of my other girlfriends swoon over him." She tilted her head and looked at me curiously.

"What?" I asked.

"You're different," she said.

"What do you mean?" I asked, my heart knocking like a tiny hammer in my chest.

"I don't know. You're full of surprises, like when you hit that home run. But," she said, jumping up, "that's what I like about you. Come on. Let's go listen to music and talk."

I followed her into the house, feeling deceitful, feeling as if I really didn't belong, but I wasn't upset so much about lying to my new friends as I was about lying to myself.

The truth was, the only time I felt honest was when I was playing softball or some sport. The real me couldn't be hidden.

Harrison would be disappointed. I wouldn't even come close to striking out.

8
Bases Loaded

We lost our next game, but not because I struck out or the other team got so many hits off me. Our team made too many errors, the big one being Cora Munsen's dropping of a fly ball with two on base. The way she looked at me afterward gave me the feeling she had done it on purpose just so I wouldn't look good. Coach Grossbard might have thought so, too. Afterward, in the locker room, she kept asking Cora why she dropped it.

"The sun wasn't in your eyes. You were in good position. What happened, Cora?"

"I don't know," Cora said, eyes down.

"Well, I don't understand. Anyone could have caught that ball," the coach insisted.

Cora was silent.

"Maybe she was too anxious," I said. "That's happened to me. I think about throwing the ball before I catch it."

It really didn't happen to me, but I'd seen it happen enough times to other girls. Cora looked up quickly.

"Yes," she said, grateful for the suggestion. "I think that was it."

The coach still looked suspicious. "Let's be sure it doesn't happen against Westgate next Saturday. We've never come close to beating them, and they shut us out the last three times," Coach Grossbard said.

"It won't," Cora promised.

The coach put up posters with the words "Get Westgate" on the locker-room walls during the week. I soon realized there was a real rivalry between the two schools, and pressure began to mount toward Saturday. It was hard for me to keep my mind on my piano lessons and modeling lessons while doing my homework and attending practices.

During Wednesday's piano lesson, Professor Wertzman had a tantrum.

"You seem to have forgotten everything. Such mistakes are not made by someone who is supposedly practicing!" he accused.

He jumped up and paced at the piano, shaking his head and looking at me furiously.

"I'm sorry," I said. "I'm trying."

"No, you're not trying. I know when a student is trying. I made your mother promises, and you're making it impossible to keep them," he declared.

Tears clouded my eyes. I lowered my head and waited for his fury to die down.

"I'll be a laughingstock," he muttered. "I have a reputation to protect. My reputation is my livelihood!"

"I'm trying," I moaned. "I'll try harder. I promise."

He stared at me with a look that made me feel as if I wasn't fit even to be in his presence. My lips began to tremble. Just then, Pamela entered. Right after dinner, her beautician had come over to do a treatment on her hair that she said would make it look fuller and richer. It didn't look any different to me.

"What's going on in here?" she asked, her hands on her hips.

The professor looked at me and shook his head. "I must have the full cooperation and attention of my student if I am to succeed," he said, shifting his eyes toward me.

"Brooke, aren't you trying?"

"Yes," I said. "I am. I'm not as good as everyone thinks, that's all."

"Who thinks that?" the professor muttered. "You can't be any good if you don't practice and pay attention. You are not practicing enough," he insisted.

"I do practice. I do," I said.

"Are you saying she needs more practice?" Pamela asked.

"At the rate she is going, more practice is definitely needed. I would like to see her add at least another four hours a week," he prescribed.

It hit me like a tablespoon of castor oil or a whip across my back. "Four more hours! When could I do that?"

Pamela stared coldly at me. "I think," she began slowly, "considering the sacrifices and the expense Peter and I are undertaking for your benefit, you could at least find the time. She'll practice an additional four hours every Saturday from now on," she declared firmly.

The professor looked satisfied.

"I can't practice any more on Saturday, especially not this coming Saturday. It's the biggest game of the year!"

"Game?" the professor asked, looking at Pamela.

"Don't listen to anything she says, Professor Wertzman. Please, give her instructions on what you want her to practice and what you expect her to accomplish this coming Saturday."

She turned back to me, her eyes like cold stones. "I'm filling out the application for the pageant's first audition tonight, Brooke. You have to be ready for every event. No," she said as I went to speak. "I don't want to say another word about it."

"But Saturday is very important. Everyone's depending on me," I blurted despite her order.

She stared and then looked up at the ceiling as if she were in great emotional pain. Without looking at me, she continued, "If there is any further problem or if the professor complains to me again, I will call Mrs. Harper and tell her you are forbidden from being on any team, baseball, checkers, anything," she threatened, her eyes still on the ceiling. Then she pivoted on her high heels and went clip-clopping down the hallway.

The professor turned to me. "Turn the page," he ordered, "and begin again."

The tears in my eyes made the notes hazy. I sucked

in my breath and tried to swallow down the lump that was stuck in my throat, but it clung like a wad of chewing gum. I could hardly breathe. Still, I did what the professor asked. It was more like torture now, his breath on my face, his groans and slaps on the piano, but I endured every moment, terrified that he would complain to Pamela again.

As soon as the lesson ended, I rose and ran from the room. I charged up the stairs, my feet pounding the steps so hard the beautiful stairway actually shook. When I got to my room, I slammed the door behind me and sat at my desk fuming. I was too angry to do any homework.

Minutes later, there was a knock.

"Come in," I called, and Peter opened the door.

"I saw you fly by the den and heard the house coming down over my head. What's today's crisis?"

"The professor thinks I'm doing terrible and wants me to add at least four more hours of practice. Pamela said I have to do it on Saturday, too, and I have the biggest game of the year on Saturday. She said if I made any more trouble, she would tell Mrs. Harper to keep me off all the teams. It's not fair!" I cried.

"That does sound severe," he agreed. Then he looked at me with his eyes brightening. "What about getting up earlier and practicing before you go to school?"

"Practicing isn't going to help me. I'm no good at piano," I moaned.

"If you do it, I'll make sure Pamela doesn't call Mrs. Harper," he said.

Another negotiation, I thought, another deal arranged by my lawyer foster father. I was getting up earlier now to do my makeup because Pamela wanted me to look beautiful. I might as well not go to sleep, I thought. But what choice did I have? A foster child who was soon to be legally adopted was like someone without any rights or even feelings. If I wanted parents and a home and a name, I had to be obedient. Pamela talked about my auditioning for the pageant, but what I was really doing was auditioning to be her daughter.

"Okay," I said. "I'll practice in the morning before breakfast, too."

"Great. Another crisis solved," he announced with a snap of his fingers, and went downstairs to tell Pamela how it would be.

Despite my enthusiasm and determination, my new busy schedule took its toll on me. It was most difficult during my morning classes. I felt as if I was dragging myself through the halls and plopping into my classroom seat like some old mop. Twice in English class, I actually dozed off for a few minutes, and Mr. Rudley had to step up to me and shake my shoulder after asking me a question. My eyes were open, but I hadn't heard him. I apologized, of course.

Somehow, I came to life at softball practice. Maybe it was being back in the fresh air. It was the third week in May now. The foliage was full, lush, and richly green. Two nights of rain during the week brought out the mayflies, however, and most of the girls were complaining. The ground was soft, even damp in spots. We all looked grimy by the end of a practice, mud splattered on our uniforms, faces, and hands, our hair sweaty, bug bites on our arms and necks.

None of it mattered to me. I felt I was at home, but my teammates wanted Coach Grossbard to have the field sprayed and dried. Everywhere these rich, pampered girls went in life, they expected someone would change things cosmetically to please them or make things easier.

However, when I returned home that afternoon and Pamela saw the little red blotches on the back of my neck, she went into a hysterical fit. At first, she thought it was caused by something I might have been eating. She accused me of sneaking candy bars at school. Then she thought I might be having an allergic reaction to something and started for the telephone to call her dermatologist. When I told her it was just a few mayflies, she stopped and stared at me as if I was crazy.

"Mayflies? Mayflies. Bug bites! That's disgusting. Get upstairs and into the tub immediately. Don't you realize how this could play havoc with your complexion, and you with a pageant audition only weeks away?"

"The bites don't last long. Next time I'll wear some bug repellent," I said calmly. That only made her more furious.

"You don't just spray chemicals on your skin like that. Do you see me doing such a thing? I thought I told you to study me, be like me. Upstairs," she ordered, and followed me. She surprised me by directing me to her bathroom instead of mine. There, she made me strip and go into her steam room. She flicked a switch, and the steam began to pour out until I could no longer even see the door. I felt as if I was being cooked and screamed that I had had enough, but the steam kept coming. I found the doorknob and discovered I couldn't open it.

"Pamela?" I called. "It's too hot!"

The steam continued. I lay down on the floor, because that was the coolest place, and waited. Nearly ten minutes later, I heard the steam stop, and the door was opened.

"Out!" she cried.

I was dizzy and thought I might be sick, but still I stood there while she inspected my body.

"Good," she said.

"It was too hot in there."

"It has to be that way to get out the poisons. Now you need your bath."

Joline had been called to prepare it. After I got into the tub, Pamela began to scrub my skin with a stiff brush, making it redder in spots than the bug bites, I thought. She poured all sorts of different oils into the water and shampooed my hair with such vigor I thought my scalp would bleed.

I stepped out, exhausted, when she told me to, and I barely had the strength to wipe myself down. I was taking too long, and she yelled at me to hurry up.

"Blow-dry your hair," she ordered. Before she wrapped the towel around me, she suddenly stared at my body with more interest than ever.

"What's wrong?" I asked.

She shook her head. "It's still happening. In fact, it's getting worse. You look too . . . masculine. You don't have any soft places. Even your breasts are like little puffs of muscle." She grimaced, twisting her mouth, her eyes filling with concern. "I want you to see my doctor."

"Doctor? Why?"

"I don't think you're developing right," she declared. "I'll make an appointment."

"I feel fine," I said.

"You don't look right to me. Maybe you need some feminine hormones. I don't know. Let the doctor decide," she said, and left me.

I was almost too weak to hold the hair dryer. When I'd dressed, I headed downstairs for dinner. The only way I could be more listless was to be asleep. Peter was away on another trip, and there was even a possibility he would not be back in time for the big game on Saturday. Pamela sat at the table and lectured me about the importance of protecting my skin.

"There is just so much makeup can do," she declared, "and some of these pageant judges get so close, they can see the smallest imperfections. Don't think that doesn't play a role in their decisions. It does. They see an ugly blemish on your neck, they'll drop you a place no matter how well you do in the other categories, especially the male judges." She stopped to take a breath and then continued with her criticism. "Why aren't you eating?"

"I lost my appetite because I was in the steam room too long," I said.

That threw her into a new tirade. "It's not the steam room. Removing poisons should make your body more efficient. It's that stupid softball, standing out there in the hot, destructive sunlight, letting yourself be feasted upon by bugs, filling your pores with dirt. And you're not using the hand cream enough," she added.

She stared at me, her fingers thumping the table as Joline moved as quietly and as quickly as she could around us, removing plates, straightening silverware, filling the water glass. I stared back at her. Not a hair was out of place. Her makeup was perfect. She looked ready for a professional photo shoot. It occurred to me that she made a bigger effort to look pretty than the effort most people made to do their jobs well.

Afterward, my piano lesson was grueling. Professor Wertzman seemed to sense my exhaustion as soon as I began. Instead of taking it easier on me, he made me do all my exercises repeatedly, finding fault with everything as usual. At one point, he became so annoyed, he actually slapped my left hand. He didn't hurt me, but it was so surprising and sharp, I felt an electric jolt in my heart and lost my breath for a moment.

"No, no, no," he said. "No, no, no. Again. Again!"

As usual, I was nearly in tears by the time the lesson ended. When I went up to my room, I just sat dazed and looked at my remaining homework. I didn't have the energy to open the book, much less begin the written work. I fell asleep at the desk and woke with a start when I heard my door open.

"What are you doing?" Pamela demanded.

I rubbed my eyes and looked at my open textbook. "Just finishing some math," I said.

"I want to check your skin," she said, and inspected my neck. "I'm calling Mrs. Harper in the morning and making a formal complaint about all this. They shouldn't be permitting you girls out there until those bugs are gone."

"No, please don't do that, Pamela. I'll keep my neck covered. I promise. There won't be any bites on me tomorrow. Please," I pleaded.

"Ridiculous," she said. "All of it. Beautiful girls exposing themselves to such damage. Sports are for boys. Their skin is tougher than ours. Their muscles are bigger."

"Lisa Donald and I beat her cousin Harrison and his friend at tennis the other day," I pointed out.

She stared at me again with that strange look in her eyes, a mixture of concern and bewilderment. "I have heard where some girls because of hormone deficiencies actually think like boys. I'm beginning to wonder if you have this medical condition. Instead of taking pride in beating them at tennis, you should be taking pride in the way they look at you, at how you attract and capture their attention," she lectured. "Your doctor's appointment is next Tuesday, after school, so make sure you come right home."

"I don't need to see a doctor," I complained.

"I'm your mother now, and I'm telling you I want you to be checked by a doctor." She smiled cruelly. "I know you're not used to having someone care this much for you, Brooke, but that's what it means to have parents. You should be grateful and not rebellious. I'd like to hear a thank you once in a while instead of this constant stream of complaint. It's all because of your stupid involvement with that softball team."

"I'm grateful. I just don't understand why I have to see a doctor. I'm not sick or anything."

"Sometimes we go to see the doctor to prevent sickness. Don't you understand that? Well?"

"Yes," I said, taking a breath and looking at my textbook.

"Well, then?"

"Thank you, Pamela."

"That's better," she said. "Oh," she said at the door. "Peter called. He won't be home in time to attend the mosquito feasting this Saturday. You'll have to arrange for transportation. I'm going to my dermatologist for a special Saturday appointment. He has something brand-new, a breakthrough rejuvenating skin treatment he wants to show me. Good night," she added, and left.

I felt more dazed than tired now. My mind was reeling, all her statements, declarations, and ideas bouncing around like loose tennis balls. I knew I had done a poor job on my homework, and when it was returned to me a day later, I was given a failing grade.

"If you don't pull your grade average up on the next unit test," Mr. Sternberg told me in front of the rest of the class, "you might not be able to participate in extracurricular activities next year."

I knew that meant all sports.

My heart felt like a deflated balloon. I looked at some of the girls. All but Heather looked concerned for me. She was smiling, her green eyes of envy brightening like the tips of two candle flames. Even Cora Munsen felt sorry for me. After class, as we all left the room, she caught up with me in the hallway and whispered, "If you need any answers next Monday, just look at my paper."

She sped away as Rosemary Gillian stepped behind me to whisper, "If you need your social studies homework, you can copy mine during lunch."

I laughed to myself, remembering Mrs. Harper's introductory remarks.

Girls at Agnes Fodor don't cheat. They were the special girls, the cream of the crop, the sophisticated, privileged, and cultured girls from the best families.

Sorry, Mrs. Harper, I thought. The only thing really special about Agnes Fodor's School for Girls were the lies woven into the fabric of the school's emblem.

9
Smile!

We had our biggest crowd attend the Saturday game. It couldn't have been a better day for a softball game. The sky was ice blue with an occasional cloud that looked like a puff of smoke. There was just enough of a cool breeze to keep everyone comfortable in the stands.

Because I had no ride, Rosemary had her brother David come by with her to pick me up. David did not attend a private school. I thought that was odd until he explained he had made friends with kids who attended public school and didn't want to leave them.

"I've got some friends over at Westgate, too," he told me soon after I got into the car. "They said there's more excitement about this game than some of the boys' games. For the first time in years, there might be a real contest."

As it turned out, that was an understatement. The

girls at Westgate were stronger and more determined than any others we had played. It had become a question of honor for them to defend their school's string of victories against Agnes Fodor. How could anyone lose to a school full of spoiled, rich, bratty girls?

But our team was determined, too. Coach Grossbard gave a great pep talk.

"Everyone out there thinks you're all a bunch of namby-pambies. They'll expect you to crack under pressure and fall apart just as we have in the past, but there's a new spirit here, and each and every one of you has improved," she said, gazing my way. "I'm proud of you girls. Go out there and show them what you're really made of."

We cheered and took the field. I did my best pitching and kept them to a single hit through the first five innings. The problem was their pitcher, a tall, dark, brown-haired girl with a body so muscular that it would put Pamela into a faint. She threw bullets over the plate. I struck out twice. No one was able to get a hit. Cora managed a fly ball, but it floated right to their center fielder.

An error on our side put a girl on base for them at the top of the last inning. The next girl struck out, but the next hit was a short fly that fell between second base and our center fielder. Her throw managed to keep their runner on third. One of their better hitters came up. I took deep breaths and looked at the crowd. There was a hush of expectation. Some people looked as if they were holding their breath. I spotted Mr. Rudley in the stands. He smiled at me and held up his thumb. It would have been nice to see Peter there cheering me on, too, I thought.

My first pitch went wide, but my second was in the low portion of the strike zone, and the batter went after it and missed. She fouled off my next pitch. Then she hit a hard line drive right at me. I stood my ground and caught it even though it stung right through my glove. Instantly, I spun and threw the ball to first. Their runner had gone too far and couldn't get back in time. It was a double play.

Our fans roared. Parents, siblings, and friends were standing and cheering us as we came off the field. It was still anyone's game. Then our first batter struck out on three pitches, and our confidence began to fall. No one said it, but I could practically hear people thinking that we would be the ones who wore out first.

I was up fourth, but someone would have to get on base. Heather was up next. She struck out with her eyes closed, backing away from the plate so much she brought laughter and sarcasm from the other side.

"What's the matter, honey, you afraid you'll mess up your makeup?"

"Afraid you'll ruin your nose job?"

"Watch yourself. That ball's got your name on it: Chicken Girl."

Laughter rippled through the crowd in waves. Despite our good showing, they still saw us as a joke. I saw how my teammates were taking it to heart. If we didn't do something now, we would surely lose, I concluded.

Eva Jensen was next at bat. I stopped her on the way to the plate.

"She's pitching a little more inside. Just step back and try to hit it to right field," I suggested. She nodded and took her stance. The first pitch was too low, but the second was right where I expected it would be. Eva stepped back and swung. It was a solid hit that bounced hard in front of the first baseman. She misjudged it, and it went over her head and into right field. We had a runner on first.

I looked at Coach Grossbard, who had heard me give Eva the advice.

"She's smart," she said, referring to the pitcher, "but she's not going to give you anything good."

I nodded and went to the plate. Once again, a hush came over our fans. The pitcher tried to get me to go after two pitches that were low and away, but I held back. The next pitch was coming in perfectly over the outside corner. It was the sort of pitch that required strength to hit. I leaned to the right and came around, catching the ball just down from the top of the bat enough to get a solid connection.

It soared.

And soared over the left fielder's head, and it kept going, clearing the fence. I had hit a home run.

I had been to ball games at public school, especially exciting basketball games when the crowd's roar was so high and loud my ears rang. That was the way it was now. As I rounded the bases, our side was screaming so loud it actually made my ears hurt. Mr. Rudley had a big, wide grin on his face, and Coach

Grossbard . . . Coach Grossbard had tears of joy streaming down her cheeks as I passed her between third and home plate.

Cora gave me a hug that nearly cracked my ribs. Everyone on the team was around me, Heather hanging on the perimeter with a plastic smile on her face. I couldn't remember when in my life I was more excited and proud of myself. The crowd was full of appreciation, but sadly, neither my new mother nor my new father had been there to see it. I was as alone as I had ever been, even now, even when I wanted parents so much it made my heart ache.

Lisa Donald announced a victory party at her house. Everyone on the team was invited, of course, even Coach Grossbard. It was to be a barbeque. When I returned home, I rushed into the house, hoping my invitation to Lisa's might get Pamela to see how important all this was to me and perhaps make her proud of my accomplishments finally.

Instead, I found her in a mad tizzy. Peter wasn't coming home as early as she had expected, and before I had a chance to tell her anything, she cried, "Everything's falling apart!"

"What's wrong?" I asked, standing in the entryway, holding my glove and the winning ball in my hand. Everyone on the team had signed it, Coach Grossbard's signature biggest of all. The date of the game was there as well.

"Your pageant audition has been confirmed, but how I could have forgotten the most important thing, I don't know. It's probably because of all the turmoil surrounding your piano lessons," she concluded, popping my bubble of excitement.

"What important thing?" I asked.

"Your pictures! Your photographs! Oh, where is he? Where is he?" she cried toward the doorway.

"Who? Peter?"

"No, not Peter. The photographer. I told him to be here and get set up before you returned. I want the pictures taken in the atrium outside the living-room patio doors. Those flowers will provide a colorful background. It will just look more . . . royal and make you seem more of a princess. Well, why are you just standing there?" she screamed. "Go upstairs and get the grime out of your skin. Bathe, shampoo, and start on your makeup. We've got to be ready in an hour."

"Don't you want to know what happened at the game?" I asked.

"Game? What game? You mean the, what do you call it, softball game?"

"Yes. We won. I hit a home run in the last inning and won the game. It was like the World Series or something. There were a lot of people there, more than ever, teachers, too. I pitched great. There's a party to celebrate at Lisa Donald's house. Everyone on the team is coming. Our teachers and parents are invited, too."

"Who has time for that? Are you mad? This photo shoot will take hours. We can't submit just any pictures to the pageant judges. These have to be professional, photos taken the way a model takes them. Would you stop wasting time and go up and get ready.

I'll be along to choose what you should wear. Of course, we'll have you wear more than one outfit. And the bathing suit I bought you last week. Go, go, go," she cried, waving at the stairway.

I gazed down at the softball. What was the point of showing it to her? She might have it thrown into the washing machine. I started up the stairway.

"Can we at least go to the party when we're finished?"

"We'll see," she said. "I can't be thinking about any of that right now. Joline! Joline!" she cried.

"Yes, ma'am."

"Get up there and draw her bath. Quickly."

"Yes, ma'am," Joline said, and hurried to the stairway. She passed me by and was in the bathroom, fixing my bath of oils before I even took off my uniform.

I just sat there, dazed. I was certainly in no mood to pose as a model for beauty pageant pictures. I had come home on a cloud and now felt as if I was being dragged by my hair to be propped up on some stage surrounded by strangers, gaping at me with numbers in their eyes.

Naturally, I wasn't moving fast enough for Pamela. When she came bursting into my room, I was just sitting at the vanity table to blow-dry my hair.

"Aren't you ready yet?" she screamed. "You can run like the wind around those stupid bases at a ball game, but when it comes to getting ready for something really important, you're a turtle," she fired at me as she crossed the room to my closet.

"My ball game *is* really important," I insisted, pride

flooding into my spine. She ignored me and rifled through the clothes hanging in my closet.

"I want something with color, and yet I want to make a simple statement of your beauty."

"I'm not beautiful," I muttered, mostly to myself.

She heard me, though, and whipped around. "Stop that! I don't want to hear that anymore. I told you, if you tell yourself you're not beautiful, you won't be. Attitude comes through. Why have I been working so hard with you, training you on how to sit, to walk, to talk, to hold your head, even to turn your eyes, if I didn't believe you were beautiful? Pictures don't lie, either, so you had better change your attitude before you go downstairs. I want to see that effervescence, life, youth, your eyes radiating with confidence. Stop staring at me!" she yelled. "Get your hair brushed and your makeup done!"

"Okay," I said.

"Don't say okay. Say yes. Don't you remember what I told you? Okay is too . . . inferior," she declared for lack of another term.

She pulled out what she wanted me to wear and then found my new bathing suit.

"The photographer has arrived. He's a highly regarded professional. He's setting up in the atrium right now. I'll discuss with him what you should wear first and then return. By the time I do, you should be ready to put on your dress. Understand?" she demanded.

"Yes, but if we do finish in time, can I go to the victory party? Please?"

"We'll see," she said, and stormed out of the room. I gazed at the clock. The team members and their families were just starting to arrive at Lisa's, and I was trapped at home. My only hope was to cooperate and get it done as fast as possible.

I was ready when Pamela returned. She told me to put on the light blue dress with the V-neck collar. She made sure my padded bra embellished my small bosom and then brought me a thin string of her own pearls to wear. After I was dressed, she stood me in front of the mirror and fixed my hair.

"You look flushed. I knew this would happen. I knew you would get too much sun out on that ball field and ruin your complexion," she said, and made me sit while she adjusted my makeup until she was satisfied. It took almost a half hour.

"When is Peter coming home?" I asked on the way down.

"I don't remember," she said. "Later," she muttered. I was hoping he would arrive before the photo shoot ended and would agree to take me to the party.

The photographer was a pleasant young man with dark curly hair. His name was William Daniels. From the way Pamela had raved about him, I expected someone much older and more experienced. When William began, however, I saw that he really knew what he was doing. Every time Pamela made a suggestion, he calmly pointed out why it wouldn't work, why the lighting would be wrong, why my profile wouldn't be as complimented, or why the backdrop would lose its value.

William sensed how tense and unhappy I was immediately and did what he could to make me relax.

"Don't fight it," he whispered while he was adjusting my posture. "We'll get finished faster if you relax and just let it happen."

He was right, of course, and I stopped wishing and hoping it would be over.

"Great, good. That's it," he kept saying. Pamela relaxed more, too.

I hurried upstairs to change my dress, but when I returned, Pamela didn't like the way my hair had lost its shape and made William wait while she brushed it again until it satisfied her.

We had been working nearly an hour and a half. I knew the party was in full swing at Lisa's by now, and I imagined they were all wondering when I would arrive. Heather was probably telling them that I wanted to make a special entrance and was being late deliberately. That was something she would do.

Pamela had even more problems with my bathing suit picture. As soon as I put on the suit, she groaned.

"Can't you stop those muscles from popping out in your legs?"

"I'm not doing anything," I said.

"Is there anything you can do?" she asked William.

He studied me a moment, adjusted my stance, and shook his head. "She's got a great little body, Mrs. Thompson. I don't see why you want to hide it."

"They'll think she's one of those women bodybuilders or something. Who wants an Amazon to be Miss America?" she snapped. "Relax your arms," she told me.

I tried to stand as loosely as I could, but nothing I did satisfied her.

"They'll hate this shot," she muttered.

"Let's just see," William said. "I might be able to touch it up here and there."

"That'll work for pictures, but not when she's walking on the stage in the flesh," she moaned.

He stared at her, waiting.

"All right, all right. Do what you can," she said with a wave of her hand, and he began.

Finally, the photo shoot ended. I ran upstairs to change into a pair of slacks and a blouse. I was back before William had put away all his equipment.

"Can we go to the party now, Pamela?" I asked, barely containing my excitement.

"I have a horrible headache from all this tension and trouble," she said, shaking her head. "It would take me hours to get ready for any public appearance."

"But . . . everyone's expecting me. I promised I'd be there. Please," I begged.

"I can drop her off," William offered.

I looked at Pamela.

"Fine," she said tightly.

"Thank you, Pamela. Thank you," I cried, and actually helped William get his equipment loaded just so we would leave faster.

"What's the occasion for the party?" he asked me as we drove off.

I told him, and he smiled, very impressed. Why couldn't my parents be this way? I thought. He told me about himself, that he was married and had a pair of twin four-year-old girls.

"They're as cute as two peas in a pod," he said.

"I'm always taking pictures of them, as you can imagine, but I wouldn't want them to be in any beauty pageants. They're even having pageants for five-year-olds these days, dressing them and putting makeup on them to make them look older. It's out of hand."

"I don't want to be in one, either," I muttered.

"I could tell," he said, smiling. "But, hey, if it wasn't for people like your mother, I wouldn't be making a good living," he added, and laughed.

Talking to him helped me relax. When he saw the Donalds' house, he whistled. "Don't you hang out with fancy people," he teased. "As they say, it's better to be born rich than born."

If he only knew the truth, I thought, and laughed to myself. I thanked him for the ride and stepped out of the car.

Being late did result in a big welcome for me. As soon as I was spotted, the party came to a hush, and then they all shouted my name and cheered. Everyone rushed over to congratulate me. Many of my teachers were there. Even Mrs. Harper was there and gave me a restrained look of approval. Lisa's cousin Harrison, speaking to me with respect in his voice, tried to get me to be nicer to him. My heart was too full of joy to dislike anyone. To me, this was the greatest day of my life, and this was the best party I would ever attend, maybe even better than my wedding. Nothing could put a dark cloud over this day, I thought.

I was wrong.

10
Sheer Satisfaction

I felt as if I was floating above the party and not really a part of it. Never in my life had so many people thought so highly of me. At my public school, there were many girls who were good at sports, and I was always seen as just one of those girls from the orphanage, which was something that diminished my achievements.

I couldn't help feeling special here. I lived in a house as big as or bigger than most of the other girls'. I wore clothing that was just as expensive as, if not more expensive than, theirs. No one could look down on me and lessen my achievements with the simple words, "One of them."

I knew I was letting my head get too big. Lisa's brother and his friends had me surrounded most of the time. I was still wearing what anyone else would probably call stage makeup. I imagined everyone thought I had doctored up my face just for the party. I was too embarrassed to tell my girlfriends about the beauty pageant, so I said nothing.

However, I saw the looks of envy on some of my classmates as the boys vied for position, tried to do me favors, get me food or something to drink, and then tried to impress me with their stories and jokes.

Soon after I arrived, Lisa and Eva pulled me away, and we joined the other girls in the house to giggle and talk about the boys. For the first time in my life, I felt like somebody in the eyes of my classmates. I could even put up with all of Pamela's demands just so I could keep this moment and this opportunity.

Later, shortly before the party was drawing to its conclusion, Heather stepped up beside me and leaned over to whisper. "I've got to talk to you," she said. "I have something very important to tell you that can't wait."

"Now?"

She nodded and walked away. Heather had been ignoring me most of the evening, so I was surprised at her urgency. I followed her until we were far enough from everyone to speak privately.

"What is it?" I said, gazing back at the party. I wished it could go on forever, the music, the lights, the great food and excitement.

"I just overheard my aunt talking about you," she said.

It was as if we were in a movie and suddenly the camera stopped and the picture began to melt on the screen. The party actually turned hazy as my eyes clouded with fear.

"What do you mean?" I asked in a breathy, thin voice.

"I know you're an orphan and your parents are not really your parents," she said. "You never even saw your real mother, and you don't have a real father. You know what they call someone without a father?"

I shook my head. "I don't want to hear it," I said.

She smiled coldly. "I just thought you should know that I know," she said, full of self-satisfaction. Her smile faded and was quickly replaced with a look of rage. "No wonder you play sports like a boy."

"What does that have to do with anything?"

She smirked as if I should know. "Just don't act like such a big shot around me," she warned, and walked away.

My heart was pounding. The me I imagined floating above the victory celebration slowly sank down to earth. With trembling legs, I rejoined the party, but I didn't really listen to anyone or hear the music. Every once in a while, I caught sight of Heather staring at me and smiling, her eyes full of satisfaction.

In fact, I was grateful when Peter arrived to take me home. He was introduced to people who immediately congratulated him on my achievements.

"I'm so sorry I missed the game," he told me as we started for the car. "From the way everyone was talking, you were really something. Didn't you tell Pamela? She didn't mention a word of it when I stepped into the house."

"I tried, but she was too concerned about my photographs. I almost missed the victory party," I complained.

"She just doesn't realize . . . I'll explain it to her," he promised. "Slugger," he added with a big smile. He sensed something wasn't right. "What's wrong?"

"I'm just tired, I guess," I told him. I desperately wanted to keep anything from spoiling this day and this night.

"No wonder. Catching up on schoolwork, keeping up, learning how to play piano, bringing the girls' softball team to victories . . . talk about an overachiever. I'm proud of you, Brooke. I really am," he said.

It made me feel better. Pamela was already in bed when we returned. He hurried up to tell her more about the ball game and make her understand. I went to bed, and when my head finally hit the pillow, I felt as if my body had turned to lead. I sank into a deep sleep and didn't wake up until the sunlight hit my face in the morning.

Peter received a phone call early in the morning that ruined his Sunday. Even before I went down to breakfast, he had to leave to go to his office. It made Pamela angry, and she was in a sulk. I spent my time catching up on studying for exams. I didn't get half as many phone calls as I had expected. Peter didn't get home until nearly dinner, and I could tell that there was still a lot of tension between him and Pamela. It was one of the quietest meals since I had arrived.

All of it caught up with me that night, and I fell asleep with my books in my lap. When I woke Monday morning, it was later than usual, so I had to skip my piano practice and I didn't spend half as much time on my makeup. Fortunately, Pamela was sleeping late and didn't get a chance to inspect me as she often did before I went off to school. She did, however, leave word with Peter to remind me that I had a doctor's appointment after school tomorrow. I told him I thought it was silly. There was nothing wrong with me.

"It doesn't hurt to get yourself a checkup," he said. "Think of it as that."

If there was a compromise in the wind, Peter would smell it, I thought. Anyway, at the moment, he was obviously avoiding any more arguments with Pamela.

I felt something different in the air soon after I attended homeroom. Everyone has to come down from a peak of excitement, I thought, and this was what it was like. We were back to our usual day of work. The victory was already fading into the past, and there were looming final exams to consider and new work to do.

I was late for lunch because I had remained after class to talk about a math problem. When I arrived in the cafeteria, I heard what seemed like a little hush in conversation, and when I looked at the girls, some of them dropped their eyes guiltily. Why? I wondered. I got my food and joined my new friends at the table.

"I thought Mr. Brazil was going to keep me right through lunch period," I said, laughing. "You know how slowly he talks." Eva smiled, but no one else did.

I started to eat and noticed everyone was being rather silent. "Is something wrong?" I asked.

No one replied. It was as if I wasn't even there. The bell rang to move on to class almost before I had finished my lunch. Everyone started to move away.

I reached out and seized Lisa's wrist. "What's the matter with everyone today? They act like someone died," I said.

She gazed at the girls who were moving toward the door. "Someone did," she quipped.

"What does that mean? Who died?"

"Many of the girls think you're a phony," she replied coolly.

"A phony? Why?"

"Because you never told anyone you were adopted," she said.

"Oh," I said, looking at the back of Heather Harper's head. She was laughing loudly. "Well, why did I have to announce that?" I asked.

"You didn't have to announce it, but you didn't have to pretend you were someone you're not," she replied.

"Yes, I did," I snapped back at her. "Especially here, where everyone judges everyone by how much money her father makes or how big her parents' house is."

"That's not true."

"It is," I insisted.

Lisa glared at me. "You probably knew how to play tennis all along, too," she said. "You made me look stupid."

"What?"

She started away.

"I didn't know. How could I know? Do you think we had a tennis court at my orphanage?" I shouted at her. Some of the other girls looked back, but no one remained to walk to class with me.

Less than forty-eight hours ago, I thought, I was a school hero. Today, I'm a school pariah. Once, when I complained that some of the other kids at my school made me feel inferior, one of my counselors at the orphanage told me sometimes you're respected more because of the nature of the people who dislike you. She was right. If anything, I was angry at myself for trying too hard to be like these girls. No matter how much money Pamela and Peter had, how much money they spent on my clothes, how many pageants I would enter, how big our car and our house were, I would never be like these girls. I felt as if I was born and had lived in a different country. I practically spoke a different language.

I put my head down and went forward. I worked hard in my classes the rest of the day. I ignored everyone. Most of the other girls were polite, if not overly friendly, but even my teachers seemed different to me. Maybe it was my imagination. Maybe I was feeling sorry for myself. Suddenly, I had little to look forward to.

My dark, heavy mood was lifted from my shoulders when I went to physical education class. Coach Grossbard called me to her office before I dressed for gym. She was sitting behind her desk with a huge grin on her face.

"I just received a nice phone call a half hour ago and waited for you to attend class," she said.

What could this be? I wondered. Did she just find out I was an orphan, and that somehow made her happy?

"What does it have to do with me?" I asked.

"Everything," she said. "You were chosen by the league to be on the all-star team for the county's all-star game. In fact, you're probably going to be the starting pitcher."

"Really? All-stars?"

She nodded. "I never had a pupil make an all-star team before. Congratulations, Brooke," she said, rising. Instead of shaking my hand, she hugged me.

I couldn't help crying.

"Hey, this is supposed to be a happy occasion," she said, laughing, but there was just too much emotional baggage for me to carry. I bawled harder. "What's wrong, honey?" she asked, making me sit.

I told her as quickly as I could. She sat back and listened, her face turning red with anger. "They should call this place Agnes Fodor's School for Snobs," she said. "You must not let them get you down. They're all just jealous, that's all."

"No, they're not," I said. "There's nothing to be jealous about. They have real families."

"You're twice the person any of them are, honey. Real families or not. People are going to judge you for yourself and not because of your family name. You'll see," she promised. "If you don't feel like dressing for class today, you can skip it," she said. "Just rest up."

"No," I said, brushing the tears from my cheeks and taking a deep breath. "I'll be all right."

She smiled. "All-star. Wow!" she said.

It did buoy me, and I felt much stronger when I left the building than when I had entered. The word hadn't gotten out about me yet, but I didn't think my new so-called friends would be as happy about it as they would have been a few days ago. I tried not to think about it.

Pamela wasn't home when I returned. I went to my room and started on my homework, but my excitement was so great I couldn't concentrate very well. Finally, I heard footsteps on the stairway and stepped out to see Joline coming up, her arms loaded with packages. Pamela followed soon after.

"I had to get myself some new things to wear to the pageant," she told me when she paused in the hallway. "It's important that I stay in fashion, too. They take pictures of the mothers and daughters."

"I have something to tell you," I said. I knew how important it had been to her that no one knew the truth about me. "The girls have found out about me. They know I'm a foster child in the process of being adopted."

"What? How could that happen?"

"Heather Harper overheard her aunt talking to someone and told everyone," I said. "They're a bunch of snobs. I hate them. I hate that school, except for Coach Grossbard. Even the teachers are looking at me differently," I wailed.

She stared, furious. "Wait until I tell Peter. We'll sue her for being a gossip," she declared.

"What good will that do me?" I asked, but she didn't reply. She turned and charged back down the stairway. A little over an hour later, Peter came home. I heard their raised voices below and went down to find them in the den. Peter looked overwrought, his face flushed, his hair disheveled.

"There's no ground on which to sue anyone," he told me as soon as I entered.

"I don't want you to do that, Peter. It wouldn't help," I said.

"She's right, Pamela. Let's forget about it."

"I won't forget about it. That woman is going to get a piece of my mind. I'll speak to the trustees. She should be fired for doing this."

"It's over and done with," Peter said.

"I don't want to go there next year," I said.

Pamela looked up sharply. "What do you mean? Where would you go, a public school?" she asked, her lips twisted.

"I don't care. I hate those girls. And soon they're going to be even more jealous of me," I added.

Peter raised his eyebrows. "And why is that?"

"I've been selected to be on the county's all-star team. I'm going to be the starting pitcher in the game," I told him.

He beamed a wide grin. "Brooke, that's fantastic! I'm so proud of you!" He stood up and hugged me.

"What kind of an accomplishment is that?" Pamela muttered.

"It's the biggest, most important thing that's ever happened to me," I said.

She smirked and shook her head. "I can't take all this tension. It's bad for my complexion," she complained. She stood. "I need to sit in my electric massage chair before dinner."

"Well, I'm thrilled for you, honey. When is the game?" Peter asked.

I told him, and Pamela stopped walking out. She turned and looked at me. "What did you say? When is that silly event?"

I repeated the date.

"You can't go to that," she said. "Don't you realize what that date is? Have I been talking to myself for weeks and weeks? That's the date of your audition for the pageant. It's all arranged."

"No," I said, shaking my head. I looked at Peter, but he looked worried. Surely, he would come up with one of his ingenious compromises, I thought. "I've been selected from all the girls in all the schools. It's a great honor."

"That's no honor," Pamela declared. "How can you compare throwing a softball to winning a pageant?"

"I don't care. I'm playing. I've been chosen. I'm not going to the pageant."

"You absolutely are," she said. "I'm going to the phone immediately and call that big-mouth principal. I'll tell her that I absolutely forbid your participation, and if she doesn't obey me, I'll warn her that I'm going to the trustees about her gossiping."

"Pamela," Peter said softly.

"What? You're not thinking of permitting her to go to the ball game instead of the pageant, are you? Look at all I've been doing, what we've spent, the piano lessons, the work, the pictures!"

"Maybe we can get her a different audition," he said, still speaking softly.

"You know we can't do that. You know how hard it was to arrange for this." She turned to me. "You're going to the pageant. Forget about that ball game. You're a girl. You're a beautiful young woman. You're not some . . . some Amazon. I won't have it!" she screamed. "I'm Pamela Thompson. My daughter is going to be a pageant winner."

"No, I'm not. I'm not," I yelled back at her, and ran out of the den.

"I'm calling Mrs. Harper right now," she screamed at me as I charged up the stairway. "I'm calling her! You can put that game out of your mind, Brooke. Do you hear me?"

I slammed my door closed and locked it. Then I threw myself on my bed and buried my face in my pillow until I couldn't breathe.

Why did this have to happen to me?

I sat up and stared at my image in the vanity table mirror. Why was I born if I was to suffer like this? Why did people have children they didn't want?

When Pamela came to the orphanage and saw me, she didn't see me. She saw herself. She saw what she wanted me to be, and then she brought me here and tried to make me into the girl she had seen. I'm not that girl. I'll never be that girl, I told my image in the mirror.

The makeup I had been wearing had streaked under

my tears. I wiped the lipstick off and then, in a rage, went into the bathroom and washed my face until my skin burned. Afterward, I came out and looked at myself again. I practically ripped off my blouse and tore away the padded bra. I rifled through my drawers until I found the faded pink ribbon my mother had left with me, and I tied up my hair. Then I put on my blouse again and sat fuming.

I heard footsteps outside my door.

"Why is this door locked?" Pamela cried.

"I don't want to talk to anyone," I said.

"I just got off the phone with Mrs. Harper. You can forget that game. It's all taken care of. Now, stop this nonsense immediately. I want to talk to you about the audition. I have other things to explain."

The tears streaked down my cheeks again. My shoulders felt so heavy.

Everyone looked down on me at the school, and now I was losing the one big accomplishment I had achieved. Coach Grossbard would be so disappointed, too.

"Brooke! Do you hear me?"

I felt something shatter inside me. It was as if my body was made of glass and the glass had cracked. Soon, I would just crumble to the floor, and when she did come in, she would only find a pile of broken pieces.

"Brooke!"

The more she yelled, the more I felt as if I was coming apart. I reached out and seized the scissors in front of me, and then, taking fistfuls of my hair into my hand,

I began to hack away at the strands, dropping clumps of it on the table, cutting and snipping away above the old, faded ribbon, slicing my hair without design until I could even see my scalp showing in places.

Pamela was pounding on the door, screaming my name, threatening, lecturing. I could hear Peter behind her, pleading, asking her to calm down.

When I was finished, I laid the scissors down softly on the table, rose, and quietly, like a shadow, floated across the room to the door. I unlocked it and then opened it.

When she saw me, her eyes nearly exploded. Her mouth opened and closed without a sound at first, and then she put her hands against her own temples and screamed louder than I could ever imagine myself screaming. Her effort turned her face blood red, and her body shook violently, denying what she saw, refusing to believe.

Peter stepped around her to look at me and fell into shock himself.

Pamela's eyes went into the top of her head. She threw her hands toward the ceiling and collapsed into his arms.

I closed the door softly.

Epilogue

"It's better for you," Peter said.

The grandfather clock's ticking seemed so much louder.

Peter sat across from me in the plush living room, his hands clasped as he leaned toward me. He looked very tired, his perennial tan had faded, and his hair was slightly messed up. He wore no tie. His collar was open and his brown sports jacket undone. I almost felt sorrier for him than I did for myself. I knew how bad a time he was having with Pamela. A parade of doctors and health-related people had come through the house, marching up the stairs to her room to give her massages, skin and hair treatments, nutritional guidance. There was even a meditation specialist who spent hours with her. She claimed I had aged her years in minutes and it would take months to cure the degeneration. She even complained of heart trouble.

I had yet to say another word to her or she to me.

"No one wants to make you live where you're uncomfortable," Peter continued. "Or go to school where you're unhappy," he added.

I looked at him, and he had to look away.

People who lie to themselves have a hard time looking at other people directly. They are afraid that their eyes will reveal the self-deceptions.

After my tantrum, Peter wanted to take me to a doctor, too. I refused. Actually, I felt fine, even somewhat stronger. It was as if I had thrown a weight off my shoulders. I had been trying to fit myself into a mold that simply did not fit. What I wished at this moment was that I had my old clothes back. I still wore my old ribbon around my head. I wouldn't take it off.

Peter sat back thoughtfully. The clock ticked.

Sacket appeared in the doorway. "The car has arrived for Miss Brooke, Mr. Thompson. Should I begin to load the trunk?"

"Yes, please, Sacket," Peter said.

I had told him that I didn't want my new things, but Peter insisted I take them. "What you do with them afterward is your business, Brooke, but they are yours."

I was adamant about not taking a single tube of lipstick. The way I felt, I didn't know whether I would ever put on any makeup again.

"Are you all right to travel?" Peter asked me.

I nearly laughed. I looked away and then stood up. He had hired a limousine to take me to the foster home. All I knew was it was a group foster home run by a couple who used to run it as a tourist house. Supposedly, there were at least a dozen children of various ages already there. Peter was told, and he tried to convince me, that it was only a temporary situation. Other, more personalized homes were being sought, and I would soon have another set of foster parents, maybe even adoptive parents.

I couldn't help thinking about my mother and dreaming that she was the one waiting for me outside. She had heard about my situation, and she had come from wherever she lived to claim me. Now she was waiting outside in her car, and in a moment I would set eyes on her for the first time.

It was a wonderful fantasy, one that helped me walk with determination and confidence, something Pamela would be proud to see, I thought. That brought a smile to my face and confused Peter, who watched me with a strange half-smile of his own.

"I've arranged for you to have some money," he told me at the door. "It's been deposited in the bank."

I almost said, "I earned it," but instead held my tongue and stepped outside. It was a gray, overcast day with a stiff breeze that lifted the remaining strands of my hair from my forehead. It had been Peter's idea to buy me a baseball cap. I put it on.

He had spared no expense on the limousine, I thought. It was a long, sleek black car with a driver in uniform. He stepped out and waited.

"You're an exceptional young lady, Brooke," Peter said. "Don't let anyone try to convince you otherwise.

Whatever you set your mind on doing, I'm sure you'll do. Maybe you'll become a lawyer someday and come to my firm."

"I don't think so," I said.

It wiped the smile from his face. He looked sad enough to cry. "I wanted better things for you," he said. "I hope you believe that."

I nodded. Then I looked back toward the stairway. Pamela wouldn't even know I'd left, I thought. What did it matter? We had never really become mother and daughter, not in the way I had dreamed we would.

Peter leaned forward to kiss me on the forehead. "Good-bye, Brooke," he said. "Good luck."

"Thanks," I muttered, and walked down to the car. When I looked back, Peter was still standing in the doorway. The breeze lifted his hair. He raised his hand, and then, as if hearing himself paged, he turned quickly and went back inside.

We drove off. The driver tried to make conversation, but I wouldn't answer any questions, and soon I was riding in silence, listening to my own thoughts. A little less than two hours later, we pulled up in front of the group foster home, a place named the Lakewood House. It was a very large two-story house of gray clapboard with a wraparound porch. I realized it was very quiet because all of the children were probably at school. The driver began to unload my luggage just as a tall man with dark hair that fell over his forehead came around the corner. He had a pickax over his shoulder and his shirt off. His shoulders were thick with muscle, as were his long arms. His hands looked like steel vises. The fingers easily held the tool when he paused to swing it down.

"Louise!" he shouted. He stared at me. "Louise!" he screamed again, this time followed with striking the side of the building with the flat side of the pick-ax. I imagined it must have shaken the building and everything inside.

Suddenly, the front door opened, and a tall brunette with shoulder-length hair came hurrying out. She looked about fifty, with soft wrinkles on the sides of her eyes and over her upper lip, wrinkles that would have given Pamela the heart attack she claimed I had almost given her. Louise had young, vibrant-looking, friendly blue eyes, however.

"Sure she brought enough?" the big man asked, nodding at my pile of suitcases and bags.

"We'll find a place for everything," Louise assured me.

"Not in the room she has," he corrected.

"We'll figure it out. Hi, honey. My name's Louise. This is my husband, Gordon. He looks after the place. Did you have a long ride?"

"No," I said.

"She wouldn't feel a long ride in a car like that, anyway," Gordon said, drawing closer. He stood gazing at me as he wiped his hands on his pants.

"You're lucky. You have your own room. You don't need to share at the moment, but Gordon's right. There's not enough closet space for all this," Louise said, looking at the luggage.

The driver slammed the trunk.

"What'd ya get for something like this?" Gordon asked him.

"A hundred and fifty," the driver answered quietly.

"Maybe I oughtta go into the limo business," Gordon muttered.

"Be my guest," the driver said, and got into the car. We didn't say good-bye since we never really said hello. I didn't even know his name, and I doubted if he knew mine.

"Who's supposed to carry all this inside?" Gordon asked.

"I can do it myself," I said. "Don't worry about space. There's a lot I don't want."

He stared at me with a sharpness and then smiled. "Independent, huh?" he asked.

"Let's get her settled in first, Gordon. Then we'll all get to know each other."

"Can't wait," Gordon said, and sauntered off toward the garage.

"Gordon's not used to having children around the house," Louise explained. "We ran this as a prime tourist resort. But that was before the resort business began to suffer," she continued, and explained her history and the building's as we took in some of my things and I settled in my room. Then she showed me around the house, where the dining room was, the game room, the kitchen, explaining what went on in each during the heyday of the resort period. There were pictures on the walls of guests and employees. I did think it was interesting and almost felt as if I had come to a hotel.

But that was a feeling that wouldn't last long.

"I'll get you into school tomorrow," Louise promised. "For now, why don't you rest and wait for the others to come home? You'll make lots of friends here," she predicted.

I didn't say anything. The overcast sky was beginning to break up so that patches of blue were visible here and there. The breeze was still strong but warm. I walked the grounds and sat at the top of a small hill, looking down at the lake. There were interesting, beautiful birds to watch. I was so deep in my thoughts, I almost didn't hear the school bus arrive and the voices of other children. I smiled at the sight of them. The house seemed to come alive when they entered, as if it was a big, loving mother opening its arms.

Soon, some curious children came looking for me. I imagined Louise had told them. A small girl with beautiful gold hair and a face that belonged on a doll walked behind an older, taller girl with thick glasses who carried a textbook and notebook. They paused a few feet from me.

"Louise said you just arrived," the girl with the glasses began. "I'm Crystal. This is Janet Taylor. You can think of us as your welcoming committee," she added dryly.

I laughed.

They drew closer.

"My name's Brooke," I said.

"This is actually my favorite spot," Crystal said. "As long as the weather's good, I like to start my homework here."

I nodded and gazed at Janet, who seemed so shy she had to sneak looks at me. I smiled at her, and slowly she smiled back. Then they sat, and the three of us looked out at the lake. The sun was breaking out now, and its rays felt wonderful on my face. It was washing away all the false faces I had worn.

Crystal and Janet stared at me but remained quiet. I knew they had been through the system. We were like soldiers who had fought similar wars and knew that we didn't have to rush to get to know each other. We would have lots of time, because all the promises of new homes that had been made to us would fade in the days to come.

I didn't care. I couldn't think about that now. I was looking beyond the lake.

I could hear all the voices, the cheers, and the screams. I was up at the plate, looking at the pitcher and then back at Coach Grossbard. She closed her eyes as if in prayer and then opened them and smiled. I took a deep breath and dug in.

Almost as soon as I had hit that ball, I knew it was going to be a home run. It carried my hope with it as it soared higher and higher. I didn't care if I forgot everything else, lost all my recent memories, as long as I could close my eyes and relive that moment.

As long as I could come around those bases toward home.

Raven

Prologue

"I never asked to be born," I threw back at my mother when she complained about all the trouble I had caused her from the day I was born. The school had called, and the truancy officer had threatened to take Mama to court if I stayed home one more time. I hated my school. It was a hive of snobs buzzing around this queen bee or that and threatening to sting me if I so much as tried to enter their precious little social circles. My classes were so big most of my teachers didn't even know I existed anyway! If it wasn't for the new automated homeroom cards, no one would know I hadn't gone to school.

Mama kicked the refrigerator door closed with her bare foot and slapped a bottle of beer down so hard on the counter it almost shattered. She tore off the cap with her opener and stared at me, her eyes bloodshot. The truancy officer's phone call had jolted her out of a dead sleep. She brought the bottle to her lips and sucked on it, the muscles in her thin neck pulsating with the effort to get as much down her throat as she could in one gulp. Then she glared at me again. I saw she had a bruise on the bottom of her right forearm and a scraped elbow.

We were having one of those Indian summers. The temperature had reached ninety today, and it was nearly October twenty-first. Mama's hair, just as black as mine, hung limply over her cheeks. Her bangs were too long and uneven. She pushed her lower lip out and blew up to sweep the strands out of her eyes. Once, she had been a very pretty woman with eyes that glittered like black pearls. She had a richly dark complexion with distinct, high cheekbones and perfect facial features. Women shot silicone into their lips to get the shape and fullness Mama's had naturally. I used to be flattered when people compared me to her in those days. All I ever dreamed of being was as pretty as my mother.

Now, I pretended I wasn't even related to her. Sometimes, I pretended she wasn't even there.

"How am I supposed to scratch out a living and watch a twelve-year-old, too? They should be giving me medals, not threats."

Mama's way of scratching out a living was working as a barmaid at a dump called Charlie Boy's in Newburgh, New York. Some nights, she didn't come home until nearly four in the morning, long after the bar had closed. If she wasn't drunk, she was high on something and would go stumbling around our one-bedroom apartment, knocking into furniture and dropping things.

I slept on the pullout couch, so I usually woke up or heard her, but I always pretended I was still asleep. I hated talking to her when she was in that condition. Sometimes, I could smell her before I heard her. It was as if she had soaked her clothing in whiskey and beer.

Mama looked much older than her thirty-one years now. She had dark shadows under her eyes and wrinkles that looked like lines drawn with an eyebrow pencil at the corners. Her rich complexion had turned into a pasty, pale yellow, and her once silky hair looked like a mop made of piano wire. It was streaked with premature gray strands and always looked dirty and stringy to me.

Mama smoked and drank and didn't seem to care what man she went out with as long as he was willing to pay for what she wanted. I stopped keeping track of their names. Their faces had begun to merge into one, their red eyes peering at me with vague interest. Usually, I was just as much of a surprise to them as they were to me.

"You never said you had a daughter," most would remark.

Mama would shrug and reply, "Oh, didn't I? Well, I do. You have a problem with that?"

Some didn't say anything; some said no or shook their heads and laughed.

"You're the one with the problem," one man told her. That put her into a tirade about my father.

We rarely talked about him. Mama would say only

that he was a handsome Latino but a disappointment when it came to living up to his responsibilities.

"As are most men," she warned me.

She got me to believe that my real father's promises were like rainbows, beautiful while they lingered in the air but soon fading until they were only vague memories. And there was never a pot of gold! He would never come back, and he would never send us anything.

As long as I could remember, we lived in this small apartment in a building that looked as if a strong wind could knock it over. The walls in the corridors were chipped and gouged in places, as if some maddened creature had tried to dig its way out. The outside walls were scarred with graffiti, and the walkway was shattered so that there was just dirt in many sections where cement once had been. The small patch of lawn between the building and the street had turned sour years ago. The grass was a sickly pale green, and there was so much garbage in it that no one could run a lawn mower over it.

The sinks in our apartment always gave us trouble, dripping or clogging. I couldn't even guess how many times the toilet had overflowed. The tub was full of rust around the drain, and the shower dripped and usually ran out of hot water before I could finish or wash my hair. I know we had lots of mice, because I was always finding their droppings in drawers or under dressers and tables. Sometimes, I could hear them scurrying about, and a few times I saw one before it scurried under a piece of furniture. We put out traps and caught a couple, but for every one we trapped, there were ten to take its place.

Mama was always promising to get us out. A new apartment was just around the corner, just as soon as she saved another hundred for the deposit. But I knew that if she did get any spare money, she would spend it on whiskey, beer, or pot. One of her new boyfriends introduced her to cocaine, and she had some of that occasionally, but usually it was too expensive for her.

We had a television set that often lost its picture. I could get it back sometimes by knocking it hard on the side. Sometimes, Mama received a welfare check. I never understood why she did or didn't. She cursed the system and complained when there wasn't a check. If I got to it first, I would cash it at my mom's friend's convenience store, and get us some good groceries and some clothes for myself. If I didn't, she hid it or doled out some money to me in small dribs and drabs, and I had to make do with it.

I knew that other kids my age would steal what they couldn't afford, but that wasn't for me. There was a girl in my building, Lila Thomas, who went with some other girls from across town on weekends and raided malls. She had been caught shoplifting, but she didn't seem afraid of being caught again. She made fun of me all the time because I wouldn't go along. She called me "the girl scout" and told everyone I would end up selling cookies for a living.

I didn't care about not having her as a close friend. Most of the time, I was happy being with myself, reading a magazine or watching soaps whenever I could get the television set to work. I tried not to think about Mama sleeping late, maybe even with some new man in her room. I had gotten so I could look through people and pretend they weren't even there.

"You just better damn well go to school tomorrow, Raven. I don't need no government people coming around here and snooping," she muttered, and wiped strands of hair away from her cheek. "You listening to me?"

"Yes," I said.

She stared hard and drank some more of her beer. It was only nine-fifteen in the morning. I hated the taste of beer anyway, but just the thought of drinking it this early made my stomach churn. Mama suddenly realized what day it was and that I should be in school now, too. Her eyes popped.

"Why are you home today?" she cried.

"I had a stomachache," I said. "I'm getting my period. That's what the nurse told me in school when I had cramps and left class."

She looked at me with a cold glint in her dark eyes and nodded.

"Welcome to hell," she said. "You'll soon understand why parents give thanks when they have a boy. Men have it so much easier. You better watch yourself now," she warned, pointing the neck of the beer bottle at me.

"What do you mean?"

"What do I mean?" she mimicked. "I mean, if you got your period coming, you could get pregnant, Raven, and I won't be taking care of no baby, not me."

"I'm not getting pregnant, Mama," I said sharply.

She laughed. "That's what I said, and look at what happened."

"Well, why did you have me then?" I fired back at her. I was tired of hearing what a burden I was. I wasn't. I was the one who kept the apartment livable, cleaning up after her drunken rages, washing dishes, washing clothes, mopping the bathroom floors. I was the one who bought us food and cooked for us half the time. Sometimes, she brought food home from the restaurant, when she remembered, but it was usually cold and greasy by the time she got it home.

"Why'd I have you? Why'd I have you?" she muttered, and looked dazed, as if the question was too hard to answer. Her face brightened with rage. "I'll tell you why. Because your macho Cuban father was going to make us a home. He was positive you were going to be a boy. How could he have anything but boys? Not Mr. Macho. Then, when you were born . . ."

"What?" I asked quickly. Getting her to tell me anything about my father or what things were like for her in those days was as hard as getting top government secrets.

"He ran. As soon as he set eyes on you, he grimaced ugly and said, 'It's a girl? Can't be mine.' And he ran. Ain't heard from him since," she muttered. She looked thoughtful for a moment and then turned back to me. "Let that be a lesson to you about men."

What lesson? I wondered. How did she think it made me feel to learn that my father couldn't stand the sight of me, that my very birth sent him away? How did she think it made me feel to hear almost every day that she never asked to have me? Sometimes, she called me her punishment. I was God's way of getting back at her, but what did she consider her sin? Not drinking or doing drugs or slumming about—oh, no. Her sin was trusting a man. Was she right? Was that the way all men would behave? Most of my mother's friends agreed with her about men, and many of my friends, who came from homes not much better than mine, had similar ideas taught to them by their mothers.

I felt more alone than ever. Getting older, developing as a woman, looking older than I was, all of it didn't make me feel more independent and stronger as much as it reminded me I really had no one but myself. I had many questions. I had lots of things troubling me, things a girl would want to ask her mother, but I was afraid to ask mine, and most of the time, I didn't think she could think clearly enough to answer them anyway.

"You got what you need?" she asked, dropping the empty beer bottle into the garbage.

"What do you mean?"

"What I mean is something to wear for protection. Didn't that school nurse tell you what you need?"

"Yes, Mama, I have what I need," I said.

I didn't.

What I needed was a real mother and a real father, for starters, but that was something I'd see only on television.

"I don't want to hear about you not going to school, Raven. If I do, I'm going to call your uncle Reuben," she warned. She often used her brother as a threat. She knew I never liked him, never liked being in his company. I didn't think his own children liked him, and I knew my aunt Clara was afraid of him. I could see it in her eyes.

Mama returned to her bedroom and went back to sleep. I sat by the window and looked down at the street. Our apartment was on the third floor. There were no elevators, just a windy stairway that sounded as if it was about to collapse, especially when younger children ran down the steps or when Mr. Winecoup, the man who lived above us, walked up. He easily weighed three hundred pounds. The ceiling shook when he paced about in his apartment.

I looked beyond the street, out toward the mountains in the distance, and wondered what was beyond them. I dreamed of running off to find a place where the sun always shone, where houses were clean and smelled fresh, where parents laughed and loved their children, where there were fathers who cared and mothers who cared.

You might as well live in Disneyland, a voice told me. *Stop dreaming.*

I rose and began my day of solitude, finding something to eat, watching some television, waiting for Mama to wake so we could talk about dinner before she went off to her job. When she was rested and sobered up enough, she would sit before her vanity mirror and work on her hair and face enough to give others the illusion she was healthy and still attractive. While she did her makeup, she ranted and raved about her life and what she could have been if she hadn't fallen for the first good-looking man and believed his lies.

I tried to ask her questions about her own youth, but she hated answering questions about her family. Her parents had practically disowned her, and she had left home when she was eighteen, but she didn't realize any of her own dreams. The biggest and most exciting thing in her life was her small flirtation with becoming a model. Some department store manager had hired her to model in the women's department. "But then he wanted sexual favors, so I left," she told me. Once again, she went into one of her tirades about men.

"If you hate men so much," I asked her, "why do you go out with one almost every other night?"

"Don't have a smart mouth, Raven," she fired back. She thought a moment and then shrugged. "I'm entitled to some fun, aren't I? Well? I work hard. Let them take me out and spend some money on me."

"Don't you ever want to meet anyone nice, Mama?" I asked. "Don't you ever want to get married again?"

She stared at herself in the mirror. Her eyes looked sad for a moment, and then she put on that angry look and spun on me.

"*No!* I don't want to have no man lording over me again. And besides," she said, practically screaming, "I didn't get married. I never had a wedding, not even in a court."

"But I thought . . . my father . . ."

"He was your father, but he wasn't my husband. We just lived together," she said. She looked away.

"But I have his name . . . Flores," I stuttered.

"It was just to save my reputation," she admitted. She turned to me and smiled coldly. "You can call yourself whatever you want."

I stared, my heart quivering. I didn't even have a name?

When I looked in the mirror, whom did I see? No one, I thought.

I might as well be invisible, I concluded, and returned to my seat by the window, watching the gray clouds twirl toward the mountains, toward the promise of something better.

That promise.

It was all I had.

1
A Rude Awakening

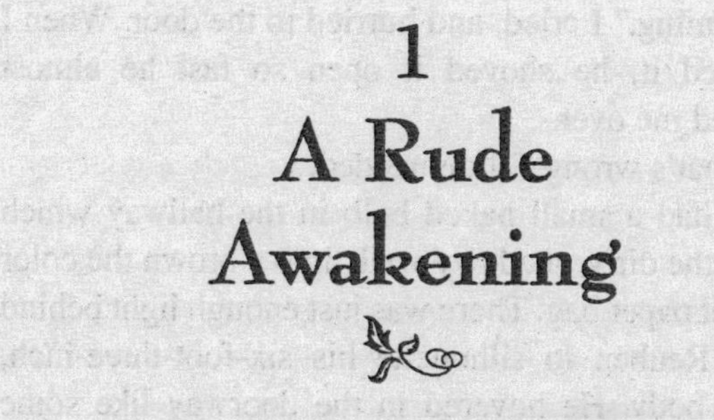

I woke to the sound of knocking, but I wasn't sure if it was someone at our door. People pounded on the walls in this apartment building at all times of the day or night. The knocking grew sharper, more frenzied, and then I heard my uncle Reuben's voice.

"Raven, damn it, wake up. Raven!"

He hit the door so hard that I thought his fist had gone through. I reached for my robe and got up quickly.

"Mama!" I called.

I ground the sleep from my eyes and listened. I thought I remembered hearing her come home, but the nights were so mixed up and confused in my memory, I wasn't sure. "Mama?"

Uncle Reuben pounded on the door again, shaking the whole frame. I hurried to Mama's bedroom and gazed in. She wasn't there.

"Raven! Wake up!"

"Coming," I cried, and hurried to the door. When I unlocked it, he shoved it open so fast he almost knocked me over.

"What's wrong?" I demanded.

We had a small naked bulb in the hallway which turned the dirty, shadowy walls into a brown the color of a wet paper bag. There was just enough light behind Uncle Reuben to silhouette his six-foot-three-inch, stocky body. He hovered in the doorway like some bird of prey, and the silence that followed his urgency frightened me even more. He seemed to be gasping for breath as if he had run up the stairs.

"What do you want?" I cried.

"Get some things together," he ordered. "You got to come with me."

"What? Why?" I stepped back and embraced myself. I would have hated going anywhere with him in broad daylight, much less late at night.

"Put on some light," he commanded.

I found the switch and lit up the kitchen. The illumination revealed his swollen, sweaty red face, the crests of his cheeks as red as a rash. His dark eyes looked about frantically. He wore only a soiled T-shirt and a pair of oily-looking jeans. Even though he had an administrative job now with the highway department, he still had the bulky muscular frame he had built working on the road crew. His dark brown hair was cut military short, which made his ears look like the wings on Mercury's head. I used to wonder how Mama and Uncle Reuben could be siblings. His facial features were large and pronounced, the only real resemblance being in their eyes.

"What is it?" I asked. "Why are you here?"

"Not because I want to be, believe me," he replied, and went to the sink to pour himself a glass of water. "Your mother's in jail," he added.

"What?"

I had to wait for him to take long gulps of water. He put the glass in the sink as if he expected the maid would clean up after him and turned to me. For a moment, he just drank me in. His gaze made me feel as if a cold wind had slipped under my robe. I actually shivered.

"Why is Mama in jail?"

"She got picked up with some drug dealer. She's in big-time, real trouble this time," he said. "You got to come live with us in the meantime, maybe forever," he added, and spit into the sink.

"Live with you?" My heart stopped.

"Believe me, I'm not happy about it. She called me to come fetch you," he continued with obvious reluctance. It was as if his mouth fought opening and closing to produce the words. He gazed around our small apartment. "What a pig sty! How does anyone live here?"

Before I could respond, he spun on me. "Get your things together. I don't want to stay here a moment longer than I have to."

"How long is she going to be in jail?" I asked, the tears beginning to burn under my eyelids.

"I don't know. Years, maybe," he said without emotion. "She was still on probation from that last thing.

It's late. I have to get up in a few hours and go to work. Get a move on," he ordered.

"Why can't I just stay here?" I moaned.

"For the simple reason that the court won't permit it. I thought you were a smart kid. If you don't come with me, they'll put you in a foster home," he added.

For a long moment, I considered the option. I'd be better off with complete strangers than with him.

"And for another reason, I promised your mother." He studied my face a moment and smiled coldly. "I know what you're thinking. I was surprised she gave a damn, too," he said.

My breath caught, and I couldn't swallow. I had to turn away so he wouldn't see the tears escaping and streaming down my cheeks. I hurried into the bedroom and opened the dresser drawers to take out my clothes. The only suitcase I had was small and had to be tied together with belts to close. I found it in the back of my closet and started to pack it.

Uncle Reuben stepped in and looked at the bedroom. "It stinks in here," he said.

I kept packing. I didn't know how long I would really live with him and Aunt Clara, but I didn't want to run out of socks and panties. "You don't need all that," he said when I reached into the closet for more clothes. "I don't want roaches in my house. Just take the basics."

"All I have is basics, some shirts and jeans and two dresses. And I don't have roaches in my clothes."

He grunted. I never liked Uncle Reuben. He was full of prejudice, often telling Mama that her problems began when she got herself involved with a Cuban. He liked to hold himself higher than us because he had been promoted and wore a suit to work.

I had two cousins, William, who was nine, and Jennifer, who was fourteen. William was a meek, quiet boy who, like me, enjoyed being by himself. He said very little, and once I heard Aunt Clara say the school thought he was nearly autistic. Jennifer was stuck-up. She had a way of holding her head back and talking down her nose that made everyone feel she thought she was superior. Once, when I was five, I got so frustrated with her I stomped on her foot and nearly broke one of her toes.

I finished packing and scooped up a pair of jeans and a sweater. Uncle Reuben stood there watching me as I walked past him to the bathroom to change. When I came out, he had my suitcase in his hand and was waiting in the doorway.

"Let's go," he urged. "I feel like I could catch some disease in here."

He, Aunt Clara, and my cousins lived in a nice A-frame two-story house. Mama and I didn't visit that often, but I was always envious of their yard, their nice furniture and clean bathrooms. William had his own room, and Jennifer had hers. The house was in a smaller village far enough away from the city so that I would have to go to a different school.

"Where am I going to stay?" I asked Uncle Reuben as I slipped on my sneakers.

"Clara's fixing up her sewing room for you. She has a pullout in it. Then we'll see," he said. "Come on."

"Should I just leave everything?" I asked, gazing about the apartment.

"What's there to leave? Old dishes, hand-me-down furniture, and rats? I wouldn't even bother locking the door," he muttered, and started down the stairs.

I paused in the doorway. He was right. It was a hole in the wall, drab and worn, even rotten in places and full of apologies, but it had been home for me. For so long, these walls were my little world. I always dreamed of leaving it, but now that I actually was, I couldn't help feeling afraid and sad.

"Raven!" Uncle Reuben shouted from the bottom of the stairway.

"Shut up out there!" someone cried. "People's trying to sleep."

I closed the door quickly and hurried down after him. We burst into the empty streets. It was still dark. The rest of the world was asleep. He threw my suitcase into the trunk of his car and got in quickly. I followed and gazed sleepily out the window at the apartment house. Only one of the three bulbs over the entryway worked. Shadows hid the chipped and faded paint and broken basement windows.

"It's lucky for you I live close enough to come and get you," he said, "or tonight you'd be on your way to some orphanage."

"I'm not an orphan," I shot back.

"No. You're worse," he said. "Orphans don't have mothers like yours."

"How can you talk about your sister like that?" I

demanded. No matter how bad Mama was, I couldn't just sit there and listen to him tear her down.

"Easy," he said. "This isn't the first time I've had to come rescue her or bail her out, is it? This time, she's really gone and done it, though, and I say that's good. Let it come to an end. She's a lost cause." He turned to me. "And I'm warning you from the start," he fired, pointing his long, thick right forefinger into my face as he drove, "I don't want you corrupting my children, hear? The first time you bring disgrace into my home, that will be the last. I can assure you of that."

I curled up as far away from him as I could squeeze my body and closed my eyes. This is a nightmare, I thought, just a bad dream. In a moment, I'll wake up and be on the pullout in our living room. Maybe I'll hear Mama stumbling into the apartment. Suddenly, that didn't seem so bad.

We drove mostly in silence the rest of the way. Occasionally, Uncle Reuben muttered some obscenity or complained about being woken out of a deep sleep by his drunken, worthless sister.

"There oughta be a way to disown your relatives, to walk into a courtroom and declare yourself an independent soul so they can't come after you or ruin your life," he grumbled. I tried to ignore him, to go back to sleep.

I opened my eyes when we pulled into the driveway. The lights were on downstairs. He got out and opened the trunk, nearly ripping my suitcase apart when he took it out. I trailed behind him to the front door. Aunt Clara opened the door before we got there.

Aunt Clara was a mystery to me. No two people seemed more unalike than she and Uncle Reuben. She was small, fragile, dainty, and soft-spoken. Her face was usually full of sympathy and concern, and as far as I could ever tell, she never looked down on us or said bad things about us, no matter what Mama did. Mama liked her and, ironically, often told me she felt sorrier for her than she did for herself.

"It's a bigger burden living with my brother," she declared.

Aunt Clara had light brown hair that was always neatly styled about her ears. She wore little makeup, but her face was usually bright and cheery, especially because of the deep blue in her warm eyes and the soft smile on her small lips. She was only a few inches taller than I was, and when she stood next to Uncle Reuben, she looked as if she could be another one of his children.

She waited for us with her hands clasped and pressed between her small breasts.

"You poor dear," she said. "Come right in."

"Poor dear is right," Uncle Reuben said. "You should see that place. How could a grown woman want to live there and let her child live there?"

"Well, she's out of there now, Reuben."

"Yeah, right," he said. "I'm going back to bed. Some people have to work for a living," he muttered, and charged through the house and up the small stairway. The banister shook under his grip as he pulled himself up the stairs. He had dropped my suitcase in the middle of the floor.

"Would you like a cup of warm milk, Raven?" Aunt Clara asked.

"No, thank you," I said.

"You're tired, too, I imagine. This is all a bad business for everyone. Come with me. I have the sewing room all ready for you."

The sewing room was downstairs, just off the living room. It wasn't a big room, but it was sweet with flowery wallpaper, a light gray rug, a table with a sewing machine, a soft-backed wooden chair, and the pullout. There was one big window with white cotton curtains that faced the east side of the house, so the sunlight would light it up in the morning. On the walls were some needlework pictures in frames that Aunt Clara had done. They were scenes with farmhouses and animals and one with a woman and a young girl sitting by a brook.

"You know where the bathroom is, right down the hall," she said. "I wish we had another bedroom, but . . ."

"This is fine, Aunt Clara. I hate to take away your sewing room."

"Oh, it's nothing. I could do the same work someplace else. Don't you give it another thought, child. Tomorrow, you'll just rest, and maybe, before the day is out, we'll go over to the school and get you enrolled. We don't want you falling behind."

I hated to tell her how behind I already had fallen.

"Here's a new toothbrush," she said, indicating it on the desk. "I had one from the last time I went to the dentist."

"Thank you, Aunt Clara."

She gazed at me a moment and then shook her head and stroked my hair.

"The things we do to our children," she muttered, kissed me on the forehead, and left to go upstairs.

I stood there for a moment. To Aunt Clara, this room wasn't much, but to me, it was better than a luxury hotel. Her house smelled fresh and clean, and it was so quiet, no creaks, no voices coming through the walls, no footsteps pounding on the ceiling.

I got undressed and slipped under the fresh comforter. The pullout was firmer than ours, and the pillows were fluffy. I was so comfortable and so tired that I forgot for the moment that Mama was in jail. I was too tired, too frightened, and too confused to think anymore. I closed my eyes.

I opened them again when I felt someone was looking at me. It was morning. Sunlight poured through the window. I had forgotten where I was and sat up quickly. William was standing there gaping at me.

"Mama says you're going to live with us now," he said slowly.

I scrubbed my face with my palms and took a deep breath as it all came rushing back over me.

"William, get your rear end back in here right now and finish your breakfast," I heard Uncle Reuben shout.

William hesitated and then hurried out. I lay back on my pillow and stared up at the ceiling.

"Your mother's in jail," I heard Jennifer say from the doorway.

I just turned and gazed at her. She had her light

brown hair tied back with a ribbon. She was a tall girl with a large bone structure that made her look heavier than she was. Aunt Clara's features were overpowered by Uncle Reuben's, so that Jennifer's nose was wider and longer, as was her mouth. She had Aunt Clara's eyes, but they seemed out of place in so large a face. She was wide in the waist, too. Whenever I saw Uncle Reuben with her, however, he always treated her as if she were some raving beauty. There was never any question in my mind that he favored her over William. William was too small and fragile, too much like Aunt Clara.

"That's what your father says," I replied.

"Well, he wouldn't lie about it, would he? Jesus, what an embarrassment. And now you're going to be in my school, too," she complained.

"Well, I don't want to be," I said.

"Just don't tell anyone about your mother. We'll make up some story," she decided.

"Like what?" I asked dubiously.

She stood there, staring in at me and thinking. "I know," she said with a smile. "We'll say she's dead."

2
Cinderella's Nightmare

"Who do you think you are, some princess?" Uncle Reuben bellowed from the doorway. "Everybody's up and havin' breakfast. Clara ain't gonna be waitin' on you."

"I was getting up," I said. "I didn't realize how late it was. There's no clock in this room, and I don't have a watch."

"No clock? I'll make sure I get you a clock. Those kind of excuses won't work here."

"It's not an excuse. It's the truth," I said.

He stood in the doorway with his hands on his hips. Then he glanced down the hall and stepped into the sewing room.

"We're going to set some rules down in concrete right now," he declared. "First, from now on, you're up before everybody. You set the table for breakfast, and you put on the coffee. Before you head off for school, make sure the table's cleared and the dishes and silverware are put away. When you come home from school, I expect you to help Clara around here. I want to see you cleaning the house, washing windows and floors. You'll help her with the laundry, too. This ain't a free ride just because your mother is a major screw-up, understand?"

I glared at him.

"When I ask you a question, I expect an answer. You need discipline. You're like some sort of wild animal livin' over there in that hole with that drunk of a sister of mine. That's all ended today, hear? Well?"

"I wasn't living like a wild animal," I shot back.

He smirked. "It looks like I'm going to end up bein' your legal guardian. That means you report to me, and I'm warning you right now, Raven, I don't spare the rod and spoil the child. Understand? Well?" He brought his large hand up. The palm looked as wide as a paddle.

"Yes," I said. "Yes."

He was practically standing over me, his face dark red with fury. I had no doubt he would strike me if he saw fit to do so, and I was afraid.

"Raven," he muttered with a twist in his lips. "What kind of a name is that to give a girl, anyway? She must have been drunk the day you was born."

"I like my name," I insisted. He was terrifying, but I had some pride.

He stood there a few minutes longer, gazing down at me. I pulled the comforter up to my shoulders, but I felt as if he could see right through it.

"I know you're growing older and growing fast, and I remember what happened to your mother, how she was when the boys started looking her way. You better not be taking the same road. I don't want you corrupting my Jennifer, hear?"

I turned away, the tears in my eyes making it impossible to look up at him anymore. I wasn't some disease. I wouldn't infect his precious Jennifer.

He grunted and left the room. I could hear him telling Aunt Clara what he had told me, what he wanted to be my chores. She didn't argue. A little while later, I heard him leave with Jennifer and William. I waited and rose.

"You hungry, dear?" Aunt Clara asked as I went to the bathroom.

"Just a little," I said.

"Coffee is still warm, and I have eggs if you want, even oatmeal."

"I'll take care of myself, Aunt Clara. Please don't think you have to wait on me," I said.

"Don't you worry about that," she said.

I got dressed and found myself some cold cereal. Aunt Clara poured me some orange juice and sat with me as I ate.

"Reuben's bark is worse than his bite," she said, trying to reassure me. "He's just upset with the surprise and all. Don't pay no mind to all those orders he gave."

"I don't mind helping out," I told her. "I did most of it at home, anyway."

"I bet you did." She nodded and sipped some coffee.

"Aunt Clara, what's going to happen to my mother? Is she really going to jail for a long time?" I asked.

"I don't know. Reuben mumbled something about them maybe putting her in a drug rehabilitation program, but we'll have to wait and see. You know, it's not her first time getting herself into big trouble," she added.

I nodded. There was no sense pretending it wasn't true or living in a dream world. Mama was in very big trouble, and that meant I was in trouble, too. Who wanted to live here with a cousin like Jennifer and an uncle like Uncle Reuben? I'd rather be in the streets.

"You just rest up a bit, honey," Aunt Clara said. "You've been through a terrible shock. After I tend to some chores, we'll have lunch, and right after that, I'll run you over to the school to get you enrolled, okay?"

"I'll help you with your chores, Aunt Clara. It's what Uncle Reuben wants, anyway," I said, "and it will help keep the peace."

"Ain't you the smart one?" she said, smiling. She tapped my hand. "Just sit here and finish your breakfast first."

She left and went upstairs. When I was done, I washed all the dishes and cleaned the table. I joined her just as she was starting on Jennifer's room. I paused in the doorway, shocked at the mess. Clothes were strewn about, and there was a dish with leftover apple pie on the floor by the bed, where the phone had been left as well. I imagined she had been sitting there talking to some friends and eating the pie, but why did she just leave it? Wasn't she worried about mice and bugs?

The bed was unmade, and the bathroom she shared with William looked as if someone had had to leave in a hurry. Makeup was uncovered, the sink was still full of cloudy water, an open lipstick tube was on its side, the toothpaste was uncovered with some of it dripped onto the counter, a washcloth dangled over the doorknob, and there were magazines on the floor by the toilet. The shower door was open, a wet towel on the floor beside it.

Aunt Clara began to clean up without making a comment about the mess.

"Why does she leave her room and bathroom like this, Aunt Clara? Talk about living in a pig sty," I muttered. "I guess Uncle Reuben doesn't look in here often."

"Oh, he does," Aunt Clara said with a deep sigh. "And I've been after her, but Jennifer . . . Jennifer's a little spoiled," she admitted.

"A little? This looks like spoiled rotten," I said, but I pitched in and helped. I cleaned the bathroom until it looked spotless, even washing down the mirrors that were smudged with lipstick and makeup.

William's room was actually more organized and cleaner. The messiest thing was his unmade bed. After I straightened up his room, I went down and cleaned up the sewing room. I put the pullout back together so it didn't look like a bedroom. With my few things neatly put away, no one would even know I had slept there.

"You don't have to do that every day," Aunt Clara commented. "You can just close the door."

"I'm sure Uncle Reuben wouldn't like that," I told her.

She didn't argue. Even though he wasn't here, his shadow seemed to linger. The way Aunt Clara looked over her shoulder, it was almost as if she believed the shadow would tell him things we had said.

After we cleaned up the bedrooms, she began to vacuum the living room. I polished some furniture and swept the kitchen floor. I had to keep busy so I wouldn't think too much about Mama sitting in jail.

"You are a good worker, Raven. I hope some of your good habits will spill off onto my Jennifer," she said, but not with much optimism.

She prepared chicken salad for our lunch, and we sat and talked. I really didn't know much about her. She described where she had been brought up and how she had met Uncle Reuben. She said he had just started working with the public works department, and she had just graduated from high school.

"He was like an Atlas out there on the highway. With his shirt off and his muscles gleaming in the sunlight. He was a lot trimmer then," she recalled fondly. She laughed. "One day, he pretended to have road work right in front of my parents' house just so he could visit with me. We got married about four months later. My mother hoped I would at least go to a secretarial school, but you're impulsive when you're young," she remarked, and looked very thoughtful for a few moments. Then she shook her head and patted my hand. "Don't you go jumping into the arms of the first man you see, honey. Stand back, listen to your head instead of your heart, and take your time."

It seemed to me that every woman I ever met gave me the same advice. I was beginning to believe that love was a trap men set for unsuspecting women. They told us what we wanted to hear. They wrote promises in gold. They filled our heads with dreams and made it all seem easy, and then they satisfied themselves and went off to trap another innocent young woman. Even Aunt Clara, who had married her young sweetheart, discovered she had gotten caught in a trap. Uncle Reuben ruled his house like an ogre, turning her into a glorified maid instead of putting her up on a pedestal as I was sure he had promised. She just shook her head and threaded herself through her days like a rat caught in a maze.

After lunch, she drove me over to the school. It was smaller and seemed quieter than mine. The principal, Mr. Moore, a stout, thick-necked man of about forty, invited us into his office. He listened to Aunt Clara and then called his secretary and dictated orders quickly.

"I want you to contact her previous school, get the guidance counselor, get her records sent here ASAP, Martha," he said. I was impressed with his take-charge demeanor. "I suppose you know that we'll have to get some sort of instructions from Child Welfare as to her status. You and your husband are going to be her legal guardians, of course."

"Yes, of course," Aunt Clara said.

"She'll do fine," he concluded, gazing at me. "I know this isn't easy for you, but you should consider what it will be like for your new teachers. They have the added burden of bringing you up to par in their classes. The subjects might be the same, but everyone has his or her way of doing things, and there are bound to be differences. Some teachers move through the curriculum faster than others."

"I know," I said.

He nodded, staring at me a moment with his eyes dark and concerned. Then he smiled.

"On the other hand, you have a cousin attending classes here. She should be of great help. Your daughter is a year older than Raven?" he asked Aunt Clara.

"Yes."

"Not a big difference. You'll have similar interests, I'm sure. She can help fill you in on our rules and regulations, too. Keep your nose clean, and we'll all get along, okay?"

I nodded.

Mr. Moore suggested I attend classes immediately. "No sense wasting any more time. She can still sit in on math and social studies. She'll get her books in those classes, at least," he said.

"What a good idea," Aunt Clara agreed.

A student office assistant brought me to math class and introduced me to Mr. Finnerman, who gave me a textbook and assigned me the last seat in the first row. Everyone looked at me, watching my every move. I recalled how interested I used to be when a new student arrived. I was sure they were all just as curious.

One girl, a black girl who introduced herself as Terri Johnson, showed me the way to social studies and introduced me to some other students along the way. She called me "the new girl." As we approached the social studies room, I saw Jennifer coming down the hall with two girlfriends at her side. The moment her eyes set on me, she stopped and moaned.

"That's her," I heard her tell them as she passed by without saying hello.

It was worse when social studies class ended and I had to find the right schoolbus home. Jennifer didn't wait for me, and when I found the bus, she was already seated in the rear with her friends, pretending she didn't know me. I sat up front and talked to a thin, dark-haired boy named Clarence Dunsen, who had a bad stutter. It made him shy but also very suspicious. When he did speak to me, he waited to see if I was going to ridicule him. I looked back at Jennifer, whose laugh resounded through the bus louder than anyone else's.

Please, Mama, I thought, be good, make promises, crawl on the floor if you have to, but get out and take me home, take me anywhere, just get me away from here.

"I got news," Aunt Clara said as soon as we entered the house.

"What?" I gasped, holding my new textbooks tightly against me.

"Your mother's not going to jail."

"Thank God," I cried. I was going to add, "And good riddance to you, Jennifer Spoiled Head," but

Aunt Clara wasn't smiling. She shook her head. "What else, Aunt Clara?"

"She has to be in drug rehabilitation. She could be there for some time, Raven. They won't even let her call you until her therapist says so."

"Oh," I said, sinking into a chair.

"It's better than it could have been," Aunt Clara said.

"Great. I have an aunt in drug rehabilitation," Jennifer whined. She turned her eyes on me like two little spotlights of hate. "You better do what I said and tell everyone your mother is dead," Jennifer warned.

I just looked at her.

"Don't talk like that, Jennifer," Aunt Clara said. "And you should know your cousin helped me clean your room. See if you can keep it that way."

"So what? She should clean our house. You heard what Daddy said. She's living off us, isn't she?" Jennifer fired back.

"Jennifer!" Aunt Clara cried. "Where's your charity and your love?"

"Love? I don't love her. It was hard enough to explain who she was. Everyone wanted to know why she's so dark. I had to tell them what her father was," she complained.

"Jennifer."

"You're not better than me because your skin's whiter," I charged.

"Of course, she isn't," Aunt Clara said. "Jennifer, I never taught you such terrible things."

"It's not fair, Mama. My friends are all wondering about our family now. It's not fair!" she moaned.

"Stop that talk, or I'll tell your father," Aunt Clara said.

"Tell him," she challenged, smirked, and walked up the stairs.

"I don't know where she gets that streak of meanness," Aunt Clara muttered.

I gazed up at her. Was she that blind or deliberately hiding her head in the sand? It was easy to see that Jennifer had inherited the meanness from Uncle Reuben.

"I'm sorry," Aunt Clara said.

"Don't worry about it, Aunt Clara. I'll be fine with or without Jennifer's friendship."

The door opened and closed, and William came sauntering in. He looked up at me with shy eyes.

"How was your day in school, William?" Aunt Clara asked.

He dug into his notebook and produced a spelling test on which he had received a ninety.

"That's wonderful! Look, Raven," she said, showing me.

"Very good, William. I'll have to come to you for help with my spelling homework."

He looked appreciative but took the test back quickly and shoved it into his notebook.

"Do you want some milk and cookies, William?" Aunt Clara asked him.

He shook his head, glanced at me with as close to a smile as he could manage, and then hurried up to his room.

"He's so shy. I never realized how shy. Doesn't he have any friends to play with after school?" I asked, watching him leave.

Aunt Clara shook her head sadly.

"He stays to himself too much, I know. The counselor at school called me in to discuss him. His teachers think he's too withdrawn. They all say he never raises his hand in class. He hardly speaks to the other students. You see him. He looks like a turtle about to crawl back in his shell. I don't know why," she added, her eyes filling with tears. I felt like putting my arm around her.

"He'll grow out of it," I said, but she didn't smile.

She shook her head. "Something's not right, but I don't know why. I took him to a doctor. He's healthy, hardly even gets a cold, but something . . ." Her voice trailed off. Then she turned to me with teary eyes and asked, "What makes a young boy behave like that?"

I didn't know then.

But I would soon learn why.

Only I wouldn't be able to find the words to tell her.

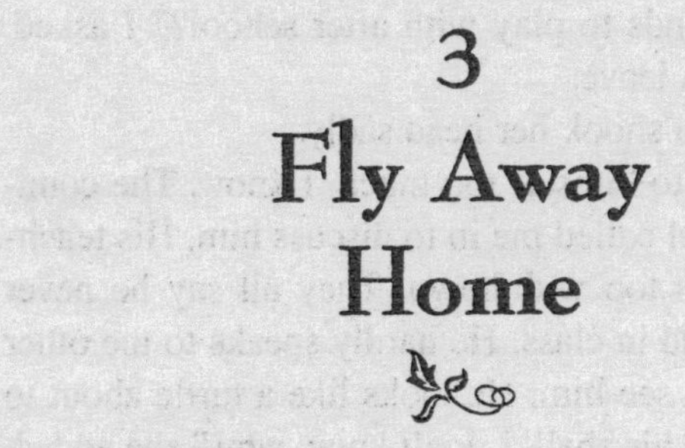

3
Fly Away Home

"Drug rehabilitation," Uncle Reuben muttered as he chewed his forkful of sirloin steak. Whenever Mama and I had steak, it was usually warmed-up leftovers she had brought back from Charlie's. "That's a waste of government money," he continued, chewing as he talked. He seemed to grind his teeth over the bitter words as well as his meat.

"It's not a waste of money if it helps her," Aunt Clara said softly.

He stopped chewing and glared at her.

"Helps her? Nothing can help her. She's a lost cause. Best thing they could do would be to lock her up and drop the key into the sewer."

Jennifer laughed. I looked up from my plate and fixed my eyes on her.

"Stop staring at me," she complained. "It isn't polite to stare, is it, Daddy?"

Uncle Reuben glanced at me and then nodded. "No, it ain't, but how would she know?"

Jennifer laughed again and smiled at me. My meat tasted like chunks of cardboard and stuck in my throat. I stopped eating and sat back. "I'd like to be excused," I said.

"Like hell you will, until you finish that," Uncle Reuben said, nodding at my plate. "We don't waste food here."

Jennifer cut into her steak and chomped down with a wide smile on her chubby face, pretending to savor every morsel. "It's delicious," she said.

"It's not polite to talk with food in your mouth," I said quickly.

William looked up with a gleeful smile in his eyes. Jennifer stopped chewing and swung her eyes at Uncle Reuben. He continued to scoop up his potatoes, shoveling the food into his mouth as if he had to finish in record time.

"I have a homemade pecan pie, Reuben. Your favorite," Aunt Clara said.

He nodded as if he expected no less. They're all spoiled, I thought.

"I got an eighty on my English test today," Jennifer told him.

"No kidding? Eighty. That's good," Uncle Reuben said.

"I have a chance to make the honor roll if Mr. Finnerman gives me a decent grade in math this quarter," she bragged.

"Wow. Hear that, Clara? That's my little girl making her daddy proud."

"Yes. That's very good," Aunt Clara said. "William came home with a ninety in spelling," she added.

William looked at Uncle Reuben, but he just continued chewing with only the slightest nod. "I guess I gotta go get the paperwork done on her," he said finally. "Everything go all right with the school?"

"Yes," Aunt Clara said. "She's enrolled."

"What kind of grades you been getting?" he asked me.

"I pass everything," I said, looking away quickly.

"I bet," he said. "Your mother ever ask you how you were doing in school?"

"Yes, she has," I said with indignation. He curled his lips. "She had to sign my report card, so she saw my grades all the time."

"You never forged her signature?" Jennifer asked with a smile that could freeze lava.

"Why? Is that what you do?" I fired back.

"Hardly. I don't have to do that. I pass for real," she said. "Daddy signs my report cards, don't you, Daddy?"

"Every time," he agreed. He pushed back from the table and stood. "If she's going to waste food, Clara, you see you don't give her as much to start. I work hard for my money to pay for everything," he added, directing himself to me.

Even though my stomach was protesting, I forced myself to swallow the last piece of meat and another forkful of green beans.

"I want to catch the news. Call me when coffee and pie is ready," he added, and left the kitchen to go watch television.

My eyes followed him out, and then I looked at William, who was staring at me sympathetically. I smiled at him, and his face brightened.

"I gotta go do my homework, Ma. I don't have to do anything with the dinner dishes anyway, right? You got her," Jennifer said, nodding at me.

"You should still help out, Jennifer."

"I can't. You heard Daddy. He wants me to make the honor roll. Don't you want me to finish my homework?" she whined.

"Of course."

"Okay, then," she said, jumping up. "I'll come down later for a piece of pie."

She left the kitchen. Aunt Clara shook her head sadly.

"I'll help," William said. He started to clear the table with me.

"You want to see the birdhouse I built?" he asked me when we were finished.

Aunt Clara smiled at me, happy William was emerging a little from his shell.

"Sure," I said.

"It's up in my room. I made it myself," he said. I followed him up to his room, and he took it off the shelf. It was a triangular-shaped house with dried corncobs attached to the outside.

"I glued all those on," he said, showing me how secure the cobs were.

I handled it gently. "This is wonderful, William. It must have been hard to build this from scratch. How long did it take?"

"A couple of days," he said proudly. "As soon as I save up enough, I'm going to buy some binoculars so I can see the birds that come to my house up close. Do you know anything about birds?"

I shook my head, and he went to his desk to get an encyclopedia of birds. It contained brightly colored photos of birds, their habitats, and the type of food they ate. He then showed me another book that had instructions on building birdhouses.

"That's the next one I want to build." He pointed to a double-decker birdhouse.

"That's beautiful. You can build that?"

"Sure," he said confidently. "I'll let you know when I get the materials, and you could watch if you want."

"Thanks," I said.

He gave me his best smile, one that truly brightened his eyes.

"I better start on my homework," I told him.

I left, and as I passed Jennifer's door, which was partly open, I saw her curled on the floor, talking on her phone. I paused, and she looked up at me.

"What are you doing, spying on me?" she snapped.

"Hardly," I said. "But I thought you had to do your homework, or are you taking a course in gossip?" I continued down the stairs, my heart pounding. I heard her slam her door closed behind me.

Since the sewing room was so close to the dining

room, I could hear Uncle Reuben's conversation with Aunt Clara while he had his coffee and pie.

"We're not going to go and spend a lot of money on new clothes for her. I want to see if we can get some sort of government help. I think if you take in a kid, they give you some support money."

"She needs things, Reuben," Aunt Clara said softly. "Shouldn't you go back and see what else she has in the apartment?"

"What good would that do? We'd only have to have it deloused."

"You can't just let her wear what she has," Aunt Clara insisted softly.

"Okay, okay, get her a couple of things. But I don't want you spending a lot of money, Clara. We got Jennifer, who needs new things. You see how fast she's growing."

"Maybe Jennifer will share some of her things with Raven," Aunt Clara said.

He grunted and then added, "If she does, you make sure Raven is clean before she puts anything of Jennifer's on."

"Oh, she's clean, Reuben. She's really a very nice young lady, despite her life with your sister."

"We'll see," he said. I heard him rise. "Make sure she cleans all this up before she goes to sleep. I want her to appreciate what she gets here."

"She does."

He didn't respond. I heard him go back into the living room and turn up the television. Then I went to help Aunt Clara.

"You don't have to do this, Raven," she whispered. "There's not much left. Go do your homework."

"I didn't have that much, Aunt Clara. I have to meet with my teachers for a while after school each day for the next week to catch up. When will we know when Mama can talk to me?" I asked.

She shook her head. "I don't know, honey. Reuben will find out more tomorrow."

"He should have made more over William's spelling test," I mumbled. "And an eighty isn't such a great grade."

She looked at me with not so much fear in her eyes as cautious agreement. "I know," she said. "I've been after him to spend more time with William."

"I'm not so sure that would help," I muttered, mostly to myself. If she heard, she didn't respond. Then she paused and looked as if she saw a ghost. I turned.

Uncle Reuben was standing in the doorway.

"She should do that herself, Clara. You need to come in and rest," he ordered, his eyes burning through me.

"There's nothing left to do, Reuben."

He continued to stare. Had he heard me?

"All right, Reuben. I'm coming," she said. She wiped her hands on a dish towel and left the kitchen. He let her pass, glanced at me again, and then followed her.

From what I had seen already, I realized Uncle Reuben whipped his family around this house with a look, a word, a gesture. He was the puppet master, and they jumped when he tugged at their strings.

I felt as if he was tying strings around my arms and legs, too, and soon I would be just another puppet.

After finishing my homework, I made my bed and changed into the one nightgown I owned. Lying there and staring out through my one window at the stars that popped in between passing clouds, I thought that somehow I had been turned into Cinderella without the magic slipper or fairy godmother. There would be no magic in my life.

Once, I spent my time dreaming about far-off places, beautiful houses, handsome young men, gala dances, beautiful clothes and jewels. I was in my own movie, spinning out the scenes on the walls of my imagination. It took me out of the small apartment.

I had to laugh.

Here I was, out, with a family, going to a new school, and what did I dream of?

Getting back to my small apartment.

I actually grew to like the new school. Because my classes were much smaller, the teachers took more time with me, and I also began to make some friends. Jennifer continued to avoid me as much as possible, but I began to accept it. From what I saw of the friends she had, girls who were mostly like her, selfish, vain, and sneaky, I more than accepted it. I welcomed it. There were much nicer kids to know.

Jennifer was far from the goody-goody she pretended to be in front of Uncle Reuben, too. She was right in there with the girls who smoked in the girls' room, and from what I was told and what I saw, she often cheated on her homework and tests. I could see that her teachers weren't very fond of her, either. Terri Johnson told me she knew for a fact that Jennifer and her friends went on shoplifting sprees at the mall just for the thrill of it. Here she was, a girl with parents, a nice home, and all, and she wasn't any better than the girls I had known who came from broken families and who lived in much more unpleasant places. I wondered what Uncle Reuben would do if he found out any of this about his precious perfect daughter.

One day in the cafeteria, Jennifer paused with two of her friends at my table. I stopped talking and looked up at her.

"You've fallen behind on the laundry," she said. "I need that blue and white blouse tomorrow. See that it's done."

My mouth fell open as I looked from her to the smirking faces of her friends.

"Why don't you wash it yourself, then?" I shot back.

"You're supposed to be earning your room and board, aren't you?"

"What about you?" I countered.

"I don't have to. I have parents," she replied smugly. "Just get it done, or I'll tell Daddy," she threatened, and walked off laughing.

Terri looked down, embarrassed for me.

"She's a spoiled brat," I said. I wanted to say a lot

more, but it was hard to talk. My words got choked in my throat because it was tight from fighting back my tears.

"I'd rather live with a snake than that," Terri offered, and the girls at my table all laughed.

"Yeah, well, that's what I'm doing," I muttered, "living with a snake."

When I got home from school that day, I found her precious blue and white blouse in the hamper. Before I put it into the washing machine, I poked a hole in the shoulder of the blouse with the pointed end of my math compass. After dinner on Tuesdays, Aunt Clara and I folded and ironed clothes. She didn't notice the hole in the blouse, and she brought everything up to Jennifer's room. It wasn't until the next morning, when I was sure she was going to wear it just to show off at school, that we heard her scream.

I had already risen and gotten dressed. Aunt Clara was with me in the kitchen preparing breakfast.

"What in the world . . ." She hurried to the foot of the stairway.

Jennifer was on the landing in her skirt and bra, holding up the blouse.

"Just look at this, Ma. Just look."

"What the hell is it?" Uncle Reuben demanded, coming from his bedroom and buttoning his shirt.

"There's a hole in my favorite blouse, and she did it. She did, Daddy!"

She showed him the blouse. He looked at it and then down the stairs at me.

"Did you do this?"

I shook my head. "I didn't even see it, or I would have told Aunt Clara," I said.

"Why would Raven do such a thing?" Aunt Clara asked.

"Because she's jealous," Jennifer cried.

"I don't even like that blouse. It's too old-fashioned, like something a grandmother might wear," I said dryly.

"It is not! Everyone's wearing these blouses. You don't know anything about style!"

"Please, Jennifer," Aunt Clara said, "stop yelling."

William came out and looked at everyone, his face full of surprise. I smiled at him, and he smiled back.

"If I knew you put a hole in this . . ." Uncle Reuben threatened. He looked at the blouse again. "I don't know how this kind of a hole would get in there."

"Bugs can do that," I said. He looked up sharply.

"We don't have bugs, or at least we didn't before you came," he said. "Clara?"

"Oh, I'll just buy her a new one today, Reuben."

"I'd better not see anything else like this," he warned. He gave Jennifer the blouse back and returned to his bedroom to finish dressing. Aunt Clara went back to the kitchen, and Jennifer and I looked at each other.

"You'll be sorry," she said. "I'm going to wear it anyway and let everyone know what you did."

"Suit yourself," I said. "You'll only make a bigger fool of yourself."

I winked at William.

"What are you laughing at?" she snapped at him, and ran back into her room.

For the first time in a long time, I had a great appetite and ate a big breakfast. Even Uncle Reuben was impressed at how I didn't leave a crumb.

4
A Close Call

When we boarded the schoolbus on Thursday, I had my arms full. Jennifer had to do a social studies project, and she had chosen to make a large visual chart, but there was a good reason she had made that choice. One of her girlfriends, Paula Gordon, who was talented in art, came over and really did most of it. Jennifer pretended she had done it all, and when she showed it to Uncle Reuben on Thursday morning, he raved about it as if it were something a famous artist like Rembrandt or that artist who cut off his ear for his girlfriend might have done. I thought any one of the birdhouses William made in his wood shop all by himself was twice the accomplishment, and yet I never once heard Uncle Reuben even mention them, much less praise him about them.

As usual, Jennifer basked in the compliments her father tossed like wedding rice over her. When we got ready to leave the house, she was very concerned about getting her precious project to school undamaged. She surprised me by pausing at the door, and in the sweetest voice she could manage, she asked me to do her a favor. I saw she had made sure to ask in front of Uncle Reuben.

"You know how rough the kids are on the bus, Raven. I have to protect my chart. Can you please carry my books, my notebooks, and my lunch bag for me? Please. Someday, I'll do you a favor," she promised, flicking her eyelashes at Uncle Reuben.

What else could I do but agree? I felt like some slave walking behind her, my arms laden with my books and my lunch bag as well as hers. She paraded down the sidewalk and onto the bus, holding her chart up high enough for everyone to see.

"Someone make a place for Raven. She's carrying my things for me," she announced.

It wasn't necessary. I always sat with Clarence Dunsen. She just wanted everyone to know that she could get me to do things for her.

When we arrived at school, she surprised me by taking only the books and notebooks she needed for her morning classes.

"Bring everything else to lunch. I've got to carry this around until social studies," she said in front of her friends, who stood there with thin smiles and laughing eyes.

"Why don't you just bring it to social studies now?" I asked her.

"And take a chance that someone might sabotage

it? Never. Remember what happened to Robert Longo's ant farm in science class?" she asked her entourage. They all nodded. "Someone poured water in it and drowned all the ants."

"I wonder who would do that," I said dryly.

"Thanks, Raven," she said, taking her morning class books and shooting off before I could refuse.

I lugged her things along with mine to my first class.

"How come you have two lunches today?" Terri Johnson asked me in English class. I told her, and she raised her eyebrows sharply, the skin in her forehead forming small furrows.

"She's just trying to show off," I said, but Terri still looked suspicious.

"She could ask one of her slaves to do that. Those girls would be glad to do her favors. I've seen it. I don't know what she's up to, but as my granny tells me all the time, a snake can't be a rabbit," she added.

I laughed, but later I began to think a little more about it, too. Just before class ended, I looked at what I thought was Jennifer's lunch bag, only I noticed my name was on it. Why would that be? I wondered.

I opened what was supposed to be Jennifer's lunch bag. We usually had the same thing. I knew because I had helped Aunt Clara make the lunches. There was an extra small pack wrapped in wax paper in hers. I glanced up to be sure Mrs. Broadhurst wasn't looking my way, and then I unwrapped the wax paper.

A cold but electric chill shot through my heart. I had seen this before. I knew what a joint was. I had seen and smelled pot around my old apartment. Lila Thomas had tried to get me to smoke it with her once.

I looked over at Terri. She saw immediately from the expression on my face that something was wrong. I lowered my hand to the side, looked at the teacher, and then opened my hand. When I looked back at Terri, she was nodding with satisfaction. Five minutes before class ended, the real reason Jennifer wanted me to carry her lunch was clearly revealed.

"Excuse me, Mrs. Broadhurst," the student office volunteer said from our doorway. "Mr. Moore would like to see Raven Flores immediately. He wants her to bring all her things, too," she added.

"Raven," she said, nodding at me. I glanced at Terri, whose eyes were filled with worry. I smiled and winked at her to reassure her.

I scooped everything into my arms, glanced once more at Terri, and followed the student volunteer. As I left the classroom, I stuffed the wax paper and joint into my bra. I had seen girls do this at my old school. No one would look there. It was a very serious thing to strip-search a student. Male teachers were terrified of even suggesting such a thing, and the girls knew it.

Mr. Moore was standing at his desk when I entered his office. He gazed at me and then nodded at the student volunteer.

"Close the door," he told her. She glanced at me with interest, stepped out, and did so. "Sit," he ordered, nodding at the chair. I sat quickly, and he stood over me.

"It has always been my policy to handle my problems in house, if possible," he began, gazing at me quickly to catch my reaction. "That doesn't mean I don't tell parents what goes on. I have an obligation to do that, but the rest of the world doesn't have to see our dirty laundry."

"What do you want from me?" I demanded.

His eyebrows hoisted with surprise at my courage. "I know you've had a poor background and upbringing, and that goes to explain poor behavior, but you're at an age now when you will be held accountable for your actions, young lady. I can assure you of that."

I looked away, my eyes fixed on one of his plaques, and waited.

"If there is something illegal in your lunch bag, I want you to take it out now, leave it on my desk, and go to class. Later, we'll discuss it, and believe me, that is a major favor I'll be doing for you."

My heart thumped, and then I smiled. I leaned down and opened my lunch bag, slowly taking out the sandwich and the cookie. Then I turned the bag inside out and placed it next to the food. I waited.

"What about that bag?" he asked, nodding at the other.

"That's my cousin's, even though my name is somehow on it. I was doing her a favor. Her arms were full of books and her social studies project."

"How do I know that's hers if your name is on it?" he asked.

"You don't, but we have the same lunch, so it doesn't matter," I said, and took out the sandwich and the cookie. I did the same thing with her bag, turning it inside out, and waited.

His eyes went from the harmless contents to my books and then to me.

"Can I at least know what you're looking for?" I asked.

"Never mind," he said. "Put all that back."

I did so slowly. "I don't think it's fair for me to be singled out for no reason," I said. "It's embarrassing to be called out of class like this."

His shoulders shot up as if I had snapped a rubber band in his face. "I have a very big responsibility here," he said. "Many young lives are in my hands, and"—he lifted a thick folder—"I have read your records from your previous school. Frankly, if you did all this here, I would consider having you taken to family court. I'm not surprised your mother's in prison."

"I haven't done anything wrong," I shot back at him.

"We'll see," he said.

"Who told you I did?" I asked.

"That's none of your concern. Very well, return to your classes," he ordered. "And just remember," he said, tapping my previous school record folder, "I'll be keeping my eye on you."

I got up quickly and left his office. The bell had rung, so the secretary had to give me a late pass. When I got to my next class, Terri looked up expectantly. I nodded and smiled to let her know everything was fine. After class, I told her what I had done and what had happened.

"She tried to set me up and get me into trouble."

"It doesn't surprise me. Jennifer and her friends are always getting other people in trouble," Terri said. "You better watch your back."

"I will, but she'll find out she should watch hers, too," I said.

At lunch, Jennifer and her friends walked over to my table.

"I'll take my lunch," she said.

"I don't know which one is yours," I said. "Somehow, my name is on both bags. Luckily, we both have the same thing." I handed it to her. She looked at the girls and then at me.

"I heard you were called to the principal's office," she said. "Why did he want to see you?" She smiled at the girls. "I hope you didn't embarrass my parents."

"No, it was fine," I said, taking a sip from the straw in my milk container. "He just wanted to know what we were having for lunch. He said he heard we had the best homemade lunches," I added, and bit into my sandwich.

Even her friends had to laugh. She fumed, her face so crimson I thought the blood would shoot out of the top of her head like a geyser, and then she pivoted on her heels and marched away. Terri and the girls at my table laughed so hard that others in the cafeteria stopped talking to look our way.

"I guess there's a little snake in you, too," Terri said.

"What else? She and I are cousins, aren't we?" I said, and that made everyone laugh again.

But I wasn't finished, not yet, not quite.

On Saturday, Jennifer went off with her friends right after breakfast as she usually did on Saturdays. Aunt Clara tried to get her to take me along, but she resisted and complained.

"She doesn't have the same friends I do," she moaned.

"What does that mean?" Uncle Reuben asked quickly, fixing his eyes on me sharply. "Who are her friends?"

Jennifer shrugged. "She hangs out with black people. I suppose because she's so dark."

"No," I said. "I hang out with people of color who happen to be nice and not phony."

"Oh, and that's supposed to mean my friends are?"

I shrugged. "Because I'm new in the school, everyone is warning me about them," I said as nonchalantly as I could.

Her face looked as if she was facing a wall of fire. Before she could stutter out a response, Aunt Clara spoke. "You two should get along," she said. "You're just about the same age."

"I don't want Jennifer hanging out with any troublemakers," Uncle Reuben said.

"I don't hang out with troublemakers," I insisted. "It's just the opposite."

"Why can't she go with Jennifer and be with young people, too?" Aunt Clara asked softly.

"It's all right. I'm fine," I said.

I don't know why Aunt Clara suggested I go along anyway. She knew that Uncle Reuben would be home and would be watching to make sure I did my chores.

Jennifer wouldn't lift a finger, and she certainly wouldn't have wanted to wait for me.

Shortly after Jennifer left, Aunt Clara and I began our weekly cleaning of the house. William wanted to help with the vacuuming, but Uncle Reuben chastised him.

"That's woman's work," he growled. "Let them do it. Why don't you go play baseball or football instead of spending all your time in your room?" he complained, which only sent William back to his room.

I gazed at Aunt Clara to see if she would speak up for William, but she looked away quickly and continued to clean. We went upstairs to start on the bedrooms, and I began as usual with Jennifer's mess. It was worse than ever, now that she knew I had to do most of the cleaning. Aunt Clara felt sorry for me and joined me in Jennifer's room. She started with making the bed. When she lifted the pillow, she stopped and stared down. I kept picking up clothes that had been flung about with apparent glee. A blouse actually dangled off the top of the vanity mirror.

"What's that?" Aunt Clara asked.

"What?"

I turned and watched her put the pillow down and then pluck the joint between her fingers. She smelled it and looked at me. I approached and leaned over to smell it, too. Then I looked at her, my eyes wide, my head shaking slowly.

"Is this what I think it is?" she asked.

"Yes," I said. "I'm afraid so, Aunt Clara."

"Oh, dear. Oh, dear me. Oh, no. I'll have to tell Reuben." She hurried out of the room and down the stairs. Moments later, I heard Uncle Reuben come charging up, his footsteps so hard on the steps the whole house shook.

"What's going on here?" he demanded.

I stepped out of the bathroom, my arms full of wet towels for the laundry.

"I don't know," I said.

"Who put this there?" he demanded. Aunt Clara came up behind him. I stared at him.

"I really don't know, Uncle Reuben," I said.

"You didn't do it?"

"She was working on picking things up when I found it, Reuben. She didn't put it there," Aunt Clara said, and started to cry.

"And I suppose you don't know nothing about it?" Uncle Reuben followed.

I shook my head.

Uncle Reuben's eyes grew small and then widened. He gazed at Aunt Clara and then at me.

"We'll see about this when she gets home," he fired. He shot another angry look in my direction and then left the room.

"Oh, dear," Aunt Clara said. "Oh, dear, dear." She followed after him.

I set down the towels, looked at Jennifer's picture on her dresser, the one in which she had the most conceited grin on her face, and smiled myself.

Jennifer's reaction was predictable. As soon as she was confronted with the evidence, she burst into tears and pointed her right forefinger at me like a pistol.

"She did it. She did it to get me into trouble," she accused.

Uncle Reuben nodded. "I've been thinking so," he said.

"How could I do it? I wasn't in your room until I went upstairs with Aunt Clara to clean the mess," I said quietly.

"You must have done it before."

"Why?"

"To get me in trouble," she whined.

"Why would I do that?" I asked. "Why would I stoop so low as to put something like that under your pillow?"

She stared at me hatefully. Then she turned to Uncle Reuben. "Daddy!" she moaned.

"Jennifer's never done anything like this before," he said. "I'd bet you have."

"You'd lose," I said.

"Daddy, I didn't do it," Jennifer cried, stamping her foot.

"All right. All right. I believe you." He thought a moment. I could see there was an inkling of doubt in his mind. "We'll let it go for now, but I'll be on the lookout for any more trouble, even the slightest. If I find drugs in this house again, I'll bring the owner to the police. That's a promise," he said, directing his words mostly at me.

Jennifer looked satisfied and glanced at me with an expression of contentment. "I'm tired," she said. "I have to rest before I go to the movies."

She hurried away. Nothing more was said about it,

but when we left for school the next day, she hurried up to me before mounting the steps to the bus.

"I know you did that with the joint."

"It was yours. You accidentally left it in your lunch bag, but I got it out in time so you wouldn't get in trouble. I thought you would appreciate my hiding it for you," I said, pretending to be dumb.

She stared at me, and then her eyes filled with cold understanding before she stepped onto the bus. Later, I told Terri, and the two of us had fun telling our other friends. Jennifer avoided me most of the day. It was one of my best days at the new school, but I was still wishing it would all come to an end. I had had enough of Uncle Reuben and battling with Jennifer.

My hopes died a quick death when we got home that afternoon. Jennifer refused to talk to me on the bus and walked slowly so I would get to the house first. As soon as I entered, Aunt Clara stepped out of the living room, her hand clutching a handkerchief to her mouth.

"What's wrong?" I asked. Jennifer came up behind me.

"Your mother," Aunt Clara said. "She's gone and run off from the rehabilitation clinic. She's a fugitive."

"Great," Jennifer said. "Maybe she'll come for you, and you can run off together."

"Stop that talk!" Aunt Clara cried in a voice so sharp and shrill even I took note. "I won't have it."

Jennifer's eyes filled with tears. "You care more about her than you do me," she accused. Aunt Clara started to shake her head. "Yes, you do. But I'm not surprised," she added, and flew up the stairs.

"I should leave," I murmured, looking after her.

"Where would you go? You have to be with family," Aunt Clara insisted.

Family, I thought. That's a word I'll never understand.

5
Behind Closed Doors

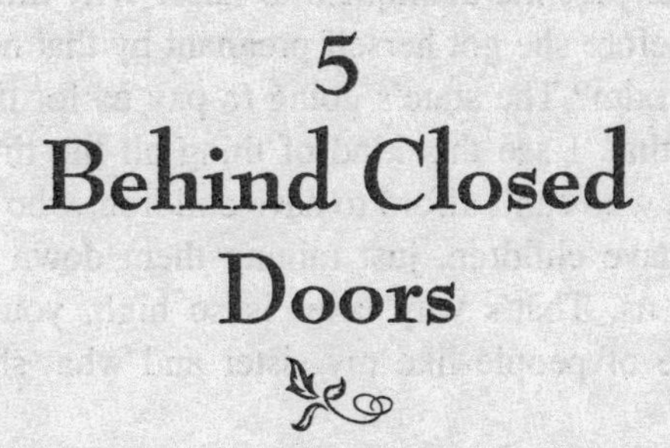

"Can you believe it?" Uncle Reuben cried as he entered the house. "The police came to my office, came to see me at work! The police! Everyone sees them and wants to know what's going on. My sister, I had to tell them, has run away from her drug rehabilitation center, violated court orders. She's some kind of fugitive, and the police came to see if she's contacted me. I can tell you this. If she does have the nerve to contact me, I'll turn her in. She's dragging us all down with her!"

I was in my room trembling, but I could hear him slamming things around in the kitchen.

"Please don't get yourself so upset, Reuben," Aunt Clara pleaded.

"Don't get upset?" He laughed madly. "My sister's rotten through and through, Clara. She's like some dark, rancid piece of fruit stinking up the place. Now

I got her juvenile delinquent to raise. Why didn't she think before she got herself pregnant by that no-good Cuban bum? The state's going to pay us for this. I'll see to that. I see this kind of thing all the time . . . women who can't afford to have children, who should never have children, just raining them down on the rest of us. That's why taxes is so high, you know, because of people like my sister and what she produces."

"You've got to stop this, Reuben. You'll get yourself sick," Aunt Clara said.

"Sick? I am sick, sick of it all." He groaned so loud I thought he was coming through the wall. "It's not like I didn't try to help my sister. I told her how a real man acts . . . I showed her. I showed her, all right."

"Reuben . . . I don't think you should get so worked up," Aunt Clara said. I could tell by the sound of her voice that she was nervous and wanted to change the subject.

What was Uncle Reuben saying about my mother? What had he showed Mama?

I heard him get up and walk to the stairway, pausing at my door. My heart thumped. I thought he would come bursting through the door and yell at me about my mother and how I was a drain on society. I kept my eyes to the floor and waited, holding my breath. A moment later, I heard him start up the stairs.

My eyes were burning with hot tears. I stared out the window.

Mama, how could you do this to me? Why did you run away? For a moment, I wondered if she would come here to get me, take me away from all this. I'd even hide out with her. Who was I fooling? I thought. I was probably the last thing she thought about when she fled. By now, she must be with one of her degenerate boyfriends, either hiding out or racing off to live in some hovel.

My mother seemed to be two different people to me now. Once, when I was younger, I thought of her as someone to love and someone who loved me, but somehow, somewhere, that all disappeared, and we started to live like two strangers. Maybe Uncle Reuben was right. Maybe my mother was just no good. Something had gone wrong inside her, and she could never be rehabilitated. She would never change.

Was that same bad germ inside me, too? Would I become like her someday, despite myself? Was Uncle Reuben right about that, too? I was my mother's daughter. I inherited something from her, and maybe that something was evil. I wasn't any sort of student. I had no real friends. I was afraid to have any ambitions, and so, when I tried to envision myself ten years from now, all I could see was the same lonely, lost person.

Uncle Reuben wasn't wrong. I was going to be just like my mother.

I sighed so deeply my chest ached. Then I stood up, wiped my eyes, and went to help Aunt Clara prepare dinner. She looked very tired and very sad herself. The way she held her shoulders slumped, kept her eyes down, and moved with tiny, insecure steps made her look even smaller than she was. It was as if she had shrunk inches since Uncle Reuben had come home. She was the one who looked pitiful, and yet she turned to me with sympathy flooding her eyes and shook her head.

"You poor dear," she said. "I know how you must feel. I'm sorry your mother has done these things. She should think what she's doing to you."

I didn't reply. I set the table, moving mechanically about the kitchen. I dreaded sitting at the dinner table with Uncle Reuben tonight. My throat was closing as it was. As soon as he began his tirade against my mother and complained about me, I would surely choke on anything that was in my mouth, and he would scream about my wasting the food he worked so hard to provide.

Suddenly, I felt dizzy and had to seize the top of a chair to keep myself from falling. Aunt Clara came running to me.

"What's wrong, Raven?"

"I don't know. My head just started to spin."

"You look white as a candle. Here, let me get you some cold water. Sit," she ordered, and I did so. My stomach churned. When she brought me the water, I held the glass with both hands and sipped. It did make me feel a little better.

"I want you to go lay down, honey," she said. "I don't need you to do anything. Go on. Rest. You've had a big shock."

She helped me to my feet and guided me back to the sewing room. I hadn't pulled out the bed yet, so she did it for me, and then I lay down.

"I still feel a little sick," I said.

"Oh, dear. If you're not better in a little while, I'll take you to the emergency room."

"No, I'm not that sick, Aunt Clara. I'll be all right," I promised.

She stroked my hair and felt my forehead. "You don't feel too hot, but you're very clammy. It's all emotional, I'm sure," she said. "Just rest."

She brought the glass of water in and set it beside me. I settled under the blankets and felt a little better, but still my stomach flopped. I closed my eyes again, and before I knew it, I fell asleep, only to wake to the sound of Uncle Reuben's loud voice rumbling through the house like thunder demanding where I was and why I wasn't helping to serve the meal. I started to get up, and the room spun on me, so I had to lie back.

Their voices became indistinct mumbles, and I must have fallen asleep again, because when I opened my eyes this time, Aunt Clara was standing beside the bed with a tray in her hands.

"How are you feeling now, dear?" she asked.

I blinked, rubbed my face, and sat up slowly. Fortunately, the room didn't spin.

"Better."

"Good," she said. "Here, I brought you some dinner. You have to put something warm in your stomach."

"I'm not very hungry."

"I know, but it's best to eat when you're under such a strain. Go on," she said, placing the tray in my lap, "eat what you can."

"Jesus, serving her like she's some kind of special guest," I heard Uncle Reuben spit from the doorway.

"I told you she wasn't feeling well, Reuben. I want her to get some food down."

"Of course, she's not feeling well. Who would if they were brought up the way she was? It's a wonder she's not seriously sick with some bad disease," he concluded. "We might all come down with it, and you asking Jennifer to share clothes and such with her."

"I'm just as healthy as Jennifer," I fired back at him.

He smirked. "I can just imagine what your teeth are like. When were you to a dentist last?"

I hadn't been for nearly a year, so I didn't answer.

"See what I mean?" he said to Aunt Clara. "Either we get the state to help us, or . . ."

"Or what?" I shot back at him.

"Don't you be smart with me," he said, pointing his finger at me.

"Let her eat, Reuben. There's time to talk about all this," Aunt Clara pleaded softly.

He glared at her, and she looked down quickly. "Time? Yeah, there's time," he said sarcastically. "Lots of time. My sister ain't coming back for her. That's for sure," he added, and walked away.

I started to sob, my shoulders shaking so hard I thought my heart would split in two.

Aunt Clara put the tray down and sat beside me, embracing me. "Don't cry, dear. He doesn't mean what he says. He's upset because he was embarrassed at work. Please, you'll only make yourself sicker, and then what?"

I sucked in my breath and pulled back my tears.

"Please, eat something, Raven," Aunt Clara begged.

"All right," I said. "Thank you, Aunt Clara."

I started to eat, and she left. Afterward, William came to my door.

"I'll take your tray to the kitchen for you," he volunteered.

"Thank you," I said, smiling, "but I can do it, William. It's nice of you to offer, though."

He continued to stare at me.

"Is there something wrong?" I asked him.

"Are you feeling better now?"

"Yes, I am," I said. "Your mother was right. Hot food helped."

He smiled. "Good, because I want to show you the double-decker birdhouse. It's done," he declared.

"It is? Okay," I said.

I took my tray to the kitchen. Aunt Clara, who was watching television, came rushing in. "I'll do that, Raven."

"I'm fine now," I told her, and smiled.

"And you ate, too. Good," she said. She put my dishes in the dishwasher. "You just go and do your homework, or come watch television if you like, Raven."

"I'm going up to see William's new birdhouse, and then I'll do my homework," I explained.

"Oh. That's very nice," she said.

William looked proud. "Come on," he said, and I followed him up the stairs to his room.

As I sat and listened to him explain what kind of birds would feed in his house, I felt sorry for him, sorry that his father took so little interest in what he had accomplished. He was like a flower, stunted and pale because it received so little sunlight. He almost talked as much about his father making fun of his hobby as he did about why he loved making the houses. When I showed sincere interest in him and what he was doing, he wasn't sad or shy anymore. He practically beamed with pride.

"Thank you for showing me your work, William. I bet you could sell these birdhouses. They're so perfect," I told him, gazing around at his collection. It was impressive when I realized he had done all of it himself.

He beamed and strutted about his room, showing me his books on birds, his tools and paints, and some of his other creations.

"Do you have a favorite bird?" he asked me. "Because if you do, I'll make a special house for you."

"No. I don't really know very much about birds. We didn't have many trees around the apartment building."

"Oh, I guess not," he said. "I've been hoping to build a house for every kind of bird we get around here. But it takes money to buy all the wood and stuff. And every time I talk to Daddy about my projects, he just makes fun of me." He hung his head sadly.

"I wish I had some money to help you buy supplies," I told him.

"Don't worry. I'll get the money." He thought a moment and then decided to tell me how. "Daddy drops a lot of change behind the cushions on the sofa downstairs when he sprawls out to watch television. When nobody's around, I pick up the cushions and find it. Once, I found nearly two dollars in quarters and dimes."

I laughed. "Your secret's safe with me," I told him. I leaned over and kissed him on the forehead. For a moment, he looked so shocked I thought he might cry or scream. When I turned around, I saw the cause of his alarm. Uncle Reuben was standing in the doorway.

"What the hell are you two doing in here?" Uncle Reuben's face was bright red with fury. "Raven, get away from my son. I knew you were a no-good troublemaker like your mother. And here you are flaunting yourself around and tempting my son just the way she tempted me. Well, I won't have none of it! Get out of this room right now before I drag you out!" For a second, I was too terrified to move. Then Uncle Reuben started pulling William toward him, and I knew I had to get away.

I saw William's horrified face as I ran past him and knew that I had to speak up.

"We didn't do anything, Uncle Reuben. Honest, William was just showing me his birdhouses." I was probably just making him more furious, but I had no idea why he had gotten so angry, and I was ashamed that I was leaving William to face his father's fury all alone.

Not stopping to look back, I ran downstairs and

straight into my room, shutting the door tightly behind me. I knew that Uncle Reuben would break down the door if he wanted to, but the house was quiet suddenly, and I prayed that maybe I was safe. For now.

I tried to start on my math homework, but there was no way I could concentrate with my heart still racing and my pulse pounding. What if Uncle Reuben was upstairs hurting William? What did he think we were doing, anyway?

William already lived in constant fear of being ridiculed and belittled by his father, and now it seemed that Uncle Reuben had one more thing to add to his ammunition—against both of us.

It was obvious even to me that the reason William was so withdrawn was that he was afraid. Afraid that he would get yelled at, made fun of, or maybe even worse. I knew Aunt Clara was concerned about William; she even talked about taking him to a doctor. Why couldn't she see that the reason William was so quiet and timid was that he was afraid?

What would happen if I stayed in this house where I was belittled and ridiculed as well—for my birth, for my mother, for things I hadn't even done? Would I become like William? Would I just one day disappear inside myself?

Just as I was opening my math book, Aunt Clara poked her head in the door. "Raven, are you all right?" Her eyes were all red and puffy, and I could see that she'd been crying.

"Yes, Aunt Clara, I'm fine. How is William? Uncle

Reuben didn't hurt him, did he? We weren't doing anything bad, Aunt Clara! I was just thanking William for showing me his birdhouses. We . . . we . . ." Talking about it made me upset all over again, and I began sobbing so hard I couldn't even speak.

Aunt Clara came to sit beside me on the bed. "Shh . . . I know, dear, I know. Everything will be fine."

"But, but William . . . what did Uncle Reuben do to him?" Why wasn't she answering my questions?

"He's fine, dear, but please, promise me not to speak of this again. Reuben will just get upset all over again. Promise me you won't speak of it!"

"I promise, Aunt Clara."

She stood there for a few moments, then told me not to stay up too late studying, and left. I sat with my math book on my lap and stared up at the dark ceiling. I could hear Uncle Reuben's heavy footsteps, a door close, water running, and a phone ringing. Poor William, I thought. I had seen it in his face. He was terrified. What about Aunt Clara? Had she built a wall of self-denial around herself, shutting up the dark secrets? Like a coiled fuse attached to a time bomb, sooner or later all the horror in this house was sure to explode.

I didn't want to be here before. I surely didn't want to be here now, but what choice did I have? I had no father. I had no other relatives. I felt trapped, caged in by events far beyond my control. It heightened the panic that throbbed so loudly in my heart, I thought for sure it sounded like a jungle drum beating out the rhythms of alarm.

What should I pray for? My mother's miraculous appearance? My mystery father's sudden interest in a daughter he had never known? Who was more lost than me, someone without even a real name, forced to live with people who really didn't want me?

A real rumble of thunder pounded at the windowpane and was soon followed by a downpour. Thick raindrops tapped at the window as the wind grew stronger, slapping torrents against the walls. I heard Aunt Clara rushing around downstairs shutting windows. Then I heard Uncle Reuben curse from the top of the stairs. Moments later, it was silent except for the monotonous sound of drizzle. I could feel the darkness deepening around me, wrapping itself around this house.

My cheeks felt cold. All my tears had turned to ice behind my eyes. I turned over and buried my face in the pillow as I tightened myself into the fetal position and swallowed back my fear and loneliness.

Sunlight fell on my face and woke me up just as Uncle Reuben was coming down the stairs. I flew off the bed and hurried to the bathroom. Even before I could wash my face, he was bellowing about my not being in the kitchen helping Aunt Clara prepare breakfast for everyone. It looked as if things were back to normal.

"Why weren't you up and helping?" Uncle Reuben demanded.

William entered and took his seat at the table. His eyes met mine for a moment before he looked down at his cereal and juice.

Uncle Reuben looked from William to me and slammed his fist down on the table. "I don't ever want to catch you in William's room again, understand?"

"Yes," I said, hoping that that would be the last said about last night.

"And today, again, I got to take time out of my busy schedule to look into your problems. I bet your mother never spent a minute on you. Did she ever go to the school to see how you were doing?"

I sat and began to sip my orange juice.

"When I speak to you, I want you to look at me and respond," he ordered.

"No, she never did," I said.

"I didn't think so," he said, pleased with my answer. He looked at Aunt Clara, who kept busy at the sink.

"Jennifer should come down, Reuben. She'll be late for the bus."

"She's never late," he said.

"You know she has been a few times, and you had to drive her to school," Aunt Clara said softly.

"The bus came too early those days," he insisted.

By the time Jennifer appeared, William and I had finished eating. I began to clear the table.

"Leave that," Jennifer ordered when I reached for the sugar bowl. "I haven't had my cereal yet."

"You should get up earlier, Jennifer," Aunt Clara said. "You don't have much time."

"I would if I could find the clothes I want," Jennifer whined. "Someone put my blouses in the wrong place, and my favorite skirt was shoved so far in the back of the closet I nearly didn't find it." She glared at me.

"You could put your clothes away yourself, and that way you'd know where everything is," I said.

"You're just jealous because I have more clothes than you. If you had as many as I did, you'd have trouble remembering where you put them," she said angrily. "Besides, you probably were hiding this skirt so you could wear it."

"I don't want to wear your things. I have my own clothes and . . ."

"Stop this bickering at the table!" Uncle Reuben shouted. He rose out of his seat like a gusher, his face crimson and steaming. Jennifer sat, and Aunt Clara quickly poured some coffee in a cup for her. "We never had bickering at the table before," he added, glaring at me, "but I bet that was something that happened in your house often."

"It wasn't," I said.

Aunt Clara glanced at me fearfully and shook her head gently. She wanted me to be like her, bury my head in the sand, absorb Uncle Reuben's hateful remarks, and pray that it would all end quickly.

"If I do anything of any value for you, it will be to teach you how to behave properly," he continued. "I know there are years of degenerate living to overcome, but by God, if you're going to live with us, you'll overcome them," he said, wagging his monstrous fist at me. "Why don't you watch Jennifer? Learn from her," he suggested.

I raised my eyebrows and nearly laughed. Jennifer sat there smugly, chomping down on a few flakes of cereal, sipping some coffee before jumping up.

"We've got to go, Daddy," she declared. "You can teach her how to behave later."

He grunted. William looked at me sympathetically but said nothing. I went to get my books and left the house a few seconds after Jennifer. She was already down the sidewalk, meeting her friends at the bus stop. The big topic of conversation was the upcoming school dance. The girls were all talking about which boys they hoped would ask them. Jennifer's wish list was the longest.

"She hasn't been here long, but do you think anyone will ask her?" I heard Paula Gordon whisper as she nodded in my direction.

"Who would ask her?" Jennifer said, loud enough for me to hear, and she laughed. "Oh, no, wait a minute. Maybe Clarence Dunsen will ask her."

"Yeah," Paula said. "He'll go, 'Raven, would . . . would . . . would would would . . . would . . . you . . . you . . . like to . . . to . . . gogogo . . .' "

They laughed loudly and then moved away. Their voices grew softer, more secretive. I was relieved to see the bus pull up. I hurried on. They all laughed again when they filed past and looked at me sitting with Clarence.

Funny, I thought, how girls like Jennifer attract other girls just like her. They stick together as comfortably as a pig in its own mess, I thought. It made me laugh. Clarence looked at me with curiosity. For a moment, I wished he would ask me to the dance and we would show them all up. But that was a fantasy, and in my life, fantasies were written on clouds that floated by, impossible to grasp, caught in the wind, gone as fast as they appeared.

6
He Likes Me!

I had a crush on a boy when I was in the sixth grade. His name was Ronnie Clark, and he had blue eyes that brightened with so much warmth when he smiled that he made you feel good when you were upset, and yet his eyes could darken with mystery and intensity when he looked at someone intensely or was in deep thought. I caught him gazing at me that way a few times, and it made my heart flutter and sent tiny warm jolts of electricity up and down my spine. Suddenly, I thought about my hair, my clothes, a budding pimple on my chin.

The world around you changes when you realize someone as handsome as Ronnie Clark is gazing at you with interest. Every time I moved or turned, when I rose to walk out of the classroom, even when I picked up my pen to write in my notebook, I was very conscious of how I looked. I couldn't wait to get to a mirror to check my face and my hair. I hated my clothes and regretted not watching my mother do her makeup when she did it well.

I tried not to be obvious when I looked at Ronnie, and if he caught me looking, I always shifted my eyes quickly and pretended I didn't have the slightest interest in him. Sometimes he smiled, and sometimes he looked disappointed. He was as shy as I was, and I thought it would take a bulldozer to push us dramatically into each other's path. He didn't seem to have the nerve to sit next to me in the cafeteria or come up to me in the hallway, and after a while, I was afraid that I might be making more of his gazes than there was. Nothing could be more embarrassing than thinking a boy liked you when he didn't.

One afternoon, when I was in gym class, I looked at the doorway to the gymnasium and saw him standing there looking my way. We were playing volleyball, and we were all in our gym outfits. The ball bounced close to the doorway, and I chased it and seized it, looking up at him at the same time.

"Nice," he said.

Butterflies panicked in my chest, but I gave him the best smile I could muster. Mrs. Wilson blew her whistle and shouted for me to get back into the game. Ronnie walked away quickly before she chastised him for being there, but at lunch, he came up to me in the line and told me I was pretty good at volleyball.

"You could probably be on the girls' team now instead of waiting another year," he said.

"Tell me what it's like to be on a school team," I asked him, and he followed me to the table.

We started dating soon after that, but never did much more than hold hands and kiss a few times after school. I met him at the movies one night, but he had to go home right afterward. And then, just as suddenly as it had all started, it ended. He turned away from me as if I had been just another interesting picture in a museum. Soon he was off looking at other girls the way he'd once looked at me. I felt stupid chasing after him, so I stopped looking for him, and that was about when my school attendance began to drop off anyway.

There were many fewer students at the school I now attended and only about a dozen or so boys I would consider as good-looking as Ronnie Clark. I agreed with Jennifer that I could never expect any of them to take any interest in me, but to my surprise that very afternoon after Jennifer and her friends had teased me about Clarence Dunsen, a chubby boy named Gary Carson bumped into me deliberately between classes, and when I turned to complain, he smiled and said, "Jimmy Freer likes you."

He hurried on, leaving me confused. I knew who Jimmy Freer was. He was captain of the junior varsity basketball team, tall for his age, and very, very good-looking. He was right at the top of Jennifer's wish list, and I never even dreamed he would be looking at me, but at lunch he was suddenly right behind me when I went to buy some milk.

"That's the healthy choice," he quipped. I turned and, for a moment, was too surprised to speak. "Most everyone else is buying soda."

"I don't drink much soda," I told him. "Milk's

okay." I paid for my milk and headed for the table where Terri and some of the other girls I liked were sitting, but he caught up with me.

"How about sitting with me?" he asked, and nodded toward an empty table on our right.

I gazed at the girls, who were all looking my way with interest, and then I turned and saw Jennifer and her friends staring at me, too. It warmed my heart to see the jealousy in their faces and made me smile.

"Okay," I said. He led the way and set his tray down across from me.

"How do you like the school here?" he asked, dipping his spoon into his bowl of chicken rice soup.

"It's okay."

"Is that your favorite word?" he joked.

"No. Sometimes I say it's not okay."

He laughed, and I noticed what a nice smile he had and what a perfectly straight nose. I liked the way a small dimple in his right cheek appeared when he talked. His dark brown hair was cut closely on the sides, but he let a wave sweep back from the front. He had beautiful hazel eyes, bejeweled with flecks of blue, green, and gold on soft brown. No wonder he was everyone's heartthrob, I thought, and tried to look cool and sophisticated under his gaze. I could feel the way everyone was looking at us in the cafeteria. It made me think I was on a big television screen and every little move I made was magnified. I brushed my lips quickly with my napkin, afraid a crumb might be on my mouth or chin.

"So you're living with Jennifer, huh?" he asked.

"Sort of," I said.

"Sort of?"

"I don't call it living," I told him, and he laughed again. Then he smiled, his eyes drinking me in so intently I felt as if I were sitting there naked.

"I had a feeling you were smarter than most of the girls in junior high school here."

"I'm hardly smarter."

"You know what I mean," he said with that impish gleam in his eyes.

"No, I don't."

He laughed and grew serious. "Have you been to any school basketball games yet?"

"No."

"There's a big one coming up tomorrow night with Roscoe. We beat them once, and they beat us once this year. Why don't you come?" he asked.

"I don't know if I can."

"Why can't you? Don't you believe in having school spirit?" he asked with that teasing smile returning.

"It's not that. I don't know if my uncle will let me out," I said.

He grew serious-looking and ate as he thought.

"Why?" He leaned toward me to whisper. "Did you have a bad record at the last school you attended or something?"

"Sure. I'm on the post office walls everywhere," I said. He stared a moment and then roared so hard that kids who were sitting nearby stopped talking to look at us.

"You really are something. Come on, come to the game. Afterward, Missy Taylor is having a small house party. We'll have a good time, especially if we beat Roscoe. Can I hear you say okay again?"

"I can't make any promises," I said, but I really wanted to go.

"You're old enough to go out if you want. They shouldn't keep you locked up. Jennifer's certainly not kept locked up," he added. "She'll be at the game, I bet. You can come with her, can't you?"

"I'll try," I said. "She's not happy about taking me along anywhere."

"I'll make sure she does," he said with a wink.

We talked some more. He asked questions about my life before I began living with Uncle Reuben. I didn't want to tell him too much. Jennifer had successfully spread the word that my mother had died, and for the moment, I was afraid to contradict her and create too much of a scandal. It might scare Jimmy away, I thought, and anyway, what difference did it make what the kids at this school knew or didn't know about me?

Jennifer approached me in the hallway the first opportunity she had after lunch. Normally, she wouldn't so much as glance in my direction, but her girlfriends were buzzing around her like bees full of curiosity instead of honey.

"What's going on between you and Jimmy?" she demanded as if she were a police interrogator. She stood in front of me with her hands on her hips.

"Excuse me," I said. "I don't want to be late for class."

"Don't you walk away from me, Raven," she cried, her nostrils flaring. She looked exactly like Uncle Reuben.

"I'm not walking away. Do you want me to be late and get into trouble? Uncle Reuben won't like that, will he?"

"You've got time. Answer me," she demanded.

"Jimmy who?" I said, looking perplexed.

"Jimmy who? Jimmy Freer. You were talking to him in the cafeteria," she said, amazed at my questions. She looked at the other girls, who were just as surprised.

"Oh," I said, "was that his name? He never told me. Um . . . nothing's going on, but when something is, you'll be the first to know," I added, and kept walking. I could almost hear the explosion of anger in her head.

I didn't realize that because I had been seen with Jimmy Freer, Jennifer was going to pay more attention to me. She was even waiting for me at the bus at the end of the day.

"Do you want to go to the basketball game tomorrow night?" she asked in as close to a pleasant voice as she could speak.

"What?"

"Are you deaf? I asked you if you wanted to go to the game with me, that's all."

"Sure," I said. Now I was the one who was really surprised.

"Just don't get my father angry about anything and spoil it," she warned, and marched onto the bus before

I could ask her why she suddenly didn't mind being seen with me. I found out later. One of Jimmy's friends, Brad Dillon, had asked Jennifer to the game and party. The plan was to double-date with me and Jimmy, and since Brad was on Jennifer's wish list, she was eager to get me to go and make it happen for herself. I was more surprised that Brad wanted to be with her. He was even better-looking than Jimmy, in my opinion, but as we would soon discover, the boys had their own special plans.

Jennifer really wanted this date. All that evening and the next day, she did everything she could to ensure that Uncle Reuben wouldn't stop us from attending the game. I was suddenly very important to her. She even offered to help with some of the chores and put on a big act of reconciliation, pretending to help me make friends.

Uncle Reuben had made an appointment at the social service agency and announced at dinner that he was undertaking the necessary steps to make himself my formal legal guardian. In the meantime, social services was promising to cover my health and basic needs.

"It still irks me that society has to pay for my sister's mistakes," he declared as he chomped down on a lamb chop. I thought he would consume it, bone and all, like some bulldog.

I looked up sharply. It was as if he had reached across the table and poked me with his fork.

"I'm not a mistake," I said as proudly as I could. I

was a tight wire inside, stretched so tautly I thought I might break and cry, but I held my breath and kept a firm lid on my well of tears.

Uncle Reuben paused and glared at me, the meat caught between his thick lips and the grease gleaming on his chin. Jennifer looked up nervously. Aunt Clara held her breath, and William gazed down at his food. I could almost feel the trembling in his little body.

"It's a mistake not to be prepared properly for children," he said firmly.

"My mother made mistakes, but I'm not a mistake. I'm a human being with feelings, too." I tossed my hair back. "Nobody's perfect, anyway."

"You hear that? You hear the way she talks and thinks? You'd think she would be more respectful and grateful. Here I am trying to make a new home for her, and she talks like that, insolent."

"I'm not being insolent, Uncle Reuben."

"She didn't mean it," Jennifer piped up.

Uncle Reuben raised his eyebrows and gazed at her. Even I had to pause and look at her. She flashed me a quick look of warning.

"It's hard to start in a new school with new people. I'm going to help her make new friends," Jennifer offered.

Aunt Clara beamed. "That's wonderful, dear. You see, Reuben, the girls will get along just fine."

He still had a glint of suspicion in his eyes, but he grunted and continued to eat. Jennifer began talking about the basketball game as if it was the event of the century.

"Even our teachers are going to attend. It's important to show school spirit."

"That's very nice," Aunt Clara said.

Uncle Reuben started to talk about his own school days, and for a moment, I felt as if I was really sitting at a family dinner. Aunt Clara even laughed, recalling some stories he described, but then he suddenly stopped and looked at William.

"You hear how important it is to participate in sports, William. You shouldn't spend so much time in your room. You should stay after school sometimes and join a team," he told him.

William gazed at me with desperately sad eyes.

"He's too young. They don't have teams yet," I said.

"Sure they do," Uncle Reuben snapped. "He wouldn't even go out for the Little League when he had the chance. I was going to drag him over to the field, but his mother was too upset."

"Not everyone has to be an athlete. Some people have other talents. William is fantastic at building things," I said.

"What is this? You're not here a month, and you're telling me what my son is capable of doing and not capable of doing?" Uncle Reuben cried. "She's just like my sister, with a mouth bigger than her brain. When I say something to William, I don't want to hear you contradict it, understand?" he said, slamming his fork down on the table.

"She didn't mean anything," Jennifer said quickly. "Raven, if you want, I'll help you with the dishes, and then we'll work on your math. I told you I would help you," she said, turning her back on Uncle Reuben and winking at me.

I shook my head and went back to eating. After dinner, when Uncle Reuben retired to the living room to watch television, Jennifer did help with the dishes. She stood beside me at the sink and whispered.

"Can't you keep your big mouth shut at dinner? Just let Daddy make his speeches like I do, and don't say anything," she advised.

"He bullies this family," I remarked.

"Who cares? You want him to get angry and forbid us to go to the game and the party? Just shut up." She wiped another dish and then turned and left the kitchen.

Where was the love in this house? I wondered. What makes this more of a family than what I had with my mother? Was it just the roof over their heads and the food in the refrigerator? I was beginning to think I would rather settle for the occasional good days with Mama than the constant life of tension and fear that existed in this home, but I didn't even have the choice anymore. Maybe I truly was a mistake. I was someone who could be moved and ordered about like a piece of furniture.

The next day at school, Jimmy paid even more attention to me. He walked with me in the halls between classes and sat with me at lunch. When I asked him if Brad Dillon really wanted to go out with my cousin, he just smiled and said, "I told you I would make sure you got to the game, didn't I? Let's just have a good time. I'll be looking in the bleachers for you," he promised.

Jennifer talked Uncle Reuben into driving us to the school gymnasium. It wasn't until we were almost there that she revealed we were invited to a party after the game. He almost stopped and turned around to take us home.

"What do you mean? What party?" He bellowed so loudly I thought the windows would shatter.

I sat quietly in the backseat and listened to Jennifer rattle off her lies.

"Everyone's going. It's a chaperoned party at Missy Taylor's house. We won't be late. It's a celebration," she explained.

"How come you didn't say anything about it before?" he demanded.

"We just got invited, right, Raven? Missy called us."

I didn't say anything. He wasn't going to blame me later. I was determined about that. I saw his eyes go to the rearview mirror.

"Who's this Missy Taylor?"

"Melissa Taylor. You know her father. He owns Taylor's Steak House."

"That's no more than a bar," Uncle Reuben said.

"They have a nice house," Jennifer continued.

He grunted. "I don't want you home late. Be home before twelve. How are you getting home, anyway?" he asked.

"Oh, we have a ride. Don't worry, Daddy."

He looked at her again and then at me through the

mirror. "I'm not happy about this. Who's the chaperone?"

"Her mother's there. Stop worrying so much, Daddy. You went to parties when you were our age."

"No, I didn't. I didn't even go out on a real date until I was a senior."

This time, I grunted, unable to imagine anyone going out on a date with him. He looked at me through the mirror again and drove on.

It was a very exciting game. Jimmy was spectacular, stealing the ball, making long shots, holding the team together, and keeping them within four points the whole time. He did what he promised, too: he looked into the bleachers and found me. When he smiled, Jennifer glanced at me with eyes so green with hot envy I thought she would burst into flames.

In the last minute of the game, Jimmy intercepted a pass and scored. Then one of their players was fouled but missed his shot. The ball was tossed to Jimmy, who made a long jump shot from the corner. It put the game into two-minute overtime. The crowd was excited, and the roar was deafening. When they stomped their feet, I thought the bleachers would come tumbling down and crush us all.

The overtime was just as exciting as the game, each team scoring until the last thirty seconds, when Jimmy had an opportunity to score and delayed it as long as possible. The crowd held its collective breath as the ball sailed through the air and threaded through the basket to give our school the victory. The team carried Jimmy off the court, the school's hero.

"And you're going to be with him at the party!" Paula Gordon moaned.

"I have no idea why," I said.

She exchanged a funny look with Jennifer, both covering their smiles with their hands.

Afterward, the boys joined us to watch the varsity game, but it wasn't as exciting, and during the half-time, Jimmy suggested we just leave and go to the party.

"We'll get a head start," he said.

We piled into two cars and headed for Missy Taylor's house. The weather had turned bad, and there was a constant drizzle, but rather than put a damper on our excitement, it made everyone squeal and scream as we rushed to get into the automobiles. When we arrived at the house, I discovered both her parents were at their bar and restaurant, so Jennifer's first lie was immediately evident. It was a nice house, bigger than Uncle Reuben and Aunt Clara's. Missy was an only child, and there were four bedrooms as well as a basement party room with a bar and a jukebox.

The music started immediately, and Brad got behind the bar and began to pour beer and vodka. I didn't want to drink anything, but everyone was drinking, even Jennifer, who claimed she was used to drinking vodka.

"I drink it at home and then put water in the bottle so my father won't know," she said. I actually believed her, but it wasn't long before she began to feel sick and had to go to the bathroom to throw up.

"She drank it too fast," Jimmy said. "That's the

trick, drinking slowly. You're doing all right. You know how to handle yourself, I see."

I had only sipped half a glass of beer. My mother would roar with laughter, I thought.

"Come on," Jimmy said, taking my hand. "Let's leave these losers behind."

"Where are we going?"

"You'll see," he said. He led me up the stairway to the bedroom.

"We can't just walk through her house like this, can we?" I asked.

"Sure, Missy knows. It's all right," he said. "We've had parties here before. It's a great party house, because her parents don't keep track of what we drink, and they're always out."

Missy Taylor can't have much of a family, either, I thought. I was beginning to wonder if any of the kids at school were really better off than me.

Jimmy did seem to know exactly where to go. He led me to one of the guest bedrooms. As soon as we passed through the door, he kicked it closed and embraced me. It was the most wonderful kiss I had ever experienced, long, wet, and so hard it made the back of my neck ache. As he kissed me, he brought his hands up the sides of my body to my shoulders and then kissed my neck.

"You're delicious," he said. "Just as I imagined you would be."

"I'm not something to eat," I said, trying to laugh. I was getting very nervous. I liked him, wanted him to kiss me, but he was moving so fast he made my heart pound. His hands were on my breasts, and his fingers were manipulating the buttons of my blouse. As he did that, he walked us toward the bed, and before I knew it, we were sitting on it. He brought his lips to my chest and began to work on my bra.

"Wait," I said.

"For what?"

"I don't want to do this so fast. We can get in trouble," I told him.

He looked at me with a frozen smile on his lips. "Don't worry. We won't. I have what we need. You expected I would, didn't you?"

"What? No," I said.

"What do you mean, no? You agreed to come here with me. What did you think we'd be doing, having popcorn and watching television? You know what's happening, and I know about you. Jennifer's told everyone."

"What?" I pushed him back. "What did she tell everyone?"

"Hey, what's going on? This isn't brain surgery. We're just having a good time. You've had them before."

"Not like this," I said, standing. "I don't know what Jennifer has told everyone, but I'm not what you think."

"Come on," he said. "I don't kiss and tell." He reached for my hand, and I stepped back.

"Neither do I," I said. "I'm nobody's one-night stand," I added, repeating something Mama had once told one of her lovers. As it turned out, she was often a one-night stand.

"I thought you were cooler than the girls here," he said. "Why do you think I asked you out on the night of the biggest game? Come on," he said, reaching for me again. "Don't I deserve some reward?"

"No," I said. "You deserve a kick between the legs, and that's what you're going to get if you try to pull me onto that bed," I threatened. My eyes were full of fire.

He cowered. "Fine. Get the hell out, then."

I headed for the door.

"You and your cousin are full of it," he yelled after me.

"Don't put me in the same category as Jennifer," I spit back, disgusted.

Out in the hallway, I saw Brad leaving one of the bedrooms, a smile on his face as he hurried to straighten his clothes.

"Brad, where's Jennifer? We're going home!"

"Fine, chill, I'm done with her. She's all yours." He laughed as he made his way downstairs to the party.

I pushed open the bedroom door and saw Jennifer lying on the bed, her skirt bunched up and her shirt halfway unbuttoned. She looked as if she was sleeping, but I had enough experience with my mother to know that she was passed out.

"Jennifer, wake up!" I shouted, shaking her by the shoulder. "C'mon, we've got to get out of here!"

"What? Who? Raven . . . what are you doing here? What happened?" She looked groggily around the room. "Where's Brad? We were having fun, and then the room started to spin, and I . . ."

"Come *on,* Jennifer, you have to get up!" I pulled

her into a sitting position, and she swung her legs over the side of the bed.

"Ohhh, my head! I want to go home," she moaned, clutching the side of the bed.

"We will. That's why I came looking for you. But first you better tell me what kind of stories you've been telling everyone about me," I demanded.

"Please, Raven, I just want to go home."

I could tell there was no use talking to her in this condition, so I put my arm around her and helped her to the stairs. Brad was standing at the foot of the stairs with a group of boys, and they were all laughing hysterically.

"Somebody better take us home," I said. "Jennifer's sick. We need to go now."

"Why don't you just hitchhike?" Brad suggested. Everyone laughed.

Jennifer and I made our way downstairs, and I turned to Missy Taylor who had come up from the basement to see what all the laughing was about.

"If someone doesn't take us home, my uncle will make a lot of trouble for you, especially with all this drinking going on."

She smirked. "Take them home, Brad. I don't want to get into trouble. They're too young to be here, anyway. It was a stupid idea."

"I'll say it was," Jimmy piped up from behind us.

"Come on," I urged Jennifer, and we walked to the front door.

"Let's get moving," Brad said angrily. "I don't want to miss the fun."

"Yes, we'd hate to have you miss any of the fun. Some fun," I muttered, and led Jennifer to his car. She sprawled out in the backseat.

"She better not throw up in my car," Brad said.

"You really didn't want to bring her here. Why did you?"

"I did it as a favor for Jimmy so you would come. I guess you didn't hit it off, huh?" he said, smiling. "That's okay, though, Jennifer and I had fun." Jennifer giggled from the backseat.

"No," I said, "we didn't hit it off."

"A lot of girls want to go out with Jimmy," he said as if I had lost a golden opportunity.

"Here's one who doesn't," I said.

He shook his head. "Man, where are you from?" he asked.

Yes, where am I from? I wondered, and then I thought, it doesn't matter where I'm from. It's where I'm going that matters.

7
The Party's Over

It was raining harder when we arrived home. Brad wouldn't help me with Jennifer. He just sat there waiting impatiently while I struggled to get her out of the car. She didn't even seem to realize we were getting soaked, because she wouldn't or couldn't move quickly. I practically carried her from Brad's car to the house. He shot off as soon as we were out of the automobile. By the time we reached the door, both of us were soaked. I had hoped to sneak Jennifer in and up to her room, but the moment I opened the front door, Uncle Reuben sprang from his recliner in the living room and appeared in the hallway. His eyes bulged when he saw Jennifer. She was pale, her clothes wet and disheveled, her hair messed with strands sticking to her forehead, and her eyes half closed. She leaned on me for support, and I guided her into the house.

"What the hell happened to her? What's wrong?" he demanded. "Is she sick?"

She lifted her eyes and looked at him pathetically for a moment and then suddenly burst out laughing and crying at the same time.

He turned to me.

"What's going on here?"

"She drank some vodka at the party," I said. I had made up my mind I wouldn't lie to protect her.

"What? Drank some . . . Clara!" he screamed.

Aunt Clara came rushing out of the bedroom and appeared at the top of the stairway. She wore only her nightgown. "What is it, Reuben?"

"Look at your daughter," he declared, extending his arms toward Jennifer.

She looked even more ridiculous wearing an idiotic smile and clinging to my arm. Her eyes rolled, and she pressed her hands to her stomach. "Uh-oh. I don't feel so good," she moaned.

Uncle Reuben turned to me again. "I thought you said the party was chaperoned."

"I didn't say anything. That was Jennifer," I said.

He curled his thick, dark eyebrows toward each other and narrowed his eyes into slits of suspicion. "Who gave her the vodka?"

"I'm sick, Daddy. Let me go upstairs," she pleaded.

"Oh, dear, dear," Aunt Clara cried, coming down the stairs quickly. She took Jennifer's other arm. We started toward the stairway, but Uncle Reuben reached out with his large hands and grasped my shoulders, pulling me away and toward him. He nearly lifted me off the floor as he brought his nose closer to my face and sniffed.

"You drank something, too," he accused.

"Just half a glass of beer," I said.

"I knew it. I just knew this sort of thing would happen when you came into my home."

"It wasn't my fault," I cried, and pushed his hand away from my shoulder. "Jennifer wanted to go to this party more than I did. And she knew exactly what was going to be happening there," I told him. If he only knew what else had happened—even his precious princess wouldn't be safe from his wrath.

He didn't hear a word. Jennifer stumbled on a step, and Aunt Clara struggled to keep her from falling. Uncle Reuben shot forward, scooped Jennifer up in his arms, and charged up the stairway with her as if she were nothing more than a toddler.

"Don't shake her so much, Reuben," Aunt Clara warned, climbing after them. It was too late. Jennifer started heaving again just as he reached the upstairs landing. He hurried toward the bathroom.

"Oh, dear, dear," Aunt Clara said, pressing her hands together and then to her face. She paused to look at me and shook her head. "How could this happen, Raven?"

"I think it's happened before, Aunt Clara, only you never knew," I said. I wasn't sure exactly what had happened with Jennifer and Brad, or if it had happened before with other boys, but I was pretty sure Jennifer wouldn't want her parents to know about that, either.

She bit down on her lip and started upstairs. Uncle Reuben stepped out of the bathroom.

"See to her," he ordered. "Give her a cold shower."

William had come to the doorway of his bedroom dressed in his pajamas. He wiped his eyes and looked out at the bedlam, confused. "What's going on?" he asked.

"Go back to sleep," Uncle Reuben ordered. Then he turned to glare down at me. "I want to talk to you," he charged.

"I didn't do anything," I protested, and went to my little room, closing the door behind me.

He nearly ripped it off the hinges opening it again. "Don't you dare walk away from me!" he screamed.

"It wasn't my fault, Uncle Reuben. She wanted to go to the game and the party. She talked the boys into asking us. She went right to the bar and poured herself a glass of vodka, claiming she knew how to drink, but she got sick right away. I guess she drank too much too fast trying to show off. I brought her home as soon as I could. That's the truth."

"Jennifer never went to a party like that before," he insisted. "She's never come home like this. Somehow, I'm sure this was all your doing."

"Believe what you want," I said. "You will anyway."

I turned my back on him. It was a big mistake. Seconds later, his big left hand was at my neck, and his right hand scooped up the hem of my dress. He lifted me off the floor and tossed me to the pullout, nearly knocking it over with me on it. Before I could scream, he had unbuckled his belt and pulled it off his pants. The next thing I knew, he was pulling down my panties. Then I screamed as loud and as hard as I could.

"Bitch!" he said. "Bad seed! You're not coming here and ruining my Jennifer. I'll put an end to this bad behavior right now."

The first whack of the belt shocked me more than it hurt me. I couldn't believe this was happening. With his large palm on my back, he held me down as he swung his belt again. This time, the pain shot up my spine.

"Wagging your rear at boys, going to parties, drinking and who knows what else. You are just like your mother," he said. "You should have been whipped before this, but it's not too late. No, sir." He hit me again and then again. Between my screams and my tears, I started to choke. It was useless to try to get away. He as much as nailed me to the bed with his heavy palm. He finally stopped beating me, but for a long moment he just held me down. My rear end was stinging in pain. It was as if I had been stung by dozens of wasps. I felt him move his right hand over it, but this time surprisingly softly. I wondered if he was checking to be sure he had done enough damage. Then he pulled his left hand from my back. I was afraid to turn, afraid to move. I sensed him standing there, gazing down at me, breathing hard.

"Maybe now you'll behave," he said.

I shuddered with sobs and heard him leave, closing the door behind him. For a long time, I didn't move. I remained there, with my face down, waiting for the pain to subside. Finally, it did so enough for me to turn over. It hurt to move my legs and even more to put pressure on my rear. I sprawled on my back and tried to catch my breath, wiping my face. I think I was bothered more by my outrage and loss of dignity than the stinging and aching, however. Slowly, I leaned over and pulled my panties back on. When I stood up, it was like rising from a beach or poolside and realizing you had been sunburned. My skin was throbbing, and there was a deep, sick feeling in the center of my stomach.

I wanted to open the door and scream, "How dare you do this to me?"

I actually did open it, but when I looked out at the quiet house, I suddenly became even more terrified. If he would do this, who knew what else he would do? Instead, I made my way to the bathroom and tried putting a warm, damp towel on my battered thighs and rear.

It didn't help much. I returned to my room, moving cautiously and slowly through the house. I could hear Uncle Reuben yelling upstairs and Aunt Clara's muffled sobs. I barely had enough strength to undress, and when I finally did lie down, the throbbing grew worse. It kept me awake most of the night. I think I passed out rather than fell asleep sometime just before morning.

A cold shock woke me, and I realized I was drenched in ice water. I cried out and sat up to face Uncle Reuben, who stood there with the emptied pail in his hands. The water quickly soaked right through the blanket, but I kept it close to my half-naked body.

"You get yourself up and get out there to help Clara do the weekly cleaning," he demanded. "You won't sleep late here because you carried on like a tramp, hear? I'll teach you what it means to misbehave while living with me," he threatened, speaking through clenched teeth. "I'm not your mother. None of this goes here. Now, get up!"

"I will. Leave me alone," I moaned.

He started to throw more water on me.

"Reuben, stop!" Aunt Clara cried from the hallway.

He glared at me and then nodded and left the room, pausing at the doorway to speak to Aunt Clara.

"Don't baby her, Clara. She needs strict discipline. She's no more than a wild animal."

He walked off.

When I began to move, the pain from my beaten body shot up my spine and made me cry out.

"What is it?" Aunt Clara said, coming in. "What's wrong, Raven?"

"He beat me, Aunt Clara. He beat me with a belt last night."

She shook her head in denial, but I turned on my side and lifted the blanket from my legs and rear. Then she gasped and stepped back. "Oh, dear, dear."

"Is it bad?"

"It's inflamed, welts," she cried. "Reuben, how could you do such a thing?" she asked, but far from loudly enough for him to hear. It was more as if she was asking herself how her husband could have turned into such a monster. There were other questions to ask, but this was hardly the time to suggest them, I thought.

"I'll get some balm," she said. "Just stay there, Raven. Oh, dear, dear," she muttered, and hurried out.

I collapsed back onto the pillow, my head pounding. What tortured me was not the beating I had been unfairly given as much as the realization that there was no one I could depend on now that Mama had gotten herself into even deeper trouble. Aunt Clara was too weak. I had no other relatives to run to for help. I was in a strange town in a school where I was still so new that I hadn't had time to make close friends. I was truly trapped.

"Here, dear. Let me see what I can do," Aunt Clara said, hurrying back.

I turned over to let her apply the medicine. It did bring some cool relief.

"I can't believe he did this," she muttered. "But he was so upset. He has such a temper."

"I didn't make Jennifer drink the vodka, Aunt Clara. Those kids are all her friends, not mine."

"I know, dear. I know."

"He won't believe anything bad about her," I said, turning when she was finished. She stared at me. "It's not fair, and it's not right," I continued.

"I'll speak to him," she promised, nodding.

"It won't matter, Aunt Clara. He has a bad opinion of me and my mother, and he hates me for being alive and a problem for you. I should just leave."

"Of course not. Where would you go? Don't even

think of such a thing, Raven. He'll calm down. Everything will be all right," she insisted, just as someone living in Never-Never Land would.

"It won't be all right. He'll never calm down," I said. "He's an ogre. He's more than that. I know why he favors Jennifer so much, too," I added, more under my breath. Aunt Clara either didn't hear me or pretended not to. She quickly turned away.

"I'll make us some hot breakfast, and we'll all feel better. You take your time, dear. Take your time," she said, and left before I could add a word.

I sat there fuming. All I wanted to do was get my hands on Jennifer and wring her neck until she confessed the truth. I wasn't going to let her get away with this, I thought. I took the beating that should have been meant for her.

I stepped out cautiously, hating even the thought of facing Uncle Reuben now. I heard no voices, just the clanking of dishes and the sounds of Aunt Clara moving about the kitchen. When I peered in, I saw William alone at the table. Jennifer was permitted to sleep off the effects of last night, but not me.

Anger raged up in me like milk simmering too long in a pot. I felt the heat rise into my face. Without hesitation, I turned and started up the stairs. If I had to drag her down these steps and throw her at her father's feet, babbling the truth, I would do it, I thought.

As I turned at the landing, I saw that her bedroom door was slightly ajar. I started for it and stopped when I heard the distinct sound of whimpering. Then I heard Jennifer's voice, tiny and pathetic, sounding more like a girl half her age than her usual cocky self. I drew closer, curious and confused.

"I'm sorry, Daddy. I didn't want to do it, but Raven and the other girls started to make fun of me. They said I was immature, a baby, and I shouldn't be at parties yet."

"Don't you let them say those things about you, princess. Don't you even think it," I heard Uncle Reuben say.

If only he knew the whole truth, I thought, then what would he think of his little princess?

A moment later, Aunt Clara called for me. "Raven? Are you upstairs?" Uncle Reuben heard her call me and appeared in Jennifer's doorway.

"What are you doing up here?" he demanded.

"I came up to see Jennifer," I said.

"She's not well this morning, as you should know," he said. "Just tend to your chores."

"Daddy!" I heard her cry behind him.

"Go on!" he shouted at me.

I started down the stairs, turning to look up when I was almost halfway to the bottom. Jennifer's door was closed.

"What is it, dear?" Aunt Clara said.

I looked at her for a moment and thought about telling her about last night.

"It's nothing, Aunt Clara. I'll be right down." I wasn't ready to stoop to Jennifer's level. Not yet, at least.

Aunt Clara knew something was wrong, but she didn't press me for answers. I suppose she didn't want to know about Jennifer's behavior any more than she wanted to know about Uncle Reuben terrorizing William. Deep in her put-away heart, she couldn't be happy with the person Jennifer was becoming. She had to be aware of her deceitfulness, her laziness, and her meanness. I knew she was upset about the way William shut himself off from everyone, even her, and wanted the best for her son. So what about her daughter? What did she want for her?

And then I would reconsider and stop hating her and start pitying her. I had been here only a short time. I had no idea what sort of horrible things she had endured before I arrived. It was easy to see she was afraid of Uncle Reuben, maybe even more afraid of him than I was. All he had to do was raise his voice, lift his eyebrows, hoist his shoulders, and she would stammer and slink off, pressing her hands to her bosom and lowering her head. There were times when she didn't know I was looking at her, and I saw the deep sadness in her face or even caught her wiping a tear or two from her cheeks. Often, with her work done, she would sit in her rocking chair and rock with her eyes wide open, staring at nothing. She wouldn't even realize I was around.

I never doubted she loved her children, and maybe she once had loved Uncle Reuben, but she was someone who had been drained of her independence, her pride, and her strength, a hollow shadow of her former self who barely resembled the pretty young woman in the old pictures, a young woman with a face full of hope, whose future looked promising and wonderful, who had no reason to think that anything but roses and perfumed rain would fall around her.

Some adults, I thought, fall apart, drink, go to drugs, become wild and loose like my mother did when they lose their dreams. Some die a quiet sort of death, one hardly noticed, and live in the echo of other voices, their own real voices and smiles carried away in the wind like ribbons, gone forever, out of sight, visible only for a second or two in the glimmering eyes or soft smiles that come with the memories.

Late in the day, Jennifer emerged with that triumphant sneer on her face. I was dusting furniture after having vacuumed the living room. Uncle Reuben was taking a nap. William was in his room, and Aunt Clara had gone for groceries. Jennifer plopped on the sofa and put her feet up, shoes and all. I stopped and looked at her with disgust.

"I'm so tired," she said. "Lucky we didn't have school today."

"You got me in a lot of trouble," I said. "What stories did you spread around school about me? How could you tell so many filthy lies?"

"Your reputation preceded you," she said with a laugh. "I didn't have to spread any stories."

"You're really pitiful, Jennifer. You could at least tell your father the truth."

"Yeah, right. Then I'd be in trouble," she said, and laughed. "You can keep cleaning. I won't be in your way. Just don't make too loud a noise."

"You're disgusting," I said, my anger boiling. "And in more ways than one."

"What's that supposed to mean?" she asked, making her eyes bigger. "You never drank too much, I suppose. In your house, it was probably a daily occurrence."

"For your information, it wasn't, at least for me." I stared at her a moment, debating whether or not I had the courage to say it. Finally, I did. "How could you let Brad do that to you? Don't you have any pride?"

She gazed at me, barely blinking. "What are you talking about now, Raven? What sort of lie are you trying to use to get out of trouble?" she asked.

"You know what I'm talking about, and you know it's not a lie," I said firmly.

Her expression didn't change. Then she looked away for a second before turning back to shake her head. "I don't know what you're talking about," she said, "and I'm warning you not to say anything that will make Daddy angry."

"He already got angry," I said. I put down the dust rag and undid my pants, lowering them and my panties. I turned to show her my welts.

"Ugh," she said, grimacing.

"He enjoyed doing it to me," I said, closing my pants. "He's a sadist, and he's perverted."

"Stop it!" She jumped off the sofa. "He's my father, and if he had to punish you, it was because you did something wrong. He's really kind, and he cares about me."

"You're just afraid of him. And you should be. If he knew how you really behaved, you'd get a far worse beating than I got," I said, drawing closer and staring into her face.

"Stop it!" she whispered. "He could hear you."

She stamped her foot on the floor. "What the hell's going on down there?" Uncle Reuben shouted from his bedroom.

Jennifer hesitated, staring at me with wide, scared eyes.

"Should I tell him?" I asked. "Should I tell him what really happened last night?"

She seemed to think, and then bet against me facing Uncle Reuben.

"Nothing, Daddy," she called back.

"Well, keep your voices down. I'm trying to get some rest. I didn't get much last night thanks to someone in this house," he added.

"Okay, Daddy. Raven's sorry," she said.

"You're sicker than he is," I said, shaking my head.

"You're just jealous because you don't have a father," she spit at me, her eyes narrow and hateful but also filling with tears. "You never had a father. You have a mother who is a tramp and a drug addict, and now you don't even have her," she said, gloating.

"No," I spit back at her, "but at least I still have some self-respect."

I threw down the dust rag and marched past her, practically knocking her out of my way.

"Who else would respect you?" she called after me. "You're worse than an orphan. You're nothing. You don't even have the right name! That's right, Daddy told me your mother was never even married, so don't go throwing stones. You're an illegitimate child!" she shouted.

I slammed the door closed behind me.

She was right, of course. Nothing she said wasn't true, but I'd rather be no one, I thought, than someone with a father like hers.

"Didn't I tell you two to shut up down there?" I heard Uncle Reuben scream.

"It's all right, Daddy. I'm taking a walk over to Paula's. If there's any more noise, it's not me making it," she shouted back. A moment later, I heard her leave the house, and it was all very quiet again.

I took a deep breath and went to the window. It was still gray and dismal outside. Jennifer had guessed correctly. I wouldn't tell Uncle Reuben. Why would he believe me? I'd keep her little secret. For now.

And then I saw someone on the corner standing under a sprawling maple tree. She wore a raincoat and a bandana over her hair just the way my mother often did.

"Mama?" I called, my eyes filling with tears.

The woman turned and disappeared down the next street.

I shot out of the room and rushed to the door. Then I ran down the walk and up the street to the corner, but by the time I got there, there was no one in sight. I stood there looking. Had I imagined it?

"Mama!" I screamed. My voice died in the wind, and no one appeared.

But what if it had been Mama? I thought. In my heart of hearts, I wished it had been, just so I knew she was thinking about me, just so I knew she did care a little, even if she hadn't come back for me.

Maybe, I thought, looking down the long, empty street with barely a car moving along it, maybe I wanted it so much that I simply imagined it.

Just like everything good I wanted for myself, this was only to be a dream, an illusion, another hope tied to a bubble that would burst, leaving me as lost and as forgotten as ever.

I turned and went back to the hell I had to call home.

8
Innocence Lost

The guidance counselor at my old school, Mr. Martin, once told me it's harder to look at yourself than it is to look at others. Some of my teachers had been complaining to him about me, and when I had my meeting with him and he read off the list of complaints, I had an excuse for everything. I was so good at dodging that he finally sat back, looked at me, and laughed.

"You don't believe half of what you're telling me, Raven," he said, "and you realize that when you walk out of here, you will walk out of here knowing that I don't believe you, either. The truth is, you have been irresponsible, neglectful, wasteful, and to a large extent self-destructive. You want to know what I think?" he asked, leaning forward and clasping his hands on the desk.

He had rust-colored hair and eyes as green as emeralds. Tiny freckles spilled from his forehead, down his temples to the crests of his cheeks. He always had a friendly hello for anyone. I never saw him lose his temper, but he had a way of making a troubled student feel bad about himself or herself. He spoke softly, sincerely, and acted as if he was everyone's big brother, taking each disappointment personally and asking questions that forced you to be honest.

My heart seemed to cower in my chest as I waited for him to drop his bombshell. I had to look down. His eyes were too penetrating, his gaze too demanding.

"No," I finally said, "but I guess you're going to tell me anyway."

"Yes, I am, Raven. I think you're a very angry young woman, angry about your life, and you think you're going to hurt someone if you do poorly and behave poorly. However, the only one you're really hurting is you."

I turned to look past him, to look out the office window, because I could feel the tears welling under my lids. Few people were ever able to penetrate the wall I had built around my true feelings, and whenever anyone did, I always felt a little naked and as helpless as a child.

"Your mother doesn't respond to any of my calls or letters. She's never been available to meet with your teachers."

"I don't care if she comes here or not," I snapped.

"Yes, you do," he said softly. He sat back again. "Sometimes, actually most of the time, we can't do much about the hand we've been dealt. We've got to make the most of it and get into the game. It doesn't do any good whining about it, right? You know that."

"I don't know what you're talking about, Mr. Martin. I failed some tests, big deal. My teachers are always picking on me because I'm an easy target. Other kids talk and pass notes and forget their books and stuff and don't get into half as much trouble."

Mr. Martin smiled. "When I was on the college basketball team and I gave my coach excuses like that, he would start to raise and lower his legs as if he were walking through a swamp," Mr. Martin said. "You know what I mean?"

I felt my throat close up and just shifted my eyes down.

"All right, Raven. I won't keep you any longer. You think over the things we discussed, and just know I'm here for you if you need to talk," he said.

I got up quickly, practically fleeing from his eyes and his probing questions. After I left his office, I stopped in the bathroom and looked at myself in the mirror. My eyes were red from the strain of holding back the tears. Mr. Martin was right: it was harder to look at myself, especially after he had held up a mirror of reality and truth.

Thinking back to that, I realized how much harder, if not impossible, it was for Jennifer to look at herself in a mirror. Everyone in my uncle's home suffered from the same self-imposed blindness, especially Aunt Clara, who not only turned away and kept her eyes down but also pretended she didn't know anything was wrong.

I left Mr. Martin's office feeling even more sorry for myself and a little guilty. Many of the students who behaved poorly or performed poorly left Mr. Martin's office angry at him for making them look into that mirror. I should have expected the same sort of behavior from Jennifer. After all, I had threatened to expose her to Uncle Reuben.

The rest of the weekend went as usual. I kept to myself, did my chores and my homework. Aunt Clara was always inviting me to join them in the living room to watch television, but the few times I had, I felt Uncle Reuben's eyes burning into me. When I glanced at him, he immediately looked disgusted or angry. He made me feel like a pebble in everyone's shoes. I felt as if I had to thank him for letting me breathe the very air in his house, and I knew that he would never give me anything willingly or with a full heart, not that I wanted anything from him. It hurt more that I had to depend on him for anything. This was truly what he called the burden of family relations, only it wasn't he who carried the weight of all that distress; it was me.

If I needed any reminders of the awkwardness between us, Jennifer was more than happy to provide them. She had ignored me most of the remainder of the weekend, but on Monday, as usual, she joined her friends at the bus stop, pretending I wasn't coming out of the same house with her. Our short-lived friendship to make it possible for her to attend the party was over. Ironically, because she had gotten herself sickly drunk and fooled around with Brad at Missy Taylor's, she was even more of a heroine to her friends. They were all waiting anxiously to hear the nitty-gritty details, as if throwing up your guts was a major accomplishment.

I sat in front with Clarence, but it was hard to ignore the raucous laughter coming from Jennifer and her clan in the rear. It wasn't until I was halfway through my morning that I began to understand why there were so many other students smiling at me, hiding their giggles, and wagging their heads. Just before lunch, some of them called out to me as they walked past Terri and me in the hallway.

"Heard you had a helluva weekend, Raven."

"Surprised you can walk."

"Who's next on your list?"

"Is it true what they say about girls with Latin blood?"

No one waited for a response. They just kept walking, their bursts of laughter trailing after them. The questions were tossed at me like cups of red paint meant to stain and ruin.

"What are they talking about?" Terri asked.

"I have no idea," I said. Afterward, when we sat in the cafeteria, I told her what had happened at Missy Taylor's party.

"So you rejected Mr. Wonderful," Terri said. "He's not going to let anyone know that."

"What do you mean?" I asked.

I saw Jimmy and Brad had joined Jennifer and her friends at a table, and they were all talking quickly and laughing. Once in a while, they turned to look at me. Someone made another remark, and they all roared.

They sounded like a television laugh track. I felt the heat rise in my neck and into my face.

"I don't know what's going on," I said, "but it's coming to an end."

"What are you going to do?" Terri asked as I rose from my seat.

"Watch," I told her, and started to march across the cafeteria. I heard the laughter and chatter die down and saw that heads were turning my way. Everyone at Jimmy's table stopped talking and looked up.

"I hear that you're making up stories about me, Jimmy," I said, glaring down at him.

He shrugged. "Hey, in some cases, you don't have to make anything up," he said.

Jennifer grunted, and her friends smiled.

"In your case, I imagine it's ninety-five percent invented," I said. "After spending only a few minutes with you alone, I can understand why you're always looking for a new girl."

Smiles faded. I heard someone suck in air. Jimmy turned; his face was turning bright red. "And what's that supposed to mean?"

"You're a lot better at basketball than you are at making love," I said. "I guess you waste all your talents on the court. If you don't stop making up nasty stories about me, I'll tell everyone why I left the bedroom so quickly."

For a moment, Jimmy was unable to respond. Everyone at the table turned from me to him, their eyes widening with new awareness. I knew there was no better way to make a boy like Jimmy afraid than to attack his manliness and his souped-up reputation.

"Huh?" was all he could utter.

I started to turn away when Jennifer piped up. "Stop trying to cover up, Raven. You're the one who's always fouling out," she shouted. "That's why you're here, living as a servant in my house." Her friends laughed.

I froze for a moment, feeling my spine turn to cold steel. Then I turned slowly and stepped back toward the table.

"Me? Cover up? Please, Daddy," I whimpered. "I didn't mean to throw up all over the place. Raven made me do it."

"Shut up!" she screamed.

"I'm a good girl. Daddy's little good girl," I mimicked.

Everyone held their breath. Jennifer turned so red I thought she might just burst into flames. Instead, she reached down, seized a half-eaten bowl of tomato soup, and threw it at me. The hot soup splattered my clothes and face, and the bowl crashed to the floor, shattering.

Mr. Wizenberg, the cafeteria monitor, came running over. "What's going on here?" he demanded. "Who did this?"

Everyone at the table stared at him. He turned to me. "Who threw that at you?"

"No one," I said. "It flew up on its own." I wouldn't be a tattletale, not even to get Jennifer in trouble.

Frustrated, Mr. Wizenberg sent the whole table and

me to Mr. Moore's office. Unable to get anyone to rat, Mr. Moore put us all in detention and sent letters home to each and every student's family. Naturally, they all blamed me.

Before our letters arrived, Jennifer went crying to Uncle Reuben, claiming I had started it all. This time, Aunt Clara interceded before he could unbuckle his belt.

"Don't, Reuben," she said. "It can't be entirely her fault, and you've punished her enough already."

Uncle Reuben was angrier about Aunt Clara's interference than anything, but he didn't say a word. He pointed his finger at me and shook his hand without speaking. To me, that was more frightening. He looked monstrous, capable of murder. I retreated as soon as I could and let him vent his rage to Aunt Clara.

"She is obviously the one who needs discipline, Clara. We can't keep her here if we don't try to control her bad ways. Look at all the trouble she's caused in the short time she's been with us. Don't ever interfere again, understand? Understand?" he threatened.

"Yes, Reuben, yes. I'll have a talk with her."

"Talking doesn't help that kind. She's too spoiled, too far gone. I'm her only hope," he declared.

If he was my only hope, I was long gone.

When the letter arrived, he pinned mine on the inside of my bedroom door.

"Don't you dare take this off here, understand?" he declared. "I want you to see this each and every time you walk out of this room."

"Are you pinning Jennifer's to her door, too?" I asked.

"Don't you worry about Jennifer. You worry about yourself. That's enough," he snapped.

I couldn't keep the emotion from my face, and I saw him tilt his head as he looked at me, his own eyes focusing like tiny microscopes to look into my thoughts.

"You might have Clara fooled with that sweet act you put on," he said in a hard, coarse whisper, "but I know your mother. I knew your father. I know from where you come. You can't fool me."

"If my mother was so bad, why aren't you? You're her brother. You came from the same parents. You grew up together, didn't you? You're not perfect," I said. "You've done some bad things." The moment I said that, I knew I had gone too far, but I had no idea just how far.

He stepped farther into the room.

"What did she tell you?" he asked. "Did she make up some lie about me? Spit it out. Spit out the garbage. Go on," he ordered.

I shook my head. "There's nothing to tell," I said, my heart pounding. He seemed to expand, inflate, rise higher, and grow wider.

"I never did anything to her," he said. "If I ever hear you say anything, I swear I'll tear out your tongue."

I stared at him, and then I looked down quickly. He hovered there like a giant cat. I could almost feel my bones crumbling under his pounce.

"She was disgusting, parading around naked and

saying whatever she wanted, trying to get me to give in to her evil ways. Well, I showed her. It was good when she ran off, only she didn't run far enough," he declared.

I could almost feel his hot breath on the top of my head, but I didn't move, didn't twitch a muscle. I tried to stop breathing, to close my eyes and pretend I was somewhere else. After what seemed like an eternity, he turned and marched out. It felt as if a cold draft had followed him and left me in a vacuum of horribly dark silence. I was afraid to think, even to imagine what sort of things he meant.

Suddenly, I felt I had to get fresh air. I threw on a sweater and went out. All the houses on the street and the next were well spaced apart. There were only about six or seven on each avenue. At the moment, there was no one on the street and apparently no one outside his or her home. I folded my arms under my breasts and walked with my head down, not really paying attention to where I was going. I was so deep in thought that I never realized I had crossed the street.

"Hey," I heard, and looked up at Clarence Dunsen. "Wh . . . where are you . . . you going?"

He had a garbage bag in his hand and had just lifted the lid of the can when he saw me.

I stopped and looked around, surprised at how far I had traveled.

"I'm just taking a walk," I said.

He put the garbage in the can and closed it. Then he simply stood there looking at me.

"Is this where you live?" I asked, nodding at the

modest ranch-style home. It had gray siding with charcoal shutters, a large lawn with some hedges around the walk, and a red maple tree in front. The garage door was open, and a station wagon and a pick-up truck were visible. I saw a bike hanging on the wall as well and what looked like some tools, wrenches and pliers, clipped to another wall.

"Yeah," he said. "I live in the bas . . . bas . . . basement."

"The basement?" I smiled. "What do you mean?"

"That's where I . . . slee . . . sleep and stuff," he replied. He smiled. "I have my own door."

I shook my head, still confused.

"Com . . . come on. I'll shhh . . . show you," he urged with a gesture. He took a few steps toward the side of the house and waited. I thought a moment, looked around the empty street, and then followed him to steps that led down to a basement door. He pointed. "There," he said.

"You live down there?"

"A-huh. Wanna ssssss . . . see?"

No one had ever told me about this, not even Jennifer, but then again, no one really took any interest in Clarence except to make fun of his stuttering. I nodded again and followed him down the steps. He opened the door to a small bedroom that contained a desk and chair, a dresser, a cabinet that served as a closet, and a small table on top of which sat a television set. The floor was covered in a dark brown linoleum with a small gray oval rug at the foot of the bed. Under the bed were a few pairs of shoes and some sneakers. There were two electric heaters along the sides of the room.

His clothing was tossed about, shirts over the chair, a pair of pants dangling over the door of the closet, and some T-shirts folded and left on top of the television set. I saw magazines on the floor, some books, and a few boxes of puzzles.

"Why do you have to live down here?" I asked him. The room had no windows and was lit by a ceiling fixture and one standing lamp beside the desk.

"My mom's new hus . . . husband fixed it for . . . for me so the baby could have my old rooo . . . room," he said.

The dull gray cement walls had chips and cracks in them. It smelled dank and musty. The floor rafters were clearly visible above us, and there were cobwebs in them. This was more like a dungeon than a bedroom, I thought. Why would his mother want him down here? I could hear footsteps above us, the sound of chair legs scratching the floor, and then a baby's wail.

"That's Donna Marie," he said.

I nodded and continued to look around the dingy room. "Where is your bathroom?"

"Upsta . . . stairs. You got to go?"

"No," I said, smiling. "I just wondered. You do puzzles?" I asked, nodding at the boxes on the floor.

"Yeah, sometimes. Aft . . . after I do one, I take, take, take it apart and do it again."

I laughed, and he smiled.

Just then, the door of his room was pulled open, and a tall, lean, dark-haired man in a pale white athletic undershirt, jeans, and old slippers appeared. He was unshaven and had a square jaw with a cleft chin and a thin nose under a pair of dark brown, tired eyes that brightened with interest when he saw me.

"Who the hell are you?" he asked.

"I'm Raven Flores."

"Who's this, Clarence?" He smiled. "A girlfriend?"

"Nnnnn . . . no," Clarence replied, turning a deep red. He glanced at me with terror.

"I'm just a neighbor," I said. "I'm living with my uncle."

"Who's that?"

"Reuben Stack."

His smile widened. "Reuben, huh? He never mentioned you. I work with him." He turned back to Clarence. "We was wondering why you didn't come back upstairs after you took out the garbage. It's time for dinner. I hate to interrupt," he said, smiling at me. "Come on back later, if you want."

"That's all right. I'll see you tomorrow, Clarence," I said.

"Sure you're not coming back tonight?" his stepfather asked. I ignored him and went to the door. His laughter followed me out.

I hurried back, feeling sorrier for Clarence than I did for myself. Where was this magical family in America, the one I saw on television? You can have parents and still be an orphan, I thought.

"Where the hell have you been?" Uncle Reuben asked when I entered the house.

"I just went for a walk."

"It's suppertime. You know you have to be here to help," he said.

I hurried toward the kitchen.

"Jennifer's already set the table," he said.

"All by herself?" I retorted.

"Don't get smart," he snapped. "Just help Clara bring in the food, and next time, you let someone know when you're leaving the house, hear?"

"Yes, sir," I said. I nearly saluted.

He stared daggers at me, so I continued into the kitchen, where Aunt Clara was busy getting the food into serving bowls. She worked quickly and quietly. I had the feeling Uncle Reuben had already blamed her for my not being there.

"I'm sorry I'm late, Aunt Clara, but . . ."

"Just take this in, dear," she said, handing me the bowl of mashed potatoes.

When I entered the dining room, I found Jennifer sitting back with a wide, self-satisfied smile on her face. William looked as meek and beaten down as ever, and Uncle Reuben sat in his throne, his big arms on the table, waiting like the king he thought he was.

"It's about time," Jennifer said. "I'm starving. I got the table set for you."

I put down the bowl and looked at the plates and silverware.

"Forks are on the wrong side," I said, and winked at William, who gave me a small smile. Then I returned to the kitchen before Jennifer could offer a smart reply.

It was another dinner with Uncle Reuben pronouncing his opinions about women and young people. The world was out of control. Values were being destroyed, and the fabric of the country was being torn apart. It was all the fault of women who wanted too much and children who weren't disciplined properly. No one contradicted him. I tried to drown him out with my own thoughts, but he bellowed and knocked on the table when he wanted to force home his conclusions.

All Aunt Clara could say was, "Don't excite yourself when you're eating, Reuben."

I hurried to clean up afterward. As usual, Jennifer just rose and went upstairs, not even bringing her own plate to the sink. I saw that William wanted to help, but he was afraid of angering his father, who had just finished declaring that women were getting men to do their work and that was one of the things wrong with this country.

After my chores, I went to my room to start my homework. I could hear Jennifer in the living room watching television with Uncle Reuben and Aunt Clara. Her laughter sounded loud and obnoxious to me. Why didn't they ask her about her schoolwork? I wondered. I heard the phone ring, and a few minutes later, my door was thrust open.

Uncle Reuben stood there gaping in at me.

"What?" I asked, turning from my small table.

"Where'd you go before?" he asked, stepping into the room and closing the door behind him. "Huh?"

"I told you. I went for a walk," I said.

"That's a lie. You went to the Dunsen house, didn't you?"

"I saw Clarence, and he wanted to show me his room in the basement," I said.

Uncle Reuben smiled coldly and shook his head. "You know that boy's retarded."

"He's not retarded. He just has a speech problem," I said.

"It's easier to take advantage of someone like that. What were you trying to do, seduce him?"

"No!" I cried. "Leave me alone."

"I got to get a call from one of the men who works under me gloating that he caught you with his stepson? I got to get that call? What are you doing to our reputation in the neighborhood?"

I turned away, the tears coming so fast and hard I couldn't stop them this time. I wasn't the one who was fooling around with boys, and yet I was getting accused!

"Looks like you need more than one lesson, and more than one lesson you're going to get," he said, and pulled off his belt. "Get on that bed."

"No. Leave me alone!" I cried.

"If you get on it yourself, I'll only give you six whacks. If you make me do it, it's ten," he said. He hovered between me and the door. I could never get around him. "Well? Which will it be?"

"I didn't do anything wrong," I moaned. "Please."

"Looks like ten," he said, moving toward me.

"No," I cried, holding up my hands. I got up and backed toward the bed.

"Reuben, what's going on in there?" I heard Aunt Clara ask.

"Just keep out of this, Clara, or it will go down harder for everyone," he shouted. He turned to me. I couldn't stop sobbing. I didn't want to be hit once, much less ten times. What could I do?

I went to the bed.

"Lower 'em," he ordered.

Sobbing harder, I reached under my skirt and lowered my panties. He pushed me forward and once again held me down as he whacked me six times with the belt.

"You don't go to any boy's room alone," he said. "And stay away from that retard, hear?"

I couldn't talk. I bit down on the blanket and waited. I felt him run his palm over my rear, and then I heard him march to the door and leave, closing it behind him. It took me a while to catch my breath and pull up my panties. I lay back in the bed and cursed him over and over, praying he would fall down the stairs and break his neck. I fantasized standing over his corpse, spitting on it, kicking it. I didn't think it was possible to hate anyone as much as I hated him.

My door opened again, and I turned in terror. It was Jennifer. She stood there shaking her head.

"Clarence Dunsen? You walked out on Jimmy Freer and went to Clarence Dunsen?"

"No," I said.

She smiled and shook her head. "Wait until everyone hears about this. If I were you, I would crawl under that bed and stay there," she advised, and walked away, laughing.

I lay there, my body like an empty glass filling with

red liquid hate. Nearly two hours later, I heard them all go upstairs to sleep. I waited a little longer, and then I went to the door, my hands clenched in fists, my chest so tight my heart had trouble beating. Quietly but determined, I marched up the stairs. It was dark and still. Uncle Reuben and Aunt Clara's door was shut, as were William's and Jennifer's. I could hear Jennifer talking softly on her telephone and then laughing.

I opened the door, and she looked up from the floor where she was curled.

"What do you want?" she demanded.

"If you spread that story about me," I said, "I will tell your father what really happened the night of Missy's party."

I closed the door and walked down the stairs, somehow forgetting and ignoring the pain from my belt beating.

9

I'm Not Going to Take It

Jennifer was so quiet the next morning, she made me nervous at breakfast. She wouldn't look at me, and if she did have to gaze my way, it was as if she was looking right through me. She looked tired, her eyes dark. I imagined she had been sleeping on my threat, and it had played like a pebble under the sheet, causing her to toss and turn, flitting through her nightmares.

My hands fluttered around so that I nearly dropped a dish. Uncle Reuben was poised to pounce if I did. He kept looking at me with sparks in his eyes when I rattled cups and saucers. Jennifer kept her eyes down. Every once in a while, she would lift her chin, and I saw her puckered little prune mouth drawn up like a drawstring purse. She ate and gathered her things together with barely a syllable escaping from those tight lips.

"Are you feeling all right, Jennifer?" Aunt Clara finally asked her. I wasn't the only one who noticed a marked difference in her behavior. Usually, she didn't shut up, blabbing like someone who loved the sound of her own voice and expected everyone else to adore it as well.

Jennifer stabbed me with her nasty glare immediately after Aunt Clara's question. I half expected her to burst out with new accusations, revealing my threat. I braced myself in anticipation.

"I'm fine," she said. "I'm just tired."

"I hope you're not coming down with anything," Aunt Clara said.

Uncle Reuben's eyebrows jerked upward as if pulled by strings. "Everyone's been healthy in this house up until now," he muttered.

Did he really see me as some sort of walking, talking germ, a carrier of disease and illness, someone full of infection and decay?

"Maybe you should stay home today," Aunt Clara suggested.

"Oh, no," Jennifer said with a deep and painful sigh, "I have tests to take, and I just can't afford to miss any work."

Please spare me, I wanted to say. Since when did she care one iota about her work? She either cheated or borrowed other people's homework, and if she could find a way to get out of a test, she wouldn't hesitate. Suddenly, poor Jennifer was going to be the martyr? Now I did think what I ate would come back up. I rose from the table, clearing off dirty dishes.

Jennifer was out of the house ahead of me as usual. With the chores I had to complete—helping with the breakfast dishes, cleaning the table, organizing and fixing my little room—I nearly missed the bus. Aunt Clara hurried me along, and I charged out of the house, running down the sidewalk just as the last student boarded. As usual, there was an empty seat next to Clarence. He looked up timidly, and I smiled and sat beside him. Jennifer was in the rear with her friends.

"I'm sor . . . sorry about my . . . my . . . stepfa . . . fa . . . father," Clarence said. "He's a jerk."

"It's all right, Clarence. Don't worry about it. I didn't think much of him," I said.

"He's got a nas . . . nasty mind. He made a lot of jokes after," Clarence said.

"Where's your real father?" I asked.

He shrugged. "I don't know. Maybe he's in California. I can't hardly remem . . . remem . . . ber him anymore," he said sadly, and looked out the bus window.

There was a slight drizzle, the drops flattening against the glass and then spreading out wider to form what looked like spiderwebs. Gray skies made the morning seem more dismal than usual. Everyone on the bus was subdued. The conversations were quiet, and there was little laughter. When I gazed back, I saw Jennifer glaring my way, holding her books and bouncing with the bus. Even her normally buoyant and noisy friends looked half asleep.

The school became darker and darker inside as the clouds thickened outside. Some of the corridors weren't as well lit as others, and it felt as if I were moving through tunnels to get to my classes this particular morning. As the rain grew stronger and pounded in sheets against the school walls and windows, students grew sleepy. Even the teachers seemed to struggle with enthusiasm for the work.

Just before lunch, however, the rain stopped, and a bit of sunshine broke through. It washed away the drowsiness, and voices grew louder. Students walked faster, teased and joked with each other.

At lunchtime, Terri and I headed for the cafeteria, talking about an upcoming movie. I used to go to the movies once in a while when I lived with my mother, but now I didn't know when I would get to go again.

Suddenly, we heard a burst of loud laughter from a corner of the corridor. At least a dozen or so boys were gathered in a huddle. When they turned, I saw that Jimmy was there. I stiffened instinctively, but as the boys continued to separate, I discovered they had been surrounding poor Clarence Dunsen. He looked terrified.

"Here she . . . she . . . come . . . comes, Clarence," Jimmy said. "Why don't you tell her how much you la . . . la . . . love her," he shouted, and all the boys laughed.

"Leave him alone," I ordered.

"We're not bothering him. Clarence was just telling us about your rendezvous in his bedroom the other day," Jimmy said loudly enough for everyone around us to hear.

"You bastard," I told him, which only made him and the boys laugh harder.

I hurried into the cafeteria, Terri trailing quickly behind.

"What's that all about?" she asked.

"My cousin has been at it again," I said, fuming. I threw my books on the table and folded my arms.

"Don't do anything violent," Terri advised. She nodded toward Mr. Wizenberg, who was watching me like a nervous rabbit. I searched for Jennifer and found her holding court at a table across the cafeteria. She looked so self-satisfied, I felt like ripping out her eyes.

The boys erupted into the cafeteria behind Clarence, who tried to get to his usual table. They were chanting behind him.

"I la . . . la . . . la . . . love you, Ray . . . Ray . . . Raven."

The whole cafeteria turned, and Clarence, who was bright red, dropped to his seat and stared down at the tabletop.

"Quiet!" Mr. Wizenberg shouted. "I said *quiet!*"

The boys stopped and spread out to their tables, laughing and congratulating themselves with pats on their backs. Jimmy went to Jennifer, and they had a good laugh together.

"What's going on?" Terri asked.

I told her what had happened, but I didn't say anything about telling Uncle Reuben about Jennifer and Brad. I couldn't get myself to fall to Jennifer's level. Maybe she had known that all the while. When she rose to go to the lunch line, I jumped up.

Terri seized my forearm. "Careful," she warned. "You'll get suspended this time for sure."

I nodded but charged forward. "You're a horrible person, Jennifer," I said, pushing my way behind her. "Don't you care who you hurt?"

"I don't know what you're talking about. I didn't tell anyone anything," she said, flipping her hair back. "Clarence bragged about you and him to a couple of his friends, and it got out."

"That's a lie. You're such a liar." I stepped closer to her, and she backed away.

"If you cause any more trouble, Daddy will put you in the street," she warned.

"I'd rather be in the street. There's less dirt."

A surge of panic ran through her eyes as she looked around to see if anyone was really listening to us.

"Don't you dare say anything terrible about me or my family, Raven. Don't you dare," she said in a weak whisper.

"You're so disgusting," I said, shaking my head. Some of the girls did pause to listen. I hesitated.

"Don't worry," I said. "I won't get down in the mud with you."

She smiled, crooked and mean.

I left her and returned to my table, frustrated, raging, my anger simmering my blood into a rolling boil.

"Easy," Terri said, putting her hand on my arm and nodding toward the rear. Mr. Wizenberg had come up right behind me. He rocked on his heels a moment with his hands behind his back, and then he glared a stern warning at me as he continued across the cafeteria.

"Everyone thinks I'm the cause of trouble here," I moaned. "It's not fair."

"She'll get hers," Terri predicted. "Someday."

For now, that had to be how I would leave it. I went to my classes after lunch, the rest of the day moving more quickly. I was relieved when the last bell rang and we headed for the buses to go home. This time, when I boarded the bus, I hesitated. I knew if I sat with Clarence, Jennifer and her friends would make more fun of him. It was for his benefit that I passed him by. He looked up at me with sad eyes. I tried to smile to indicate it was better I didn't sit next to him today. He seemed to understand, and I moved deeper into the bus, finding an empty seat. No one sat beside me.

We started for home. At first, there was just the usual sound of chatter and hilarity, but suddenly, there was a shrill laugh I recognized as Jennifer's. I turned just as she and her friends began their chanting.

"I la . . . la . . . la . . . love you, Ray . . . Ray . . . Raven."

A sea of laughter swept over the bus. Everyone was smiling, and soon everyone was into the chant. The bus driver looked confused, a silly smile on her lips. She was a stout woman named Peggy Morris with hair chopped short about her ears. She wore flannel shirts and jeans and had the sleeves of her shirt rolled to the elbows. Despite her tough appearance, I always found her pleasant and friendly.

I looked at Clarence. He slapped his hands over his ears and rocked in his seat.

"Stop it!" I shouted, which only brought more laughter. "You idiots. Stop!"

They chanted louder. I was hoping Peggy Morris would do something, but she was too involved with a car that was slowing and speeding erratically in front of us.

Suddenly, Clarence shot up from his seat and screamed like a wounded animal. His voice reverberated through the bus, but instead of bringing the chanting to a halt, it drew more laughter and then louder chanting. Clarence covered his ears. I was yelling for them to stop, too. It all sounded like bedlam, like a bus filled with insane people. Peggy had just started to turn, slowing the bus down, when Clarence surprised everyone by deliberately smashing his fist against the window. The first slam brought the chanting to a halt. I could barely utter a sound, my throat choking up.

"Clarence!" I managed, but he did it again, harder this time, and the glass shattered.

He stood there, the blood streaming down the side of his arm. Girls screamed. Even some of the boys cried out. Peggy Morris jammed her foot on the brakes and pulled the bus to the side just as Clarence fell backward. She caught him before he rolled over the railing and onto the bus steps.

Everyone grew deadly quiet. I made my way down the aisle. Peggy shouted for me to hand her the first aid kit, and I hurried to do so. She opened it and pressed a fistful of gauze against Clarence's hand and arm. Then she looked up at me.

"Go out and get to a phone," she said. "Call for an ambulance. Quickly!"

When she opened the door, I shot down the steps and into a convenience store on the corner. The man behind the counter called 911 for me, and I returned to the bus. Everyone remained subdued, even Jennifer. The driver did the best she could to stem the flow of blood. Clarence lay there with his eyes closed. What seemed like an hour but was only minutes passed before we heard the sound of an ambulance followed by a police car. Chatter began again as the paramedics boarded the bus quickly, heard what had happened, and tended to Clarence. Moments later, they were carrying him off the bus on a stretcher. As soon as he was placed in the ambulance, Peggy Morris returned and stood with her hands on her wide hips, glaring angrily at everyone, her face still pale from the shock and excitement.

"I don't want to hear another peep," she said shakily. "Not another peep."

She started up the bus, and we rode to our stops in funereal silence. My heart was thumping. I had a revolting nausea whirling in my stomach. When our stop appeared, I rose and walked slowly down the steps.

"Thanks for your help," Peggy Morris said. I nodded and got off.

As I started up the sidewalk, Jennifer whipped past me, pausing only to say, "You have only yourself to blame."

It took every ounce of restraint to keep from rushing up behind her to seize the back of her hair and pull out every strand as I kicked and pummeled her sneering, ugly face. But I knew I could never sink to her level, no matter what. I would never be that evil.

Uncle Reuben knew about Clarence before he came home that night. Clarence's stepfather had been called at work and had to rush over to the hospital. Uncle Reuben didn't know any of the details, but I saw from the way he looked at me when he asked questions that he assumed I had something to do with it.

"What happened?" he began.

"Clarence went nuts," Jennifer said.

"Why?"

"The kids were teasing him, and he went nuts. He's nuts anyway," she said.

"What do you mean, they were teasing him? How were they teasing him?"

"Making fun of his stuttering," she said.

"That's all?" he followed, still eyeing me suspiciously.

"I don't know, Daddy. I wasn't paying attention. Suddenly, he smashed his hand into the window. Now, isn't that nuts?" she cried.

"How horrible," Aunt Clara said.

"Was he bleeding?" William asked.

"A lot. That's why they had to get the ambulance," Jennifer told him. William grimaced and looked to me.

"Mighty strange how all these terrible things are suddenly happening," Uncle Reuben declared.

Afterward, Jennifer had the nerve to come to tell

me she had done me a favor. "I protected you," she said, "so don't go blaming me for anything."

"How did you protect me?" I said, amazed at her boldness.

"I didn't tell Daddy why Clarence was being teased. He'd be real mad then, so you just better be nice to me, or . . ."

I shook my head. "I'd rather be nice to a rattlesnake," I told her. "You and Uncle Reuben deserve each other."

"I'll tell him you said that," she threatened. "You want another beating?"

"Leave me alone."

"I need some of my blouses ironed, and I don't have the time," she said. "I'll send them down with William, and you better not damage them, or else."

Later that evening, I heard Uncle Reuben tell Aunt Clara that Clarence's stepfather had called. He said Clarence had to have twenty stitches and was being kept in the hospital for observation. He said he might even have to go to the psychiatric ward.

"I don't know how yet," he concluded, "but I'm sure Raven had something to do with this."

"Oh, Reuben, no. She wouldn't," Aunt Clara assured him.

"I'll find out. Trouble, that's all she is, trouble just waiting to happen. Damn my sister. She should have been sterilized."

What a horrible thing to say, I thought, but I did feel just terrible about Clarence. In a strange sort of way, I supposed I was responsible. If I hadn't let him talk me into showing me his basement room, the kids wouldn't have made up the chant. I bring disaster to everyone I touch, I thought. Uncle Reuben isn't so wrong.

Clarence's self-inflicted wound and the entire event on the bus were the big topic of discussion at school the next day. The kids who had tormented him didn't feel any remorse. If anything, they behaved as if they had helped bring out his mental illness. Now he would be where he belonged . . . in a nut house. They were so smug I couldn't stand it. Clarence did not return, and in my way of thinking, he was the one who was better off.

Later that week, Clarence's stepfather somehow found out about the subject of the chanting and teasing, and he told Uncle Reuben. When he came home, armed with the knowledge, he wore a look of self-satisfaction on his face. He proudly announced to Aunt Clara that I was indeed the cause of the trouble. For the time being, he seemed content being proven right. Aunt Clara retreated even more deeply into her shell, and Uncle Reuben's tyranny raged unchecked. He was what he wanted to be, king of his own home, supreme judge and jury, and we existed only for his pleasure and comfort.

My chores were increased. I wasn't permitted to go anywhere with anyone on the weekends for at least a month. No after-school activities, parties, not even a trip to the shopping mall. Aunt Clara put up little or no argument. A cloud fell over the house, even more dark and oppressive than the ones that had preceded it.

I waited and hoped for news of my mother. Nothing came. All Uncle Reuben would say was that she was on everyone's most wanted list.

"Why should she show her face around here?" he declared with a cold laugh. "She's got a brother assuming her responsibilities."

My mother had done many cruel and stupid things to me, but the worst, I thought, was leaving me with her brother.

I couldn't imagine how things could get worse.

But they could.

And they did.

10
Home Alone

Being confined to the house while everyone else was out doing things on the weekend wasn't actually all that bad. I would have enjoyed it even more if William, who seemed to enjoy my company more than he did anyone else's in the family, had been able to stay home, too. However, Aunt Clara took him to the mall to buy him new clothes and a new pair of sneakers Saturday afternoon. Jennifer went to a matinee with her friends. Before she left, she stopped to gloat by the sewing room, where I was ironing clothes.

"Everyone's meeting for pizza, and then we're going to the movies. I'm sitting with Brad," she bragged, "so no matter what you think, he really is interested in me."

"I'm happy for you," I said dryly.

"If you weren't so mean to me, I might get the kids to like you, too," she offered.

"Me? Mean to you?" I smiled. "Do you really believe that, or do you think I'm that stupid?"

"I think you're that stupid," she said, pulling her thick lower lip into her cheek.

"You know," I said, spinning around on her, "I came here feeling sorry for myself and even envying you. You have parents, a nice house, a very nice little brother. You seemed to have everything I ever wanted, and then I got to know you better and see what really goes on here, and now you know what?"

"What?"

"I feel sorrier for you than I do for myself," I said, and turned back to my ironing.

"I have no idea what you're talking about. You're nuts, just like Clarence. I don't know why I even bothered trying to be your friend," she snapped.

"Becoming your friend is like becoming friends with a black widow spider," I retorted.

She spun on her heels and charged out the front door, slamming it so hard the whole house shook and the windows rattled. I smiled to myself, turned on the radio, and started to enjoy my solitude. Uncle Reuben had already left to bowl with his team. There were so few times when I had a chance to be alone and not feel I was being watched or judged.

I had to face the fact that my mother would never come for me or be able to take me to live with her again. When she was caught, they would put her in a real jail this time, and even if she behaved and was released, she would probably be released to another drug rehabilitation clinic. After that, she still might not be allowed to have me live with her, and who knew if she would even want the responsibility?

Perhaps I should stop fighting reality, I thought. I was only hurting myself. I was like someone bound with piano wire, struggling and squirming to be free and only tearing myself to pieces. I had to learn to ignore, to look the other way, to pretend, to make up my own world. Maybe Aunt Clara wasn't all wrong behaving as she did. At least she found some peace in her life by deliberately blinding herself to the unpleasantness in her family. She was able to go on, to face every new morning with fresh hope.

I was really like someone caught in a strong current being carried downstream. I could struggle and struggle, desperately try to fight the water and only waste my strength, or I could turn in the direction the water was flowing and try to swim a little faster than the current. Maybe, if I stayed even a few inches ahead of my fate, I would feel some sense of purpose, some meaning and identity, and be able to think of myself as real, a person with a name, with some control over what would happen to her. The current couldn't go on forever and ever. It would take me someplace, drop me at some shore, and if I endured and stayed strong, I would be able to stand on my own two feet and then, then, make a new life for myself.

That was the only hope I had, the only choice left. Realizing it was like lifting a weight from my shoulders. I actually began to feel good and swayed my body to the music as I worked. I sang along with the singers. I went to the kitchen and poured myself a soda and returned to my room to finish the ironing. After that, I thought I would take a shower and just spend the rest of the day reading, catching up with my English assignments.

It was turning out to be one of the nicest days I had spent living with my uncle and aunt. I laughed to myself realizing that the reason it was so nice was that no one else was home. I washed my hair in the shower and then sat before the small mirror in my room and dried my hair, first with a towel and then with Aunt Clara's blow dryer. My hair was truly my crowning glory, long and thick. My mother always coveted my hair, moaning about her own thin, split strands and then running her fingers through my hair and bringing it to hers as if touching mine might transfer some of the richness to her own.

I sat there in the blue cotton robe Aunt Clara had given me and fantasized, dreaming myself into scenarios with a handsome young man who would come along and see me for myself, fall in love with me, and sweep me away from all this. Why couldn't I be a real Cinderella? Somewhere out there surely was a young man destined to be my lover, my husband, my prince, a young man who would see my strengths as well as my beauty and want me at his side forever and ever.

I was in such a reverie, actually hearing the music, the voices, feeling the wind in my hair as we drove along picturesque country roads, laughing, kissing, and promising our love to each other, that I never heard Uncle Reuben come into the house, nor did I hear him come into my room. It wasn't until he was actually standing behind me, swaying, his eyes glassy, that I realized he was there. I spun around on my chair and looked up at him.

"Getting yourself all dolled up for someone else, are you?" he asked with a cold, crooked smile on his face.

"No. I did all my chores and just wanted to clean up and do my homework," I said. I couldn't believe how timid I sounded. I was wrapped so tightly inside my heart could barely beat.

"Get clean? You?" He shook his head and snorted. "You're dirty through and through," he said. "All the soap and hot water in the world couldn't clean you up."

"That's not so. I'm not dirty!" I insisted.

"You're your mother's daughter. You've proven that in just the short time you've been here," he responded. "Seducing that retarded boy," he muttered.

"I didn't do that."

"Go on with you," he said, waving his hand. "You'll never change. It's just bad blood."

"If there's bad blood in this family," I said, making my eyes small, "it's more in you than in my mother and me."

He stepped back and blinked as if I had reached up and slapped his face.

"Z'at so?" he said. "You still have a big mouth, eh?" He wobbled as he stared down at me. I could smell beer on his breath. It churned my stomach. "I oughtta just throw you out or turn you over to the court and let them put you in one of them orphanages."

"I wish you would. Then I would tell everyone how awful you are—how you terrorize your family with threats and beatings," I blurted.

This time, his eyes widened, and he opened and shut his mouth without a sound. He wobbled, and then his face reddened.

"What are you talking about? What kind of filthy lies have you been spreading? Who did you tell such stories?"

"Nobody," I said. "Yet."

Despite his unsteady stance and his dull, dizzy look, he managed to bring his hand around so quickly and accurately that he struck me across the cheek before I had a chance to lift my arm to protect myself. The blow stung, and the force of it drove me off the seat. I fell to one knee. Before I could turn to stand, he had the back of my robe up as he pulled me closer.

"Naked? Naked sitting here?" he cried.

"It's supposed to be my room," I wailed.

"With the door wide open? You're a tart, a tease, just like your mother was. I'll have to teach you the same lesson I taught her. I'll show you what happens to girls like you."

He reached down and seized me at the waist, lifting me as if I weighed nothing and dropping me on the bed.

"No!" I screamed. "Don't touch me!"

He slapped me sharply across my buttocks and then sat beside me as he pulled my robe up farther until it was at my waist.

"That's all you do want is to be touched," he said, suddenly in a softer voice. Nevertheless, that frightened me more. I felt an icy chill travel up my spine, and I turned to get away, but he rested his heavy torso against my ribs and back, and I was pinned beneath him.

I felt his hand on my rear end again and then down between my thighs.

"Just like your mother, all you want is to be touched," he said. I jumped and screamed when his fingers traveled to where I hesitated even to touch myself. "You're bringing shame into my home," he muttered as he continued.

Then, as if he had suddenly realized what he was doing, he stopped and slapped me again.

"Everyone at the bowling alley was talking about the Dunsen boy and what you done. It was embarrassing. They wanted to know what sort of niece I had living with me. You don't listen. You keep being bad," he said. "I've been too easy on you."

He leaned forward and found my hairbrush. The first blow stung so badly I really did see stars. Lights flashed in my eyes. The pain spread out along my back and sides as if I were a plate of glass, shattering. He hit me again and again; his aim was off so that some of the blows fell on my thighs, each taking the breath out of me. When he was finished, he remained on the couch, breathing hard over me.

"You'll get worse if you do another bad thing. I'll burn the skin off you, understand?"

He pinched the flesh under my buttocks harder and harder. "Understand?"

"Yes," I cried. "Yes."

"Good. Good," he said, rising. "Don't you go crying to Clara about this, either, understand? If you do . . ."

I didn't move until I heard him stumble out of the room, closing the door behind him. When I did move, I couldn't believe the burning and the pain. It was the worst beating of all and the most degrading.

I groaned, turned over on my back, and lay there staring up at the ceiling. It was how Aunt Clara found me later. She thought I was sick, and I told her I was just having a bad time with my period. She believed that and let me be, offering to do all the preparation for dinner. As if he wanted to play along, Uncle Reuben did not challenge my story. Jennifer couldn't care less and never even poked her head in to tell me how much of a good time she had had with her friends. William looked in on me, and I tried desperately to hide my pain and agony from him, but he seemed to sense it anyway. His eyes were full of suspicion and fear.

Later, when I came out of my room to join them at supper, I did walk like a girl who was suffering menstrual cramps. Aunt Clara talked about how terrible it was that modern medicine could find cures for almost everything but that.

"Maybe that's because most doctors are men," she muttered.

"That's nonsense, women's lib propaganda," Uncle Reuben piped in, and then went into one of his tirades about the standards in our society crumbling with all the liberal movements in politics and government.

I went to bed early and spent most of the next day in my room lying in bed. The pain went so deeply this time that it changed from a stinging to an aching. I ate little and slept as much as I could. The next morning, Monday, Uncle Reuben did order me to get up and help with the morning chores.

"And don't try to stay home from school, either," he warned. "I know you did a lot of that when you lived with my sister. She probably lost track of the days," he added.

Walking was still painful, but I was terrified that he would think of another excuse to hit me if I didn't obey him. I boarded the bus and rode silently to school. During my morning classes, I had to fidget and squirm a great deal to find comfortable, less painful positions. Only Mr. Gatlin noticed and asked if I had ants in my pants. That drew laughter and more whispering and teasing in the halls between classes.

My real problem was in gym class. I tried using my period as an excuse, but Mrs. Wilson wanted me to suit up anyway and stand at the sidelines. I pleaded, but she was insistent.

"My girls always suit up," she claimed. "Those are my rules. No loafers here," she added. She watched me leave her office, and minutes later, while I was changing, she came into the locker room and spied on me.

"My God," she cried, "what happened to you?"

I spun around, holding my uniform to my chest. The welts and black-and-blue marks on my upper thighs were still quite vivid, especially where Uncle Reuben had pinched me.

"Nothing," I said.

"That's far from nothing. You get your clothes on, and you go right to Mrs. Millstein this minute," she ordered.

"But . . ."

"Do what I say," she screamed. She looked horrified as I began to put my school clothes back on. Then she left to go to her office. By the time I arrived at the nurse's office, Mrs. Wilson had called and Mrs. Millstein was waiting, prepared for what she would find.

"Come in, Raven. Please," she said when I opened the door. She had me go into one of the private rooms. "Mrs. Wilson told me about your injuries. Do you want to show them to me?"

"I'm all right," I said.

"I'm sure, but just in case there is something else to do, it might be a good idea to let me see them. Okay?"

I hesitated. And then suddenly, the whole world seemed to come apart for me. I couldn't control myself. The tears that had welled up in my eyes time after time, tears I had driven back or shut off, flooded, poured out of me with no restraint. I began seemingly unstoppable sobbing. Mrs. Millstein had to help me to the chair.

"There, there now, Raven. I'm sure it's not as bad as all that," she said.

"It is," I cried. I lifted my skirt slowly, and she looked at the bruises. Then I stood up, and she examined the others.

"How did this happen, Raven?" she demanded in a firm voice. Again, I hesitated. "You must tell me, Raven. Who did this to you?"

I took a deep breath. Did it matter anymore who knew and what sort of a horrible life I had? I sat again and stared at the floor. The tears dripped off my chin.

"Raven?"

"My uncle," I said in a tired, defeated voice.

"How did he do this?"

"He beat me with a hairbrush," I said, "and he pinched me after . . . after . . ." My tears rushed out again. My chest felt as if it would cave in and crush my heart. Mrs. Millstein fed me tissues and then took my hand.

"Tell me slowly, Raven. Take your time, but tell me everything. I'm here to help you, sweetheart. Go on," she said, kneeling in front of me and holding my hand. "What else did he do to you, honey?"

"After he began to beat me, he touched me where he shouldn't," I blurted. "Then he hit me with the brush until I nearly fainted."

"Did this happen before?" she asked.

"Yes," I moaned. "Last time, it was with a belt." I started to cry softly.

She stared quietly for a long moment, and then she stood up. "Just rest now, Raven. You're going to be fine," she said. "I'll be right back."

Everything that happened afterward happened so quickly it all blurs together like a movie running too fast in my head. Soon afterward, a woman from the children's protection service, Marjorie Rosner, arrived, and Mrs. Millstein urged me to describe what had happened to me. She questioned me in more detail, and then she and Mrs. Millstein went off to confer. Minutes later, I was escorted out and taken to a doctor who examined my injuries and gave Marjorie Rosner a written report. All the while, things were buzzing around me, telephones ringing, policemen arriving, and then I was taken to a temporary foster home run by an elderly couple. They provided me with a hot meal and a place to sleep. I didn't think I would, but the moment my head hit the pillow, I drifted off, feeling my body sink into the mattress.

In the morning, Marjorie arrived and explained that I was going to a courthouse to be questioned by a family court judge. She warned me that my aunt and my uncle might be in the courthouse as well.

"Your uncle was questioned by the police, as well as your aunt," she told me.

"What about what he said he did to my mother?"

"Let's just concentrate on you for now," Marjorie told me.

I was so frightened I could barely walk to Marjorie's car. She kept reassuring me that everything would be all right.

"He'll never lay a hand on you again, Raven. I promise," she said.

When we entered the courthouse, I saw Aunt Clara sitting alone on a bench in the corridor. She had her head down, her hands in her lap. She looked so small and lost. I felt sorry for her. When she heard us in the hallway, she looked up. Her eyes were bloodshot, her face pale.

"What have you done, Raven?" she asked in a tiny voice.

"It's not what she's done, Mrs. Stack. It's what your husband has done," Marjorie Rosner said.

"He wouldn't do those things," she said. "He wouldn't." She looked up at me hopefully.

"I'm sorry, Aunt Clara. I think you know he would," I said.

Aunt Clara brought her small fist to her mouth to stop the cry that strangled in her throat.

Marjorie moved me ahead. I looked back just before we entered the judge's chambers. Aunt Clara had her hands over her face and was rocking gently on the bench like someone in great pain. My heart felt like a lump of lead.

"I hate hurting her," I said.

"You're doing the right thing, Raven. Just answer the judge's questions," Marjorie said.

I sucked in my breath and stepped in, feeling like someone on a roller coaster who was just reaching the top of another incline. In moments, I knew I would be raging downward, holding on for dear life, closing my eyes, screaming, wondering where the next turn would take me.

Epilogue

Uncle Reuben denied everything, of course. He admitted beating me but claimed that I was so rotten to the core he had no choice. The judge didn't believe him and certainly had no intention of placing me back in Uncle Reuben's home. With my mother gone and no other relatives who could bear responsibility for me, I became a ward of the state. It was what Uncle Reuben had predicted for me all along, so in a way, I suppose he got what he wanted.

I felt sorrier for William and Jennifer, since they had to stay in the home, and told Marjorie so. She thought William eventually might be the one who came out of the family's self-imposed cocoon and eventually helped everyone, especially Aunt Clara.

"In therapy," Marjorie said, "it will all be exposed."

I didn't know whether to believe her or not, and at the moment, I couldn't think about anything else but what was happening to me. She saw how anxious I was and decided she would be the one to bring me to the new foster home herself.

"It's one of our best facilities," she explained the morning she drove me there. "It used to be a small hotel, and the couple who ran the hotel, Gordon and Louise Tooey, now run the home. The grounds are beautiful, and there is lots of room in the building."

She made it sound as if I was going away to summer camp. She said there were other girls my age, and the school I would be attending nearby was one of the better schools in the state.

"Prospective adoptive parents come by frequently, too," she told me.

I didn't know if I wanted another mother. I had never had a father, and my experience with Uncle Reuben made me anxious about being in anyone else's control.

Why would someone come along now to adopt me, anyway? I thought. If I were a woman looking for a child to adopt, I would try to find one who was relatively young, one I could teach and develop. I wouldn't want a daughter who had lived the life I had already lived.

Marjorie saw the pessimism in my face but nevertheless talked continuously about the bright future that awaited me. She promised me that the worst was behind me. She assured me that the state would make sure I was never in the hands of someone as perverted and cruel as my uncle or as troubled as my mother.

"We don't let just anyone take in one of our children," she said, as if the state were a gigantic mother hen with eyes that really saw and examined and knew each and every one of her young chicks.

I was too tired and too depressed to argue or even to care. This would be the third school I would attend in less than six months. There would be new faces, faces with distrustful, cautious eyes. The hardest thing in the world was making a real friend, developing a relationship with another human being who trusted you and cared for you and had confidence that you trusted and cared for her as well. I really never had a friend like that, and now I wondered if I ever would.

A little more than an hour later, we drove up to a place called the Lakewood House. The first thing Marjorie had told me proved to be true. It was a very large building with the biggest wraparound porch I had ever seen. Marjorie helped me with my things and gazed at the grounds. She took a deep breath as if the air was fresher.

"Isn't it beautiful here? Look at the lake back there and the flowers. It's very nice that these people decided to become foster parents and share all this."

Why would they? I wondered.

We started up the steps. There was a screen door, and the door behind it was open. We heard a woman's voice.

"Coming," she cried.

Marjorie opened the screen door, and we faced a tall brunette with shoulder-length hair. She looked about fifty, with vibrant and friendly blue eyes.

"This is Raven Flores," Marjorie said. "Raven, meet Louise Tooey."

"Hi, darlin'," Louise said, reaching for my free hand. "You just come right in. I know all about you," she continued in a soft, sad voice. Her eyes actually became teary. "What we are doing to our children," she remarked to Marjorie, and shook her head. She smiled at me again. "Come on. I'm going to introduce you right away to your roommate. Her name's Brooke, and I'm sure you two will be fast friends. We're like one big family here. We all look out for each other."

I gazed at Marjorie, who nodded and smiled again. I couldn't help being skeptical. I was like the girl who had so many unfulfilled promises that one more just weighed her down deeper into a well of sadness. I'd rather not be promised anything, I thought. Disappointment lingered in the shadows, hungry, eager, ready to pound on my little bit of hope.

"Louise," we heard, and looked up the stairway. "The toilet is running over again."

A tall, thin girl with braces and stringy dark hair looked down at us, her hands on her hips.

"And I wasn't the last one in there," she added quickly. "Please tell Gordon."

"All right, dear. Don't worry. I'll get him." Louise laughed. "They get so nervous when something goes wrong. Gordon fixes everything so quickly. He should. He's been doing it long enough. I'll just take Raven upstairs," she told Marjorie, "and then come down to meet with you in the office."

"Fine. Good-bye, Raven," Marjorie said, hugging me. "You're going to be just fine," she said.

"I don't know why," I said. "I've never been before."

She and Louise exchanged troubled looks, and then I followed Louise up the stairs. The tall girl watched us for a moment before turning to hurry down the corridor. I imagined it was to announce my arrival. We stopped at a room on the left, and Louise knocked.

"Yes?" a voice called.

Louise opened the door.

"It's just Louise, Brooke, with your new roommate that I promised."

"Lucky me," Brooke replied. She looked up from the table upon which she had a tape recorder with its casing apart. It looked as if she was repairing it. When she set eyes on me, however, her head snapped around in a double-take, and she stopped what she was doing.

"This is Raven. Raven, this is Brooke. You two are about the same age, so I imagine you have a lot in common."

"I doubt it," Brooke said.

I smiled at her. "I doubt it, too."

"Oh. Well, Brooke will tell you all about the Lakewood House and introduce you to the other girls on the floor, won't you, Brooke?"

"Do I have a choice?"

"Of course you do, dear."

"Come on," she said in a tired voice. "I'll fill you in on Horror Hotel."

"Brooke!"

"I'm just teasing, Louise. You know that," Brooke said.

"Of course you are. My girls love it here," Louise said. "I'll just go finish with Marjorie, and then I'll see you soon after," she told me. "Make yourself at home, dear."

She stepped out, closing the door behind her.

Brooke and I stared at each other a moment.

"You meet Gordon yet?" she asked. I shook my head. "I thought you looked too calm."

"Why? What's he like?"

"He's big, ugly, and mean. Otherwise, he's okay," she said.

I started to smile.

"Haven't you been at other homes?" she asked.

"Just overnight at one. Before that, I've lived with family."

"Family? What happened?"

"It's a long story," I said dryly, "with a bad ending."

"Not yet," Brooke said.

"Excuse me?"

"The ending. It's not written yet."

I shrugged. "What are you doing?"

"Trying to fix Butterfly's tape recorder. Someone dropped it off the stairway. I think I know who."

"Butterfly?"

"She's across the hall with Crystal. You'll meet them soon. Put your stuff away. You can have half the closet and half the dresser. The bathroom's down the hall."

"Thanks," I said.

"Don't thank me. Thank the state."

She fiddled with the tape recorder as I put things away.

Someone knocked.

"Enter Sesame," Brooke cried, and two girls entered, one small and dainty and the other wearing a pair of glasses with lenses thick as goggles. They both stared at me.

"We heard your roommate arrived," the taller, very intelligent-looking girl said. Her eyes were beady and intense. "I'm Crystal, and this is Janet. We call her Butterfly."

"Hi," Janet said softly. She looked like a doll magically brought to life. Why wouldn't someone have snatched her up by now? I wondered.

"Her name's Raven," Brooke said. "She's had a terrible family life, and she's overjoyed about being brought here."

"Now, don't get her more depressed," Crystal ordered. "We do fine here."

"Sure we do. We're the Three Orphanteers," Brooke said.

"Now four," Crystal corrected.

Brooke looked at me. "That's up to her," she said.

I laughed. "What was it you said, do I have a choice?"

Brooke laughed. Butterfly beamed a smile, and Crystal shook her head.

"Let's go down and get some slop," Brooke decided, standing.

"Slop?"

"Lunch," Crystal said. "And it's not that bad."

"I like to think of it as bad so I get pleasantly surprised," Brooke said. "Come on."

I started out with them. Crystal fell back.

"It's hard in the beginning," she said, "but you'll see. You get used to it."

"It can't be any worse than where I've been," I said.

She nodded. "That's what we all hope."

She walked faster to take Butterfly's little hand, and we descended.

Out beyond the Lakewood House, in homes across the country, girls our ages were having their lunches, or gathering with friends, or sitting with their families. Their dreams weren't much different from ours. Could anyone look at us and know we had only ourselves now? Was there a look, a gesture, a sound in our voices that betrayed our loneliness?

I did see it in the other three, the distrust, the fear, the hesitation. I supposed that in a real sense, we were sisters, born under the same small and distant star, surrounded by darkness, waiting, watching, desperately trying to keep our light bright.

How many fewer smiles would we have? How many fewer laughs? How many more tears than all the safe and loved girls our ages? What did we do to be brought here to this place?

At the bottom of the stairway, they waited for me to catch up.

"Stick close," Brooke ordered. "You're one of us now."

"I think I've always been," I muttered.

Brooke smiled.

Butterfly looked sad.

Crystal looked thoughtful.

We continued down the hallway, together. Four of us closing ranks, hardening, gathering the strength with which to do battle against loneliness.

Firing up our precious star.

Read all the books in the Orphans series by

Brooke

Butterfly

Crystal

Raven

Runaways

Pocket Books

3005